"RECKON WE'RE IN FOR HELL NOW!"

"Hyar they come!" bawled a scout from a wagon seat.

Suddenly pandemonium broke loose. Couch had at last been surprised. His men were awake, but not all in line, and when a horrid medley of Indian screeches rent the air, only one-third of the caravan opened fire.

Buff dove under a wagon, gun thrust forward, his hair stiff and his skin tight and cold, while the blood gushed back to his heart. The melee of yells and shots was deafening. Red flashes lit up the dark night, through which swift wild forms sped by. The caravan had to fight once more.

Books by Zane Grey

Arizona Ames
The Arizona Clan
Black Mesa
The Border Legion
Boulder Dam
The Call of the Canyon
Code of the West
The Deer Stalker
Desert Gold
Drift Fence
Fighting Caravans
Forlorn River
The Fugitive Trail
The Hash Knife Outfit
The Heritage of the Desert
Horse Heaven Hill
Knights of the Range
The Light of the Western Stars
Lone Star Ranger
Lost Pueblo
The Lost Wagon Train
The Man of the Forest

The Mysterious Rider
Raiders of Spanish Peaks
The Rainbow Trail
Rawhide Justice
Robbers' Roost
Rogue River Feud
Shadow on the Trail
Stranger from the Tonto
Sunset Pass
Thunder Mountain
To the Last Man
The Trail Driver
Twin Sombreros
Under the Tonto Rim
The U.P. Trail
Valley of Wild Horses
Wanderer of the Wasteland
Western Union
West of the Pecos
Wilderness Trek
Wyoming

Published by POCKET BOOKS

ZANE GREY
FIGHTING CARAVANS

PUBLISHED BY POCKET BOOKS NEW YORK

Cove art by Murray Tinkleman

 POCKET BOOKS, a Simon & Schuster division of
GULF & WESTERN CORPORATION
1230 Avenue of the Americas, New York, N.Y. 10020

ISBN: 0-671-83272-7

First Pocket Books printing March, 1980

10 9 8 7 6 5 4 3 2 1

POCKET and colophon are trademarks of Simon & Schuster.

Printed in the U.S.A.

1

One bright June day in 1856 the driver of a covered wagon halted on the outskirts of Independence, Missouri. All spring he had traveled with wife and child to reach this frontier post. They were tired and needed a rest before undertaking the long overland journey westward. So he chose for camp a shady spot in a grove where a brook ran deep and still under grassy banks.

This sturdy, middle-aged teamster answered to the name of Jim Belmet. He hailed from Illinois and, like many of his kind, came of pioneer stock. The West called irresistibly.

There were other camps along the stream. Columns of blue smoke curled upward. The ring of ax on hard wood resounded through the grove. Covered wagons lumbered along the dusty road toward the post.

"Mary, what'll you need from town?" asked Jim, when he had finished the necessary labors around camp.

His wife was a robust, comely woman, just then active round the camp fire.

"Ham or bacon. Bread or flour. Coffee an' sugar," she replied.

"Hey, Clint!" he called to his son. "Want to go in town with me?"

"Naw," refused the boy, a blond stripling of twelve years. He had a freckled face, clear, steady, gray eyes, and an intent and quiet manner beyond his age. He was barefooted, and on the moment appeared to be trimming a long slender willow pole.

"You'd rather fish, hey?" inquired the father.

"Betcha I would," returned Clint.

Jim turned to his wife with a gleam of humor on his weatherbeaten face. "Wal, what you make of that lad? Here we've been travelin' for months an' at last we've got to Independence. Why, this here town will be like a circus! An' Clint would rather fish!"

"Reckon Clint takes after my father, who was a great hunter an' fisher," she said. "It's just as well, considerin' where we're goin'."

Clint thereupon was left to his own devices. Evidently he well knew what he was about, for he soon had his fishing rig ready. Next he spaded up the damp ground near the water, where he found worms for bait.

"Mom, you'd like some fish for supper?" he called.

"Reckon I would, sonny. But surely there's no fish in that ditch."

"Betcha. You'll see." Whereupon Clint glided under the shady trees along the banks of the still stream. He had not made a vain guess. Few indeed had been the campers who had not been of the same mind as his mother, for Clint found little indication that anyone had angled along this bank. From every hole he pulled out a fat golden sunfish or a wiggling catfish.

As he approached the next camp he espied a little girl sitting on the bank. She had pretty brown hair, rather curly. Her face was bent over her lap, which appeared to be full of clover. Clint was shy about girls. His first impulse was to go back the way he had come; however, the urge of fishing was stronger and he went on.

Now it chanced that the hole almost under the girl's bare feet was the best Clint had found. Here he caught the biggest sunfish. Then, one after another, he captured seven more. Thereafter bites began to slacken. Looking ahead, he saw where horses had been in the water, spoiling it for further fishing. He strung the sunfish on his forked willow stick.

"How do!" spoke up the little girl, shyly.

Clint gave her a civil reply. She appeared to be younger than he, which fact mitigated his embarrassment.

"I never saw anyone who could catch fish like you," she exclaimed, admiringly.

2

Clint did not realize it, but that was probably the only speech which could have detained him. More, it caused him to look at her. Her eyes were dark and bright, most disconcerting to look into. But something compelled him to.

"Me? Aw, I'm not so good," he replied, and suddenly conscious that he was awkwardly twisting his body, he sat down upon the grass. Strangely, too, he felt loath to leave.

"Oh, you must be!" she went on, round-eyed and earnest. "I heard my daddy say there wasn't any fish in this river."

"Well, there are, only it ain't a river. . . . Do you like fish?"

"To eat? Yes, I do. I'm so sick of greasy fat bacon."

"All right. I'll clean a couple of these sunfish for you," offered Clint, and bounding down to the water he whipped out his knife, and made the very best job he could of dressing his largest two sunfish. These he impaled on a fork of willow and climbed back up the bank. She had leaned over on hands and knees to watch him, and her look stirred something unaccountable in him.

"There now. You tell your mother, or whoever's your cook, to salt 'em, an' fry quick without any flour or meal."

Clint did not catch her murmured thanks, and he was divided between a hope she would go and a fear that she might not stay. But she sat back and gazed at him in the friendliest way.

"What's your name?" she asked.

"Clint Belmet."

She repeated it and giggled. "Funny name, but it's prettier 'n mine."

"What's yourn?"

"May Bell."

"Why, that's an orful pretty name!"

"It's so silly. . . . Have you a brother or sister?"

"No. There's just me an' paw an' mom."

3

"Just like me. . . . Isn't it dreadful? . . . My mother says I'm spoiled. Are you?"

"I reckon paw thinks so. Where you from?"

"Ohio. We lived on a farm."

"We did, too, back in Illinois. I didn't like it. But I sure like this travelin' west. Don't you?"

May mused over that seriously. "Sometimes I get homesick."

"Huh! What'd you do back home?"

"I went to school. Ever since I five. I liked that. . . . Did you go to school?"

"Four years. Paw says he'll betcha it's all I'll ever get. I'll be darned glad."

"Where's your paw takin' you?"

"West. He doesn't know where."

"My daddy says the same thing. Don't you think they're a—a little crazy?"

"Mom says paw is plumb out of his head."

"I—I wish we was travelin' west together," said May, boldly.

"It'd be—nice," replied Clint, confronted with the most amazing circumstance of his life.

Just at that moment Clint heard his mother calling, and as he arose, another call, evidently for May, came from the adjoining camp. She got up and gingerly lifted the fish on the willow branch. Clint wanted to say something, but he did not know what.

"I'll tell my daddy if—if you'll tell yours," May said, eagerly.

"Tell—what?" stammered Clint.

"That me an' you we want to travel west together. Ride on the front seat sometimes together. Won't it be lovely? . . . Will you tell your daddy?"

"Sure," gulped Clint, appalled at the strangeness of the truth this little girl had made him see. Then they separated, and she was not alone in looking back.

Clint found his father had returned from town, so excited about something that he scarcely noticed the fish Clint proudly exhibited. His mother listened seriously while she went on preparing supper. Clint took his fish down to the brook and cleaned them, ponder-

4

ing over what might have happened. He guessed it had only to do with the further journey west. And returning to the camp fire, where he quietly helped his mother, Clint soon learned that they were to join one of the great freighting caravans for which Independence was famous on the frontier.

"Reckon it'll be safer in a big wagon-train than a little one," was the only comment Clint's mother made.

After supper Clint was both thrilled and mortified to espy the little girl, May, coming into camp with a tall man. It happened that Clint was helping his mother wash the cooking utensils; he did not, however, choose to desist just because of the company. May smiled brightly and nodded mysteriously while the man with her addressed Clint's father.

"My name's Bell—Sam Bell, from Ohio," he announced.

"Howdy! Mine's Jim Belmet. Hail from Illinois."

"This's my little girl, May. She met your boy today by the brook. An' I've come to have a confab with you."

"Sure glad to meet you an' the little lady," responded Jim, warmly. "An' here's my wife an' my boy Clint."

After a few more exchanges Bell came out frankly with the object of his visit.

"Independence was about as far as my figgerin' went," he said. "Course I knew I was goin' farther west. But how an' when I didn't calculate much on. Now I'm here an' I've got to decide."

"Wal, I was just in your fix when I got here," replied Belmet. "It didn't take me long, though. I'm goin' to haul freight over the Santa Fé trail."

"Freight? You mean all kinds of supplies needed at the posts an' forts overland?"

"Sure. I'm goin' to haul for the Tillt Company. They have big warehouses here, where you can buy hosses, oxen, wagons, guns, tobacco, leather goods, all kinds of grub—in fact, everythin' from a paper of pins to a bag of candy. Tillt has stores an' agents all along the old trail from Independence to Santa Fé."

"Freighter, eh? What kind of a business is it?"

"Good pay. I aim to take wages while I look for a place to settle down on out West."

"Sensible idea, 'pears to me," returned Bell, thoughtfully. "How much capital does a man need?"

"Not much, considerin'. Tomorrow I'm buyin' one of them big freight wagons an' two teams. You can buy oxen cheaper."

"What'll you do with the outfit you came in?" asked Bell, pointing to the covered wagon.

"Wal, take it along, I reckon. Mary can drive, an' Clint here is no slouch with hosses."

"Belmet, I guess I'll do the same thing," returned Bell, with enthusiasm. "How many's goin'?"

"Seventy-five so far, Tillt's agent told me. The more the merrier—or safer, I should say. Injuns, you know, all the way across. Our caravan will be under Captain Couch. He's a guide an' scout. Reckon there'll be twice seventy-five wagons when we start. . . . Bell, you don't want to start across the plains alone. Better throw in with us."

"Oh, daddy, please go with them!" implored little May.

"Well, daughter, if you feel that way, why don't you ask yourself?" queried Bell, curiously and kindly.

"May we—we go with you?" shyly asked the child of Belmet.

"Why, bless my heart! We're only too glad. Clint, tell this young lady you'll be delighted."

But Clint was tongue-tied.

"It's settled, then," rejoined Bell, as if relieved. "Suppose you all come over to my camp an' meet my wife."

On the way across the grove Clint and May fell behind and gravitated toward each other. He felt her looking up at him.

"I like your daddy an' mamma. An' I hope you'll like mine," she said.

"Course I will—I do."

6

"I forgot. . . . How old are you?"

"Goin' on thirteen."

"Oh, you're so much older. I'm only ten. But you don't mind, do you?"

"What—mind what?"

"Me bein' so young an'—an' little?"

"Aw, that's all right."

"An' you'll let me set on the front seat with you—sometimes—when you're drivin'?"

"Betcha I will."

"Oh, lovely!" She clapped her hands in glee. "We'll ride an' ride. I won't be lonesome no more. We'll look an' look way, way over the grass—so flat an' far. Won't we?"

"Reckon there won't be nothin' to do but look," replied Clint, with a superior air.

"But, oh, when the Injuns come! They will, won't they?"

"Paw laughs an' says no. But mom shakes her head. . . . Yes, the Injuns will come."

"Ooooool! . . . But I'll not be afraid, ridin' with you," she said, and slipped a cool little hand in his.

2

The long wagon-train wound like an endless white-barred snake across the undulating plain.

The ox-teams, with massive heads bowed, swayed ploddingly, hauling the canvas-covered prairie schooners; the heavy freight wagons with their four horses were held to the slower pace of the oxen. This caravan was two miles long, consisting of one hundred and thirty-four wagons. The road over the Santa Fé trail was yellow, winding and full of dust; on each side, as far as eye could reach, stretched the endless prairie, green and gray, waving like a sea.

In the slow, patient movement of this caravan there lay the suggestion of an irresistible tide of travel westward. It held an epic significance. Nothing could halt it permanently. Beyond the boundless purple horizon beckoned an empire in the making. Behind the practical thought of these teamsters, behind the courage, the jocularity, the endurance, and the reckless disregard of storm, thirst, prairie fire, and hostile savages, hid the dream of the pioneer, the builder.

They were on their third day out from Independence and already the prairieland had swallowed them. On all sides lay monotonous level. Red-tailed hawks sailed over the grass, peering down; from ridges came the piercing whistle of wild horses; barren spots showed little prairie dogs sitting up on their haunches, motionless, near their holes, watching the train go by; wolves skulked away to merge into the gray; and jack rabbits seemed as many as the tufts of grass.

Somewhere near the middle of that caravan Clint Belmet proudly sat on the seat of his father's covered wagon, reins and whip in hand. His mother had relinquished the driving to him. She was not well and lay back under the shelter of the wagon cover. At twelve years of age, Clint had been given a man's job. The first day out his father had kept close watch on him from behind, as had Sam Bell from in front. But their concern gradually lessened.

On this third day Clint knew happiness as never before. He had been trusted; he had justified the faith of his elders; he was a part of something which he felt was tremendous. A heavy rifle leaned beside him against the seat. The first time he had been instructed to shoot it in camp, he had been knocked flat on his back; the second time he had held fast, to Sam Belmet's satisfaction. Clint would not be afraid to shoot it again. Young as he was, he divined the significance of a rifle in overland travel. Nights around the camp fires, listening to the freighters, the guides, the hunters, had propelled him far beyond his years.

Wonderful as had been these last days, this one surpassed all. The sun was gold; the breeze warm and dry and fragrant; the prairie grass waved and

8

shadowed; a rich thick amber light lay like a mantle over the plain, in the distance growing darkly, deeply purple; the sky was a blue sea, crossed by the white billowing sails of clouds. The roll of the heavy wheels, the clip-clop of the steady hoofs, made music to Clint's ears. But surely the sweetest thrill of all came from his companion, little May Bell, who sat close beside him on the driver seat.

Twice before she had shared this prominent place, but this time she and Clint were alone. She was under his protection. Jack, his dog, was curled at May's feet.

"Look," said May, for the thousandth time. "Isn't it lovely?" And she pointed ahead to the long curve of the caravan, winding over the plain, the leaders already beyond an undulation.

"Sure is," replied Clint, nonchalantly.

"Just think! Daddy said I could ride all day with you—if you'd let me. . . . Will you?"

"Reckon I will," rejoined Clint, hiding his own satisfaction.

"You're a regular driver now," went on May, admiringly, peeping from under her sunbonnet.

"Ah—huh."

"I'm glad. You're so strong an' smart an'—an' everythin'. . . . How far do we go today?"

"I heard a teamster tell paw it was nigh onto twenty-two miles to Fish Creek, our next camp. That's a pretty big drive. We made only eighteen yesterday."

"Oh, it seemed we came so far. But I love the ride. You can drive slower if you want to. . . . Clint, do you want it to end?"

"What?"

"This ride?"

"I ain't in no particular hurry."

"Mother says I'm too excited. I don't eat to suit her. An' I dream awful. Yell in my sleep."

Clint laughed and flicked his whip. "Ha! betcha you have somethin' to yell about before we get there."

That sobered her, though not for long. She was eager, curious, full of joy of she knew not what. Her childish mind was reveling in the adventure and beauty, while reaching out toward the dream of her elders, to the unknown future.

"It's awful far to Fort Union?"

"Reckon so. Near a thousand miles."

"Oh, then we'll be *weeks* on the road?"

"You bet."

"Daddy is goin' to leave mother an' me at the fort. Will you come there often?"

"Every trip out an' back."

"Oh, I'm glad. I won't feel so awful—then. . . . Clint what's goin' to become of us?"

"Become of us? What do you mean, May?"

"I don't mean just now—or on this ride. But after. . . . Just look! It's so awful, terrible big—so far across —this prairie. What's on the other side?"

"Didn't you study geography?"

"No."

"Well, we come to the Rocky Mountains. An' cross them, too!"

"Ooooo! how wonderful! But can we ever climb mountains?"

"There's a pass—a place to go through."

"I'm glad for the poor oxen. I saw one that had bloody shoulders. . . . But, Clint, what'll we all *do* way out West?"

"Work."

"How?"

"Well, I heard Captain Couch talkin' to paw. My, he's a man! He said we'd all fight Injuns first, then kill off the buffalo, before we'd go to farmin'."

"But, Clint—women like me can't fight Injuns an' kill buffalo!" expostulated May, bewildered.

"Why not—when you grow up?"

" 'Cause it—it's not ladylike."

"Well, by golly! you'll have to. The women have to help. Mom has a lot of spunk. She will. An' kids like you——"

"I'm not a kid," she interrupted, with indignation.

" 'Scuse me. Anyway, you're goin' out West, ain't you? It'll not be like back home. You'll have to pitch

10

in—help your mother—learn what you can—work an'
grow up an' get married. Every girl will have to do
that much or the West won't——"

Here Clint floundered while May stared up at him
aghast.

"Married? *Me!*" she gasped.

"Why, sure! You're no better'n anybody else."

"I—I didn't mean I was."

"I should think you'd want to be a pioneer's wife
some day."

"What's a pioneer?" asked May, fascinated.

"Well, I reckon a pioneer is like what paw will be.
He'll go ahead, out where there's nobody. An' more
men like him will come. They'll fight the Injuns an'
bears an' buffaloes, cut down trees, build log cabins,
plow an' plant an' reap. Make the land so more people
will come. That's a pioneer."

"I like a pioneer. . . . Clint, will you be one?"

"Reckon I'm slated for a pioneer, sure enough. I'd
like to raise horses."

"Clint, I'll grow up an' be a pioneer's wife," burst
out May.

"Ah-huh. You will if you're worth your salt."

May slipped a not altogether timid hand under
Clint's arm, and she peeped roguishly up from under
her sunbonnet.

"Would you have me, Clint?"

"What for?"

"For your pioneer wife? Course, when I grow up.
It won't be long now. I'm ten years old. . . . Would
you?"

"Reckon I would—come to think of it."

"But you'd be *glad* to?"

"Sure," replied Clint, hastily.

"We'd have to fall in love first, wouldn't we?" mused
May, with a dreamy smile.

"Well, it'd be more proper, but pioneers can't wait
for everythin'."

"Then, Clint—I promise," said May, very solemnly.

"All right, May. I do, too."

And so these children rode on the driver seat of the

11

prairie schooner, across the grassy plain, gazing with the hopeful eyes of youth over the purple calling horizon, in their innocence and romance true to the great movement of which they were a part.

Sunset, a wide flare of gold, brought the caravan to a halt along a heavily timbered creek bottom. This was Fish Creek, an ideal place to camp. Grass was abundant and firewood for the cutting. Horses and oxen were unhitched, to be turned loose in charge of twenty guards. The scene was a bustling one of camp life on a huge scale. All along the line merry shouts and voices sounded, the axes rang out, the fires sent up blue smoke, and soon fifty groups of hungry travelers sat cross-legged on the ground.

Clint was as hungry as anybody, but he remembered to pick out some choice morsels of food for little May. After supper he and May, with Jack at their heels, walked along between the wagons and the creek. For all they could see they were the only two children in the caravan. And women were almost as scarce. The grizzled freighters, the long-haired scouts, the sturdy pioneers all had a keen and kindly eye for the youngsters, and some of them shook their heads gravely.

Darkness came on apace. The camp fires flickered down. Guards patrolled the line. Coyotes began their mournful chorus. Clint crawled into the tent he shared with his mother, and went to bed without disturbing her. His father slept in the canvas-covered wagon. Presently Clint's dog came in and curled up at the foot of his bed. Soon all was quiet outside, and the flickering shadows on the tent faded.

Clint was up with the break of day. He had learned to love the early dawn. And to his disappointment he discovered that Fish Creek was not felicitously named. When he got back to camp empty-handed his father and Mr. Bell laughed at him. But little May gave him a smile that was recompense.

Soon the caravan moved out toward the west. They made twenty miles that day, and almost as many the next. On the sixth day buffalo were sighted far to the south. All Clint's yearning eyes could make out was

12

a long, dim, dark line. That night the camp was pitched upon the level plain, some distance from a watercourse. Clint was quick to grasp why the wagons were drawn in a circle, close together, with openings at two ends. They formed a huge corral. The horses and oxen were put out under guard, and shortly after dark driven back and inside the corral. The men roped off the tents.

"Paw, what's that for?" asked Clint, pointing to the mass of stock inside the circle.

"Injuns, sonny, the scouts say," replied his father. "From now on we'll always be on the lookout."

Clint went soberly to bed and did not soon fall asleep. Jack seemed to act queerly, cuddling so close to him. Clint thought of his mother and little May. But nothing happened and soon he fell asleep.

Next morning, Captain Couch issued orders for drivers to stick close together, to keep on the move, and watch the head and tail of the caravan.

Clint knew mischief was afoot. When he climbed to his high seat and took up the reins his heart was in his throat. The caravan started briskly, each wagon close on the heels of the one in advance. The mounted scouts rode far ahead and the rear guard fell behind. Driving was no fun that morning for Clint Belmet. Once May Bell waved a little hand at Clint. How white her face looked! The strong pull on the reins prevented Clint from waving back, but he knew she understood that.

Nevertheless, the hours passed, the miles grew in number and nothing happened. Clint felt an easing of the strain. He drove as well as any of the teamsters, though his arms ached. Toward afternoon low clouds of dust moved across the prairie. Again Clint saw the dim black line, and did not need to be told it was a vast herd of buffalo. It moved, and therefore was not so far away. He was thrilled anew, and awed, and watched till his eyes were tired.

Much to his relief, halt was called long before sunset. His roving eye swept the prairie. A green fringe of cottonwood trees, down in a dip, showed where there were water and wood for camp use. The caravan, however, drove into a compact circle, high up on the level. Every team was turned in, so that the wagon-tongue just missed the rear of the wagon in front.

This camp was no jolly picnic party, but serious business. Horses and oxen were unhitched and taken under strong guard down to water, and allowed to graze until sunset. Clint saw horsemen silhouetted black against the skyline—the scouts of the caravan on watch. At supper his father and Mr. Bell and the other men looked worried, and did not invite questioning. Clint found no chance to talk to May.

Darkness settled down quickly that night. There was no afterglow. Thin clouds masked the wan stars. Camp fires were extinguished, and what little conversation the men indulged in was low. No bells on the horses this night!

Clint's keen ears caught the speech of an old teamster: "Redskins somewhars, so Couch thinks. Pawnees or Arapahoes, likely. Wal, we kin stand it, jest so long as they're not Comanches."

The boy's intent mind recorded that name—*Comanches*. He crouched beside the red embers of the spread fire and listened. Men sat around, smoking and whispering, and finally were silent. The horses could be heard munching the grass.

"Sonny, better go to bed," advised his father. "There'll be fifty men on guard."

But Clint lingered. He thought his dog Jack acted more strangely than the night before. Jack was a shepherd, and what he did not know Clint thought was scarcely worth knowing. The coyotes might have caused Jack's fur to stand stiff. Yet he did not bark. Suddenly Clint caught a sharper, wilder sound from out in the blackness. It was a beast of some kind. Again it came—a deep full bay, like an unearthly hound might have rendered. The yelps of coyotes ceased.

"What was that?" whispered Clint to a man sitting near him.

"Prairie wolf, an' he shore can sing," was the reply. "We're gittin' out whar the wild begins, lad."

Clint sustained his first fear of the night, the gloom, the loneliness, and the unknown. With Jack close at his heels he slipped back to his mother's tent. It had been pitched between the two wagons, with the heavy freighter on the outside. If his mother was awake, she gave no sign. Inside the tent it was pitch black. Clint had a strange sensation—as if he had awakened with the cold of a nightmare upon him. Crawling to his blankets, he pulled off his boots and coat, and slipping in he covered up his head. He felt Jack settle down at his feet. Then all grew still except the throbbing in his breast.

After a while he uncovered his face so that he could breathe freer. All seemed silent as a grave. Clint tried to fall asleep, but in vain. The night bore some strange oppression. Jack felt it, for he was restless. He crawled close up to Clint and licked his hand. The horses were not moving.

Finally Clint dropped off to sleep. He was awakened by the dog. Jack was standing up, growling low. Clint heard him sniff. Then he went out of the tent. Clint lay awake. An owl hooted, far away and faint. Jack came running back into the tent, jumped on Clint's bed, and growled louder.

Then steps outside preceded the voice of Clint's father. "What ails that darn dog? Jack, come here."

"Paw, Jack smells somethin'," spoke up Clint.

"So you're awake, son? Well, he's sure actin' queer. Jumped in the wagon on my bed," replied Belmet.

Clint sat up. It was considerably lighter now. Evidently the moon had risen. He saw his father holding the flap of the tent open. Clint caught the gleam of a rifle.

"Jack acts like he wanted you to go with him," said Clint.

"Come on, Jack. Good dog. Hunt 'em up," called Belmet, and went away.

Right after that a shot cracked in camp, not far

15

from where Clint lay. It awakened his mother, who cried out in alarm.

"Mom, I don't know what it is, but I think Injuns," replied Clint, crawling out of bed. "Paw was just here. He took Jack."

Suddenly a rattling roar of rifle shots rang out right in camp. It appeared to string half round the circle. Clint dropped down, frightened out of his wits. Then came lighter shots, and a wild howling, the like of which Clint had never heard. His blood ran cold. A patter like hail on the tent! What could that be? More shots and hoarse shouts of men.

"My God! I'm shot!" cried Clint's mother, in a strangled voice.

"Oh, mom—mom!" screamed Clint, springing up in a panic. He saw his mother, who was on her knees, double up and sink down.

"Run for daddy—run!" she whispered, hoarsely.

Clint ran out wildly. It was pale moonlight. Men were surrounding the frightened horses. Clint saw flashes of fire from under the wagons and his ears seemed split by heavy concussions. He ran here and there, calling for his father. In his fright he fled through the opening in the circle of wagons, out to a crowd of men.

"Paw! Paw! Mother's shot," he cried, frantically.

"Who're you, boy?" queried a burly man, clutching Clint. "Who's your pa?"

"Reckon it's Jim Belmet's youngster," spoke up another man.

"Yes, he's my father. Oh, I want him! My mom's shot."

"Hyar come the men now," spoke up another man. "Jim was with them, chasin' the sneakin' devils."

Clint saw dark forms of men stridin' up, heard their low voices. Suddenly Jack bounded in sight and leaped upon Clint.

"How many did you kill?" queried the harsh-voiced man, as the party came up.

16

"Two we're sure of. They ran like deer. Got across the creek, where they had horses."

Clint recognized his father's voice. "Oh, paw! Mom's shot! Hurry!"

Belmet uttered a cry of alarm and thudded rapidly into the circle of wagons. Jack ran after him. Then Clint followed. When he reached their tent he saw a man with a lantern hurrying in. Breathless and in a cold sweat Clint spread the flaps. His father was kneeling beside a still, dark form. The man flashed the lantern over it. Clint saw his mother's face, strangely set and calm.

"Good God!" exclaimed Belmet, huskily, and bent down.

The other man lowered his lantern and placed a rough, kindly arm over Clint's shoulders. At the same time Jack whined and licked Clint's bare feet.

"Bear up, lad," said the man, hoarsely. "We're on the plains. An' them cussed Comanches have killed your mother."

3

Clint stayed in the tent, covered by his blankets. But they did not keep him warm. He seemed frozen inwardly. The dog kept close to him, trying to tell him something was wrong.

It was impossible to sleep. Every now and then Clint would raise himself to look at the still, blanketed form lying on the other side of the tent. His mother! He could not realize she was dead. When daylight broke once more this hideous nightmare would end. His father came in often.

None of the men went to bed any more that night. Clint heard their footfalls and low voices. They were not going to be surprised again by Indians.

The silver sheen on the canvas faded. There was

darkness a while, then the slow paling to dawn. At daybreak the camp was astir. Clint pulled on his boots and went out. The morning was like any other fine morning, but to Clint it was overcast by a sort of horror. He seemed stunned. He walked about. Outside the circle of wagons he saw two Indians lying stark, black-faced and terrible. Their almost naked bodies were bloody. One had a tuft of grass clenched in a tight fist.

Clint hurried back. Fires were burning, breakfast was being cooked, men were hitching up. Yet withal it was a silent camp. On all sides was the evidence of hurry.

When Clint got back to where he belonged, he saw his father and two men carrying a heavy blanketed object out of his tent. Jack came wagging his tail, but this morning he did not frolic. Clint watched the men.

Then he espied a pile of yellow earth, near a freshly dug hole. A grave! The men lowered the blanketed form. Two of them began to shovel the earth down upon it. His father knelt with clasped hands and closed eyes. Suddenly Clint realized they had buried his mother. He would never see her again. Those night devils had taken her away forever. He plunged into the tent and hid under his blankets, and it was as if he were crushed.

Presently his father called: "Come, son, we must eat an' go on. We must try to bear it. . . . The freighters tell me there are graves at every camp along the trail."

Clint got up, dried his eyes, and leaving the tent, he washed his face and brushed his hair. He espied his father at the Bell camp fire. Clint went over to sit down beside May. She looked white and scared. Mrs. Bell showed traces of tears on her face. None of them, however, mentioned the tragedy. They seemed to express the acceptance of something inevitable. Little May, seeing that Clint could eat, managed to eat something herself. The meal was brief.

One of the old scouts rode in and called: "Git up

18

an' git! Long drive today. An' we might be entertained."

"Clint, you can ride with me," said his father. "I'll find another driver for your wagon."

"Paw, if it's all the same to you I'd rather drive," returned Clint, swallowing hard.

"All right. Don't forget some grub an' drinkin'-water." His words were practical and unexpressive, but his look told volumes. As he turned away with the men one of them said, "Belmet, that lad will make a plainsman."

While Clint busied himself round the prairie schooner, the man who helped him hitch up proved quite loquacious.

"This hyar's my third freightin' trip," he told Clint. "Reckon we got off easy in last night's brush with the redskins—Comanches, too!"

"Did our men—kill many?" asked Clint, biting his lip.

"Nineteen. Reckon we'd not done so well but fer a dog——"

"Dog!" interrupted Clint. 'That was my Jack."

"Wal, he's a smart dog, an' you can lay to thet. We was all lined up with guns cocked when the varmints charged. We poured it into them hot an' heavy. You ought to have seen them wilt. This mawnin' we found nineteen bodies. I found six myself. One reddy was alive, an' I busted him over the haid with my gun. Wal, we hauled them down to the crick an' dug a big hole. Cap Couch an' two of his scouts scalped every last Injun. Funny aboot thet. These old plainsmen shore hate redskins, an' raise the ha'r of every darn one they can. After thet we throwed the Injuns in the hole an' covered them up. Cap Couch strung all the scalps on a buckskin thong an' hung the bloodin' things up on his wagon."

"Did we lose any—men?" asked Clint, curiously thrilled despite his stunned condition.

"Nope. But two got hurt. Jim Thorn has a bullet in

19

his laig, an' Tom Allen has a bad cut on his arm. But thet's all."

Clint climbed to his seat and waited for the wagon ahead of him to pull out. The horses were skittish. Clint had all he could do to control them. Soon the caravan was in motion. Clint felt a rending in his breast. He was leaving his dear mother here on this lonely prairie. He sobbed aloud. As he drove past her grave, marked by a rude cross of wood, his eyes were dim. He fought the weakness that threatened to prostrate him. He had been trusted with all his father's belongings and his best horses. The winding road shone in the sunrise like a yellow thread across the prairie.

It was well Clint had a hard team to drive that day. The effort sustained him. He had to attend to a job which was not a slight one even for a man. The road had bad places. The pace-makers had been ordered to move as fast as possible. Clint's father was behind, and sometimes on down grades the big freight wagon rolled alarmingly close. When the caravan halted Clint was amazed to find they had reached Council Grove, the first stage-coach post on the line. The wounded men were left there to be taken back to Independence.

Next morning Clint was astonished to learn that the Bells were going to remain at Council Grove for the present. He was too full of grief to feel the loss of little May, yet the way she cried at parting touched him.

"Don't—forget—my—promise," she whispered, and Clint assured her he would not, and indeed he believed he would always remember her tear-wet eyes.

The Couch caravan went on, strengthened by more wagons joining at Council Grove. That day passed. Again Clint slept the deep slumber of weariness. Then days and nights swept by as swiftly as the rolling of the wheels. He had his work and it was all but too much for him. Yet he held on, and while he grew stronger, more accustomed to his arduous task, the

20

dread misery in his breast gradually softened to sorrow.

On the twenty-ninth of June the caravan reached Fort Larned, where a stop of a week was to be made. Clint and his father camped with most of the freighters outside the fort. It was a wonderful place, quite different from Independence. Despite his sadness, Clint could not help the curiosity and interest of youth.

Fort Larned bustled with activity. There was one large store, where eight clerks had all they could do to wait on the many customers. Clint's father told him there were nearly a hundred white hunters and trappers there to sell their winter catch of furs, and fully a thousand Indians of different tribes. Clint could see the different costumes of the Indians, but did not soon learn to distinguish one tribe from another. As for the hunters and trappers, they resembled one another closely. They wore buckskin, and Clint liked the look of them, strong, soft-stepping, lithe men, a few young, but mostly matured and grizzled, and never without their weapons.

The saloons did a thriving business, and every saloon was, as well, a gambling den. Clint's father took him into them. From that time dated Clint's aversion to gamblers. He preferred to walk the street, or go to the fort, where there were stationed four troops of dragoons and two companies of infantry, with Colonel Clark in command. Clint liked to mingle with them, and especially with the hunters and trappers. All the time he touched elbows with Indians. He avoided them as much as possible, hated them, yet always had an eye for their picturesque appearance in their tight-fitting deerskins and beaded moccasins. Some wore hats, some had eagle feathers in their black hair, some went bareheaded, and they all had buffalo robes.

Several days after Clint's arrival at the fort he was accosted in front of the store by two scouts. These men he had noted before.

"Howdy, boy! What's your name?" asked the more striking one of the two. He had wonderful piercing eyes that looked right through Clint, and he had long curling hair which fell on his broad buckskin-shirted shoulders.

"Clint Belmet," replied Clint.

"You're the lad we heard drove a freighter from Independence?"

"Yes, sir."

"Shake. . . . My name's Carson," said the scout, and he squeezed Clint's hand, which was sore from driving, so hard he had to suppress a yell.

"Put her thar. I'm Dick Curtis," said the other scout, and he repeated the hand-shaking performance.

"Lost your mother on the way?" asked Carson, his hand going to Clint's shoulder.

"Yes—sir," replied Clint, his lip trembling.

"Clint, I know how you feel," went on the scout, and there was something very winning about him. "It's hard. . . . The West needs such lads as you. Go on as you've begun. You've an eye in your head. Don't ever take to drink an' cards. An' learn that the only good Injun is a dead one."

The other scout, Curtis, patted Clint on the head, and then they passed on.

Belmet, standing at the entrance of the store with others, had been an interested spectator of this little incident. He put both hands on Clint's shoulders and looked down at him.

"Son, what did those scouts say to you?"

Clint told him, whereupon he swayed back impressively.

"Have you any idea who they are?"

"They told me. The short man was Curtis—Dick Curtis, he said. The tall one with the sharp eyes—he called himself Carson."

"Wal, I reckon. Carson. . . . *Kit Carson!* He is the greatest Indian fighter an' plainsman in the West."

"Kit Carson!" ejaculated Clint, incredulously. "I've read about him. . . . An' to think he shook hands with me! Gee! he nearly broke my fingers! . . . Paw, I'm right proud of what he said."

"So you should be. You see what this frontier life is like. Wal, a young man who takes to drink an' cards doesn't last long. So I hope you'll pay some heed to Kit Carson's advice. Reckon it was a great compliment to you."

"I'll take his advice, paw. I'll never drink an' gamble," rejoined Clint.

"Son, shake hands on that," said Belmet, with emotion.

They did not leave the fort until July 8th, when the freighters who had unloaded, of whom Belmet was one, joined a caravan returning across the plains to Missouri. It was a larger caravan, escorted by troops. Clint drove every day, and they arrived at Westport, later called Kansas City, on the 10th of August.

The largest commissary stores were located at Westport, and all incoming supplies had to be unloaded there. Belmet obtained a government contract, over which he was much elated. On August 20th he and Clint drove out with over seventy other freighters on the long eighteen-hundred-mile journey to Santa Fé. They were given an escort of ninety soldiers under Captain Payne. This government caravan had to haul supplies to every fort along the trail.

Belmet had disposed of the prairie schooner. He kept the horses, and purchased another freight wagon, a new one, painted green and red, which Clint drove. After a few days out, every man in the caravan had a cheery word for the boy and his dog, perched high on the seat, and even Captain Payne noticed him.

"Lad, I see you have a buffalo gun on the seat there," he said, quizzically.

"Yes, sir, but it's not there for buffalo," replied Clint, significantly.

On the afternoon of the sixth day the freighters camped at Cow Creek. It was a pretty spot, in the big bend of the Arkansas River. The green grove of cottonwoods and the shining water appealed strongly to Clint, but he had no time to indulge in his favorite sport. The wagons, as usual, were driven in a circle, the pole of one under the rear end of another, with three wagons left out to form a gateway for the stock to get in and out of the corral.

Horses and oxen were outside, feeding on the thick grass, under a heavy guard. Presently they were observed to be moving fast. The guards were hurrying the stock back to camp, and one rider came ahead shouting, "Indians! Indians!"

Captain Payne ordered his soldiers to mount, and the freighters to stand ready to repel attack. Then he climbed on top of a wagon with his field-glass. He took a long look.

"Nothin' to worry us," he announced, presently. "Pawnees an' Comanches fightin' each other."

"Wal, we shore hope they assassinate each other," remarked an old soldier.

"Johnny, come up an' have a look," called the Captain to Clint. "It's a sight worth seein'. An' it doesn't happen often."

Clint climbed up with alacrity and eagerly accepted the field-glass. With naked eye he could see the running horses, the flying manes, the flash of color, of smoke and fire. But the distance was too great to hear guns. When he got the glass focused upon the battling tribes he stood transfixed, with nerves and veins tingling.

On a hillside over a mile away several hundred Indians were engaged in a terrific running fight. It was plain that a larger party was pursuing a smaller, in the direction away from the camp. Naked red bodies, plumes and spears, flames of red and puffs of white, the level racing of wild mustangs, the plunging of horses together, the rearing of two with their riders fiercely fighting, the falling of Indians to the grass and the galloping away of riderless ponies—all these the glass brought vividly to Clint's rapt eyes, and held him trembling and unnerved until the warriors passed over the hill out of sight.

Clint handed the glass back to the smiling captain.

"So they fight—each other," he said, rather low. He felt a little sick.

"Lucky for us. That saved us a fight."

"I hope the Pawnees kill all those red-devil Comanches," returned Clint, grimly, suddenly answering to what the West had roused in him.

On the following morning, bright and early, the cavalcade was on the way again, with orders to keep close together and watch sharply for Indians. Sometimes clever Indians ambushed a wagon-train and attacked in the center, causing loss of life and freight before the mounted riders and scouts, who usually rode in front and in the rear, could reach the scene of conflict. Comanches, particularly, were wonderful horsemen, attacked as swiftly as the rush of a cyclone, and then were gone. No sign of Indians, however, marred the drive.

To Clint's disappointment, the caravan passed right through Council Grove, only a few of the freighters, and these the last in order on the line, halting for a few moments. The train drove on to Fort Zarah on the Walnut River, where two days were necessary to unload supplies for that place.

"Paw, did you see the Bells when we drove through Council Grove?" queried Clint, eagerly, on the first opportunity that offered.

"No, son, I didn't," replied his father, turning away.

Clint was busy at the moment, but later he got to thinking this over, and it struck him that his father appeared unusually abrupt and noncommittal. So when time offered, Clint approached him.

"Did you speak to anyone at Council Grove?"

"Yes. I stopped for a few moments long enough to hear some sickenin' bad news. . . . Clint, I wanted to tell you before, but I couldn't. Hard as it is, though, you ought to be told."

"Somethin' happened to our friends, the Bells?"

"It sure did," replied Belmet, gloomily, and he left the task upon which he had been occupied.

"Paw—was it bad?" asked Clint, his voice thickening.

"Couldn't be no worse. . . . A week or so after we left Council Grove it 'pears Sam Bell got sick of the frontier an' wanted to go back home. There was a rumor that a gambler fleeced him out of all his cash. No one could talk him out of the idea. An' he got on the first stage for Independence. Accordin' to some the stage broke down an' the dozen or more travelers had to make camp while the driver rode back for help. There was several mounted riders with the stage, good Injun-fighters, but durin' the night the party was raided by a bunch of redskins. The grown-ups were killed, scalped, an' left naked on the plain. The stage was burned an' all valuables stolen. There was no sign of the little girl, May Bell. It 'pears sure she was carried off into captivity. . . . The stage-driver never got back at all. It was buffalo-hunters comin' the other way who fetched the news to Council Grove."

Clint stood up unflinching to this shock, and without a word he stalked into the shade and covert of a grove of cottonwoods. He had not shown it, but his heart was bursting. Hiding in a secluded spot, he let himself go. His mother—and now little May! It was too much to be borne. He broke down and wept as never before in his life. That storm racked something out of him. When it was over, boyhood had left him and there was born in him the stern, grim hatred of the red men of the plains. Clint had somehow always felt that the white men were in the wrong. They had no right to usurp the hunting-grounds of the Indian tribes, to take their domain from them. For that was what this invasion amounted to. Up to the hour of his mother's murder Clint had secretly felt sympathy for the savage tribes of the West, who must, no matter what was said to the contrary, some day be driven back into the waste lands to starve. But the loss of his mother, and now added to it that of little May Bell, stultified all fairness in Clint's breast.

"I'll be an Injun-killer like Kit Carson," he vowed.

4

Two days later Clint's wagon-train rolled into Fort Larned, and Clint found himself meeting scouts and hunters who remembered him, one of whom was the buckskin-clad Dick Curtis.

"Wal, lad, you shore 'pear to be growin' husky—onless my eyes are pore," said Curtis, approvingly.

"Paw says I'm runnin' up like a weed."

"How old air you?"

"Nigh on to thirteen."

"Say, is thet Injun talk?"

"Honest, Mr. Curtis. You ask paw."

"All right, I'll take your word fer it. But you shore look older. . . . An' don't call me Mister."

Curtis seemed disposed to be friendly and he took Clint around with him while he made purchases. He informed Clint that he would accompany the wagon-train as far as Fort Union, where he turned off the trail to go up into the mountains of New Mexico.

"Is Mr. Carson goin' with you?" asked Clint.

"No. Kit left some time ago. He lives at Taos, New Mexico. He's married to a Spanish woman an' he has a fine place. You be shore to go an' see Kit. He's the greatest man in these plains an' he took a shine to you."

Curtis introduced Clint to Jim Baker and John Smith, two famous frontier characters. They had been on the frontier for twenty-five years, which meant that these adventurers were among the first to cross the plains. Clint had never before seen such rough, dirty, greasy, disreputable-looking men. But for their beards and jolly talk, most of which was profane, he could not have distinguished them from Indians. Baker was married to a Cheyenne woman, Indian fashion, so Curtis said, and Smith had for wife a Comanche girl, who was handsome and could talk some English. The revulsion Clint had felt for everything pertaining to the Comanche tribe apparently did not extend to her. Clint thought her pleasant and more interesting than her renowned trapper husband. Smith had made a good deal of money buying furs from the Indians and selling them to the whites.

"Clint, there're some short drives when the Old Trail starts uphill out yonder," said Curtis, "which means we make camp early. Do you like to hunt?"

"Yes, but fishin' comes first."

"Me, too. But a feller has to get fresh meat. Have you got a rifle?"

"Yes. It's an old buffalo gun."

"Wal, thet'll do fer buffs, but you need a lighter gun fer deer an' turkey. An' say, there shore are plenty of them when we begin climbin' the divide. Fer thet matter you'll see deer all the way now, an' a mess of buffalo. How about buyin' a rifle? An' you'll shore want a knife. What'd you scalp your first redskin with?"

"I—I won't scalp him."

"Haw! Haw! Wal, then, what'll you skin your first buffalo with—or deer?"

"I've got a penknife."

"Clint, you're on the frontier now. You want a blade thet'll go clean through a redskin's gizzard an' stick out far enough to hang your hat on. Come, we'll go in Tillt's store an' I'll pick out a gun, a knife, an' I reckon a buckskin shirt."

"But, Mr. Curtis, I—I haven't any money," replied Clint. "Paw's got my wages."

"Wal, you can get what I spend an' give it to me. An' I'll shore tell yore paw somethin'."

When Clint emerged from that crowded store he felt that it would take only a puff of wind to blow him sky high. He simply could not walk naturally. And when he and Curtis reached Clint's camp it was no wonder that Jim Belmet stared a moment and then burst out, "For the land's sake!"

"Paw, this is my—my friend Dick Curtis," said Clint, loftily.

"Howdy, Belmet!" greeted the trapper, extending a

brawny hand. "Reckon you be'n neglectin' this youngster. He's shore the Kit Carson stripe an' there ain't
no sense in holdin' him down."

The caravan, still under escort of Captain Payne,
took what was called the Dry Trail. It cut off about
two hundred and fifty miles, but was not safe for an
unescorted train, and without scouts who knew where
to go for water.

Several days out from Fort Larned the perceptible
heave of the prairie land began in earnest. How vast
the slow, endless rise of grass! It was no longer green,
but gray and, in more barren spots, a bleached white.
No better feed, however, could have been found. Clint
did not grow accustomed to the boundless expanse.
More and more it fascinated him. As he drove on he
watched the plain, and his keen eye seldom went long
without espying bird or beast of some kind. Travel
was slow, because of the grade, and uphill driving was
easier, at least for the drivers. The road appeared to
wind more than formerly, owing to frequent washes
and gullies that had to be headed. Clint believed he
drove and watched for days without seeing a bush or
a tree. When camp was reached nothing but buffalo
chips could be found to burn. These made a first-rate
fire. Clint was always ready to gather this fuel, for
anything that led him away from camp had an attrac-
tion. Buffalo were sighted often, though so far off that
Clint could scarcely believe his eyes.

He lost track of days. The endless prairie had engulfed Clint. Already he seemed to have traveled
twice the eighteen hundred miles the guides claimed
lay between the Missouri and Sante Fé.

One day they arrived at the Crossing of the Cimmaron a full two hours before sunset. Curtis suddenly
confronted Clint, rifle in hand, and with a grin that
electrified Clint.

"Chuck the work. Grab your gun an' come with
me," said the scout.

"What's up?" queried Clint.

"Buffalo, an if we hustle we'll git a shot before any

29

of these fellars. . . . No, don't fetch the army rifle. Grab thet old buffalo gun. . . . Good! She's loaded. Now follow me."

Following Dick Curtis was easier said than done, Clint soon discovered. The plainsman started off at a lope, led down into a swale under a hill, and soon placed the camp out of sight and sound. When he slowed to a walk it was none too soon for the panting Clint. His breast was throbbing, hot and wet. The old buffalo gun weighed a hundred pounds. Presently Clint glanced up from the hunter's heels to observe that he was making way up a grassy draw, warm and fragrant. They jumped rabbits, coyotes, and once a heavier beast which made a commotion in the grass.

Finally Curtis began to crawl, motioning Clint to do the same. The plainsman was not very communicative while on a stalk. Clint had to bite his tongue to keep from asking what it was all about. He would have preferred a little preparation. Curtis was too sudden. Clint had little confidence in his own marksmanship, and it seemed likely that he would be directed to shoot at something presently.

Curtis ceased crawling and looked back, his face shiny with sweat.

"Don't blow so hard," he whispered. "An' you move as noisy as a cow. . . . Boy, we're huntin', an' there's some buffalo less 'n a hundred feet."

"Oh—no!" gasped Clint, suddenly limp.

"Shore are. Can't you hear them nippin' grass? Git your breath now. They haven't winded us."

Clint had more to get than his breath. Was not this genial frontiersman taking too much for granted? Clint drew in deeper and deeper breaths, expanding his lungs until he thought he would burst; and he fought with all his might the threatened collapse of what seemed to be his whole interior being.

Curtis touched him and crawled on. Very softly Clint followed, keeping his rifle off the ground and his head beneath the crest of the tall grass—no slight tasks. But he had almost recaptured his breath. The hunter wormed his way flat, like a snake, and made

30

no more noise than a snake. Clint believed he was doing better when suddenly he reached Curtis's side.

"Look," whispered his guide, parting the grass.

They had come out on the brow of the slope. Clint's startled gaze took in what seemed a mountain of black woolly fur right before him. He shook like a leaf and his heart gave a great bound, then seemed to stop. The black thing was an enormous bull buffalo, standing almost broadside, with his huge head up. He had heard or scented them.

"Aim behind his shoulder," whispered Curtis. "Low down . . . lower. There! Freeze on him. . . . *Now!*"

Clint knew he could hit the beast, but what would happen then? As one in a dream he leveled the heavy rifle, rested on his knee, strained with his last ounce of will to stiffen, covered the hairy space indicated— and pulled trigger. Boom! The tremendous kick knocked Clint flat and the gun fell in front of him. He heard a rumbling. Then he scrambled up, ready to run. The scout was laughing uproariously.

"Aw! I missed him!" cried Clint, in despair.

"Nary miss," replied Curtis, giving Clint a slap on the shoulder. "You hit plumb center. He walked off a few steps, gave a heave an' a groan, an' keeled over. The rest of the bunch ran off the other way, which was darn lucky fer us. . . . But I thought you'd shot thet buffalo gun?"

"I had. Only now I forgot to hold it tight. . . . I'll betcha I'll never forget again."

"Wal, lad, you didn't disappoint me," returned Curtis, with satisfaction. "An' Kit Carson will shore be tickled when I tell him. Come now an' take a look at your first buff."

When he rose, Clint observed the bull lying prone scarcely a hundred feet distant. He had gone only a few steps. Other buffalo showed a quarter of a mile off, ambling away. Clint ran forward with a sensation of mingled awe, delight, and regret. The eyes of the buffalo were glazing over, his tongue stuck out, and blood was streaming into the dry ground. Round and round the dead beast Clint walked, looking again and

31

again at the great black head with its short shiny dark horns, the shaggy shoulders and breast, the tufts of hair down the forelegs. It was far larger than any ox in the caravan. It had an unpleasant odor, somehow raw and wild, wholly unlike that of domestic animals. Clint stared with gaping mouth until the practical Curtis called him to action:

"Wal, you can break in your new knife. We'll skin him. I'll pack the hide back to camp an' you can pack a hunk of rump beef. We'll sure have rump steak fer supper. My mouth is waterin' now."

Clint was to learn the ardous difficulties of skinning a tough old buffalo bull. But the two of them accomplished it before sunset and, heavily burdened, they labored back to camp by a short cut over the ridge.

The two heavy guns and the generous cut of buffalo meat were about all Clint could carry, and Curtis staggered along under the roll of hide. Upon reaching the line of campers they were hailed vociferously. Before they got far there was a string of hungry freighters making a bee line in the direction of the dead buffalo. Clint received a strong impression of the savory nature of rump steak.

When they arrived at Clint's camp Curtis threw the huge hide down with a thud.

"Thar! It shore was a 'tarnal load!"

Belmet and his contingent crowded around, to stare at Clint and the scout, and to ask questions in unison.

"Nope. It was Clint who shot him. I only packed in the hide," replied Curtis.

"Say! You mean to tell us that boy killed this buffalo?" demanded Belmet, incredulously.

"Shore he did. Made a slick job of it."

"Aw, go wan," retorted an Irish teamster, derisively.

"Dick, we all know you're given to tricks," said another man.

"Why, thet lad might lift a buffalo gun to his shoulder, but if he shot it he'd be knocked into a cocked hat."

"Well, I was," laughed Clint, speaking for himself.

"Fellars, he made a clean shot—plugged the old

bull right through the middle; but he forgot to freeze on the gun, an', wal, I thought he was goin' clear down the hill."

"Haw! Haw! Haw!" they roared.

"Clint, did you shoot him—honest?" asked Belmet, in a manner that showed he would believe the boy.

"Sure did, paw."

"Belmet, I'm thinkin' we'll call him Buff," said Curtis, with a broad grin, as he took his rifle from Clint.

Right there Clint Belmet received the nickname that was destined to become known on the plains.

"An' I'm sure invitin' myself to your camp fer supper," continued Curtis. "There won't be a grease spot left of our bull, an' I can't afford to miss my hunk of rump steak."

"You're welcome," returned Belmet, heartily.

"Wal, Buff," added one of the wags, addressing Clint, "next camp I'm askin, you to take me huntin'."

As the calvacade drew well up on the slope toward the mountains, which began to show like dim vague clouds above the horizon, deer grew numerous. They traveled mostly in small herds and were quite tame. They would move away out of range, then stand to gaze at the wagons. Clint noted how the long ears stuck up. He saw several large groups, and once, as the caravan wound along a river on the edge of Colorado, a herd of at least two hundred trooped up out of the hollow. They made a spectacle Clint would never forget.

"Jest like pets," remarked an old freighter. "Pity to shoot them. I never do onless I'm hungry."

Clint's opinion coincided with this. He reflected, though, that he had never heard anything approaching such sentiment spoken on behalf of the buffalo. Clint considered that strange, and after pondering over it he concluded the vast and countless numbers of buffalo dwarfed any value they might have. He wondered if it would always be so.

Day after day the caravan plodded on. How short the

33

days and what little progress the wagons made! Yet the miles counted. One camp, for the most part, resembled all the other camps, and their number seemed innumerable. They all had names, but Clint forgot those that did not associate themselves in his memory with some especial feature or incident.

The prairie seemed endless. Clint felt that he was crossing the whole world. Yet the level plain, and the rolling prairie, and the heaving upland, all everlastingly gray and lonely, never palled upon his senses. It was home to millions of buffalo, and deer, wolves, antelope, and myriads of smaller animals, and to the nomadic savage tribes who lived upon them. To look back down a gradual slope that dimmed to a purple haze fifty miles away always swelled Clint's heart. Far back there somewhere was the grave of his mother. He never forgot that. Both the distance and the event of her death seemed remote.

One night when they reached camp late, Dick Curtis said to Clint, "Wal, Buff, if it's clear tomorrow, about noon you'll see the Rockies."

All the next morning, which was sunny and bright, Clint's keen eyes, as he drove along, sought to pierce the wall of haze that rose above the horizon. At midday dim shapes began to emerge. They darkened and lifted. Gradually they took form. Mountains tipped by white clouds! They roused an indefinable emotion in Clint. After a while he made the astonishing discovery that the white cloud crown was snow. The high peaks were snow-tipped. How tediously the horses and oxen moved on! Clint longed to fly to where he could see the Rockies clearly.

The approach, however, was so gradual that changes in the view came almost imperceptibly. Clint grew weary, watching and yearning. The prairie was wonderful, but the mountains! What could he call them?

On the third day, as the wagons topped a ridge they had been ascending all morning, Clint gazed over broken yellow and gray foothill country that led up to the grand bulk of the divide. It was Clint's first sight of

34

the real grandeur of the Rockies. Black bulk heaving to the white peaks that pierced the blue! Mountain after mountain, peak after peak, ranged away into the purple obscurity of the north. Southward a lofty butte hid the range. Somewhere between that butte and the mountains must lie the pass over which the caravan had to go. It looked impossible. Clint followed the winding yellow road, down and around and into the foothills. Who had been the first to travel it? Clint knew it had been an old buffalo trail, then an Indian trail, next the trail of the explorers, then of the trappers, then the gold-seekers, and now the freighters, of whom he was one. But the first white men who trod that old trail—how intrepid, how magnificent! Clint had a vague conception of their spirit and their greatness.

To Clint's dismay, the mountains soon retreated and became lost to his view. That sunset he camped in the foothills. They were rocky, yellow, bare eminences, with but few trees and these scrubby. The air was cold and the night wind came keen down the draw. Clint enjoyed a wood fire once more.

Next day the uphill grind went on, and it was a wearing winding between yellow hills, hot when the sun shone down direct.

It took four days like this one to cross the pass into New Mexico, and the only interesting feature about the whole climb was its culmination.

But once out in the open again, in the high country that gave promise of rugged beauty and wildness, Clint once more thrilled to the journey. At last the caravan drove into Fort Union. This was a small but important post, commanded by Major Greer, with four companies of dragoons. It was the principal distributing point for all of New Mexico.

Dick Curtis took leave of Clint here.

"Wal, Buff, I'm packin' up into the hills to trap all winter. Hope to see you along the old trail somewhere in the spring."

"Good-by an' good luck," said Clint. "I wish I was goin' with you."

"Sometime, when you're older, I'd like to have you. Friends part out here an' don't always see each other again. . . . When the time comes for you to draw a bead on a redskin, remember Dick Curtis."

Half the load of the freighters was left at Fort Union, and when they resumed the journey the wagons were light. This made travel easier on men and animals. The trail from the fort wound along the course of the Colinas River, the first mountain stream in Clint's experience. It was low and clear, and in some places there were deep pools where, according to one of the freighters, mountain trout abounded. Clint longed to have a try for them, but no opportunity afforded. Travel was fast and the soldiers were on the alert. Apache Pass was soon to confront them—one of the most dangerous points along the whole length of the overland trail. Many a massacre had been perpetrated there.

Clint had no curiosity to see it. The mere idea of an Indian attack had a twofold effect upon him—to prickle his skin tight and to form a burning knot within him. The sensations were antagonistic and diverse.

But he could not help seeing what lay open to view. The caravan halted some distance from Apache Pass, while scouts went forward to reconnoiter. Clint saw a narrow defile leading between high narrow cliffs of yellow stone. The stream led in there and so did the road. It did not take much acumen to grasp that it was a perilous place for wagon-trains and a perfect setting for an ambuscade. The hills on each side were rough and covered with brush. Concealment for a large body of Indians and their horses was possible on both sides of the Pass.

One of the teamsters was holding forth to a group of companions. The manner in which he pointed to the Pass and surroundings indicated familiarity. Clint joined the circle.

"Yep, I was in thet fight here over a year ago," he was saying. "I guess I was. Look here—an' here." He showed scars on his head and arm. "There was a big train, a hundred wagons about, an' some old Indian-

36

fighters. We got split up by accident, an' some of us drove into the Pass before the others showed up below here. Wal, I was among the bunch thet went in first. An' soon we thought hell had busted loose. They'd let *us* get well in before startin' the ball, an' then they shot right down on us. Wal, the rest of our men heard the shootin' an' they came a-runnin'. The Indians—they was Apaches, the worst red men thet ever lived—were all on the right-hand side an', as it proved, had their horses down in the draw there. When the shootin' an' yellin' were at their highest naturally them Apaches didn't see or hear our seventy-odd men who were comin' up back. Thet is, they didn't see them first off. Wal, they made a runnin' fight for their horses an' left twenty-seven dead an' crippled Indians behind. The crippled ones didn't stay crippled long! . . . We had nine dead an' a lot hurt, some bad, an' I was one. We'd got off wuss if we hadn't piled off at the first fire an' hid under the wagons. We could have held them off, too. . . . Wal, since thet last fight there hasn't been a big caravan go through without a company of soldiers."

"An' quite right thet is," spoke up another freighter. "But one of these days a wagon outfit will risk it. Apache Pass hasn't seen the last of its bloody massacres. Kit Carson himself told me thet."

In due time scouts returned, reporting the coast clear and that passage could be made without risk. Whereupon the caravan proceeded. Clint was all eyes. Apache Pass was a tortuous crack in the hills, dark and yellow, almost haunted. The shallow stream flowed over the roadbed. Clint pictured the scene of the massacre, and when he emerged once more into the open he was in a cold sweat.

Beyond the Pass the road climbed over beautiful slopes of gray grass, almost silver, that led up to isolated cedars and on to thick woods of piñon and at last the dark-green pines. Deer and antelope trotted in plain view. Huge rocks loomed up here and there; a flock of wild turkeys spotted the gray slope, oblivious of the passing cavalcade. From the heights a

37

breeze blew down and ravens breasted it, swooping, sailing as if in play.

The days multiplied and passed swiftly, as if by magic. Such marvelous country inspired Clint more than the purple plains. New Mexico appeared white and black, though the grass that looked white at a distance was really gray, and the black of the timbered ridges and ranges was a dark green. It was a wild and fragrant country. The smell of cedars, piñons, pines, and sage was new and intoxicating to Clint.

Starvation Peak near Las Vegas struck Clint even more wonderfully than had the first sight of the Rockies. It was an isolated green peak, sheering to a steep butte of rock, scantily spotted with cedars, and level on top.

Clint asked an old freighter the reason for its name.

"Wal, it's an interestin' story, an' true enough, I reckon," replied the plainsman. "In the early days, I don't know how fur back, but 'most two hundred years, some Spaniards got in a fight with Injuns. Apaches, I suppose, though I ain't sartin about that. Wal, the Spaniards took to the peak thar. Climbed it an' fought from on top. They had grub an' water for a spell, an' no doubt they was expectin' help from somewhar. But it never came. The Injuns surrounded the peaks, keepin' such watch as only Injuns can. An' they starved the Spaniards to death. Thet's why it's called Starvation Peak."

"Spaniards? They're white people, of course," replied Clint, thoughtfully. " 'Pears to me the whites are payin' dreadful high for this West."

"Right you are, Buff. But any old plainsman like me will tell you the whites haven't begun to pay what they'll have to."

Las Vegas was such a rough town that Clint's father would not allow him much liberty, especially at night. Between Las Vegas and Santa Fé there were two stations, San José and Barrel Springs. The Spanish atmosphere and color of Santa Fé were delightful to Clint, and he appreciated the comparative quiet of this very old town.

The wagon-train unloaded here, and then drove out along the river several miles, to good feed, wood, and water, and there located camp for the winter.

"Six months an' more, son," announced Belmet. "We've work, of course, but I'm worryin' about your schoolin'."

"I fetched some school books, paw, an' I'll go through them. If I get stuck can't you help me?"

"Wal, I ain't so all-fired smart, myself. But mebbe there's some one in the outfit who can."

"How about huntin'?" queried Clint, anxiously.

"Fine. I inquired of a trapper in town. Buffalo, an' turkey right along the river here. An' up in the hills bear an' lion, also deer. We won't want for fresh meat anyway."

"I saw a lot of Indians in town," returned Clint, weighing the fact doubtfully.

"Yes, but there are six troops of dragoons at the fort. They're out an' around a good deal, I'm told, an' the Injuns won't bother us."

"I'd never trust an Indian."

"Good," said Belmet, with satisfaction.

That very day numerous Indians visited the camp. They were friendly. Couch, the train boss, gave orders for everybody to feed them and be otherwise kindly disposed. Clint was both repelled and attracted by the Apaches. He never would be able to abide the Comanches, no matter how friendly.

5

The erection of camping quarters was a matter of preference. Some of the freighters lived in their wagons, others pitched tents, and a few took advantage of the abundance of wood to build cabins. Clint and his father belonged to the last and smallest contingent.

They were new to log-cabin construction, as their neighbors most jocosely informed them.

"Buff, what is thet thar shed you're puttin' up?" queried the old plainsman who had taken a liking to Clint.

"Shed? It's a log cabin," replied Clint.

"Shore it ain't to live in!". .

"Hey, Belmet," asked another friend, "air you a carpenter?"

"Them logs don't gibe," remarked a third.

Belmet took it all good-naturedly and turned to Clint: "Say somethin' to them scallywags."

Clint had a retort ready: "Are you goin' to be freighters all your lives? Aren't you ever goin' to be pioneers?"

"Reckon thet's the idee, of course," replied one.

"That's why we're learnin' to put up a log cabin."

It was early October and beautiful weather, with a frosty nip at dawn, sunny mornings, warm hazy Indian-summer afternoons, and cold nights. The cottonwood leaves had begun to change from green to gold. Far up the dark slopes patches of yellow told of the frost at work on aspens. Down in the gulches and valleys there were touches of red and bronze.

Clint was longing to go hunting, but kept faithfully at work.

One afternoon about three o'clock a stranger appeared at the Belmet cabin. He did not have a prepossessing appearance and looked hot and hurried.

"Can I buy a hoss?" he asked.

"Reckon you can, an' cheap, too. We've gone into winter camp," replied Belmet, leaving his work.

It happened that Couch came up just then, accompanied by another man whom Clint knew only by sight. They might have been following this stranger; at least they were curious.

"What's this fellow want?" asked Couch, abruptly, of Belmet.

"Says he wants to buy a hoss."

Couch turned his sharp gaze upon the stranger. "What's your name?"

40

"Miller. Hank Miller," was the reply.

"Where you from?"

"Santa Fé."

"Why didn't you buy a hoss there?" queried Couch, waxing suspicious.

"No time," returned the other, nervously.

"Huh! Had trouble?"

"Reckon I had."

"What about?"

"Wal, I was gamblin' an' got accused of cheatin'."

"Any truth in thet?"

"No. I called them all liars."

"Ahuh. An' what happened?"

"They jest went for me—the three men I was playin' with, an' some outsiders. I had to throw my gun."

"Hurt any of them?"

"Don't know. Sure left town in a hurry. . . . But see here, you're takin' up my time. I want a hoss an' saddle. I'll pay. I'd had one but for your interference. Who'n hell are you, anyway?"

Couch pulled his gun.

"Hands up, right quick."

The man who called himself Miller turned pale and was not slow to obey.

"Belmet, relieve Mr. Miller of them shootin'-irons. I notice he's packin' two," went on Couch, briskly.

Clint's father took the two guns, and also a knife.

"Sanderson, you stay here with Belmet an' watch this man while I ride into Santa Fé. Don't let him loose."

Couch got on his horse and rode away. As soon as he was out of sight Miller gave a lunge and broke free from Sanderson. He knocked Belmet down and started to run. Quick-witted Clint stuck out his foot. The man tripped and fell headlong. Whereupon two very angry freighters pounced on him, handled him severely, tied him securely, and roped him to a wagon wheel.

"Helluva way to—treat—a fellar," panted Miller, balefully. "I tell you I'm honest. But I'm—afeared of

41

—them gamblers. . . . Give you a hundred—dollars to let—me go."

"Shut up or I'll bust your head," returned Belmet, darkly, feeling of the bruise on his chin. "Say, Sanderson, what happened after he biffed me?"

"Buff tripped him, an' he shore went pilin' to the dirt," replied Sanderson, with an appraising eye on the youngster.

"Clint, you doggoned son-of-a-sea-cook," ejaculated Belmet, in mingled wonder, pride, and concern, "I'm plumb worried about you! Always doin' things!"

"But, Belmet, I'd bored the fellar but for Buff upsettin' him," interposed Sanderson, taking Belmet seriously.

Clint went back to work then, leaving the two guarding the prisoner. Couch arrived in quick time, with the sheriff and two deputies from Santa Fé.

"Reckon you're wanted," said the sheriff to Miller. "Thar's a dead man in town thet somebody has to account for, an' a crippled one who might identify you. Come along. . . . Cut him loose, men."

They led Miller away, like a beast on a halter, and Belmet and Sanderson hurried to saddle horses to accompany them, as did other curious freighters. Clint had no wish to go. He thought the man might be dishonest, but felt sorry for him. Resuming work, Clint busied himself until sunset and then quit for the day. He never failed to watch the sunset. It was never twice the same. Today there were heavy broken clouds and much gold and rose, with wonderful shafts of light shooting down into the purple valley.

Before dark Belmet rode in, and after attending to his horse he joined Clint. His customary smile was wanting.

"Paw, I got supper ready to cook," said Clint.

"Sorry I'm late. Bet you're hungry. But I'm not. I'm sick as a dog."

"What happened, paw?" queried Clint, hurriedly.

"The crowd in town hanged that fellow we caught here. An' I saw it. My, I'm glad you didn't come!"

"Hanged him? Aw! What for?"

42

"He was a gambler, a cheat, an' a bad egg. Killed one man an' wounded another. He was identified. Then a bunch of men, reckon about twenty, took him away from the sheriff. An', Clint, they strung him up in a jiffy, before I knew what was goin' to come off. Hanged him right in the plaza! An' he's hangin' there now."

Clint visualized his father's words. It was on the tip of his tongue to say he wished they had never come out West, but he checked himself. That would not have been honest. Despite the hardships and the shock of his mother's murder, he could not say he hated this wild and terrible frontier. Something strong and stange was at work deep within him.

In a few more days the cabin was habitable and Clint and his father moved in their belongings. Then the envy of their neighbors afforded much satisfaction. If the weather remained normal there would be a month or more before the snows came, and longer before winter set in cold.

For days the valley and the hills had been resounding to the reports of the freighters' rifles. They were killing game for the winter supply of meat. So that when Clint and his father started out to do their hunting they had to go father afield. The buffalo and deer had been driven away. Indeed, it turned out that the buffalo had sought a low altitude, and the hunters had orders not to go too far from camp.

Clint shot at a good many bucks before he hit one. Sight of a big blue deer, his long ears up, his white tail shining, acted so powerfully upon Clint that his gun wabbled, his eyes blurred, his hands trembled, and he simply could not shoot straight. Still he kept on trying. The hunters made fun of him and advised him to take out the heavy buffalo gun. The day came, however, when his bullet sped true, and a fine buck pitched high in the air and, plunging down, rolled over to dig his horns into the earth.

Wild-turkey hunting, however, appealed most to Clint. He could not quite determine why, but he imagined because it was the hardest work, the most fun, and turkey meat was the best to eat. Clint's father, using a shotgun, had bagged several turkeys. They had roast turkey, which settled the matter for Clint. A "drumstick," as he called the leg, or the breast of wild turkey, was food, Clint unblushingly averred, of which he could never get enough.

But hitting a running wild turkey with a rifle was a feat that required considerable skill. Somewhere Clint had heard that to shoot wild turkeys with a shotgun was pot-hunting and not sport. Clint aspired to be a real hunter, so he stood by the lighter of his two rifles and spent not a little of his money for ammunition.

High up on the mountain slope above camp Clint found wild turkeys. Deer did not seem to frequent this range to any extent. It was a hard climb, but not far from camp, and Clint's father and Captain Couch permitted him to go, provided he would not stray over the ridge.

The early morning, before the sun was up, found Clint, crackling the frosty grass and breathing a cloud of steam, bound for his favorite spot. This was a wide level bench, grassy in spots, with clumps of piñon trees. It happened to be a good season for piñon nuts—a somewhat infrequent occurrence. And these nuts were beginning to fall from the trees, which fact attracted the turkeys. Two or three large flocks frequented this feeding-ground. Any early morning Clint could count on finding them. No matter how often he shot—which was a disgraceful number of times without bringing a feather—the turkeys would come back. This attested to the sweetness of piñon nuts.

Now Clint had it forced upon him that he knew little or nothing about hunting wild turkeys. One of his advisers in camp had said: "Find where they roost." Another counseled: "Ketch 'em at their water hole." A third averred: "You gotta learn to call turkeys. Make a caller out of the wing bone of a turk, an' practice till you can gobble an' cluck an' put to beat the band. Then you can hide an' call. The turkeys will come right up to you, an' you can take your pick." Clint's father laughed at his importunities and said: "Take the shotgun loaded with buckshot an' knock 'em over."

44

Clint acted on all the advices except the last, and he began to have admiration for turkeys. They had so far always seen or scented or heard him before he got within range. The smallest of the tree flocks consisted of about fifteen gobblers. They were huge, wary birds. They were the most beautiful wild things that he had seen. Most were dark, purple-breasted, with a long beard, and a small cunning red head, dark in the back, flecked with brown, and they had a spread of reddish-white tail that dazzled Clint. A few were bronze, and one, conspicuous for his enormous size, was more white than bronze. Many times Clint had come within rifle-shot of this old flock, but when he espied them they were all on the run. And couldn't they run! He would shoot and run and shoot and run, all to no avail.

The second flock was larger in number, and consisted of the sober-colored hens and yearlings; and the third, which must have contained a hundred, were all apparently young turkeys.

One day Clint made a lucky shot into this third flock and he killed a young gobbler of about fifteen pounds. With glee and pride Clint packed his first victim down to camp. He exhibited it proudly to his father and their immediate neighbors, then he picked and dressed it and hung it from the eaves of the cabin, where it would thoroughly cool. Next morning it was gone.

"Cat got it," said his father, "or maybe a coyote."

"Nothin' with four feet ever stole my turkey," stormed Clint, in a rage. "Look ahere!" And he pointed to the tracks of a man in the soft ground. "That's not my track, paw."

"By jiminy!" ejaculated Belmet, scratching his head. Evidently he wanted to laugh, but dared not.

"I'll trail that cat, b'gosh!" declared Clint, and right there began his education as a tracker. It availed little, however, for although he followed those tracks across to an adjoining tent and made sure of the culprit, he did not recover his turkey.

The next day Clint killed another gobbler from the same flock, and that night at supper he and his father put it where there was no danger of having it stolen. In fact, Clint ate until he had made up for the one he had lost.

Having acquired the knack of surprising the younger turkeys, Clint brought one in on several occasions. Next he shot a fine big hen out of the second flock. Ambitious and determined then, he devoted his energies and cunning to the great gobblers.

For several days he was destined to defeat and considerable humiliation. Finally he managed to secure an easy shot, which he missed. He characterized this as a case of "turkey fever." Then, the very first thing next morning, he had a snap shot, and knocked over one of the huge gobblers. The others roared away on the wing, a stirring and beautiful sight. The one he had hit began to thump and flop at a great rate. It made a tremendous racket. Clint dropped his gun and made for the tumbling monster. As he reached for it he received a buffet from a wing that almost caused him to lose his balance.

To his dismay the gobbler got up and ran. Clint darted after. He was fast on his feet, but the turkey was faster. By a desperate effort Clint bent low and grasped. He caught hold, but his hand came away full of beautiful tail feathers. This added to his eagerness and discomfiture. He chased that gobbler until he fell down from exhaustion.

On the descent to camp Clint was a sadder and wiser hunter. He decided to resort to strategy. Accordingly, he arose very early and climbed the slope before daybreak, and when the light came and the east burned red he was well concealed in the thickest and most likely piñon tree on the bench.

This morning he had gotten there first. From far up the slope, among the pines, came a gobble-gobble. With a start he sat up alert, watchful. The morning was still. He heard the swish of heavy wings, then the thud of a turkey alighting on the ground. These sounds were repeated. The birds were coming down from their roost. Would they go to drink or feed first? Clint was mighty curious, but he believed they would feed before going to water.

He waited, watching, listening with all his keenness. So long a time elapsed that he feared his plan would be futile. His legs grew cramped and he found it expedient to move. Suddenly he heard a scratching. There was no mistaking that sound. Craning his neck, he peered through the foliage and espied, not fifty yards away, the whole flock of gobblers. Clint nearly fell out of the tree, so rapturous was he. Then he sternly sought to control his excitement. What a magnificent sight! They were picking and scratching along right toward him. Never a moment was there when at least one gobbler did not have his head up, peering around. They looked as big as ostriches and as wild as anything Clint could imagine. But they had not the slightest suspicion that all was not well for their morning's feed.

It so happened that Clint did not have to turn to bring his rifle into action. Slowly he raised it to his shoulder. With his heart pounding audibly against his ribs he aimed at the gobbler in best view. The bird at that short distance was as large as a barrel. Clint vowed he would not miss. But the gobbler did not stand still. Then when Clint again got a bead on him, another and a larger turkey obstructed his aim. It took a stifling moment for Clint to realize that this was even better. When he looked at the closer turkey his eyes popped.

This gobbler was the lordly white-and-bronze leader of the flock. Clint had a violent urge to yell his elation. But he had sense enough left to realize he must shoot first. As he lowered his gun a trifle he snapped a twig. The great gobbler jerked up. *Put-put! Put-put!* Clint saw his keen little black eye. He knew he had been discovered, but not soon enough, for he froze on that aim and pressed the trigger.

The gun banged. A tremendous flapping followed. Clint could not see for smoke. He listened. The whir of wings and crashing of branches ceased. His elation suffered a violent collapse. Then he dropped down out of the tree. There lay the huge white-and-bronze gobbler, his tail feathers spread and fluttering.

For once blood and death caused Clint no pangs. He gloated over his prize. "Ain't he a whopper? Aw, what'll paw say now?" And when he essayed to lift the immense bird he experienced a most profound surprise. He had to take two hands to the job, and then it was not easy.

Clint tied the gray, clawed feet together and twisted the string round a stout stick. Lifting the gobbler, he drew it over his back. But he found he could not hold the weight with one hand, so he stuck his rifle barrel between the legs of the turkey and tried, successfully this time, to lift it over his back. And then the red head dragged in the grass. Although the whole walk back was downhill, his burden grew so heavy that he had all he could do to reach camp. And when Clint laid that gorgeous wild turkey in front of his father and their camp associates, he enjoyed revenge for the many times they had poked fun at him.

"Wal, we'll shore hev to call him Turk now," remarked one.

Report of hostile Kiowa Indians along the eastern border of New Mexico put an end to Clint's hunting. As to that, the approach of winter would very soon have the same effect. Moreover, Clint had to abandon a cherished hope of riding to Taos to call on Kit Carson and of seeing the famous Maxwell Ranch, which was reported to be the most interesting and wonderful place on the frontier.

Presently Clint settled down to his books and labored over them hours on end. A majority of the camp chores fell to his hands, because little by little his father, along with many other freighters, found diversion in the gaming dives of Santa Fé. Belmet was not a drinking man, nor an inveterate gambler, but the loss of his wife had struck him deeply and the monotony of camp life palled on him. All of which worried Clint exceedingly. He fed the stock, chopped and hauled wood, built fires. What with this work and his studies the days and weeks flew by.

When spring came and the roads dried up, Captain Couch and his followers took a contract to haul furs, buffalo robes, and pelts for Aull & Company. While the men were busy packing, which was no slight task, a caravan of seventy men happened along from Taos. These freighters were mostly old frontiersmen. The two caravans joined for the long and dangerous haul east, and in the aggregate there were one hundred and forty-four men. Such a company was practically immune from raids.

This long wagon-train left Santa Fé the last of May. They made slow progress at first, saving the oxen for the heavy part of the road.

They crossed the Pecos River and camped at Mora, the ranch of a Colonel St. Vrain, one of the oldest frontiersmen then living. He had come west in 1819, hunted and trapped for years, fought through the war with the Navajos in 1823, became major of a regiment in the Texas invasion of 1842, and a colonel in the American invasion of 1846, and had retired from the army in 1849, to reside on his ranch. Clint met the old frontiersman, who looked like a southern planter. He had a pronounced interest in boys, to which fact Clint could have attested.

Travel on to Fort Union was slow, uninterrupted, and uneventful. Some days were raw and chilly. Clint did not have any liking for the dust storms. At Fort Union a government caravan was making ready for the drive east to Fort Leavenworth. Captain Couch decided to wait for it. Clint had four more idle days to watch frontier life at the post. In one instance he saw considerably more than was good for him, as he had the bad luck to be witness to a knife fight between two men.

An entire troop of dragoons made ready at Fort Union to escort this unusually large caravan. The freighters were jolly. No fear of Indians this drive! The wagons rolled down upon the plains, and once more, for days on end, Clint gazed out over the prairie, with the vast circle of boundless horizon calling.

49

Clint remembered the camps and many landmarks he had become familiar with on the way out.

When they reached Council Grove the government caravan took the road to Fort Leavenworth, while the remainder went on toward Westport Landing. Thus Clint did not pass the scene of his mother's death and burial. But that place was not so very far, as distance counted on the prairie, and for several days Clint was prey to melancholy.

Captain Couch's caravan unloaded at Westport, then proceeded out along the Missouri River to camp and rest and feed the stock. Always that was a paramount issue. The weeks of steady pulling wore out the animals.

While fishing one day in a creek that flowed into the Missouri, Clint was approached by a lad about his own age, who announced that his uncle had joined the freighters and was going to take him along. His great glee was manifest. Clint looked at the lanky, red-headed, freckle-faced boy with considerable disfavor, solely because he had apparently the most ridiculous misconception of this freighting across the plains. Far, indeed, was it from fun.

"My name's Tom Sidel," he confided, agreeably. "I know yours. It's Clint Belmet."

"Howdy! Who told you?" replied Clint, drawing in his fishing-line. No one could talk and fish at the same time.

"Your dad. He knows my uncle. An' he said he was glad we were goin' to freight goods, because I'd be company for you."

Tom made this statement with a humility and a hopefulness not lost upon Clint. He was disposed to be friendly, though he had his doubts about this boy.

"Reckon it'd help some—if you are up to a man's job," replied Clint, with a matured air.

"I'm strong, but 'course I couldn't be a driver yet," said Tom. "Not many boys of thirteen could."

It appeared that the lad was approaching this connection more satisfactorily to Clint.

"Can you shoot?" queried Clint.

50

"No, nothin' to brag of. But mebbe you could teach me. I heard about your huntin' an' the names you got—Buff an' Turk. Think I like Buff better."

"How are you with an ax?"

"Uncle says I'm just no good," rejoined Tom, frankly.

"Will you be afraid when the Indians raid us?"

"D—do—do they? Is it a—a sure thing?" faltered Tom.

"Sure. Next drive out we'll have a fight. You see, every night when we camp we drive the wagons in a circle, close together, except at one end, where we leave a hole for the stock. We couldn't risk lettin' the horses an' oxen feed outside. An' we keep twenty guards watchin' all night. Sometimes even then the Indians slip up on us. They did once, an' if it hadn't been for Jack, my dog here, we'd have been killed an' scalped. . . . I—I lost my mother."

"Aw! She was killed?" burst out Tom, awed.

"Yes. Shot right through. She sent me runnin' after paw, who was out fightin'. An' she died after we got back."

"I'm very sorry. I lost my mother, too. But not Indians. An' I haven't any dad, either."

Clint was won now. This Tom Sidel seemed likable, and, after all, he did not seem to possess the conceited and bragging traits that Clint had imagined he might.

"Well, what you goin' to do when we're set on by Comanches or Kiowas?" went on Clint, dryly.

"*Do?* Golly! like as not I'll crawl under the wagon, or suthin'."

Whereupon Clint admitted Tom into the sanctity of his friendship.

"Where you from?" asked Clint.

"Lived in Chicago till last year, then went to my uncle's in Iowa."

"City boy, huh?"

"Yes, but it wasn't my fault."

"How about school?"

"I've passed the Fourth Reader."

"Whew! You're two years ahead of me. . . . Tom,

51

I've got an idea. I'll take you in hand on drivin', shootin', fightin' Indians, work round camp. An' you take me in hand on studies. I can do history, geography, grammar. But 'rithmetic stumps me. An' I ought to learn a little 'rithmetic."

"It's a bargain, Buff," replied Tom, gladly. "But the debt will be all on my side."

Upon the return of the lads to camp, they happened on an important meeting between Couch and Major McLaughlin. The talk took place at Belmet's tent, and the officer's business was to arrange the hauling of government supplies to Fort Wise, Colorado.

"Glad to take the job, major. But I haul only under escort," replied Couch.

"I can't spare soldiers just now."

"Sorry, sir. I won't tackle thet job these days without escort. The Comanches are raidin' an' the Kiowas on the warpath."

"I could send a detachment to catch up with your train," suggested McLaughlin.

"I'll not accept the contract unless I have a whole troop to start out with."

"All right, Couch. I'll have to find soldiers. By the time you're packed I'll have them ready."

But he did not have them, and Couch refused for three days to start out unescorted. The frontiersmen upheld him, but the new freighters, unexperienced and eager to earn the high wages, wanted to risk it. But Couch was obdurate. At length a detachment of soldiers rode in from Fort Leavenworth, and next morning the caravan started.

Clint had graduated now to a big freight wagon, and the prairie schooner was only a memory of the past. He discovered that he did not now think so often of his mother. The canvas-covered wagon was associated with her. On the high seat of the freighter Clint had as companion the only other boy in the caravan, Tom Sidel, and it was impossible for Clint not to share something of Tom's wild excitement. The first day passed as had a single hour when he drove alone. Tom was full of possibilities. His looks were deceiving.

And as the days multiplied Clint grew attached to this lad.

The caravan, consisting of eighty wagons, crossed the Little Arkansas River, and then the Walnut, went on for a stop at Fort Zarah, then Bent's old fort. During this period two bands of Indians rode up within sight, wild, swift riding, sinister, and colorful, and espying the long line of mounted soldiers, they wheeled away.

When Tom Sidel saw his first hostile Indians he gripped Clint with both hands, and the freckles stood out brown on a very white face. He greeted sight of the second band with more courage, and after a creditable performance received a lecture on Indians from Clint. It presently occurred to Clint that in the event the caravan was attacked he would personally have a great deal to live up to. When the thought clarified in his mind, Clint ceased his masterly harangue.

It took the caravan six weeks to reach Fort Wise. Here the soldiers at once departed on the return trip to Fort Leavenworth. This left Couch in a predicament. A wagon-train of supplies was ready for the trail, but no escort. He tarried there waiting, and trying to decide what to do.

Fort Wise appeared to Clint identical with all the other forts on the plains, with the exception of Fort Larned. But to Tom Sidel it was the heaven of a lad's adventurous dreams. Clint boldly led Tom everywhere and had many a laugh at his expense.

That night Couch held a council with his men anent the disturbing predicament they were in. The feed around Fort Wise was scant and poor; the stock was getting gaunt. It was necessary to go somewhere, and Couch favored loading the heavy consignment of freight, much of it in valuable pelts, and starting back to Westport.

"Wal, it's an even break," said the most experienced of the plainsmen. "We may miss redskins an' then ag'in we may not."

"McLaughlin played me a dirty trick," fumed Couch. "He must have ordered them soldiers to start

53

back at once. . . . If we stay here much longer we'll lose half our stock."

"You're the boss," was the cool comment of each freighter. No one would take the responsibility of advising a move without soldiers.

Couch threw up his hands and swore roundly:

"We'll load an' move!"

6

Gray plain, winding yellow road, scouts far out in front, wagging oxen and fretting horses, so Clint saw four long anxious days drag by.

On the afternoon of the fifth day two dots appeared rising over the horizon. As it chanced, hawk-eyed Clint saw them first far to the south. They moved. Too high for buffalo! They were horses with riders coming fast. Clint shouted to the driver ahead and he shouted to the one before him; thus word quickly reached Couch and the scouts. No halt was ordered, but the wagons grew closer.

The riders proved to be two white men, arriving on wet and heaving horses.

"Whar's your boss?" queried the spokesman of the two.

"I'm Couch," returned the boss. "Who are you an' what do you want?"

"My name's Powell," returned the other, hurriedly. "In charge of an emigrant train goin' to Texas. There was fifty-six of us—thirty-four men, fourteen women, an' eight children. Just at daybreak we was jumped by a bunch of Injuns. But we'd been lookin' fer it. We'd spotted Injuns followin' us fer days. We was ready, an' we gave them such a hot fight thet they give it up. We seen your caravan an' began pullin' across country, an' we rode out ahead to see if you'd go in camp an' wait for our train to come up."

"Shore we will. Reckon you've got some casualties?"

"Five dead an' some hurt. I don't know how many."

"Too bad, but you're damn lucky. You'd better throw your outfit in with ours."

"Much obliged, boss. We'll shore be glad to."

"Pull a circle," yelled Couch to the drivers, and soon the wagons were wheeling round in the protective formation.

While Clint was helping pitch their individual camp, Tom came running, his eyes wide, his red hair sticking up.

"Buff, is it true?" he asked, excitedly. "Is there a wagon train comin' that's been fightin' Injuns?"

"Reckon it is, Tom. Our boss wouldn't be campin' for fun. An' those two riders who come in an' told us, they looked honest to me. But all the same you see the scouts out ridin' on guard. We can't be surprised."

Clint was not so excited as Tom, though just as anxious and curious. And he was among the first to see the Texas emigrant train come in sight on the rolling prairie. Then it took two hours for it to reach camp.

The band had twenty-eight wagons, all new, good horses, a few yokes of oxen, and some mighty formidable-looking Texans. It was no wonder, Clint thought, that they had routed the Indians. The more Clint saw of Texans, the better he liked them. He had heard it said they were a long-legged, sandy-haired, loose-mouthed, gun-throwing breed of men that made the best friends and worst enemies.

Couch was ready for the wounded, with his chest of medicines, bandages, hot water, and the few instruments he used. He had a considerable skill for a layman, and as on other occasions he called on Clint to stand by.

"Wash your hands clean, you owl-eyed buffalo-hunter," he ordered Clint, who was watching the men helping the wounded from a wagon.

Tom Sidel stood his ground, though the pale faces and bloody bandages manifestly affected him, but when they lifted out a little girl whose eyes were closed he fled.

The little girl had an arrow wound in her leg above the knee. Two men, one of them young, also suffered from arrow wounds, one in the arm, the other in the shoulder. They were not serious and both men were joking. A fourth man had a bullet hole in his middle, about over his stomach. He was unconscious. Couch turned him over to see where the bullet had emerged, then he shook his head as if he could do nothing.

The little girl opened her eyes and smiled wanly. She was not frightened.

"Does it hurt bad, little lady?" inquired Couch as with big deft hands he removed the bloody rags.

"Not now. . . . Am I goin' to die—mister?" she whispered.

"Die! Goodness! child, you ain't bad hurt!" replied Couch, heartily. "You're just cut a little."

"Honest Injun?" asked the child, hopefully.

"Reckon the redskin who done this to you was a very dishonest Injun. But I know what you mean. Just shut your eyes, lass, while I wash an' bind your cut."

"Boss, we couldn't stop the bleedin'," said the man who had lifted the girl down from the wagon. Evidently he was her father. The look in his eyes hurt Clint. What tortures these pioneers endured! Clint wondered if any of them realized, before starting out on the plains, what might be in store for them. Still, nothing could stop pioneers.

"Wal, it's only a flesh wound," replied Couch, with satisfaction. "No artery cut. She's weak an' sick, but in no danger at all."

The father spoke grateful incoherent words. When the girl's wound had been attended to she was laid aside on blankets. She opened her eyes, smiled at Clint, and said it had not hurt much. Somehow she reminded him of little May Bell. The old pang twinged in Clint's breast. Where was May and what was happening to her?

When Couch had attended to the arrow wounds of the two men, the third, the one with the ugly bullet hole in his abdomen, had expired.

Clint saw the Texans bury their six dead, and cut down two cottonwoods to roll over the single grave.

Next day they joined Couch's caravan and traveled with it as far as the Cimmaron Crossing. Then they asked for a map of the dry trail, so they could find water on their ninety mile cut-off, and despite Couch's advice, continued their journey on to Texas. Clint waved to the children, with whom he had become friendly, until the wagons rolled over a ridge out of sight.

"Humph! Wonder will I ever see any of them again!" soliloquized Clint. Meetings and separations on the plains were sudden, strange, and violent, but the more poignant for that.

Tom Sidel had waved with Clint, affected in similar degree. "Buff," he said, feelingly, "I don't like the idee of you goin' one way an' me another."

Couch's caravan had further good luck on this eastward trip. At Fort Larned they fell in with another wagon train of sixty-five freighters bound from Fort Union to Westport. They proceeded together, completing the long journey at the end of the summer. Couch's freighters had done well and were satisfied to continue. Then they went into winter camp on the Missouri River, not far out of Westport.

Belmet and Tom's uncle, John Sidel, joined forces on a deal for feed for horses and oxen. They bought two hundred acres of cornstalks from a man named Judson, and turned the stock in there. It became necessary, however, to guard the animals, and fetch them back to camp at night. There were twenty-five men in Belmet's outfit. They built a large corral on the river bank, and by cautious guarding did not lose any stock to the thieves rampant in that section. Such labor, and the mending of wagons and some little hunting for meat in the brakes of the river bottom, kept the men busy all winter.

Clint and Tom went to school for five months. It was a happy interval for both boys. They had plenty to eat, warm clothes, and outside of school hours had a good time hunting rabbits with Jack. Nevertheless, Clint missed his mother more than when he was out on the trail. Perhaps the comfort, the leisure, and the school work brought her back closer.

He grew big and strong that winter.

Couch told Belmet, "Buff will be a buster some day."

Card sharpers often visited the camp, where they were not welcomed, at least by the majority of the freighters. Clint painted a sign, *Gamblers not Wanted,* and nailed it up in a conspicuous place, after which the undesirables gave them a wide berth.

Clint's favorite dish was rabbit cooked in a Dutch oven with potatoes and onions. He used to take a peep, lifting the iron lid so that he could see and smell the stew. This always irritated his father, who was a capital cook and who did not like to have the red coals of fire disturbed.

The months rolled around, like the rolling of the slow caravan wheels across the prairie in summer. By the middle of May Captain Couch had loaded up again for Aull & Company, with merchandise for all the trading stations across the plains. It was a large and important consignment. Reports drifted in that the Comanches and Kiowas were more troublesome than ever.

Couch secured a detachment of ninety-five soldiers under Captain Stevenson, and the long journey began. Commonplace as were these freighting departures, there was always a crowd of relatives, friends, and well-wishers gathered to see the caravan start out. It had such singular import.

Early in June they struck the old trail for Santa Fé. At Big Timbers they found evidence that a large encampment of Kiowas had wintered at this favorite spot. This was not conducive to good cheer. Those savages were somewhere on the rampage.

The mornings broke sunny and pleasant, the prairie waved away boundlessly, the long leagues rolled under the wheels, the sunsets burned gold on the grass, and the cool, clear, starry nights passed. Not an Indian was sighted on the long journey to Fort Larned.

Here the soldiers turned back for Fort Leavenworth, while Couch waited for a caravan, on the way from Fort Aubry to Santa Fé. Owing to the scarcity of soldiers and the increase of the many freighters and other wagon-trains, it was imperative that caravans depend upon one another as much as possible. Couch waited for the Aubry train, and, indeed, so long was it in arriving that ill rumor was rife.

It got in, however, the biggest and hardest crew of freighters Clint had ever seen—one hundred and five men, all experienced Indian-fighters. Their train boss had been a sergeant of artillery in the Texas invasion of 1842. His name was Jim Waters, and the long-haired old prairie-dog was a delight to Clint.

Waters had a cannon in his caravan. It had been used in many a fight with Indians, and the roar of its fame had spread from the Missouri to the Pecos. The first thing Clint and Tom did was to go have a look at that cannon. It shone like the back of a watch case. The boys both yearned and dreaded to see it shot.

Couch threw in with Waters. This made a caravan of one hundred and seventy-nine armed men, and, including the cannon, a most formidable body.

Jim Waters' words to Couch passed from lip to lip: "Satock is out thar layin' fer us, so you-all know what to expect."

Satock was the notorious chief of the Kiowas who harassed the western border from 1855 to 1863. This year, late in 1856, had seen the rise of his activities. The country from Fort Union to Santa Fé and over the Vermigo River was crisscrossed by Satock's bloody trail. There were records of attacks on escorted caravans and important wagon-trains, but many small bands of reckless pioneers had vanished and never were heard of again. During this period Satock's Kiowas and the Apaches no doubt massacred many of these adventurers. Lucky was the caravan of any kind that crossed Satock's range without a fight.

The third day out from Fort Union, at noon, a large band of mounted Kiowas appeared from over a ridge. They were not more than a mile away.

"Pull a half-circle," yelled Waters, and that trenchant order was promptly executed.

Clint's position was next to his father's wagon near the center of the half-circle. Tom was with him on the seat. The horses and oxen were headed inward. The cannon was run in front, loaded with slugs, ready for action. The gunner, Bill Hoyle, an ex-soldier, stood laconically beside it, fuse in hand, with Waters, Couch, and others behind. One hundred and seventy-nine rifles were in hand, and that did not count the two held by Clint and Tom.

"Wal, boys, it's Satock all right," announced Waters, grimly. "I shore know the old — — — —!"

Clint estimated there were more than a hundred Indians, perhaps considerably more, because they rode in a compact mass, naked and red, feathers flying and weapons glinting, their savage faces gleaming in the sunlight.

"Boys, they're wantin' to parley," said Waters. "Reckon it's jest a trick to see how we're loaded. But no fear of attack now."

Clint heard that to his immense relief, and the explosion, almost the gasp, that Tom gave vent to was very eloquent. Clint stole a quick glance at Tom, and he was not so scared himself that he could not laugh.

The band of Kiowas halted at about sixty yards, just outside the limit Waters said he would allow them. Then four riders came on again. The leader was a lean, sinewy Indian, naked except for moccasins and breech-clout. He carried a rifle across his saddle. His horse was a ragged, fiery mustang, fittingly wild for such a master.

The four rode up within thirty paces, then halted. Clint saw the swarthy lineaments of the savage chieftain—a dark, crafty, evil visage, record of terrible deeds. If he had ever been a noble red man the time was far past. Hate of the whites breathed from every line of him. He raised a hand with superb gesture.

"Me Satock," he announced.

"Shore. We saw you first," replied Waters, with biting humor.

"We friends white men."

"Wal, if you're friends let us go on."

"Want some eat."

"Satock, we can't stop now to feed you Injuns. We must go on," returned Waters, testily.

Satock slipped off his mustang. He was as slippery as an eel. Again he held up his hand, and gave his rifle to one of his companions. He stepped forward without the slightest hesitation, his gleaming, burning, gloomy eyes taking in the cannon, the watching men.

"Me Satock. Me big chief. Me good friend. Me want sugar," he said.

"Somebody give him some sugar," ordered Waters.

Couch went to the nearest supply wagon, and after some tearing in packs, assisted by the teamster, he returned with a small bag of sugar, which he placed in the outstretched hand of the chief. Now Satock did not smile, nor accept the sugar with thanks. He simply snatched it.

"Me want coffee," he said, in his deep guttural voice.

At Couch's call the teamster fetched a sack of coffee, which was likewise turned over to the savage.

"Me want tobac," said Satock, in precisely the same tone.

That, too, was given to the chief, who received it as if it was his due.

"Thet's all, Satock," rejoined Waters, no longer conciliatory. "Get on your hoss an' go."

Satock strode back to his horse. It was noticeable that he mounted in a single agile action, without letting go of the three bags. He received his rifle from his companion, and still kept possession of the sugar, coffee, and tobacco. This fact did not in the least detract from his savage dignity.

They rode back to their band, and then, keeping the same distance away they made a complete circle of the caravan.

Curses were not wanting from the angry Couch and others of the frontiersmen, but Waters kept silent until Satock, with his warriors, disappeared over the ridge of waving grass.

"Thet damn rascal is up to somethin'," declared Waters. "We'll go on to the Pecos. Look sharp, every man-jack of you."

By four o'clock that afternoon the caravan was in camp on the Pecos River. As small a circle as possible, with the wagons drawn up close, was placed out in the open. Everybody worked. Firewood in large quantities was brought up from the river bottom. The stock was grazed under guard and driven into the circle before dark. The cannon was set pointing from the gap in the circle. A number of cooking fires blazed brightly, and after supper a big camp fire was built in the center, around which stood and sat and lay most of the men.

Clint heard Jim Waters say: "We haven't seen the last of Satock. You can shore gamble on thet an' be a winner. I've been on the frontier for twenty years. There's a red devil in all these tribes, but I reckon Satock has got them skinned. He's as mean as——! . . . We'll have to put on double guard. Now, Couch, how about your outfit?"

"You're boss, Jim," replied Couch. "I'll answer for my outfit takin' orders an' doin' their duty."

"All right, Captain," returned Waters, consulting his watch. "You take forty men for the first guard. Have Bill Hoyle relieve you in three hours. I'll relieve Bill at two o'clock. An' thet'll fetch us to daylight. . . . Then, I'm no calamity howler, but I know these Kiowas, an' we've got to be on guard every minute of our watch—or we'll never reach Santa Fé with our scalps on."

Belmet was one of the chosen for the first watch. Clint remained up with him, sitting by the bright fire, watching, listening, and keeping his dog Jack close beside him.

Hoyle and his men came on at midnight. Clint went to bed with his father. They were soon asleep. Some time later Clint awoke with a queer feeling. He reached over to put a hand on Jack. But Jack was gone. Clint sat up. As the bed had been made in the open and the night was clear, Clint could look all around. No Jack in sight!

Clint shook his father.

"Paw, I'm afraid somethin's wrong," whispered Clint.

"What makes you think that, Clint?" queried Belmet, anxiously.

"Jack is gone. I'll look for him."

"Don't go outside the corral."

Wherupon Clint searched around among the tents and beds, and then round the camp fire. None of the men on guard had seen Jack.

"Mr. Waters, my dog would not leave me," said Clint, earnestly, to the frontiersman. "Somethin's wrong. Jack could smell an Indian a mile."

"Thet's good. We'll watch all the sharper," replied Waters. "You go back to bed and try to get some sleep."

Clint did not take this kindly advice. He wanted his dog. He knew that Jack had never left him unless something was wrong, and he felt certain that was the case now. Accordingly, he searched among the stock. Not finding Jack there, Clint returned to his wagon and crawled under it out into the prairie grass. A bright moon shone. Clint called his dog, and he whistled. Something moved in the tall grass. Clint dropped flat, suddenly stricken with terror. Then he heard a whine. Jack came searching for him. Clint sat up and patted the dog. His hair stood up and he growled.

As Clint crawled back under the wagon some one stuck a gun in his back.

"It's the lad an' his dog, boss," said the man.

Waters reprimanded Clint sharply for the risk he had taken.

"But I was huntin' Jack," replied Clint. "He was out there growlin'. I tell you, Mr. Waters, Jack can smell an Indian."

"Couch, damn if I don't think there's truth in the boy. Listen to thet dog! . . . Wal, we'll play it for a hunch, anyway."

Waters had all the men called. The fire was extinquished and every one of the caravan became a guard. Most of the men were armed with a Colt's revolving rifle, a new weapon capable of firing seven shots in two minutes.

"Boys," said Waters, "if you have to shoot, don't waste ammunition. Make every shot count. If Satock an' his redskins tackle us, it's either them or us. An' I'd a heap sight it'd be them. Now spread out an' watch."

Clint went with his father and lay down just inside their wagon. He tied Jack on a string. Presently Jack grew restless and pulled and growled.

"Paw, they're comin' sure. Jack knows," whispered Clint.

Belmet got up and went to tell Waters. This caused Waters to stand up on the hub of a wagon wheel and search the prairie with his field-glass. The moonlight made the night almost as day.

"Injuns comin' all right," announced Waters. "Good fer thet dog! . . . Couch, step up an' take a look."

Couch replaced Waters on the wheel and held the glass for several moments of suspense.

"About two hundred, more or less," he said, presently turning to Waters. "They're comin' low an' easy, guessin' to surprise us."

"Wal, they'll get the surprise," returned Waters.

"Couch, send a man along the wagon line thet way, an' you go the other. Tell the men to expect an attack in short order, but to lie low an' not shoot till they hear me yell."

"How about the cannon?" asked Couch.

"Hoyle has charge of thet. He'll not fire it unless the redskins break inside the circle. . . . I'll have another look through the glass. Lucky it's moonlight."

Presently Clint, who raised his head to look, could not see a man, except his father beside him. They were all under the wagons, hiding, watching.

Not long after that several Indians appeared, cautiously approaching the caravan. Evidently they were reconnoitering to see if there was an opportunity to attack. Soon they vanished as silently as they had come.

After that every succeeding moment was fraught with greater suspense and fright for Clint. He had difficulty in keeping Jack quiet.

A long wait followed. The Kiowas were in no hurry. An owl hooted down in the river bottom. It might have been a signal. Next came the whistle of a night hawk. No doubt every listening man on guard heard that lonely, suspense-breaking cry. Following it, Clint saw a line of Indians rise out of the grass and come on in order, crouching and slow.

Clint lay stiff and cold against the wheel of the wagon, with his rifle at a rest on a spoke. The palms of his hands were slippery with sweat. He heard his father whisper, but could not distinguish what. Closer stole the Kiowas. They gleamed in the moonlight. Every second Clint expected to hear their hellish yell as they charged.

But instead of that the silence was split by Waters' stentorian roar:

"Fire!"

The hundred and seventy-nine Colts roared as one gun. But Clint had forgotten to either aim or shoot his.

7

Then the white men reversed the action of their rifles, making ready for another volley. No blood-curdling yell! No rush of agile plumed savages! When the smoke drifted away from before the waiting defenders of the caravan, fleet vanishing forms, like shadows, could be discerned in the moonlight. They disappeared without having fired a gun or shot an arrow.

Waters and his allies crawled out from under the wagons, and a large knot of them collected round him and Couch.

Clint Belmet, dazed, and with palpitating heart, followed his father.

"Haw! Haw! We shore didn't need our cannon," roared Waters.

"What you make of it, Jim?" asked Couch, more anxious than elated.

"Kiowas, all right. They got the surprise of their lives. Sneaked off like coyotes."

"They might be hidin' out there in the grass," suggested an old frontiersman.

"Not much. Them as are out there now are good Injuns . . . Boys, spread along the line an' search for bodies. But don't go far."

Careful search of a belt of grass all along the line and for a hundred paces out failed to discover one single dead Indian.

"Packed their dead an' crippled with them. Injuns will always do thet," averred Couch.

"Wal, I'll be doggoned!" ejaculated Jim Waters. "I'd have gambled on layin' out jest one hundred an' seventy-nine."

"You'd have lost your bet, boss," interposed the old frontiersman. "Shootin' by moonlight is turrible deceivin'. Things look close an' clear, but they ain't.

"Shore. But all the same we must have plugged a

few," replied Waters, stubbornly. "Anyway, we'll watch an' wait till daylight. Build some fires, boys."

Clint Belmet, shivering around the camp fire his father built, was a pretty sober boy. He realized that he was just recovering from a trance no less than panic. And shame swiftly followed his other feelings. Even Jack seemed to be looking at him askance. Clint was inordinately proud of his dog. Had not Waters just a few moments since passed the camp fire to say, "Clint, thet dog of yours saved our scalps."

While Clint was sitting there toasting his shins, who should come up but Tom Sidel, gun in hand, stalking as Clint most certainly had never seen him stalk before.

"Hullo, Buff! I was looking for you all over. Wasn't it great?" he burst out, dropping the butt of the rifle on the ground and standing as the hunters were wont to stand in leisure moments.

"Wasn't what great?" queried Clint, bewildered.

"Why, the Injuns slippin' up on us."

"Humph! Not so I noticed it."

"The way we chased them first off! Say, I heard our boss say it was the best stand-off he'd ever been in."

"We was only lucky," responded Clint, pessimistically.

"Don't say was when you should say were," protested Tom. "Buff, it wasn't all luck."

"Tom Sidel, if it hadn't been for my dog Jack, your gory scalp would be hangin' on a Kiowa's saddle right this minute."

"I ain't so damn sure," replied Tom, who was slow to realize antagonism in the boy he revered.

"Don't swear," complained Clint, irritably. "That's worse than bad grammar."

But Tom was not to be talked or frowned down. "Buff, I'll bet you plugged one," he said, in a tense whisper, leaning down.

"Plugged one what?" demanded Clint.

"One of them d-dinged Kiowas. Mebbe old Satock himself. It'd just be your luck, an' then you'd be more famous than ever."

"*Me* famous? . . . Faugh!" exploded Clint. Nevertheless, Tom's indestructible faith in his idol had begun to operate on Clint's mood.

"I'll bet you will be—if not tomorrow, then some day. . . . You shore knocked a Kiowa over, didn't you, Buff?"

"Tom, I'm downright sure I didn't."

"Aw, I'll bet you did! Uncle John says I hit one, an' so does Jackson, the teamster who was next to me."

"*What?*" gasped Clint.

"I guess I've downed my first redskin, Buff," replied Tom, solemnly. "It was this way. There's deep grass just out from our wagon, an' a little step in the plain. I was restin' my gun on the wheel, all ready, finger on trigger, when all of a sudden Injuns rose right up close, like ghosts. My gun was pointed right at one. Just then we heard Mr. Waters yell. An' I pulled trigger before anyone else down our way. I couldn't see what happened, but Uncle an' Jackson positively saw my redskin go down like a fellar who's knocked down."

"Shake hands," said Clint, with emotion. "An' you wasn't scared?"

"Who said so? Scared! Why, Buff, I was so scared my teeth clicked, my mouth watered, my throat choked up so I couldn't swallow. I was colder'n ice all over. An' deep inside was the most awful feelin' I ever had in my life."

That honest confession from Tom made a man out of Clint. All of a sudden he felt free of something sickening.

"Tom, you've said it. That's exactly how I felt, only worse. . . . An' I couldn't shoot. I forgot I had a rifle."

"Bah! Don't come that on me, just to make me feel good," returned the loyal Tom.

At daylight Jim Waters called for volunteers to trail the Indians. All the freighters wanted to go. He chose fifty men.

"Let me have your dog," said Waters to Clint.

"Jack won't trail anythin' without me," replied Clint, eagerly.

"All right. Come along an' fetch him on a rope."

They trailed the Indians to the river, and found many tracks where they had crossed. Couch pointed to the marks in the sand where something heavy had been dragged. Next Waters found blood on the leaves. The men crossed the river, which was shallow, and taking the trail again, followed it up into a cotton-wood grove. Here Jack got to trailing so fast that he dragged Clint with him ahead of the others. Where-upon Waters hurried to grasp the rope from Clint's hands.

Presently they came to a glade where the Indians had left their horses while they went on to attack the caravan. Horse tracks and dung were all over the glade, and fresh marks on the saplings, where the bark had been eaten off. The trail of the horses led out of the river bottom, up on the plain, and headed north.

"Raton Pass," declared Waters. "Wal, we'll shore have the pleasure of meetin' up with old Satock again."

The freighters hurried back to camp, where break-fast was ready, and after that the caravan was soon on the move. They drove until early afternoon. Waters chose the best available spot to stave off another raid, which manifestly he expected.

Forty men were sent out with the stock, and ten picked scouts rode out to look for Indians. About sundown the several scouts who had gone north came hurrying in with news everybody expected.

"Injuns comin," they announced.

"Heigho! A freighter's life is a merry one," sang out a wag.

"Tolerable busy, too, if you want my idee," contributed another.

"Roll the cannon out, boys," yelled Waters. "Hoyle, have powder an' slugs ready. Rest of you at your posts. If it's a bunch of Kiowas, we'll begin to shoot first, an' give them terbaccor after."

The approaching band, however, turned out to be cavalry, eighty-five men under Captain Graham, bound from Fort Wise, Colorado, to Santa Fé.

Clint was on hand to hear Waters and Couch greet the leader of the cavalrymen.

"Howdy, Jim!" said the captain, a ruddy-faced, square-jawed soldier of long service. "We took you for a bunch of Indians."

"Wal Captain, we can shore return the compliment," laughed Waters, and pointed to the ready cannon.

"Captain Graham, we were attacked by Kiowas last night, in the moonlight," announced Couch. "We drove them off, an' they never fired a shot. But we've been expectin' another attack today, an' sure one tonight."

"So it was your caravan Satock jumped," said Graham. "You were lucky. We passed Satock today. He had about one hundred an' twenty Indians. They had a good many wounded and were a pretty sore bunch. Passed us and went north toward Raton. We knew, of course, they'd been up to some devilment, so we took their back trail. Found freshly dug ground covered with a lot of rock. They had buried a good many dead. So you must have given Satock a hard knock. It's not likely they'll tackle your caravan very soon again."

"That's good. Wal, Captain, get down, you an' your soldiers, an' have supper with us."

"We'll camp here and go on with you to Santa Fé," returned Graham.

This good news, added to the remarkable luck attending the caravan of late, put the freighters in a happy frame of mind. They prepared a bountiful supper for Graham's cavalry, after which soldiers and freighters squatted round camp fires for that most unusual circumstance—a pleasant evening while on the trail.

Captain Graham had been on the plains for many years, first in Indian campaigns, secondly in charge of numerous caravans of 'Forty-niners on their way to the California gold strike; and later performing the same army service for the caravans of freighters.

"I don't see that conditions on the plains are any better than years ago," he remarked. "Lately they're worse. The Indian tribes are growing bitter. Arapahoes, Pawnees, Comanches, Kiowas, Apaches, all these southern tribes have grown steadily in hostility toward the white. When you come to think of it, you can't blame them. On the whole, the white invasion of the West is a deliberate steal. The time will come— not so far distant, in my estimation—when the Indians will grow to desperation. Some day the Sioux will be as bad as the Apaches. These old Indian chiefs, like White Wolf, are wise. They see the handwriting on the wall. They have trusted the white man, to their disillusionment. And if these wise old chieftains can band their tribes together, which they are trying to do, it will take a whole army to make the West safe. But some of these tribes have hated one another for hundreds of years. They will not easily be reconciled. That is hopeful for the whites."

"Wal, Captain, I shore agree with you 'cept not blamin' the Injuns," rejoined Waters, puffing his pipe. "You see, I've got a hunk of lead in my hip, shot there by a redskin, an' it doesn't improve my disposition. Injuns are just varmints to me."

"That's not a very broad attitude, Waters," replied the cavalry officer. "If you had stayed home, where you owned your land, instead of riding out with guns across the red man's country, you wouldn't be carrying that bullet around, and also a cantankerous disposition. Most of your frontiersmen are like that. But take a man like Colonel Maxwell. He hasn't an Indian enemy on the plains. He treats every redskin the same as he does a white man. He told me something interesting last time I was at his ranch. He said one of the chiefs told him that it was the future the Indians feared. They see these wagon-trains of furs, pelts, and buffalo hides go trailing back East, and to them the sight is prophetic of the future. Some day the white men will

71

go in to kill the buffalo on a great scale. And that will bring war between red men and white men. The Indian lives on the buffalo. He knows it. That conflict will come, but not for twenty years or more."

"Meanwhile, for us, haulin' freight an' fightin, Injuns is about all we can look for," replied Waters.

"It's all in the day's work," added Couch.

"Well, men, you can hardly say it's monotonous, even if it is the same old thing over and over again," said Captain Graham, with a laugh. "Traveling and fighting! That is all there is to the Great Plains these days, and all there will be for some time to come."

"Some day, Captain, these Great Plains will be great farms," said Couch, thoughtfully. "It's rich soil all the way across. Plenty of water. Wonderful pasture for stock. Shore millions of men could prosper."

"Yes, and they will, but not until the Indian and the buffalo are gone," concluded Graham. "Personally I shall be sorry to see both vanish, as they must, when the tide of progress moves westward. But long before that time comes there's going to be war between the North and South."

"Wal, we won't argue aboot that," replied Waters. "You're a Northerner an' I'm a Southerner, an' I reckon we don't think no more alike than the Pawnees an' Comanches."

"Jim, you an' Captain Graham better talk Injun till we get to Santa Fé, anyway," interposed Couch. And when the laugh subsided he continued. "It's late an' we better turn in."

Clint Belmet, who had been sitting before the fire with eyes and ears open, went thoughtfully to bed, deciding that he admired and liked Captain Graham better than any one he had met on the frontier, unless it was Kit Carson.

"Paw, didn't you cotton to that Cap Graham?" asked Clint.

"Sure did. I'm glad you saw an' heard him. Try an' remember what he said," replied his father.

"No fear of me forgettin'. He talked just like a book. . . . An', paw, I hear more an' more about this

Colonel Maxwell an' his ranch. Will you let me go there some day? They say *anybody* is welcome to come an' stay as long as he likes!"

"Reckon you can, mebbe this trip out," yawned Belmet, sleepily. "Go to sleep, you owl!"

The cavalry escorted Waters' caravan on to Santa Fé, and then, without a day's rest, hurried to the rescue of an emigrant train reported coming in from Texas.

The fur company in Santa Fé and Westport, for which Waters and Couch were hauling, had a huge consignment of stock to send back to the Missouri. Consequently Clint's cherished hope of visiting Maxwell's ranch could not materialize. He had to work like a trooper during the few days' stop at Santa Fé, and the rest and good time of former trips were wanting.

Waters, owing to the luck of the caravan with Satock, decided to risk a short cut to St. Calra Springs, which drive was accomplished in twelve days. The next was over an old trail seldom used any more, owing to the difficulty in finding water, and this led down Purgatory Valley to Bent's Fort. The caravan made it in twenty-five days. Only three of these days required a very long drive from water to water; the first being twenty-one miles, the second twenty-four, and the last, the longest Clint ever drove, totaled twenty-seven miles. On this whole short cut they had no fuel but buffalo chips. They did not see an Indian.

At Bent's Fort the leaders of the caravan were advised to wait and rest a few days, because White Wolf, the Apache war chief, was in the vicinity on the warpath. Two troops of dragoons were out trying to locate the Apaches and fetch them in. But Waters and Couch, trusting to their big caravan of experienced drivers and fighters, proceeded toward Council Grove.

While they were in camp on Cottonwood Creek, twenty Pawnees suddenly appeared, as if they had dropped out of the sky, and rode in.

"Wal, of all things! More Injuns!" ejaculated Waters, dryly.

"By thunder! they've got nerve!" added Couch. "Mebbe they're just a scoutin' party."

The Pawnee chief, who looked as lean and dry as leather, ran an appraising eye over the wagons.

"Heap big train! Heap men?" he said. "Heap!"

"Yes, we got three hundred men an' five cannon," replied Waters, in cheerful tones that brought smiles to the faces of his men. "Here's one of them. It will kill two hundred Injuns in one shot. . . . Look! I'll cut down that tree in one shot."

The Pawnees might not have understood Waters word for word, but they certainly got the gist of his meaning, and they looked skeptical, not to say scornful. Finally the Pawnee spokesman replied, "White man dam' big liar!"

Waters simulated great anger.

"WHAT! . . . *You call me liar?*" he roared, in outraged dignity. "I'll show you. . . . See that tree. I'll cut it down in one shot. Then you take back callin' me liar—or I'll turn my cannon on you."

He pointed to a tree nearly eighteen inches through. It was a young green cottonwood. Then he bade the men roll the cannon out. Hoyle brought the fuse and more ammunition. The freighters, not neglecting their rifles, crowded forward in suppressed glee. The Pawnees began to look impressed. Some of them edged away.

Waters carefully sighted the cannon and touched it off. BOOM! It made a terrible roar. The concussion appeared to shake everything near at hand, especially the Pawnees.

The cottonwood tree fell, not cut off cleanly, but effectually enough to make good Waters' boast. Waters had been clever enough to run the cannon pretty close to the Indians, so that they would feel and hear a terrific shock. They did. And that no doubt had as much to do with their discomfiture as the felling of the tree. They rode away a good deal faster than they had come. Then the boisterous merriment of those grim freighters was a spectacle to behold.

Waters' caravan continued its overland journey to the Missouri without seeing any more Indians. Thus another record was added to the list of the old brass cannon.

Aull & Company owned a large tract of pasture and cornfield in the river bottom, part of which was fenced. The freighters made a deal whereby they paid five hundred dollars for it, with the understanding that if they loaded for Aull the next spring they would get half of it back, and if they returned from Santa Fé with Aull's pelts intact they would receive the other half.

All the members of the caravan regarded it as a very good deal, whether they hauled Aull's freight or not. Feed for stock was at a premium on the Missouri. They spared every man available to work on repairing the fence, and in twelve days had it in such condition that they no longer needed to worry about the horses and oxen.

Belmet bought some lumber and a stove. He and Clint built a board frame, over which they stretched the tent. They laid buffalo robes on the floor and otherwise added to their comfort for the long winter months. Belmet also invested in books and magazines, and spent most of his time reading. Clint and Tom made a serious business of studying together, each teaching the other the subject in which he was most proficient. On pleasant days they took their guns and followed Jack through the thickets of the river bottom, a procedure that elicited great fun and also added materially to the larder.

So the winter passed, and when spring came Waters loaded freight for Santa Fé and Couch loaded for Fort Wise, Colorado. But the two caravans pulled out together, passed Wasarus Creek, went on to Diamond Springs, crossed the Little Arkansas, and then undertook the long drive to Cove Creek, where they ran right into a large band of Indians that evidently was lying in ambush under the creek bank. But frontiersmen like Waters and Couch were seldom trapped.

The savages, about three hundred strong, were painted and had on feather war bonnets. Seeing they were discovered, they leaped on their mustangs and charged like a tornado, yelling like a horde of demons.

The freighters had time to get half prepared, and Jim Waters stood beside his cannon, ready to spread destruction in their ranks, should they attack. Evidently the Indians were loath to close in, and instead they adopted one of their old tricks of galloping close, yelling hideously, and waving their buffalo robes and red blankets in an attempt to stampede the stock. It almost succeeded as far as the horses were concerned.

But on their second circle of the caravan, Waters selected a massed bunch of Indians and fired his cannon into it. The thunder of the report and the wide swath of destruction turned the tables on the Indians, and they were the ones to suffer a stampede.

Clint gasped at the *mêlée* and the wild chorus of yells and snorts. Mustangs by the dozens went down with their riders; others tore away, riderless; some kicked in frantic terror, dragging at the crippled Indians who still clung to them. Yet so wonderful and loyal were these savages, that those who were capable endeavored to save the wounded ones and to carry off their dead. The steady rifle fire from the freighters did not daunt them.

Then, BOOM! went Waters' cannon again, this time more heavily charged with powder and slugs.

The discharge, ruthless as shrapnel, flung devastation into the middle of that plunging *mêlée* of Indians and mustangs. The freighters lowered their rifles, prone to pity. Even Jim Waters made no move to reload the cannon. And the able-bodied Indians, profiting by this restraint, got horses and cripples straightened out and beat a hasty retreat.

Search discovered the bodies of sixty dead Indians

and eighty dead or crippled horses. It was the most complete rout Waters had ever engineered. He ordered the injured horses shot, but left them and the dead Indians unburied on the plain.

The men straightened out the teams and by brisk driving reached Fort Zarah at three that afternoon. Waters reported to Captain Selkirk the conduct of the Pawnees. A detachment of fifty dragoons was sent out on their trail.

Then the double caravan drove on to Pawnee Rock, to Ash Creek, and Pawnee Forks, and in six days more went into camp at the Cimmaron Crossing for the last time together. It was rather a sad encampment. A hundred and seventy freighters who had driven, camped, and fought together for months, and had made a success out of every trip, found the fact of parting something to deplore. They stayed up late that night. Next morning they arose at dawn, but, owing to more and yet more hand shaking, the sun rose and still the caravans did not separate.

Waters crushed Clint's hand and said: "Buff, this don't seem right, you leavin' us to get along as best we can without you an' Jack."

"But, Mr. Waters, you have the cannon," replied Clint, significantly.

"Good luck, lad. You've a head on your shoulders. You'll be a great frontiersman some day."

And so at last the caravans parted, Waters taking the dry trail to Santa Fé and Couch pushing north to Fort Wise. For many miles and hours Clint's keen eye marked the long winding wagon-train moving at a snail's pace across the plains. He thought the one drawback to an overland freighter's life was the ever-recurring farewell to beautiful and interesting places, to friends and comrades, and to loved ones.

Fort Wise, at this season, was full of Indians, trappers, and hunters, trading off their winter's catch for provisions, clothing, ammunition, and tobacco. This was the undesirable time to visit the Colorado fort. Captain Couch moved out as soon as he had unloaded, and when the caravan reached good grazing-ground

77

he made camp to rest and feed the stock and hunt buffalo.

That afternoon Belmet and John Sidel returned to camp in a wagon with three fine hides and almost half a ton of meat. Clint had a hand in preparing the hides. They were stretched on the ground, pegged down at the corners, and scraped until all the meat and fat were off. They used the brains of the buffalo to help in the tanning process, and if this was properly done over a period of four days, they could expect a hide that would not get hard or stiff.

At Timpas Creek, the next camp, an enormous herd of buffalo impeded and finally halted the progress of the caravan. As travel was impossible, Couch ordered another day there. Many buffalo were killed by the freighters, who shot from their wagons. Belmet and Sidel secured five. All day the herd rolled by, a mighty sea of shaggy beasts, far as eye could see on both sides. At sunset the last stragglers passed, followed by the wolves and coyotes that always attended a herd of buffalo.

8

One night in camp, at the end of an eight-day drive free from the sight of Indians, only four guards were stationed on duty.

"All peaceful," announced Couch. "Let's turn in."

Late that night Clint was aroused by having his blankets pulled. He jerked up. Jack was doing it, and growling besides. When Clint spoke he awakened his father.

"What's the matter, Clint?"

"Jack up to his old tricks. Look at him! Listen!" whispered Clint.

They watched the dog. He ceased both pulling and growling, but it would have been a dense fellow indeed who could not see that Jack wanted them to go outside.

"Injuns, I'll bet," muttered Belmet. "It never pays to play safe on this prairie. Grab your gun, Clint."

They slipped out in their stocking feet, rifles in hand. It was bright starlight, very still, and the very air seemed charged with portent. They followed the dog.

The four guards were sound asleep beside the burned-out camp fire.

"Don't wake them," whispered Belmet, in a sore tone. "We'll let Couch do that."

Jack led them to the farthest corner of the corral formed by the wagons, fully a quarter of a mile from the fire. Then he wagged his tail as if to say, "Here it is."

Belmet cautioned Clint to be still, and he knelt to hold the dog. Clint heard a faint noise on the outside of the wagon. It sounded like a ripping of canvas. Clint looked up at the white cover barely discernible in the darkness. It seemed to billow out slightly. Belmet evidently heard and saw the same, for he stealthily led Clint and Jack back a hundred steps or more. Then he put his lips to Clint's ear: "Go wake Couch. Tell him. Wake the men an' have them come here, but not to make any noise. Don't tell Couch about the sleepin' guards. He'd likely shoot them. Hurry now. I'll watch."

Clint ran fleetly on his errand. A touch awakened the doughty Couch. Clint told him where to go to find his father, then he ran to awaken the guards. They were mighty sheepish and the alarmed. In less than ten minutes Clint had all the freighters around his father. They held a whispered colloquy. Couch did not believe there were Indians around, but he said they had better proceed as if there were. He sent out three scouting parties, of ten men each, in different directions. Couch, Belmet, Clint and the others lay down on the grass and waited.

It seemed to Clint that an age passed. Then he was transfixed to hear an owl hoot—*who—who—whowho!*

right out of the wagon to which Jack had led him and his father. From the creek below came an answering call.

Couch hit Belmet on the back and cursed under his breath. "You men hear thet?"

"You bet," replied Belmet. "What'll we do? Wish we had a cannon."

"Redskins again," said another, resignedly.

"Nary redskin," replied the old frontiersman. "No Injun is as crazy as thet."

Couch advised his men to crawl under the wagons so they could command the prairie. Clint saw a tiny flare of flame like a lighted match down by the creek bank. Others saw it, too.

"Where in tarnation are them scoutin' parties?" growled Couch. "We can't move around much."

"Listen!" burst out Clint, quivering. "I hear horses comin' . . . Must be Injuns. Jack smells somethin'."

"Ahuh. I see the horses. . . . Men, too. . . . Don't act like Injuns," said Couch.

"They ain't Injuns," rejoined the old frontiersman.

Next Clint heard heavy thuds up by the wagon that Jack had led them to investigate.

"Listen!" whispered Couch, hoarsely. "I'm a horned sinner if some gang ain't robbin' the wagon!"

A coyote wailed out a lonely cry, the genuineness of which Clint would have vouched for. The dark objects out on the plain worked closer, making to the right of the watching party. They halted perhaps fifty feet outside of the wagon in question. Several men, like shadows, left the horses and moved in toward the wagon train.

Jack tore loose from Clint and dashed back under the wagon to the inside of the corral. Clint crawled after him. Just then on the outside of the caravan a man yelled, "HANDS UP!"

Immediately the sound of hard angry voices and a violent tussle rent the air. Then a rush of feet. Clint rose and ran after Jack, just discernible in the starlight. Before Clint reached him a man leaped down from the wagon. Jack jumped at the man and they

80

went down together. Clint, rushing up, saw them sprawling on the ground. He caught the gleam of a blade. Whereupon Clint promptly hit the fellow on the head with the rifle butt. That stunned him. The dog let go. Then Belmet arrived, panting and excited, and grasping the situation he sat astride the fallen man and tied his hands and feet.

"Watch him, Clint, while I see what's goin' on outside."

The robber did not come to, or else he feigned unconsciousness, for he never moved.

It developed presently that one of the three scouting parties had stolen up on the wagon which was being looted, and were lying in the grass when the other three robbers came up with eight horses. They were captured, not without a fight, but no shot was fired.

By this time day was not far distant. The east was light and the pale gray brightened. Fires were built, and preparations for breakfast begun.

As soon as it grew clear daylight Couch called, gruffly:

"Twenty volunteers to string up these robbers!"

Clint seemed irresistibly propelled to follow them down to the creek, where under a huge, spreading, black-walnut tree they halted with their prisoners.

"You fellars anythin' to say?" queried Couch, surveying the four robbers.

"Nope. You ketched us," replied one of them, laconically.

"Reckon I'd like a smoke," spoke up another. Some one gave him a cigarette, which he lighted and puffed with satisfaction.

Clint was chained to the spot in horror. This summary justice was not only the law of the freighters; it was frontier law, from which there could be no appeal. The four robbers knew it; they accepted it, and for all Clint could tell they were not even disturbed. If such marvelous courage could only have been expended in a good cause! Clint had never seen such rough, ragged, iron-visaged men anywhere on the frontier. They looked their characters.

The executioners had thrown noosed ropes over a great branch of the walnut and stood waiting, silent, hard-eyed, looking neither at one another nor at the robbers.

One of the four cursed the one smoking. "— — —! You're holdin' this up!"

The smoker flipped away the cigarette half smoked.

"Wal, Pickens, if you're in such an all-fired hurry, let her rip!"

In the speech and the coarse laugh following spoke all the wild lawless and terrible spirit of the frontier of 1857.

The robbers were forced in line, the nooses dropped over their necks.

"Five men to a rope!" ordered Couch, sternly. "Haul!"

Up shot the four men, the smallest of them fully six feet off the ground, the others about half that distance. Their hands were tied behind their backs, but their legs were free. The instant they were in the air a horrible change in face and body manifested itself. The instinct of the flesh to survive was the last and strongest. Their mouths opened wide, their tongues stuck out, their eyes rolled hellishly, and their faces turned livid. They began to kick and twist, to double up and turn halfway round. They drew up their legs until their knees touched their bodies, then kicked out frightfully. Facial expression and contortions augmented terribly with each second.

Clint uttered a loud cry and covered his eyes with his hands to shut out the awful sight. He sat there, head bowed, and his abdomen quaking with a sickness within. When he looked again the robbers were limp and quiet, and he never would have recognized their black visages.

"Men, we'll let 'em hang fer the good of the frontier," said Couch, and forthwith he produced a piece of paper which he fastened to the leg of the one called Pickens. Upon it had been written:

Freight robbers. We hung them. Jim Couch Caravan.

Upon the return to camp Clint heard Couch say to

his men: "A good job thet. Pickens was a murderer. I've run into his outfit before."

The caravan traveled on to Fort Bent, arriving there that day late. Couch reported the execution. Twenty soldiers under a sergeant were dispatched to bury the robbers.

Before that memorable day ended Couch sent for Clint.

"Lad, you an' Jack had a hand in savin' us again," he said, patting Clint's shoulder. "Leastways you saved us from bein' robbed. . . . Now here's the outfit of the robbers. You can have first pick."

"Aw, Captain, I—I don't want anythin'," replied Clint.

"Shore you do. It's your right. Ask any of the men. Kit Carson will tell you thet. We'll divide this outfit, an' you get first whack."

Thus importuned, Clint forced his attention upon the possessions left by Pickens and his allies. There were eight horses, several of them unusually fine animals, an equal number of riding saddles, pack saddles, bed rolls and saddle blankets, canteens, bags and bridles; also eight pistols, four rifles, a number of knives, lassoes, and other articles useful to frontiersmen.

"How much can I pick?" asked Clint, uncertain of himself.

"Haw! Haw!" roared the old frontiersman. "Take the boss up, Buff, an' grab it all."

"Wal, choose what you want best, but don't be a hawg," answered Couch.

Still Clint could not arrive at a quick decision; whereupon Tom stepped out and said:

"I know what Buff'd like best."

"Now what?"

"A horse. He has always wanted one."

"Wal, thet's fine. Come on, Buff. Pick a hoss, a saddle, a blanket, a bridle, an' by gum, one of the pistols."

Clint came out of his trance and pointed out the

83

horse that really had been the cause of his tongue-tied state—a thoroughbred dark-bay mare, clean-limbed and beautifully built.

"Thet one! Ahuh, you son-of-a-gun," ejaculated Couch. "I guess mebbe you can't pick the best hoss. I shore wanted thet mare myself."

The laugh went round the circle, and Couch continued: "All right, she's yours, Buff. What'll you call her?"

Clint studied over this problem a minute, then with a catch in his breath he replied, "Maybell."

"Fine an' dandy. Thet's a pretty handle. An' now, Buff, the question is can you ride her? She looks like a real hoss, boy. Remember, robbers can't afford to ride anythin' but fast hosses. Hadn't you better trade Maybell to me for one of the others?"

"Oh, I—I'll ride her or bust," replied Clint, hurriedly.

"Jim," went on Couch to Clint's father, "you pick his saddle an' outfit. An' I reckon you'd better straddle the mare first."

Clint was no stranger to saddle horses, but he had never seen so spirited and racy an animal as Maybell, even at the country fairs back in Illinois. When saddle, bridle, blanket, rope were chosen and placed on the horse for his edification he was an exultant boy. Lastly Couch picked out a silver-mounted pistol and a bag of ammunition to go with it, and stuck them in the saddlebag.

"Buff, more power to you an' Jack," he said, heartily. "Hope I can have you with me long."

The river bank opposite Chateau Island was chosen for the next camp. This was always a favorite place for travelers.

At sundown a troop of dragoons rode down the dry trail from Santa Fé, and reported a fight between Jim Waters' caravan and a band of Comanches under Chief White Bear. The soldiers had happened along just in the nick of time. The Comanches had ambushed the trail in broad daylight, and rushed on the caravan before Waters could get the cannon into play. The ambush was at Apache Canyon, which spot Clint had shivered through often enough to remember.

When the dragoons, who were trailing the Comanches, rode upon the scene of the battle, Waters had five men dead and eight seriously wounded. Waters had a bad wound in his shoulder. His caravan halted at Fort Aubry to recuperate. Clint could not help wondering when Jim Waters' turn would finally come. He was the boldest of freighters and took reckless chances.

Couch was glad of an escort for the remainder of the drive to Westport. He had expected a good long rest there, but did not get it. Colonel Danbury signed him to a contract to freight government supplies to all the forts west as far as Taos. If the freighters were delayed at any post longer than two days for unloading, the government agreed to supply hay for horse feed.

Couch's freighters went the limit so far as loads were concerned, putting on all the wagons would carry. They were paid by the hundredweight. It was the heaviest and most valuable wagon-train Couch had ever started out with; and the whole troop of soldiers furnished by the government was most welcome.

Near Wagon Mound a band of Comanches rode down on the stock like a flock of screeching hawks and stampeded the animals, driving them three miles before the soldiers could overtake them. There was no fight.

At Apache Canyon a band of Indians was lying in hiding. But the scouts were not to be waylaid, and the Utes sneaked off like coyotes in the safe.

The caravan labored on to Lamy, Santa Fé, and ended the successful drive at Taos. This was an opportunity Clint had long anticipated, and to his delight he found Kit Carson at home. The scout welcomed him with surprise and open arms.

"Buff Belmet!" he exclaimed. "You great big husky plainsman! Growed up like a weed!—I sure am glad to see you."

Carson insisted that Clint stay at his house, where he was introduced to two other famous scouts of the frontier—Jim Baker and John Hobbs. These frontiersmen had a wealth of experience to draw from and they liked to talk.

"Wal, thet reminds me," said Jim Baker, reminiscently, nodding his shaggy head. "Reckon it was in 'fifty-two, wasn't it, Kit, when Hatcher was agent here? Taos was the best fort on the frontier then. Five companies of soldiers at the fort under Major Greer. My old pard Denver was there. Wal, Hatcher rode over to the fort an' told Greer there was fifteen young warriors all painted up, trailin' their war bonnets, an' he was sure they was up to some devilment. Greer sent me an' Denver out to find out.

"We packed five days' grub, plenty of ammunition, an' hit their trail. They was goin' south at a pretty good clip, toward the only white settler near, an' he lived fifty miles an' more down on the Red River. Name was Lya Banks. You remember him, Kit. We used to call him Old Ly here at Taos. He was a squaw man, married Injun style to a Kiowa, but he was a good friend to all the whites in the valley. We rode fast on the trail of thet bunch, an' when we got near to Banks' place we saw smoke. We thought it was the Injuns' camp. Howsomever, when we went close we saw it was too much smoke. Injuns don't burn much wood.

"Wal, shore the fire was old Ly's place. We hid our horses in the timber an' stole up. The house an' shed was all burned down. No Injuns in sight. So we went up. There was the burned remains of a couple of people, but we couldn't identify them. Reckoned, though, thet one was poor Ly.

"We took the Injuns' trail again, an' late in the day saw smoke comin' from a grove of cottonwoods. We did the sneak trick an' soon was spyin' on them red devils at supper. They had a big bunch of horses an' some cattle. We counted them. Fifteen Kiowas. They was shore the bunch we was after. We watched them a while, then went back to our hosses.

"'Denver, them redskins are raidin',' says I. 'They're goin' on down the river to murder other settlers. What'll we do about it?'

"'Wal,' says Denver, 'they ain't a-goin' to murder no more settlers.'

"I says I ageed with him, but how did we know they wasn't?

"'We'll kill every damn one of them,' says Denver. 'We can do it.'

"'Shore,' says I, 'but how?'

"'Wal, we'll wait till midnight, then sneak into their camp. We each got two Colts thet're good for twenty shots. We can both shoot right an' left handed. An' we can pick 'em off as they jump up.'

"I agreed, an' Denver says he reckoned he'd take a nap. I sat ag'in' a tree an' watched the trail. About midnight I woke Denver. We had a look at our Colts. Then we slipped down on thet Kiowa camp an' crawled right among them. We made no more noise than a couple of mice. I touched Denver an' we rose to our feet, a gun in each hand. It was full moon an' we could see them Injuns lyin' like a row of fence pickets.

"Wal, Denver raised a gun—the signal we'd agreed on—an' then we let out a hell of a Comanche war whoop an' began to shoot. We stood back to back an' just stepped round as the Kiowas leaped straight up in the air. We didn't give them a chance to tackle us.

"But one Injun on the ground kicked my feet out from under me. They went up where my head ought to have been, an' I fell so hard on my back thet it jarred both guns out of my hands. I'd shot eight or nine times, anyway. . . . Thet redskin was like a cat. He jumped on me, swipin' at me with a knife. I warded off thet blow an' yelled for Denver. I heard him shootin' an' wrastlin'. Then he was suddenly quiet. The Injun swung his knife an' hit me in the neck, a little too high to kill me outright. I grabbed his arm,

87

twisted it, an' broke the bone. The knife dropped. Then I got both hands round his windpipe an' held on. When he sagged I rolled him off me, grabbed up his knife, an' cut his throat in one slash.

"I jumped up, lookin' for Denver. He was gone. All the redskins there seemed dead enough. I picked up one of my Colts. It was empty. An' in the other I found one shot left. I fired it, hopin' to get an answer from Denver. An' I did from way down the river.

"Thet Injun had given me a bad cut. The blood was pourin' down inside my buckskin. I bound it up tight an' went down the river, huntin' for Denver. After a little I called an' he answered. I found him lyin' across a log, below the bank of the river, an' I knowed he was hurt. Reckoned he'd fell off the bank on the log.

" 'Which way did they go?' I asked Denver.

" 'Right here,' says Denver, pointing. 'There was only two. An' I think one is alive yet. . . . I heard a noise an', makin' a couple of jumps, I came on thet redskin on his knees, crawlin' with a knife. I soaked him over the head with my gun an' used his own knife on him.'

" 'Wal,' I says, 'I reckon thet's about all. Get up, Denver.'

" 'I can't,' he says. 'My leg's broke.'

" 'How'd you break it?' I asked, an' Denver told me he'd fought the two Kiowas on the bank above, an' they'd all fell off on the log.

"Wal, I was in a pretty fix. First I took them two Injuns' scalps, then I picked Denver up an' packed him back to the camp, where I laid him down. I found four Injuns alive yet, so I sent them off to the Happy Huntin'-grounds, an' then I counted thirteen. These with the two down by the river made fifteen. We had them all.

"Denver had some bad cuts, one on his face bein' deep. I started the fire goin', heated some water, an' washed an' tied Denver's wounds. The Injuns had coffee an' grub, so after me an' Denver had some we felt better. I went back after our hosses. An' then I looked for the Injuns' stock. Found them all bunched together, an' I herded them down into the river bottom near the camp. Next I got Denver on his hoss, makin' a sling for his broken leg to rest in. I took the other thirteen scalps, an' strung them all on my belt. An' what with my own cut I shore was a bloody mess.

"Wal, I drove them cattle an' hosses very slow back to Banks' place. Denver stuck it out all right. I put him in a dugout, with water an' meat. Then I drove the stock into Banks' pasture. Some of the stock had slipped away on me, but I counted forty-seven hosses an' ninety-three cows, steers, an' calves.

"What I had to do then was the wust of the job, an' thet was get to the fort an' report in time to save Denver's life. I made it in fourteen hours. The major sent soldiers an' a six-mule wagon post-haste to Banks' place.

"Then he says: 'Jim, what you been up to? You had orders to report on fifteen Indians.'

"Wal, I told him.

" 'See here, scout, air you drunk or crazy? You're so cut up you're out of your head. You an' Denver never tackled fifteen Kiowas all by yourself.'

"I reached round my belt, untied the string with the fifteen scalps, an' I says, 'Major, count 'em yourself.'

"Greer took one look, an' with a crooked face he says: 'I'll take your word, Jim. I jest wanted a report to send to Washington.'

" 'Wal, Major,' I says, 'I don't care a damn what they think in Washington, but I want a doctor now.' . . . Next evenin' the soldiers fetched Denver in, an' we lay side by side in the hospital. I was up in a few weeks, but thet Kiowa left his work on me for life." Here Baker swept aside his grizzled locks and exposed a red scar fully five inches long on his neck. "Denver lay in bed five months an' all but croaked, an' it was longer before he could fork a hoss. The quartermaster bought thet stock I saved, an' me an' Denver got fourteen hundred an' eighty dollars each out of it."

"Well, Buff, what did you think of Jim Baker's story?" asked Kit Carson, with a smile, seeing Clint's jaw had dropped.

"Aw! I—I don't know," replied Clint, expelling a deep breath.

"True as gospel, Buff. I happen to know," said Carson. "Fact is, lad, truth is often stranger than fiction on this frontier."

At this period Kit Carson was about forty-seven or -eight years old, rather slightly built compared with scouts like Baker and Curtis, but the muscles rippled on him. He had a clean-shaven, fair face, keen light eyes that held a wonderful piercing quality, and altogether he looked what he was—the greatest frontiersman of the West.

Clint stayed several days at Carson's house, a long, low, wide-porched, whitewashed adobe structure. Carson's wife was a Spanish woman, dark-eyed and sweet-voiced, who took a strange liking to Clint and called him Señor Buff, much to Clint's pleasure.

Kit Carson liked to talk, at least to Clint, of his wonderful exploring trips with Frémont, the Pathfinder, whose name was inseparably linked with the West. He mentioned the first trip he made with Frémont, in 1842, when they climbed to the Wind River Range. He remembered most vividly the capsizing of Frémont's rubber boat in the rapids of the Platte River.

About the second of Frémont's expeditions Carson had a great deal more to say. The purpose of the government was to explore the country beyond the Rockies just south of the Columbia River.

In 1843, Kit Carson joined this expedition, with his friend Maxwell, on the Arkansas River, and under Carson's guidance they successfully consummated fourteen months of exploration that wholly changed the attitude of the government toward the West and opened the way for the settlers. Frémont's ambition then was to acquaint the East, and the whole world with the wonders of California.

"Buff, what do you think?" asked Carson. "Frémont told me Daniel Webster did not approve of the takin' of Texas into the Union, but had a strong leanin' for San Francisco Bay an' California. He said England would not agree to Mexico cedin' California to the U. S. Boy, I shore could tell you a lot of history. . . . It was in August, 1845, that I met Frémont's third expedition, one purpose of which was to explore California an' keep England from gettin' it away from Mexico. There were sixty men. I had my friends again. . . . Well, lad, you know, of course, how Frémont made conquest of California an' how jealous army officers run him out of the army in disgrace. That's history. They were little men an' Frémont was big. Of all the men I've known an' fought with he had the most unconquerable spirit."

9

Clint, back at Santa Fé, heard several times about mountain lions, or panthers and cougars, as some hunters called them, that had been prowling around where the stock was feeding. This was exciting news to him and Tom Sidel, but they were not permitted to go alone to hunt.

About four inches of snow had fallen, making the trailing of game easy and rapid. Belmet gathered a party of freighters to hunt the lions, and took Clint and Tom with them.

The hunting party crossed the Pecos, and before they saw any lion tracks they jumped a bunch of big gray-blue timber wolves. There were about fifteen of them, each as tall as a yearling calf, with heavy fur and bushy tails curling up over their backs. They stared at the hunters for a moment, then loped up a gulch. They had been eating from a cow which they had killed.

After trailing the wolves for five miles, one of the hunters advised a cut across to head them off, and he took a half dozen of the others, including Clint and Tom. They rounded a thick clump of cedars to run fairly into the pack. What yelling and shooting! Clint, as usual, had been on the alert out in front, and he got in his first shot a fraction of a second before the others. He downed one of the leaders, and had another shot besides. Seven wolves in all fell to the guns of the freighters. They skinned the beasts right on the spot. In Kansas City a wolf pelt brought fourteen dollars.

It might have been that the return of the hunters with seven fine wolf hides stimulated an idea in Captain Couch's mind. At any rate, he called on Belmet and said, "Jim, how'd you an Buff like to risk a little money?"

"What on, Cap?" asked Belmet.

"Wal, I was over to the fort today, an' learned a troop is ridin' up to Raton Pass. There are some villages of Comanches an' Utes. We might ride up an' drop in friendly like on the Injuns. You see, all the fur hunters come in about May. Now if we'd offer them cash for pelts I think they'd like it better than tradin' at the store for supplies. We'd just about get all their trade."

"Good idea, Cap, but have we enough money? I've only twenty-five hundred odd. How much have you, Clint?"

"About a thousand dollars saved."

"Thet's fine. What with mine an' yours an' some of the other fellars we'll let in on the deal, bet we make a haul."

Two days later Couch, Belmet, and several others rode away with the soldiers. Clint begged hard to be taken, but unavailingly. They returned in a couple of weeks, elated over promises from Chief Lone Wolf and Chief Black Kettle to fetch down all their furs and pelts and buffalo robes the latter part of April.

The Indians, as usual, kept their word, and a few of them at a time brought in their winter supply and sold to Couch. Presently the traders at the store discovered what was going on, and in high dudgeon they went to the colonel. He answered their complaint in succinct terms: "I can't stop them. It's none of my business. If they have the cash to buy furs, no one can prevent it."

Thereafter a great deal of money found its way into Couch's hands. Where the money came from was a secret. The officers at the posts were not permitted to do any kind of trading with the Indians. But it was significant that when the caravan was loaded with a large and magnificent stock of furs, it was given an escort of ninety-eight soldiers under Captain Howland and Lieutenant Wilcox, clear through to Westport.

The fur company made a good many complaints and took the matter to Fort Leavenworth military headquarters of the Southwest. The general in command sent officers to investigate, but they could not learn anything from Couch of his freighters.

"How'd you come to have such a large escort?" Couch was asked.

"I never turn a wheel without a troop."

"Whom did you ask?"

"I didn't ask anybody."

"You were hauling at your own risk?"

"Yes, sir. But half our freight was protected by Aull an' Company."

The officers had to depart without giving any satisfaction to the fur company. Captain Couch, Belmet, and the others regarded it as a perfectly honest transaction and a far fairer deal to the Indians.

Clint found himself in possession of ten thousand dollars where formerly he had owned only one. He felt rich. At this rate he would have money enough some day to go into ranching or own a trading store. That brought to mind May Bell, his little friend, who had been carried off by Indians. Clint seldom thought of her now. It seemed long ago. He could remember her eyes, dark, bright, following him, and he sighed with the sorrow of it.

Captain Couch, Belmet, and the other freighters who had profited by the fur deal traveled to St. Louis by boat to invest all their money in merchandise to trade to the Indians, white trappers, and hunters. Clint had money to invest, too, and so they took him

93

along. St. Louis was a big place. Clint had so long been used to quiet and the open spaces that he was glad to get back on the river boat. He enjoyed the ride up the swift, muddy stream.

On the vessel Captain Couch ran into Maxwell, the frontiersman so widely known; and through this circumstance Clint met him.

"Are you the Maxwell who went with Kit Carson on Frémont's explorin' trips?" asked Clint, eagerly.

"I sure am, young fellar. How'd you know?" replied Maxwell, a splendid type of Westerner, who, though past fifty, stood erect and virile, his dark face a record of his adventurous life.

"Kit Carson told me himself," replied Clint, with pride.

"Say, do you know Kit Carson?"

"I'm a friend of his."

"Then you're one of mine. You'll be welcome at my ranch any time, to stay a day or all winter. I've got ten thousand head of horses. You can have your pick."

When they arrived at Kansas City, Maxwell, who had bought a heavy supply of goods, engaged Couch to haul it for him. Early in August the caravan was loaded and ready. But an escort could not be secured. Couch, confident with his ninety-three tried and proven freighters, decided to start without one.

Couch had eighty-seven wagons loaded with his freight; Maxwell had forty-four, heavily packed. The caravan then consisted of one hundred and thirty-one wagons, four hundred and sixty-four oxen, forty horses, and six mules.

Across the Kansas River, near Smoky Hill, they sighted the first buffalo, and therefore encamped, while twenty hunters, followed by a wagon, went out after meat. They killed five, and then desisted because a scout had discovered a party of Indians near the head of the herd.

The stock was kept in close all night, but as the grass grew richly the animals fared well. Starting in good time the next morning, the freighters got away from that camp without sighting the Indians again.

Thereafter they drove along the old and familiar trail day by day, with the vast and sublime monotony of the plains on all sides, from rosy sunrise to golden sunset, on and on over the waving, gray and green, flower-dotted prairie. They came at last to the rising ground, to the Cimmaron Crossing, proceeded along the dry trail to Sand Creek, Willow Bar, McNess Spring, and so on to Round Mount, Rock Creek, and at last Point of Rocks.

The date was the 19th of November, and the camp site a favored one. Large rocks stood up twenty feet or more, from the center of which gushed a cold spring. Wood was abundant, but the grass near camp had been grazed off for a mile or more. The freighters did not like to send the stock so far, but there was no alternative. Twenty-five men, among them Belmet and John Sidel, were sent out to guard the animals and fetch them in before dark.

Broken clouds in the west obscured the setting sun, but through the rifts poured a golden effulgence that painted the prairie. There was still warmth in the air. Peace and quiet seemed to reign over the plains. Here and there, around their smoking camp fires, freighters sang and whistled at their tasks.

Clint was peeling potatoes, a job he appeared forever to have assigned him, and which he hated. "Reckon I've peeled nine million potatoes for this darn outfit!" he grumbled.

Presently Jack came running up to him, hair ruffled and bristling, eyes bright and knowing. He barked and bounded away, only to return.

"Now what ails you?" demanded Clint. Jack repeated the performance. Clint became uneasy at once. There was one thing he hated worse than peeling potatoes.

"Lie down, you scallywag," ordered Clint, trying to hope against hope. But Jack would not settle down. Clint sat there tingling. Then he heard a rifle-shot, far off. Leaping up, he ran like a deer to Couch's camp.

"Captain—my dog—smells Indians," he panted. "An' I heard a shot."

Couch did not need to be told twice. He got up and shouted: "Ho, men! Be on the lookout."

He climbed a wagon, stood on the seat, and leveled his glass. Almost instantly he uttered a loud curse and dropping the glass on the seat, leaped sheer off to the ground.

"COMANCHES!" he yelled at the top of his lungs. "They've cut our guards off from camp! Grab your guns!"

Pandemonium broke loose inside the circle of wagons. Fifty and more men resembled a swarm of angry ants dashing here and there around an antheap. They made a rush for horses, only to realize that there were scarcely fifteen horses left in the enclosure. The guards had driven out almost all of the stock to feed. Couch's mighty oath rolled away over the plain.

"Hell to pay, boys," he shouted, gnashing his teeth, his face flashing dark. "We're ketched bad. . . . Saddle up. Some of us will go. . . . Rest of you stick here."

Clint had stood rooted to the spot. He saw the men running, he heard the hoarse shouts and orders. He watched two freighters trying to get on one horse. In a few moments fifteen riders were tearing out of the opening between the wagons, with Couch leading. They turned away out of sight.

Clint's fear of his father's peril had paralyzed him, but now he broke out of the clamping spell, and leaping on the wagon seat he scanned the plain. A mile or more out the waving golden grass showed a dark blot of horses, riders, oxen, in a confused moving mass, working to the northward. The Comanches must have been hidden down in the river bottom in the brush, and at an opportune time they had cut off Couch's guards from the wagon-train, had surrounded them or were driving them farther away. Clint's blood ran cold. The Comanches were in strong force. Disaster to Belmet, Sidel, and their comrades was imminent, inevitable. Couch and his fourteen riders were racing toward the scene of the battle, but it seemed to Clint that they were not only too late, but in danger of losing their own lives.

Clint happened to step on the field-glass that Couch had left on the seat. As he stooped to take it up he saw Tom Sidel's white face at the wheel.

"Buff! Buff! Do you see anythin'?" he faltered.

"Do I? Good Lord! Jump up here, Tom," returned Clint.

Tom climbed to a place beside him. "I see! I see!" he cried. "Oh, Buff, it's good-by to my uncle John an' your dad!"

Clint got the range with the field-glass, and then it appeared that the scene of terrific struggle was only a few rods from the wagon-train. He heard Tom talking wildly and crying out, but did not distinguish what he said. There was a shouting clamor inside the circle as the freighters ran around in excitement, moving wagons, making barricades of boxes of freight, and then dashing for a look out across the plain.

Couch and his riders ran into the range of Clint's glass. They soon came within rifle-shot of the wheeling, flashing circle of Comanches, and spreading out they halted to open fire. Clint's cold, clammy horror broke to thrill on thrill as he saw the quick puffs of white smoke.

It appeared that the Comanches had the guards surrounded, but not the stock. Oxen were lumbering in every direction. Unsaddled horses were running wild.

Then Clint was rudely shaken from his fascinated gaze. A freighter had jerked Tom off the seat and was reaching for Clint.

"Get down. Go back to your own wagon. Load your guns. Be ready to fight," he ordered, harshly.

Clint piled off the seat, glass in hand, and ran to his wagon. In a few swift moves he had both his rifles and his pistol and a bag of ammunition ready at hand. But where should he make his stand. The wagon wheels afforded but little protection, though better than none. If there had been time he might have built a platform of boxes high enough so that he would be protected by the wagon bed. He decided he would be better off inside the wagon. There was room enough under the seat for him to hide. Forthwith he deposited his arms in the wagon and climbed in. He still had Captain Couch's field-glass.

Panting and sweating, Clint peeped over the side of the wagon. The wide, black, moving circle out there appeared to have condensed or gotten farther away. His hand shook and he had to rest the glass on the wagon to steady it. Then he found a dimness in his eyes, that hindered vision. There seemed both a knocking and a something locked tight within his breast.

Presently the powerful field-glass brought the battle right before Clint. And it was stunning. The swift circle of Comanche horses seemed riderless, but the occasional puffs of smoke, and a closer view proved those incomparable horsemen were hanging over the backs of their mustangs, shooting from under their necks. A streaming, smoking continuous whirl! All inside that circle was a blur. Yet plain it was the circle closed inward.

Somewhat to the right Couch's men bobbed on their horses, shooting fast, moving back, it seemed. Where were the fifteen freighters who had dashed out to the rescue of the guards? Clint counted only nine.

Faster and smaller rode the wheel of Comanches. Smoke and dust and action! The gold of sunset flashed on bright moving objects. Mustangs leaped high to plunge down. The rattle of rifle-shots lessened. Suddenly all those wheeling horses appeared to have riders with upflung arms, plumes and feathers flying; the circling ceased. The movement was inward only. It was like the wave of prairie grass. Then from across the space pealed a low, wild, and hideous sound—the war whoop of the Comanches. It signaled victory. And the intricate mass seemed a lashing thicket of horses' heads, manes, riders, arms, bonnets, guns, and bows, all upflung in terrible significance.

ALL READY! *They're comin'!"* sang out the stentorian voice of one of the freighters in the line.

Clint saw Couch and his men—only seven now—riding madly toward the caravan. Another glance showed the mass of Comanches spreading out into a line in swift pursuit.

Dropping beside the wagon-side, Clint shuddered there. The glass fell from his nerveless hand. His father was murdered. He sank under the blow. He had an impulse to hide his head, so as not to see the end. Convulsion of horror and agony clamped him inert, cold as ice, like wet dead flesh.

Yet his instinct was to listen. Silence! The freighters were under their wagons, grim and silent. A faint low trampling clatter of hoofs pierced Clint's strained ears. It increased, breaking to the crack of rifles. Another sound struck fire into Clint. The swelling yell of the Comanches! Clint had heard old frontiersmen tell about the most terrifying of all human sounds—the war cry of the Comanche Indians. It swelled louder. The trampling clatter of hoofs likewise increased.

Clint's hair rose stiff on his head. At the same instant a hot explosion of blood within him galvanized all his being. Grasping a rifle with hard hands, he thrust it over the wagon-side and looked over the barrel.

Couch and his riders were close, madly riding, their horses separated, stretching low on a dead run for the caravan. Behind raced the Comanches, scarcely a hundred yards distant, riding as one horseman. They were shooting. Clint saw puffs of smoke but heard no shots. If the freighters were shooting, the reports were lost in the din. Clint dared not take aim, because Couch and riders were still between him and the Indians. But they were sweeping to the right toward the gate.

The last rider suddenly threw up his arms. His horse gave a wild plunge. Clint's keen sight registered the man's awful blank face and as he pitched off the saddle, a feathered arrow showed quivering between his shoulders. His riderless horse swept on.

Roar of heavy Colt's rifles then mixed with the yell of the Comanches. Two hundred or more, they split into two lines and sheered to right and left, closing in to encircle the wagon-train. Clint had a grim realization of this familiar manoeuvre of all plains savages. He was in that circle now. And surely the fate of many wagon-trains was at hand for Couch's freighters.

He tried to get a bead on an Indian, but he could not see any. They were riding on the far side of their horses. Then he caught glimpses of lean dark-red faces, of guns and bows, protruding from under the stretching necks of the mustangs. Also he saw puffs of smoke and flash of arrows.

Clint fired at a white mustang. Missed! How swiftly these horses flashed by! He aimed at another, tried to get a little ahead of it, and missed again. They were still quite far out, perhaps between eighty and a hundred yards. But Clint saw mustangs rear and fall. Others staggered away. The freighters were taking toll, though Clint did not see any Indians drop. They just disappeared in the grass.

He fired the Colt seven times, then dodged down to reload. He had his buffalo gun there, too, and his pistol. The din was growing deafening as the savages closed in.

Clint thrust his rifle over the wagon-side and peeped after it. They were close now, a string of racing ponies, with a red leg over each back. The white horse swept into Clint's range. He led it—fired. And with a convulsive lunge the beautiful wild creature went down to roll with kicking hoofs in the air. Clint saw its rider fall like a sack.

"Got—the—hang of it—now," muttered Clint to himself, hot and wet, his grimy hands reloading. Holding the rifle tight, he waited until a lean mustang head was aligned with his sight, then pulled trigger. Down went that beast. One after another, then, Clint shot five more horses, satisfied that he had disabled

100

some of their riders. He had half reloaded when he felt the wagon shake under him.

The next instant a hideously painted face, with eyes of black fire, protruded over the side of the wagon. A naked body rose, barred with black and white paint. Swift as light a lean arm swung a tomahawk high. Clint had no time to raise the Colt. A terrible panic seized him.

At its highest point the tomahawk paused. It quivered as behind Clint boomed a heavy buffalo gun. Then it slipped from the lean dark hand that had swung it aloft. Clint gasped back to life. He shifted his gaze down. The Comanche's visage had incalculably changed. Vacant, wild eyes set! His hand clutched at his breast. Then as he sank Clint saw a huge round bullet hole with blue edges in the center of his body.

One of the freighters, standing behind Clint's wagon, had saved his life. Clint peeped out on that side. Tom Sidel stood there, half crouching, rifle thrust forward, his hair standing up like a mane, his face black with powder. His wild roving eyes caught sight of Clint. "I got him, Buff," he yelled above the uproar.

If anything could have inspired Clint out of his panic at that awful moment, it was the sight of Tom and the fact that he had shot the Comanche with the tomahawk. Clint bent to the other side of the wagon, and completing the reloading of his rifle he peered out behind it again.

Smoke and dust overhung the prairie. Clint could not see the whole space in front. The steady reports of guns along the wagon-train grew distinct, which proved that the yelling of the savages had ceased. Mustangs were not flashing by as formerly. As the smoke lifted Clint discerned Comanches from each side riding together, farther out, to where others on foot were trying to get wounded and dead on their mustangs. They had been repulsed, apparently with great loss. And they were finding rescue of injured a losing game, for where one Indian was lifted on a horse two went down under the deadly fire of the freighters. They gave up the attempt, moved out of range, held a consultation which seemed plain as print to the freighters, and then rode off out of sight over the ridge.

Clint leaned his guns against the wagon seat and stood up. Outside the caravan, dead and crippled Indians and horses showed everywhere. Inside, groups of men around objects on the ground awoke Clint to another aspect of the situation. One of these groups —three men, all kneeling beside a prostrate form— was right next to Clint's wagon. Then he saw Tom Sidel's pale face.

With a sharp cry Clint leaped out, and plunged to his knees beside Tom. His eyes were closed; his slowly heaving breast was all dark and wet; a thin stream of blood ran from his mouth.

"Tom! Tom!" cried Clint, frantically. Then he gazed at the grim men. "Say he isn't bad hurt. . . . He saved my life. . . . One of the Comanches got on my wagon. . . . He was about to tomahawk me. . . . I couldn't move. . . . Tom shot him."

"Buff, it's tough lines. Tom is dyin'," huskily replied one of the men.

"Oh, my God! How awful! . . . *Tom!*"

The poignant cry reached Tom's fading consciousness. He opened his eyes, strange, deep, unfathomable. He smiled.

"Good-by—Buff," he whispered.

Then light and life fled. The men laid him back, covered his face, and rose and went away, leaving Clint kneeling there with Tom's limp hand in his. Under this last blow Clint seemed to lose thought for a while. He heard dully, and could see the men moving around in a hurry. It was Maxwell who aroused him.

"Lad, brace up. It's been hell, but it can be worse," he said, a kind hand lifting Clint. "We must hurry on to Fort Union before the Comanches come back. They'll come, an' they'd get us all next time."

Clint allowed himself to be led and presently could obey orders. During the next hour he learned the extent of the catastrophe.

The twenty-five guards, among whom were Belmet

and John Sidel, had been massacred to a man, stripped, scalped and mutilated. Of the freighters left, less than fifty lived, and many of these were wounded.

Sixty-nine Comanches were found on the prairie outside the caravan, twenty-three of whom were still alive. But they did not live long after they were discovered. Dead horses lay everywhere.

The freighters, under command of Couch and Maxwell, loaded seven wagons with the most valuable supplies and personal belongings, and abandoned the rest. Fort Union was not quite two days' travel. They had little hope of arriving there and sending the soldiers back in time to save the one hundred and twenty-four wagons of supplies.

Couch's last act was to spike his brass cannon, which the freighters had not had time to get into action. And he did it viciously, as if he were driving the spike into the heads of the Comanches.

It happened that Clint's wagon, which was a large and new one, was chosen one of the seven. The driver assigned to it, a man named Saunders, knew Clint and liked him; and when he cracked his whip, ready to start, he called, "Rustle an' jump in, Buff."

"An' leave Tom—here—to be—scalped an' eaten by coyotes? . . . No, I'll stay an' be—scalped with him," replied Clint, with a sob.

Saunders leaped off, and grasping a blanket off a pack he wrapped it round Tom and lifted him into the wagon.

"Thar, lad. We'll take him along an' give him decent burial," said Saunders. "Jump up, now. They're leavin'."

One of the seven wagons held two hundred and fifty of the Colt rifles, with ten thousand rounds of ammunition. These the freighters had brought to sell to hunters and trappers. It would never have done to let this load fall into the hands of the savages.

That shortened caravan halted only twice in thirty hours, and then to let the oxen and horses drink. At

Mora Creek the condition of the wounded demanded attention, so a camp was risked there.

Clint helped bury his friend Tom high above the creek, back in the grove, under a giant cottonwood. Clint hid the grave with rocks and brush. He would know where to find it if he ever passed that way again.

Clint neither ate nor slept and the night was a horror. Next day, by noon, the depleted caravan had straggled into Fort Union, and all were objects of great interest and sympathy. Dragoons were dispatched to the scene of the carnage.

"Wal, Buff, how about you?" queried Captain Couch, kindly, the first chance he had to accost Clint.

"I don't care about nothin'," replied Clint, despondently.

"Reckon you don't now. But hard as it seems, it'll pass. This frontier is a hell of a place, Buff. You know thet. An' we got to be men. Wal, here's your father's bag. We'd better open it."

Belmet's papers, two thousand dollars, a few keepsakes, and a letter written some years before composed the contents. Couch read the letter.

"Your dad leaves you in my charge till you're twenty-one," explained Couch, seriously. "Wal, I'll do my best by you, Buff. You're a born freighter an' you can throw in with me. I'll keep these papers an' the money for you."

Maxwell, too, sought Clint out, and was so kind that Clint felt a mitigation of his utter loneliness and hopelessness.

"Buff, you've got the same stuff in you that made Kit Carson an' me an' Frémont himself what we are," said Maxwell. "We are all losers at this frontier game. Some more an' some less. It's hell for a boy to lose mother an' father an' then his pal."

"I—I lost my—my sweetheart, too," replied Clint, breaking down under this kindness.

"Well! Well!" . . . Maxwell was plainly baffled by the boy's misfortunes, and at a loss for words. "I just don't know what to say, Buff. . . . But I've been thirty years on this frontier, an' it has taught me much. I've been friends with Indians from all tribes. Some of them are good Indians, though many of my friends cuss me for sayin' that. So I can't advise you to be an Indian-hater an' killer. . . . Just stick it out for the sake of the West an' for those who are to follow us."

"All right, Mr. Maxwell," replied Clint. "I—I'll stick it out."

"That's the spirit, boy. I was not mistaken in you," said Maxwell, warmly. "Now when we get to Santa Fé, I'd like you to go to my ranch for the winter. Will you come?"

"Yes, sir, thank you," rejoined Clint, gratefully.

Upon the return of the dragoons from Point of Rocks, the sergeant in charge reported that all of Couch's wagons had been burned, and piles of supplies were still burning; over a hundred dead horses lay on the plain, but not an ox, nor a dead Indian, was to be seen for miles around.

10

Clint Belmet went on with Maxwell to his ranch and spent the winter there. It was well that this good influence came to Clint at this critical period of his life. When spring returned Clint did not go out with Couch and the freighters. Maxwell advised against it. So it came about that Clint had the run of the ranch during the following spring, summer, and through winter again.

Maxwell's Ranch in 1861 reached the zenith of its fame and prosperity. There was not then, and had never been, any place like it in all the West, and nothing ever approached it in later times.

Maxwell left Illinois for the West in 1822, and became almost as great a frontiersman as Kit Carson. He went through the war with the Navajo Indians and came out a captain. He fought through the Mexican

War in 1842 and the Texas Invasion in 1846. Then he was a captain of Texas Rangers for four years. After these years of active service he retired to the great ranch he had acquired.

At that time he was the biggest landowner in America. His ranch was bounded on the north by Raton Pass for a distance of sixty-five miles; on the west by twenty-five miles of the Red River; on the east by the Cimmaron River, about fifteen miles; and south was the open prairie. Fort Union, twenty-two miles off, was the nearest settlement.

Usually Maxwell employed between four and five hundred Mexicans. He raised corn, oats, wheat, and all kinds of vegetables in immense quantities. He operated a flour and grist mill, using horse power, and furnished white flour and meal to the forts and settlements.

In 1861 he had no accurate idea how much stock he owned, but the estimate was four hundred thousand sheep, fifty thousand cattle, and ten thousand horses. Mules and burros he never attempted to count.

One of his contracts with the government required that he furnish beef to the Indian reservations in New Mexico; and another, to render the same service to the forts. He owned the largest trading and supply store in the West. He was friend alike to whites, Indians, and Mexicans, and was not known to have a single enemy among them. The Indians called him Father Maxwell. At all seasons hundreds of red men were camping on his ranch, and in the spring, when the trading of pelts was on, there were thousands. And white trappers, hunters, freighters, plainsmen were as numerous as soldiers at the fort.

Colonel Maxwell was a very handsome man, standing six feet one inch in his moccasins. He never shaved his face. He had a habit of looking anyone straight in the eyes, and his own were singularly piercing. His rare smile relieved the sternness of his face.

Never had a white man been employed at Maxwell's ranch. When a caravan camped there, which happened often, he was especially courteous to any women who happened to be with it. A vague rumor of an unhappy love affair never had any substantiation, but the sadness in his eagle eyes seemed to justify such a surmise.

The main ranch house appeared more like a white-walled fort than the home of one man. It was of Spanish design, long and low and picturesque, with a wide porch all along the front, from which one of the most magnificent views in the West always fascinated visitors. As to that, Maxwell and his guests, who were always numerous, lounged on the shady porch and gazed out across and down that gray, endless, purple-horizoned prairie, as if they could never tire of it.

His dining-room would seat a hundred, and it often did. The house and kitchen were run by old experienced Mexican women, whose quarters were wholly isolated from those of the men. No guest of Maxwell's ever saw a woman! The tables were waited upon by Mexican boys, clean, efficient, who spoke English well.

Back of the main house a splendid grove of cottonwoods shaded buildings of infinite variety. A carpenter shop, a blacksmith shop, a weaver's and a shoemaker's, a harness- and saddle-maker's, all attested to Maxwell's self-sufficiency. Beyond were the barns, the corrals, the sheds, many in number, all white and neat. And behind these the pastures spread fifty miles to the mountains.

Like other men of his type, Maxwell, called *Colonel* by his friends, was an inveterate gambler. He did not care whether he won or lost, but if he did win he was inexorable in collecting his due, if it took the very last dollar of his opponent. But if that loser or anyone needed money and asked for it, Maxwell would answer, "When will you pay this back?" Upon receiving a reply, he would invariably hand over the sum requested. Singularly enough, no man ever cheated Maxwell.

Clint Belmet was present one night in the living-room when Kit Carson lost all he had to Maxwell, a circumstance which gave that worthy great satisfaction.

"See, here, Lew, you've done me for every peso," protested Carson, "an' I've got to go home to my wife. I can't go broke."

"Sorry, Kit, but you would gamble with me. An' you know you can't play cards," replied the colonel.

"I couldn't tonight, that's sure," retorted Carson. "An' you've got to lend me five hundred."

Maxwell produced the amount and gave it to Carson, asking, "Kit, when'll you pay me back?"

"Doggone it! I don't know," returned Kit, somewhat nettled, as there were several officers from the fort present. Carson and Maxwell had been close friends for thirty years, had gone through the Mexican and Texas wars together. Both had been Texas Rangers, and they had guided Frémont on his marvelous exploring trips across the Rockies. Carson had, according to history, saved Maxwell's life several times, and Maxwell had repaid the debt at least once. Yet the colonel insisted that he know when Kit would return this five hundred dollars.

"Confound you! The next time I win five hundred from you!" exclaimed Carson.

"Which will be never," said the colonel, with one of his rare smiles, yet he seemed perfectly satisfied with Kit's promise.

The spring of this year Colonel Maxwell was very busy putting in crops, something he had to superintend himself, as the Mexican farmers were satisfactory only under direction. The ground was all high, and not irrigated, so it was important to plant early to take advantage of the spring rains.

There were two thousand Indians down in the valley, encamped together despite the fact that they were not all friendly and at other seasons might be warring upon each other. This was spring, however, and the trading of pelts had begun. The big courtyard before the store was an endless and fascinating circus to Clint. He often worked in the store, but as he was only learning the Indian languages, and as this was the rush season, he did not go behind the counters.

At Maxwell's dining-table there sat a score of trappers and forty chiefs of the various tribes, and a dozen or more officers from the garrison. Flying Cloud, a chief of the Utes, had the seat of honor on Maxwell's right. Clint sat on the left, and it was known to all who visited there that the colonel treated him as a son. To gaze across the bounteous table at that great chief was a thrilling yet doubtful pleasure for Clint. Flying Cloud had a magnficent bearing, but he was not handsome. His head was shaped like a hawk's. No proof had ever been fastened upon this Ute chieftain, but border rumor whispered that he had massacred more than one caravan. It was accepted fact, however, that he would never attack one of Maxwell's caravans. It was something to sit at that table, Clint thought, as he gazed down the line of lean, dark, fierce faces.

During this busy trading time three companies of soldiers patrolled the San Fernando Valley, which lay between Maxwell's ranch and Taos. Here lived, at least at that season, ten well-known squaw men. These renegade whites had taken Ute squaws, and Pawnee squaws and Arapahoe squaws to wife, in Indian fashion, and they made whisky to sell to the Indians. The soldiers were there to put a stop to this illicit practice, but were not very successful.

Another of Colonel Maxwell's many virtues lay in the fact that he would never sell a drop of liquor to an Indian, or invite one to drink; and if a white man under the influence of the bottle showed himself anywhere on Maxwell's land he was promptly escorted off.

It was after that very dinner at Maxwell's on the 16th of May, that the first caravan from the east arrived. Clint was present when Dagget, the leader, came up to report to Maxwell. He appeared a typical freighter, stalwart, bearded, bronzed and weather-beaten, dusty and smelling of horses.

Naturally the arrival of the first freighter that spring excited unusual interest. The men crowded around

Dagget. And presently he did all the talking, while the others listened with growing breathless attention.

The North and South were at war. What had seemed a certainty was now a reality—the Union was fighting for its very existence. Soldiers were at a premium, and none or next to none could be spared for the caravans crossing the plains. Freighters were going to be difficult to engage, and only through higher wages. The government was sending soldiers from Kansas and Nebraska to strengthen all the forts. The Union commander at Fort Leavenworth, General Hunter, had called on all loyal states and territories for volunteers.

"Well, by God!" ejaculated Maxwell, his eyes like lightning. "So Sumter was fired on an' there's war? . . . New Mexico will secede from the Union! . . . There'll be hell to pay out here on the frontier. I must see Kit Carson."

"Colonel, reckon the Mexicans out hyar won't help the situation any?" queried Dagget, shrewdly.

"No, they won't," returned Maxwell, decisively. "I can answer for mine. But there are Mexicans in Taos an' Fort Union who'll furnish arms an'. ammunition to the Indians—promise them scalps an' plunder."

"Thet'll slow up the freightin', " returned Dagget. "An' last year there was more freight than we could haul."

"Dagget, it'll be worse this year. I'll have over a hundred wagonloads. What'd you fetch out?"

"Biggest train I ever drove. Hundred an' forty-two."

"Lose any?"

"No. Got across fine. At Cow Creek we was jumped by Pawnees. They didn't stand our cannon. At Phantom Island we had a brush with some Comanches. They wasn't lookin' for us. After buffalo an' gave us a run. Next day we got stopped by a herd of buffalo thet took all day to pass. Goin' north early this year."

"It's an early spring. Any wagons besides freighters with you?"

"Yes. We fell in with a small caravan of schooners

110

from Texas. They joined us at Timpas. They had women an' children, which was worrisome."

"Ha! No wonder. I'm glad you fetched them in safe. Where are they bound?"

"Santa Fé an' Californy. I reckon we'll rest an' feed up the stock hyar fer a week or two. I've got fifty wagons of supplies for you."

"Good. I'm needin' them bad enough. When can you start unloadin'?"

"Tomorrow, I reckon. How's feed on the range?"

"Never better."

"Wal, I'm needin' some oats an' grub. We're short. Plenty of fresh meat, though."

"Come up for dinner tonight, an' fetch anybody. I want to hear more about the war," concluded Maxwell.

Everybody at Maxwell's, for that matter, wanted to hear about the war. It was the absorbing topic. It meant incalculable changes in frontier travel and life. Gambling, selling, and trading of pelts, the business of Maxwell's store, were all suspended for the time being.

Clint was vitally and peculiarly interested, with the difference that he asked no questions. He went from group to group and listened. The freighters, as a body, were inclined to be thrilled by prospects of the doubling of their earnings, and aghast at the probable necessity of freighting across the plains without the escort of soldiers.

Couch was jubilant. The tragedy of war between the Yankees and rebels did not seem to affect him.

"Wal, it means more an' bigger business," he said, rubbing his brawny hands. "We'll double up our caravans, take two or three cannons, an' blow hell out of the redskins."

"But, boss," queried one of the younger members of his clan, "haven't some of us young fellars a pretty hard choice to make?"

"What, for instance?"

"Whether we'll enlist in the army an' *which* army?"

"No," declared Couch, with startling suddenness that proved this question had been answered in his mind. "We freighters have got as big a duty an' responsibility as the soldiers. If we all enlist what's goin' to become of the forts out here, an' the settlers? Good many settlers comin' west now. If the forts had to quit, these settlers wouldn't have no protection. They'd be massacred by Injuns. . . . Don't worry none about your duty, Bill. It's sure to stick to our job."

Maxwell stroked his silky beard and nodded his handsome head. "Boys, there's a heap of sense in Couch's talk. I believe I second it without reservation. Anyway, we'll talk it out an' look at it from all sides. That's one reason I want to see Kit Carson."

Later Jim Couch happened to espy Clint listening around a group in front of Maxwell's store.

"Howdy, Buff! What're you lookin' so serious about now?" he inquired.

"Reckon everybody looks serious," retorted Clint.

"See here. I reckon I've got to recognize you as a grown-up," declared Couch. "You're shore a big husky *hombre,* but you're not twenty-one yet by some years, an' till then you're under my charge. You savvy?"

"But you wouldn't compel me to go against my strong feelin's?" protested Clint.

"Wal, no, I wouldn't. Your dad left you in my charge, but if you kicked over the traces I reckon I'd have to stand it. Only, I hope you will listen to us older heads. Maxwell backs me up. Buff, you ask him."

"I heard him stand by you."

"Buff, you can do a lot for the Union, an' more for the West, by stickin' to your freighter job," went on Couch, earnestly. "I've got several thousand dollars of yours an' next trip to Kansas City I'll bank it for you. These next few years will be rich ones for us. An' some day you can settle down on a ranch out here. . . . You stick to Jim Couch."

"I'm pulled both ways, Uncle Jim, but I reckon I

ought to stay with you because my father wanted that," replied Clint, soberly, and walked away.

Nevertheless, he had not wholly made a choice. Clint had strong patriotic leanings toward the Union. His father had anticipated the struggle between the North and the South. Often he had spoken of it to Clint, and of their duty as Northerners. Clint did not quite agree with Couch and Maxwell that his service to the freighters was as responsible as it might be to the army. He meant to talk to Kit Carson.

He strolled out across the range to get away from the crowd. He wanted to be alone, and he did not feel alone until he got out of sight of the ranch house, the Indian encampment, and the caravan of the freighters. To which end he climbed a knoll and found a resting-place under a cedar that overlooked the wide gray stretch of Maxwell's ranch and led to the white-and-black country—the wonderful New Mexico uplands.

The Rockies to the north were snowclad, and the marble fields sloped down to the timber belt, from which the forests and canyons in turn descended to the grassy open. The sunny May day was warm and pleasant, yet a breath of the cold, pure air of the heights came down to Clint. So far he had not had much experience of the mountains, except to watch them and revel in them from afar.

Out to the south and the east, over the ranges of cedar and pine and grass, there extended a blue-hazed void that was distance. It held the magic of the Great Plains. Whatever the Rockies might come to mean to Clint, they could never minimize the prairie-land. Yet, though he sensed the strange, deep hold of the low open country, he could not bring himself to admit he loved it.

But at this time of his life, a critical one he scarcely realized, the vast spread of gray grass and purple ridge and winding lines of willow and cottonwood, the home of the buffalo and the savage, called to him with inexplicable and tremendous power. Still, he had it in him to give that up for the sake of his country, if it needed him to fight. He had no home, no relatives,

113

except a few back in Illinois that had not been friendly or kind to his parents. He had no one to care for—to work for. If little May Bell had only never been lost!

Clint had to force himself out of sad and sweet reminiscence, but not before he had tried to picture May as she might have been at this time, a girl of sixteen, and probably the prettiest in the world.

Still, if he lived through the war he could return to the West and the life of a frontiersman. For that matter, he was hardly more likely to be killed by rebels in the East than by savages in the West. Clint considered the thing from both sides. It would be horrible to kill white men who had done him no injury. To kill Indians—the very thought sent a fiery thrill along his veins. Was it impossible for him to grow up and be like Maxwell, a friend to all red men? But the great rancher's mother and father and little sweetheart had never been murdered by Comanches.

Clint grew dreamy in contemplation of the scene. Gradually he ceased to ponder the knotty question of war or freighting, the East or the West, the work he loved or that which he would hate. He listened to the sough of the wind in the cedar over his head, low and pleasant, a strange sound, never anything but music. And he watched the mountains awhile.

They changed with the movement of the sun and clouds. Now one of the snowy peaks split the blue sky, and again a cloud lodged against it, enveloping it down to the fringed edge of pines. Beautiful black shadow-ships crossed the vast slopes. It was an unknown and wild kingdom to him. But the trappers and the hunters and the Indians penetrated the fastnesses of gorge and canyon and timbered saddle whence they brought the furs to trade.

Clint ended as always, however, in giving his allegiance to the lowland. At his feet the gray bleached grass was blowing in the wind; down in the valley tumbleweeds were rolling along like balls; far out over the miles the yellow dust devils were rising. The gray knolls arose, some bare, others dotted with cedars, and round hills dark with pine broke the monotony; and beyond, a vast valley, bowl-shaped and speckled, lay in the hollows between the ranges; and over the center slept the blue phantom of the distant plains; and on each side sheered up the broken slopes, on and ever upward, black-belted, red-cragged, yellow and gray with open spots, and at last the purple-black that ended abruptly in the snowy domes.

Clint spent hours there, but he arrived nowhere in decision, except that the West had chained him for all of his life.

He returned to the ranch, arriving about the middle of the day, and therefore at the busiest hour, so far as a movement of the whites and Indians was concerned. The wide road leading from ranch house to store, the courtyard, the long porch, were colorful with Indians, Mexicans, and visitors from the caravans. Those from Dagget's wagon-train were not difficult to pick out, especially the Texas contingent, among whom were women and children. They seemed to excite universal interest, especially among the Indians and the trappers.

At the store there appeared to be more business going on than during the earlier hours. Clint mingled among the customers. One blond Texan attracted his attention by reason of unusual height—he was seven feet tall, fair of hair and blue of eye, a wonderful specimen of pioneer from the Lone Star State. Clint was not short himself, but he felt small beside this giant.

Two curly-headed youngsters, boys of about five and seven, sat on some bales with hands and mouths full of candy, manifestly the first they had had for a long time. They were in a rapture that both amused and touched Clint. Far indeed from their thoughts were the hardship and the peril of the frontier.

"Howdy, Johnnie!" said Clint, by way of striking up acquaintance. The lad addressed had the friendliest kind of look and smile, but he could not talk with his mouth full and his cheeks puffed out round with candy.

115

Next Clint was taken with more than passing interest in two young women who were making purchases. He lingered to listen to their voices. They seemed excited and happy to be safe in this wonderful place, and the stern business of pioneering at that moment was far from their thoughts.

Presently others, undoubtedly of this Texan caravan, entered the store. In all Clint's experience west of Kansas City he had not seen together so many women and girls. He counted them. Nine! It amused him somewhat to realize that he would have liked to talk to them. But Clint was shy. He could not take advantage of even the friendliest glances. Still he realized that he was an object of interest, and put it down to the credit of his buckskin garb, or perhaps the gun he wore in his belt.

Presently, however, one of the young women giggled and said to her companion in a quite audible voice: "One of those trappers. Isn't he handsome?"

Clint blushed and moved away. It flattered him to be taken for a trapper, but the rest of the compliment embarrassed him and he concluded he had better leave the store.

Then he turned to go out and looked into a pair of beautiful, dark, hazel eyes that gave him a shock.

A young girl had come in, accompanied by a middle-aged woman and a stalwart young man, another Texan.

The girl seemed startled, too, probably because Clint had almost collided with her.

"Say, trapper, look out aboot where you're haidin'," drawled the Texan, with the cool, slow, Southern accent Clint knew so well.

Clint murmured an apology and stepped aside. But he did not leave the store. He wandered around, and presently from the background he looked again at this latest acquisition to the Texas group. He did not quite realize that something unfamiliar possessed him.

Soon he espied the girl again. She wore a little bonnet that was tied under her chin, and a flowing blue gown, full and long, yet which appeared unable to

116

hide her grace. She had lustrous brown hair. She did not concern herself with making purchases, and evidently was simply accompanying the others. The Texan hung rather close to her, with an evident air of proprietorship, which to Clint did not seem to be a matter of delight to the girl.

Her cheek was of a golden-tan hue with a hint of rose. Her profile was delicately drawn. Clint hoped she would turn so that he could see her eyes again. She was looking at the people all around, and in time she moved, giving Clint a full view of her face. It was not only very pretty, but somehow, in a vague and incredible way, strangely familiar, like that of a girl he might have seen in a dream.

After a moment Clint decided he was only silly and sentimental. He had not talked to a girl for years. He moved away again, but was conscious of a haunting power in that face. He desired powerfully to look at it again, and closer. That annoyed Clint, and in arguing with himself he became a little nettled. What was a pretty girl to him?

Still, he did not leave immediately, and when he stole another glance, quite instinctively, the intervening people had thinned and the young girl was staring at him. Her red lips were parted. Caught in the act, her cheeks took on the hue of her lips. Her glance wavered and fell. But swiftly it came up again. She was not smiling.

Clint lost, in some inexplicable manner, his eagerness to rush out of the store. His moccasins might have contained lead. His glance roved away casually, to fly back as if drawn by a magnet. She was still looking at him, differently now. Her color had fled. Her gaze had a strange, perplexed eagerness, wondering, wistful. Clint caught his breath. Something tugged at his heart-strings. This girl was not regarding him as had the other young women.

She seemed about to come toward Clint, when her companion checked her impulse. Clint saw then that the Texan was evidently talking rather forcefully to her, and his slight gesture seemed to indicate Clint.

The girl did not take this submissively. Her head went up, her chin tilted; and whatever her reply was, Clint would have liked to hear it. He took an instant and unreasonable dislike to this Texan. Probably the girl was his sister.

Clint reacted to this situation in a way perfectly incomprehensible to him. He knew what he was doing when he stepped forward leisurely and approached the group, but he had not the slightest idea why. If this girl looked at him again it would be astounding, and Clint felt that he could not answer for the consequences.

She did look again. Clint was now close enough to catch the strained, piercing intensity of eyes that seemed to search him through.

Just then one of Couch's freighters, Sam Black, swaggered by her on his way out of the store. Plainly the girl accosted him. Then the Texan grasped her arm.

"Let go," she said, distinctly and with spirit. She freed herself and spoke to the freighter. Clint did not catch what she said, but he guessed it had to do with him, and all the unaccountable sensations in him coalesced to a tremendous uncertainty.

Black heard her, and turned with a grin, to look where she pointed.

"Miss, you mean thet young fellar in buckskin?" he queried, in a voice easily heard all around.

She nodded eagerly and the scarlet suffused her cheek.

"Shore I know him. Haw! Haw! Reckon I ought to, miss. He belongs to my outfit. Thet's Buff Belmet."

The girl uttered a little cry, her hand going up too late to stifle it. Her eyes widened, darkened, and seemed fixed on Clint with a gaze he could not understand, yet which made his heart quake.

She glided toward Clint. She came close, closer, to peer up at him with lustrous eyes soft under which shone hope and rapture and terror.

"Buff—Belmet! . . . Who are you?" she asked in a whisper.

"Buff's a—nickname," stammered Clint. "My name's—Clint."

She put out a trembling little hand as if to touch him, to feel if he were flesh and blood, but it hovered back to her breast. The flush receded from her face, leaving it as white as pearl.

"Clint—don't you—know me?" she whispered, tremulously.

"Your eyes! Your voice!" gasped Clint, incredulously.

"Oh, you *do* remember!" she cried, and a rush of tears dimmed the rapture in her eyes.

"Miss—you're like some one—" burst out Clint, hoarsely, "but, oh, my God!—you couldn't be——"

"Yes, I could," she flashed. "I am May Bell!"

11

Clint never knew how it came that May was in his arms. But when he felt her there he hugged her close and his heart pounded against hers as he bent his face over her. It touched her hair and then her tear-wet cheek.

There was something wrong with his sight, but he felt her clinging to him, straining at his shoulders.

"Clint! Clint! Oh, thank God! I knew you were alive!" she cried out.

"An' I thought you dead!" murmured Clint, as if in a trance.

"I'm the livest girl you ever saw," she whispered against his cheek, and then her lips pressed softly, warm and quivering, in a kiss.

Clint's bliss was short-lived. A hard hand clutched his shoulders, and tore him so violently from the girl that but for a stack of boxes he would have fallen. That instant saw the end of his blurred sight. It was burned clear.

The Texan had thrust him back. Clint caught a

blaze of blue-flashing eyes. Then that hard hand, open-palmed, smote him across the mouth, staggering him again. Clint leaned against the boxes, in need of their support. Pain, suddenly added to these other bewildering sensations, hindered his faculties.

A man's burly form stalked in front of him, facing the Texan.

"Hyar! What'd you hit thet boy for?" he shouted, his voice loud in anger.

Clint recognized Couch. And following Couch the tall form of Maxwell interposed itself into the scene.

"I am Maxwell," he said, in cold, cutting accents. "This lad is my guest. Explain why you struck him."

The Texan was neither intimidated nor impressed. He eyed the men in cool disdain.

"If it's any of your business, I slapped his pretty face——"

But Couch interrupted him by knocking him down. It was then that Couch evidently saw the girl for the first time. Pale, with dilating eyes, she gazed from him to Clint, and at the fallen Texan, and then back to Clint. The big store had grown silent, except for footsteps crowding closer.

Couch stared at the girl and bent lower to peer closely.

"Lass, was it 'cause of you?" he queried, with gesture indicating Clint.

"Yes—sir," she faltered.

"Say, don't I know you?" he asked, suddenly excited.

"Perhaps you do, sir," she returned. "I know you. Mister Jim Couch."

"For the land's sake!" exploded Couch as he took the hands she held out. "I know you. . . . Your voice goes with your eyes. I never forget people. . . . You're thet little big-eyed kid who left my train at Council Grove. Years ago. . . . Jim Bell's little girl."

"Yes. I am May Bell," she replied, with smile half sad.

"Little May Bell come to life again—after we thought you was dead or worse. Growed to be a young

120

woman an' a mighty pretty one. . . . Wal, I never was so glad in my life."

Meanwhile the Texan had gotten rather groggily to his feet, and it was evident that he had no liking for the turn of events.

Maxwell accosted him again: "Stranger, you haven't explained your action."

The Texan's handsome face was marred by an expression of extreme malignity, most of which appeared centered upon Clint. But he shouldered his way through the circle of curious onlookers and left without a word.

"Maxwell, here's one of the few an' glorious surprises of the West." announced Couch, drawing May toward the rancher. "This girl's father joined my outfit at Independence years ago. The same year Buff an' his father started with me. . . . Bell left us at Council Grove, an' later started back east. His outfit was massacred to a man an' we heard his daughter was taken captive. . . . But here she is, little May Bell thet was."

Maxwell made the girl a courtly bow and warmly pressed her hand in both of his. "Miss Bell, I sure am happy to meet you. Indeed, it isn't often the frontier gives us as sweet an' glorious surprises as this."

"Thank you, sir," returned the girl, shyly.

"Buff, come out of it," interposed Couch, heartily. And as Clint shuffled forward, white and red by turns, the freighter went on. "Boy, I take it you an' May seen each other an' just sort of—of——"

Couch failed of adequate words. Clint stood tongue-tied, shifting from one foot to the other. Maxwell laughed as if he understood, and he placed his arm round Clint's shoulders. Then May Bell came to his rescue.

"I—I first saw Clint outside," she began to explain, eagerly, blushing rosily, yet brave in her anxiety to place him right before his friends. "I wondered. . . . Then I saw him here—in the store. I recognized him —yet I didn't dare believe my eyes. I—I kept looking. And I think he was curious about me. Then I asked a freighter—if he knew him. He did—he called him

121

"Buff Belmet.' . . . Then I ran to Clint. . . . I—I don't know just what happened—but Lee separated us—and struck Clint."

"Ahuh. Wal, now, thet begins to straighten things out. I'm sorry I hit this Lee fellar. But considerin'—an' anyway I never saw you. If I had, I reckon I'd had better—Wal, no! he hit Buff an' Buff is like a son to me."

Couch was plainly at a loss. Clint's embarrassment amounted almost to shame. The girl had paled again, as if at the mute query in Clint's eyes. Maxwell saw the crux of the situation and he bent to May, asking low: "It was natural for you an' Buff to be glad to see each other. But had this man Lee any right to—to separate you—an' strike Buff?"

"No!" she returned, and the single clear word had a ring. On the instant then she averted her gaze from Clint while a wave of scarlet obliterated the pale earnestness of her face.

"Wal, now," breathed Couch, in deep-chested relief. "Seein' thet's settled, tell us who you're with."

"Dear good friends. They have been—everything to me," replied May, turning to look for them.

The crowd stirred and broke its interested calm. A buxom motherly woman, ruddy and smiling of face, evidently was waiting for this moment.

"Heah we are, May," she said in a hearty voice, and with a plump elbow she nudged the tall man beside her.

May slipped away from the freighter to the unmistakable embrace of this kindly-faced woman.

"This is Mister Couch," began May, radiantly, "and his friend Mister Maxwell, I think . . . and this is Clint."

"Gentlemen, I'm Sarah Clement, an' shore am glad to meet you all. . . . Jim Couch, I've heard your name these many years. An' Lew Maxwell, I know you. . . . An' so this boy was May's playmate across the plains? . . . Clint Belmet." She gave her hand to Clint and searched his features with the shrewd, penetrating gaze

122

of a woman who had known men. "You're not the boy she has talked aboot all these years. You're a man. But I like your face."

Clint mumbled he knew not what.

Maxwell ejaculated: "Sarah Clement! . . . Could you by any chance be related to Hall Clement, who served with me in the Mexican War an' later was a Texas Ranger?"

The tall Texan stepped out and tilted back his huge black sombrero, to expose a remarkable visage that no one could ever have forgotten.

"Howdy, Cap!" he said, laconically, and leisurely extended a long arm.

"By all that's holy!—Hall Clement! . . . The Lord is good," broke out Maxwell, sonorously, and he fell upon Clement with an onslaught unusual in so cool a Westerner. The meeting was one that well might have made the onlookers wonder.

"Jim—Buff," said Maxwell, turning to the others, his eyes alight. "Shake hands with my old pard, Hall Clement. 'An' Kit Carson's pard, too, in those old Texas days. Them was the days! . . . Well, folks, it's almost too good to be true. You'll all come to dinner with me. Ask your friends. We'll make it a party."

"Wal, we won't have to be axed twice," boomed Couch, and again he possessed himself of May's yielding hand. "Forgive me, lass, but I'm uncommon keen to know what happened to you."

"It's not much of a story," replied May, her eyes shadowing. "When the Indians attacked us it was night. I ran over the bank—hid under brush. . . . They never found me. . . . When day came I crawled out. The camp was silent—all dead—the wagons burned. . . . I wandered away, half crazy. A caravan came along. They took me to Texas. . . . And there people were good to me. Mrs. Clement gave me a home—became a mother to me. . . . I went to school— grew up—and here I am."

"Ahuh! If it ain't a fairy story old Jim Couch never heard one," replied the freighter. "An' now, lass, one more question. Who's this feller Lee?"

123

"His name is Murdock," said May. "I did not know him in Texas."

Mrs. Clement manifestly considered it her duty to interfere. "Couch, this man Murdock joined us in the Pan Handle. He's not a freighter. He claimed he was goin' West to buy pelts. Like every other man you meet on the trail, he didn't tell much aboot himself. An' we didn't ask. He was good company an' attentive to us women. I liked him. An' I reckon May did too. But Hall didn't. You can talk to him. . . . Murdock got sweet on May, which was only what every one of the young bucks did, an' he was allfired jealous of her. Thet shore accounts for his actions here."

Clint found himself walking beside May, behind the older folk, who were being led by Maxwell to the house. Once out of the store, free of the curious crowd, Clint began to recover from his shame and humiliation, though the creeping paralysis of his tongue loosened its grip only slowly.

May walked beside Clint, her head reaching to his shoulder. That seemed the most astounding thing. She had been so little, and the picture of her in his memory was far removed from May Bell in the flesh today. He stole a glance at her, to find that she held her gaze straight ahead. Her color was high. As they walked along she spoke of the weather, the Indians passing, the ranch, the West. And Clint replied without in the least knowing what she said.

They were, in fact, strangers to each other, and though in the poignant emotion of reunion the link of childhood held, now they were beginning to realize.

Clint, having stolen one glance at her, ventured another. She averted her eyes and the quick blood darkened the rich golden tan of her cheek. This somehow mitigated Clint's shyness and he began to do battle with the chaos of his mind. He had been making a stupid ass out of himself, when he should have been proving that he was a freighter now, a plainsman. Nevertheless, this argument did not at once restore his equilibrium.

May had started out to talk with wild enthusiasm, but that or her stock of expressions wore out. Clint floundered in vain; he could not make conversation. They were saved from something disastrous by their arrival at the ranch house.

"Let's set out on the porch till it gets cool," suggested Maxwell.

That, for the time being, ended the constraint between Clint and May. She, with Hall Clement, and his august wife, became the center of attention. Maxwell beamed upon them. It was evident that his meeting with an old ranger comrade had recalled associations which must have been pleasant, thrilling, perhaps filled, too, with regret. He introduced the Clement party to army officers, scouts, hunters and trappers, and even to several Indian chiefs.

One of these, Lone Wolf, of the Utes, a superb warrior, always friendly to the whites, took most dignified note of May. Maxwell spoke to him in Indian language. The chief raised a slow deprecatory hand in expressive gesture that did not need words. It signified: Alas for the injustice done to the red man and the injury to the white man.

Lone Wolf offered his hand to May, who hesitatingly placed hers in it.

"How do," he said, in a deep, not unpleasant voice. He was very tall and bent his feathered head. The minute wary lines of his face indicated his age. He had fine eyes.

May acknowledged his greeting. Evidently it was an ordeal, yet she saw that this Ute was a friend of Maxwell's, and no doubt worthy of respect.

"Father—mother—gone?" he asked.

"Yes," replied May.

"How old you?"

"Sixteen."

"You married?"

"Oh no," returned May, surprised out of her reserve.

"White man slow," said the chief. "You like marry big chief?"

Maxwell led the shout of laughter. Lone Wolf's serious visage did not change, yet it seemed plain that he had a sense of humor.

"Are you proposing to me, Lone Wolf?" asked May, smiling in her confusion.

"Me like white squaw."

"Thank you. I—I must—say no."

The chieftain let go her hand and spoke to Maxwell in his own tongue, and then passed on with slow moccasined tread.

"There, May, you've had an offer at last," said Mrs. Clement, gayly.

"Mr. Maxwell, of course he wasn't in earnest?" queried May, bright-eyed and laughing.

"Lone Wolf was in fun, but he meant it, too," replied Maxwell. "That old Indian is the salt of the earth. If only they were all like him. . . . He paid you a compliment, lass. Said you were a pretty young woman an' that the white boys would be fightin' for you."

"Indeed, he flatters me," said Mary.

"Wal, I reckon Buff will have somethin' to say about thet," put in Couch, calling the gay attention to his young charge.

Clint responded to this with so deep and inward a thrill that his confusion seemed checked.

"Speak up, lad," called Maxwell, with kindly interest as well as teasing spirit.

"I reckon I will," replied Clint. He got it out deliberately and even managed to look at May, who sat wide-eyed, with parted lips. But the instant afterward he wanted the ground to open and swallow him. That instant spared him, however, for May Bell then got the brunt of the attack, which caused her face to turn rosy red.

Clint's fright had a chance to recede. Presently it occurred to him that he had asserted himself in a marvelous manner. He remembered that May Bell had not only been his childhood sweetheart, but also his promised wife. She had been forced to remember. Her sweet face was a record of that. No flashing retort!

126

No laughing denial! She was as true as steel. She endured the teasing and joined in the laugh at her expense. But never for an instant did she lift her shy veiled eyes to Clint.

His mounting confidence, his vain assurance, his strange exultation, suffered an eclipse. Two army officers joined the group, and Maxwell presented them to the party. One was a young lieutenant, Clayborn by name, handsome, debonair, a West Pointer, and very plainly an eager admirer of the fair sex. He had many qualities which Clint envied, especially his grace, his ease, and the charming affability of manner that no plainsman ever attained. May Bell was undoubtedly pleased with him. She gave him her undivided attention, smiled up at him, listened to his low conversation —compliments, perhaps love-making, and she cast down her eyes and blushed even more rosily than she had for Clint.

Whereupon Clint became prey to an absolutely new and insupportable variety of feelings. At first he was struck by a subtle shock of realization. May Bell did not belong to him. It was possible for her to admire —like—love some other person than himself. The thought seemed a sacrilege. Disloyal to May! But there was the evidence before his own eyes. How beautiful she looked! Clint's new emotion gave birth to a terrible yearning. After all, he had only been a boy playmate. She was far above him.

Suddenly he struck the descent of his vain imaginings, his hopes, and he shot down over the precipice. From the heights he plunged to the depths. He moved away from the group, no longer able to endure May's absorption in this fascinating young soldier. He walked to the far end of the porch. A deep inward burning sickness assailed his breast. What ailed him? The old familiar trouble—the black despair of the past returned tenfold, augmented by this fierce, wild pain.

Clint gazed out on the wild gray range, far over the speckled flat to the cedared ridge, rising and undulating, across the black pass between the mountains, to the purple nothingness of distance beyond. Out there,

127

months had been multiplied into years. And the beauty the solitude, the majesty and monotony of the plains, the travail that had come to him out on them, told him now that the greatest sorrow and sublimest joy of man had come to him—love of a woman. He had loved little May Bell from the hour of that meeting beside the brook; and in proportion to the labor and suffering and struggle that the years had magnified, his love had grown.

Sunset found Clint still gazing through the gray distance to the heart of his woe. Couch discovered him then and dragged him into the dining-room.

Clint shrank from the ordeal, but there seemed to be protection in the comparative darkness, and the hum of many voices, and the largest number of guests he had ever seen assembled there. He hated to look for May, because she would be under the spell of that captivating soldier, but as it seemed useless to resist, he let his eyes rove round the room. The chiefs, scouts, trappers, and hunters, already seated, occupied two-thirds of the long table. The freighters came next and there were a score or more. A number of military men had seats together, and that brought Clint's glance to the head of the table and Maxwell's especial guests for the evening. The several ladies of Dagget's caravan, including Mrs. Clement, were on the left. May Bell had the place of honor at Maxwell's right. She had removed her bonnet and looked bewitching.

To Clint's startled amaze the seat next to May was vacant. Undoubtedly that had been reserved for Lieutenant Clayborn. Clint longed to flee like the coward he was, but all the time Couch had been forcing his reluctant steps closer.

"You blockhead! Thet empty place is for you," declared Couch, and he gave Clint a shove. Its momentum carried him several steps farther. Then Maxwell, who was standing, espied him and motioned him to the seat beside May. As Clint had not quite taken leave of his senses, he managed to do as he was bidden, without excessive awkwardness. Then he squeezed his trembling hands between his knees and riveted his eyes upon his plate.

Nevertheless, he was most torturingly aware of May's presence. The seats were benches, and owing to the large number of guests they were closer together than ordinarily. Clint felt May's elbow touching his and the contact set him thrilling. He thought wildly that he must rush away and do something desperate.

The acuteness of his pangs was not soothed by May's attention to him. She had spoken when he first sat down beside her. The tone was gay, but the content escaped Clint. Out of the tail of his eye he could see her looking at him, casually, then with interest, and in a moment with more concern. No doubt his fool face betrayed him. It always had.

"Clint, isn't it won-der-ful?" she whispered, leaning a little closer.

He nodded and muttered something incoherent.

"Why—you're pale!"

Clint could just catch her voice. Everybody appeared to be talking at once.

"Clint, you don't look natural," she went on, and the sweet solicitude only increased his despair. He could not pull out now. "What's the matter?"

"I'm sick," he muttered.

"Oh, Clint! . . . Was that why you went away?"

"Yes—I reckon."

"*Where* are you sick, Clint?" she importuned him. "You're all doubled up. . . . Your hands!—*Where* do you feel bad?"

Clint loosened one of his hands long enough to indicate that his malady was situated rather high for the common ills of mankind.

"It's here—an' I'm tur-rible sick."

At this point Maxwell rapped loudly on the table and stilled the many voices. He looked the genial host, happy to give pleasure, yet he had that air of dignity and impressiveness which presupposed that gatherings of this nature at his table had their niche in frontier history.

"Folks," began Maxwell, in his resonant voice,

"there are a hundred and twenty of us at table tonight, an' that's a record for Maxwell's Ranch. It makes me glad an' proud to welcome you all. To prove to you newcomers the hospitality of the West, an' that all Indians are not scalp-hunters. I welcome you more because of the meanin' of your presence here . . . the vanguard of the settlers who will populate the West! . . . Our beautiful, rich, an' savage West. Some day, despite the hard trials, you will love it as I do."

Maxwell paused a moment as if to let that sink in, or to gain force for his next utterance. Certain it was that a benevolence beamed from his face; and those seated near might have caught a deeper something— the phantom of a ceaseless sorrow under his benign exterior.

"Our guest of honor is Miss May Bell here at my right," he went on. "She was originally from Ohio, an' when she was ten years old came with her parents to join Jim Couch's caravan, at Independence, in the spring of 1854. They left that caravan at Council Grove, an' turned back, discouraged, no doubt, by the perils an' terrors of the frontier. Small wonder! . . . Well, on the return little May lost her parents. The old, old frontier story, bloody an' terrible—a massacre. But May hid in the brush under the river bank, an' escaped. Next day emigrants bound for Texas picked her up an' took her along to the great Lone Star State. There she had the good fortune to fall under the notice of Hall Clement—long my partner on the plains—good soldier—great Ranger—an' all that is typified in the word frontiersman. . . . Sometimes it seems God forgets us, but I reckon that is not so. Anyway, God did not forget little May Bell. An' she has come West to throw in her lot with us. Mrs. Clement, who has been mother to her, has come also, an' other women of that grand Texas breed. It might be exaggeration to say that the West never could be settled without Texans. Sure it would never have belonged to the Union but for Texans. An' in this connection I grieve to say, no doubt with all of you, that war between South an' North has come. That will pass, we pray soon. An' the great West will feel the impetus of new travel an' progress. The West needs women—pioneer women. No hunger on earth is as terrible an' destroyin' as man's hunger for a woman."

Maxwell paused again, and stroked his thin fine beard, while his eyes glowed upon his guests from the last chief at the foot of the table up to the radiant young girl by his side. He smiled down upon her, and the past, far away and long ago, sweet and full of pathos, shone in that smile.

"I said before—the West needs women," he resumed. "Women who can be *true!*" How his deep voice rang the poignancy of the word! "Women who can endure an' fight an' stick. . . . I think little May Bell will turn out one. When she was ten years old—on that caravan trip I told about—she met a lad an' plighted her troth to him, as she sat beside him on the seat of a prairie schooner. . . . Our lucky young friend here—Buff Belmet, who was known to the frontier before he reached fourteen. . . . These youthful lovers were torn asunder, but though she believed he was dead, she lived on true to him. . . . An' now they have found each other again. What could be more beautiful an' hopeful than that? . . . Ladies, gentlemen, chiefs, we do not drink at table in Maxwell's house. Yet I propose in place of a toast a right hearty cheer for little May Bell."

The assembled company rose and gave vent to a mighty cheer, that was the stronger for the wild, piercing staccato note of Indian whoop.

Clint, blind and stricken, had yet been aware of May's tug at his arm, and he had arisen in order, but he was mute. And it took a more urgent tug to drag him down again.

"Friends," went on Maxwell, who had remained standing, "we have tonight a privilege an' honor seldom accorded here on the frontier—a man of God amongst us. . . . Preacher Smith, will you say grace?"

As the minister rose he appeared as sturdy and virile as any of his company. All heads bowed.

"Bless this food to our use, O Lord! . . . Bless this

131

gathering of pioneers, frontiersmen, soldiers, and red men. Bless the young people who have chosen to carve out homes in the West. . . . Bless little May Bell and the lad she chose years ago. Bless them and guide them further in faithfulness, in hope, in the glory and dream of love, in the hard trials of the frontier land. Amen!"

During this prayer Clint was uplifted and exalted out of the conflicting emotions that in the end had dulled and stunned him. Under cover of the table May took his clenched hand, and pressed it open, and softly clasped it, her palm to his, warm, pulsing, in a tenderness that even his stupidity could not misjudge.

Maxwell clapped his hands, the door banged open, and a stream of Mexican lads poured in, to spread a savory and bounteous feast before the guests. Appetite did not wait upon gaiety. Both were indulged to the fullest. And Maxwell at the head of the table watched and listened as a man whose heart was enriched by this occasion.

12

They lagged a little more and more behind the older folk. The grass slope shone silver in the moonlight. Below, the camp fires of the caravan flickered, and the long line of wagons gleamed pale against the dark cottonwoods. A hound bayed, and from the hill a coyote answered in wild defiance. Jack, trotting at Clint's heels, growled his disapproval.

At a rough place in the road Clint took May's hand. Then, when it was the last thing he wanted to do, he let go. They had not exchanged two sentences since leaving Maxwell's table. At times Clint could scarcely keep up with May without running; at others he had to wait for her.

There was enchantment in the cool sweet air. Down

in the creek the spring frogs were peeping. The smell of wood smoke mingled with the fragrance of sage. The cottonwood leaves, small and young, rustled faintly in the soft wind. The moon had just topped the black rim that looked so close, yet was far away; and the range lay blanched and lonely and beautiful under the sky.

At last Clint reached the end of the stubborn complexity that had stultified him. He felt dammed up, with an accumulation of emotions, thoughts, and words that must find freedom. But he could not free them.

They passed wagon after wagon. Somewhere a Mexican twanged a guitar and sang a languorous Spanish song. Then, to Clint's dismay, they reached the camp, where the Clements and their party waited.

"Wal, it's been good to meet you-all," Couch was saying. "I'm powerful glad you're to hang up here awhile. Good night."

Then the freighter, espying Clint, added, genially, "Buff, I reckon you needn't hurry back."

The girl trilled sweet laughter, as if she caught his import and found it pleasant. "Good night, Mister Jim Couch."

"Good night, lass," replied Couch, his voice deeper with a rich note.

"You young folks needn't hurry," said Mrs. Clement.

"Shore you must have a lot to say," drawled Hall Clement. "Climb up on the wagon seat heah. Didn't Couch tell us how you used to drive an' ride an' talk all day long? . . . Mebbe then you can find your tongues an' talk the old moon down."

Beyond the tents a little way, under a giant cottonwood, stood the wagon Clement had designated.

"May, will you come?" asked Clint, eagerly inspired.

"Come! Do you imagine I'm going to bed?"

She tripped lightly ahead of him to the wagon, and was climbing up the wheel, with her bonnet hanging over her shoulders, when Clint got there to lend her a helping hand. He leaped up beside her to the seat. It was high and the low-spreading foliage cast a shadow pierced by rays of moonlight.

Clint bent to look at her. Her dark head was bare, her hair rebellious, her eyes radiant and unfathomable in the moonlight. How terribly afraid he was of her!

"Well, Buff?" she asked, roguishly.

"Aw—you can't like that nickname," he expostulated.

"I do, though."

"Better than Clint?"

"It means a lot. Mister Couch told me Kit Carson gave it to you."

"No It was Dick Curtis, another scout—a pardner of Kit's."

"You've made a name on the frontier," she said, regarding him gravely.

"Aw, I only drove a wagon."

"I shall call you Buff—always."

"Always?"

"Don't you want me to—always?"

"May!" he whispered, with a shock. "You told him!"

"Him? Who? Told what?"

"You told Maxwell about—about us . . . on the wagon seat, like this together, years ago. . . . No one else knew. I never even told my own father."

"Oh, then you hadn't forgotten?" she asked, archly.

"Never! Never the littlest word you ever said."

His sincerity swayed her. "Yes, I told Mr. Maxwell," she returned, gravely.

"But how—why?" Clint burst out.

"That Mr. Maxwell doesn't miss much. When the handsome soldier with the dainty moustache sat down beside me—well, Buff, you changed."

"Did I? No wonder."

"I've met a good many soldiers like him. They are all the same. They make love to every girl. . . . You were so queer. *You* didn't try to make love to me. So I—well, I didn't snub Lieutenant Clayborn. . . . Presently you rushed off—and I was sorry.

Mr. Maxwell had been watching you—saw you go. He politely took me away from the lieutenant. And he said, 'Little lady, our lad Buff is hurt.' And I told him I knew it and was sorry. Then it seemed I was drawn so strangely to him. I talked—and talked. . . . I—I—told him about the time on the wagon seat—that we—we were engaged. He seemed so glad. He squeezed my hand till it hurt. Oh, Clint—I mean Buff—it'll take me a long time to get used to this new name. Ever since we parted it has been Clint—Clint—Clint. . . . Mr. Maxwell likes you dearly. He didn't say so, but I knew. And, Buff, he got some strange happiness out of my faithfulness to you. Oh, I felt it."

"I near died when he said that—about us, right out."

"Yes, I remember you had a terrible pain." She let out a little peal of laughter. "And I—silly goose—thought you had colic."

"May, it was no joke," said Clint, shaking his head. "I've had Indian arrows shot into me, but they weren't a marker to what I had then."

"What was it, Buff" she asked, edging a little closer to him.

"Reckon I didn't know then, but I do now," he returned, ruefully. "I was jealous of that handsome soldier. I had a burnin' hell inside me."

"Oh, you mustn't swear," she whispered, and slipped her hand through his arm.

"May, dear, it's a swearin' matter. I read in the Bible about jealousy. 'Who can stand before jealousy?'"

"Buff Belmet, don't you ever make me jealous," she threatened. "Oh, I'm beginning to feel that I know you. At first you seemed a stranger. But you haven't changed. You're older, of course, and quiet—and sad. . . . Dear boy Clint!"

She leaned her face against his shoulder. Clint felt tears fall upon his hand.

"Don't cry," he whispered, wanting to cry himself. "It's been hard—but now we—we—"

"Have each other," she finished when he broke off haltingly.

135

Clint reached over with his left hand and clasped hers. The instant response, warm, clinging, strengthened him to overcome his backwardness.

"We're engaged—you said?"

"Don't *you* say so?"

"Huh! I reckon. . . . But, May, be serious. Engaged people get married, don't they?"

"It's customary," she replied, with a little low laugh, nestling closer to him. "Unless—the man proves faithless!"

"Aw!"

"Go on, Buff," she whispered, thrillingly. "I think you were about to propose to me."

"Will you make fun? . . . I'm tryin' to—to——"

"Oh, I know, Buff, darling, I always knew. You were so full of things you almost burst, yet you couldn't say them."

"Reckon I'll say somethin' now—or die," he replied. huskily, moistening his lips.

"Don't die."

"May—you called me darlin'!" he ejaculated, in awe and bliss.

"It slipped out. But to be honest, I've called you that—in my mind—since—well, since I read a book full of the word, and I liked it."

"Then I call you—darlin'," he said, in hushed accents at his temerity. "There! . . . An' I must tell you somethin' else that I never said before. I should of, though, long ago. For I did. But, honest, May, I never knew it till this afternoon. . . . Bless that handsome West Pointer!"

"Buff, you are talking riddles," she rejoined, happily.

"Are you any good at riddles?" he queried, slipping his arm around her slim waist.

"No good at all," she murmured.

"I wish I could tell it the way I felt it. . . . I was lookin' away out over the blue open that's the Great Plains. An' it seemed all the work an' longin' an' fear, an' the hurt of sun an' blister an' cold, an' the bite of Indian arrows—an' the agony of my loss—all these just burst with the truth of what ailed me. . . . Little May, it was then I found out I loved you."

"Oh, Clint! . . . Oh, Buff!" she whispered, lifting her face from his shoulder. The moonlight showed it rapt and lovely, with eyes like night.

"Yes, I love you, May, an' the feelin' isn't much different from that turrible pain I had at supper."

With his left hand he drew a cord from round his neck. Something bright dangled at the end.

"Oh!—a ring!" she said, thrillingly.

"It's all I have of my mother's. Paw gave it to her when she was a girl. . . . It was too small for her in later life. But it'll fit you. Let's see."

She held out a little hand that shook, and he essayed to slip it on her finger.

"Not that one. . . . The third. . . . Oh, it fits! . . . Clint, I'll treasure it all my life."

They were silent for a while. She was lying on his breast now, her head in the hollow of his neck, her hair brushing his lips.

The moon soared, and silent night reigned. The camp fires had died. The last late freighters had sought their blankets. The coyotes had ceased their yelp and wail. Bells on the hobbled horses no longer jangled.

"May, wasn't it awful—when we met in the store?" he asked, presently.

"Awful sweet."

"Weren't you petrified with—with shame?"

"Me! I gloried in it! . . . Oh, it was all so—so *good,* until that Lee Murdock pulled me away—and struck you."

"Aw! He did. I'd forgotten," replied Clint, broodingly.

"Buff, I liked him at first. Less after he—he tried to take liberties with me. And now I hate him."

"What liberties?" queried Clint, violently.

"Oh, never mind. He only *tried.* And I slapped his face till my hand burned for hours. . . . Clint, you keep out of his way. He'd stop at nothing. Mr. Clement

137

knows something he won't tell his wife or me. I'll be glad to see the last of Murdock."

"But will you?" demanded Clint.

"We understand he leaves the caravan here. He had plenty of money to buy pelts."

"Aw, I'm glad. Let's forget him. . . . But not our meetin'. May, dearest, do you know just what you did then?"

"When?"

"At the store—just after the freighter told you I was Buff Belmet."

"Oh! . . . I guess I ran to you, didn't I?

"Ran? You flew. . . . That was the most turrible glorious moment I'd ever lived—up to then."

"And then I suppose I flew right into your arms?"

"You did!"

"Well, you had them wide open. What was a poor distracted girl to do?"

"I don't know how it happened, but all at once you were there."

"And then did you hug me—or did I hug you? One of us did, for my ribs ached."

"I reckon, maybe, I'm most to blame for that. Uncle Jim says I don't know my strength."

"I knocked your hat off, didn't I?"

"You sure did."

"And tousled your hair?"

"Yes."

"And then—before all that gaping crowd—I shamelessly kissed you, didn't I?"

"Not shamelessly, darlin', though you were as red as fire."

"It *was* shamelessly. Not that I'd have cared the littlest bit—if you had only kissed me back. . . . But, Buff Belmet, you didn't. You didn't! . . . And I shall *never* kiss you again."

"Aw, May, that's what I was gettin' at."

"Oh, I see. . . . Clint, I spoiled you back on the plains, when I was ten years old. I did all the love-making. Now if you want anything of the kind you will have to make up for lost——"

Clint closed her saucy lips with his own. When he rose from that contact she lay in his arms, wistful and surrendering, awakened to the fire and glory of love, and too honest to deny it.

"Buff, I reckon I'll have to take that back," she whispered, and lifted her arms.

At a late hour, when Clint wended his slow way back to the ranch house it seemed that the moon, the night, the earth, the universe had been created for him. He could only accept, humbly, wondering, reverent. All that he had endured lost its utter cruelty in the light of the love he felt and the love bestowed upon him.

He lingered, sitting on the doorstep of the adobe shack behind the range house. Even the dogs at the corrals were quiet, like their wild brothers out on the range. Over Maxwell's ranch hung the pale moon-mantle, mysterious and beautiful. But Clint could not think. He only dreamed over May's sweet willing kisses. Tomorrow, perhaps, he could face the realities of his new responsibilities. And he found, too, that sleep was something he did not require for a long while. As a consequence he was late at breakfast next morning, to the amusement of Maxwell.

"Buff, if you stay up late at night playin' with the ladies, you'll never make a good scout," he teased.

"I'd hate not to make a good scout," returned Clint, "but last night was worth it."

"I reckon," laughed the rancher. "Well, Buff, come to my office this mornin'. I want a little talk with you."

Clint knew that meant something private and he was puzzled, and so interested he took early advantage of the invitation. Maxwell was busy with freighters. Upon concluding his business with them he pushed a chair toward Clint, and also a box of cigars, which he immediately withdrew. "Buff, I forgot you didn't smoke. . . . Well, lad, I don't need to ask you if you fixed it up with May."

"No, sir. But it was May an' you who fixed it," rejoined Clint, gratefully.

"All's well, then, lad?"

"I never dreamed I could be so happy," said Clint, simply.

"Couch told me your age, but I've forgotten."

"Near eighteen now, Mr. Maxwell."

"Well, out here on the frontier years don't matter. An' May is sixteen. Pioneer girls marry young, which is a good thing."

"What—what you—you aimin' at, sir?" stammered Clint, red in the face.

"I've a hunch you an' May ought to get married," replied the rancher, earnestly.

"Oh! . . . W-w-when?"

"Just as quick as the Clements will let you. They adopted the girl an' they love her as their own. But I might persuade Hall. I don't savvy about the misses, though."

"Uncle Jim Couch might have somethin' to say. He has charge of me till I'm twenty-one."

"Ahuh. Jim Couch is all right, among train bosses. But he gets sore now an' then, at delays an' on important drives. Then he takes chances. An', Buff, take a hunch from me. Couch's bones will bleach on the prairie, the same as those of so many good frontiersmen. . . . An' the point is I don't want you to break that little girl's heart."

"But Mr. Maxwell—I—I wouldn't!" expostulated Clint.

"You couldn't help it if you got killed."

"Killed!"

"That's what I said. Buff, I'm not goin' to advise the freighters to quit, because my business depends on them. If the caravans stop I'm ruined. . . . Now take this confidentially. The war is goin' to play hell on the frontier. Freightin' supplies is goin' to be ten times as dangerous as ever before. The time is comin' *pronto* when a small caravan will have no chance. In a year, maybe this summer, all the Apaches, Comanches,

Kiowas, an' Pawnees will be on the warpath. An' bad white outfits are growin', Buff."

"An' you're just about advisin' me to quit freightin' overland?" queried Clint, aghast.

"Yes. For the little girl's sake," said Maxwell, and leaned his head on his hand, shading his eyes. "I'll tell you a secret, Buff. . . . Once I loved a girl like May. I stayed away too long. . . . She thought me dead, or swore she did! She married another, an' life has never been the same to me since. I don't want you to risk so much with your sweetheart."

"But May would be true," replied Clint, passionately, as if a doubt of her was preposterous.

"She was, an' she might be for a while yet—when she's so young. But a beautiful girl like May can't stay unmarried or at least unpossessed. Not out here very long!"

"That's turrible, Mr. Maxwell," ejaculated Clint, aghast.

"Man's hunger for woman is too strong. Look at the white men who marry Indian girls an' become squaw-men. Kit Carson married a half-Mexican woman. Very estimable indeed. But I'm illustratin' a point. . . . Buff, you an' May are orphans. You haven't any relations. You're just alone. You've been long unhappy. You love each other, an' you ought to get married."

"Yes, sir. But—but when?" asked Clint, feebly. He had no will to fight this glorious prospect.

"Right away. Before Preacher Smith leaves. He's on his way to California. An' I'm tellin' you, lad, preachers are scarce, an' they'll be scarcer for some years."

"Who'll I ask first?" whispered Clint.

"May, of course. An' then if she's willin', you can go to Couch. He'll consent all right, but I believe he'll kick on your quittin' the freightin' game. An', Buff, if you marry May you'll sure have to take care of her. If you wait you'll have to trust that to God, an' somebody else. I've never had a white woman on my ranch. I made that rule. But I'd have May, only for one reason. I may be ruined here, by the war. Or I might sell out. Keep this under your hat, lad. It's for you I'm thinkin' an' talkin'."

"Thank you, sir. I realize that. An' I—I'm sort of knocked flat."

"Of course you are, Buff. But I *know* this frontier. An' so does Kit Carson. He'll be here today or tomorrow. I'll bet he'll advise you to marry May an' go on to California."

"California? . . . But I love the Great Plains!" burst out Clint.

"Ah!" Maxwell threw up his hands. "More than May Bell?"

"No! No!"

"Well then go to her, an' if you can persuade her, an' the rest of them—*marry* her before it's too late."

"Too late for what?"

"Ever to do it. A few more years of caravans an' you'll be a plainsman. *Then* it'll be too late. The life will claim you. Kit Carson had to quit. An' just in time. Curtis, Glade, Rockwell—they all saw what was comin'. Jim Couch, Dagget, Grace—they've stuck at it too long. They'll never quit. An' their scalps will ornament some redskin's lodge."

"Were you ever a plainsman, Mr. Maxwell?" queried Clint.

"No. I crossed enough, though, to feel the strange fascination of the Great Plains. To understand it. Most men never find out *why*. It's the tremendous barrenness, the ever-callin', never-endin' land, the eternal monotony of the prairie, the strange loneliness —an' then the drive, the camp, the watch, the fight— these change a boy's very soul an' grip him as a man."

Clint rose, trembling in the presence of this wise and good man. "Mr. Maxwell," he said, standing straight, "as far as I can I'll take your advice. I'm grateful for such a friend as you—an' Kit Carson. But until I'm twenty-one I must obey Uncle Jim."

"An' that's right. I'll admit Couch is our hard proposition here. But he'll have you an' May an' me to reckon with. A pretty good combination! Now run along, Buff, an' tackle May."

"I'll go, but I'm plumb scared."

"What? Of that sweet, soft-eyed little thing?"

"Maybe it's because she's so—so wonderful. . . . I'm afraid I'd *have* to beg her, sir. Not *make* her do anythin'."

Maxwell laid down his cigar and regarded Clint almost hopelessly.

"You made a name for yourself when you were a boy. The boy freighter, they called you once. I heard of you long before I ever saw you. An' now you're a big husky lad, near six feet tall, an' they tell me you've stopped your share of Indians. You're a man! Well, get out of here *pronto* an' show May Bell you're man enough in love, too."

"Yes, sir—but—but what shall I do?" faltered Clint, feeling caught between contending tides.

"Catch her alone, if you have to wait till night," said Maxwell, seriously, with a dreamy light of the past in his dark eyes. "Then grab her in your arms—yank her off her feet—hug an' kiss her till she hasn't sense or desire or breath left to say no. . . . Can you try that. Buff? How does it strike you?"

"Makes me turrible weak, sir. . . . But ought I try such an awful trick when I *know* she'd say yes to anythin' I'd ask her?"

"Don't you believe it, Buff. Women are funny. You can never tell what a girl will do. Changes her mind with the wind. Like as not you'll find her makin' eyes at Lieutenant Clayborn or that Murdock fellow. He's too old an' keen for her, Buff. You keep her away from him. Mind what I say! . . . Now run. I've got men waitin' to see me. I can't spend all day on your love affair."

Clint ran all right. And Maxwell called after him.

"Buff, I wish I were you. . . . Come back an' tell me what happens."

Clint raced out, half beside himself, and then bent hurried steps across the courtyard, which was crowded

143

with idle trappers, hunters, Indians, and freighters, waiting for something to turn up.

Presently he almost bumped into Couch, who evidently had come up the slope from the camp.

"Hello, Uncle Jim! . . . What you lookin' so glum about?"

"Buff, I just had a run-in with Buell—new agent for Aull an' Company," replied Couch, fuming. "He's got ninety wagon-loads of pelt that have got to be in Westport before end of August. An' he swears if I don't take the contract an' pack at once I'll never get another with his company."

"What are you goin' to do?" asked Clint, anxiously.

"I don't know. I'm stumped."

"What do the men think?"

"They haven't heard it yet."

"But, uncle, you know you oughtn't start out now unless you have a troop of soldiers. You'll have to wait for another caravan to join you."

"Sure I know. But Dagget says he can't get along from Santa Fé for weeks. Maybe six. . . . Buff, the worst of it is Buell offered me more money per hundred weight, an' a bonus of five hundred dollars if I landed the freight in Westport by August fifteenth."

"Uncle, that's a temptin' offer, but I hope you don't accept it," rejoined Clint, seriously.

"Hey, you don't say *we!*" ejaculated Couch, testily. "That means you don't want to go."

"No, I don't, Uncle," replied Clint, quietly.

"Wal, I reckon you'll do as I say," said Couch, harshly. "I'm more than your train boss. I'm your guardian."

Couch, usually the kindest and most genial of men, could be most stubborn when crossed. And when he drank he became sullen and taciturn. Clint feared that he was somewhat under the influence of liquor.

"Uncle, I'll not disobey you."

"Wal, I'm glad to hear that. You never did. . . . Buff, it's a rotten deal. You've just found your sweetheart again, an' God knows I'd hate to separate you from her. . . . Damn the luck, anyhow."

144

Without another word Couch strode on toward Maxwell's store, leaving Clint in a worse quandary than ever. He decided he had better not be in a hurry to see May, at least until he had pondered over Uncle Jim's predicament. Freighters were going to be scarce, in spite of high pay. Couch would need all the drivers he could muster.

But the momentary setback to Clint's buoyant hopes and enchanting dreams did not persist. It would take more than predicaments, caravans, and Indians to subdue the joy in him that day. Suddenly he conceived the fine idea of going to the store to purchase May a box of the fresh candy that had come with Dagget's train. So he recrossed the courtyard.

When he glanced up, what were his amaze and consternation to be confronted by May Bell and Lieutenant Clayborn coming out of the store. She did not at once see Clint because she was looking up at the soldier. Her bright eyes, her parted red lips, her smile, lifted to this West Point officer, gave Clint a stab. She carried one of the boxes of candy Clint had imagined he was going to buy for her.

Then she saw him, and the bright eyes, the parted lips, the smile that had been for Clayborn suddenly augmented their beauty and sweetness tenfold.

Clint observed that, realized in a flash his utter foolishness, felt the rush of ecstasy at the beautiful light on her face, which was for him; but not that nor anything kept him from bowing stiffly as he doffed his hat and bolted into the store.

13

Clint stalked through the store, blind to customers and clerks alike; and he fell over sacks and bales, and out the back door, in a boiling rage with himself, with May, with that lady-killing lieutenant and the whole world.

He went by Mexican quarters, barns, corrals, only to rush back to the courtyard. His rage melted into self-pity and mortification, and they lasted through another nameless stalk, at the end of which remorse edged into his conflicting emotions. But it was too late to bank the fires of jealousy. He walked, he sat on a box, he leaned on a hitching-rail, watching like an Indian from a hill.

Presently his sore heart gave a great jump. He espied May coming out of Maxwell's house, accompanied only by Mrs. Clement. The fascinating lieutenant did not appear anywhere on the horizon, for which reason Clint decided he would allow him one more chance for his life. For Clint had whispered darkly in his soul that he would kill that soldier some day.

May and Mrs. Clement entered the store. Clint lost no time in following. And he encountered the object of his search standing somewhat apart from Mrs. Clement, who was making purchases. Clint essayed a superior air, not without misgivings, and approached the young lady.

"Good morning, Mr. Belmet," she said, distantly, when he reached her.

"Mornin'," replied Clint, gruffly, more than ever unsure of himself. He had seen this young lady only a part of one day and one evening, during which she had certainly not exhibited the character that shone from her dark eyes now.

"Didn't I see you before?" she asked.

146

"I'm not so sure. Anyways, not when I first saw you. Reckon you couldn't have seen me with a spyglass."

"Oh, you did look rather small. . . . . Are you buying anything? Don't let me detain you."

"I run in here lookin' for you," rejoined Clint, doggedly.

"That makes twice you ran in here, doesn't it? You're rushed this morning."

Clint glared at her, quite unable to meet her on common ground, though conscious that he was very much out of favor. This added to his resentment.

"Have some candy?" she asked, sweetly, offering the open box.

Clint repeated his assertion as to his reason for entering the store. And she replied, with a hint of the drawling Southern accent she had acquired, that she was there, and what did he intend to do about it.

"Did that pink-cheeked West Pointer buy you candy?" queried Clint.

"Yes. It was nice of him. I had another box left at my tent. By Mr. Murdock. It was most thoughtful," she replied, in tone and look which completely mystified Clint. A red spot showed in each cheek.

"I won't have you——" burst out Clint. The sudden flash of her eyes checked him.

"Clint, did you come in here to apologize—or bully me?" she asked, with spirit.

"Apologize! Me? What for?" exclaimed Clint.

"You were ungentlemanly, to say the least."

"What'd I do?" demanded Clint.

"You met me face to face," she retorted, hotly. "You glared at me as if—as if you'd caught me at something disgraceful. You never spoke. You never even looked at Lieutenant Clayborn. And when I called you—why you never even looked back. . . . You were rude to me and insulting to him."

"Reckon I don't agree. An' I caught you flirtin'."

"Flirting! How dare you?" she blazed.

She appeared lovely to Clint then, most marvelously desirable and unattainable, her face as pale as a pearl, her eyes black and passionate with fire. He saw

147

what his cantankerous mood had led him into, and it rendered him both soul-sick and miserably wrathful.

"Well, wasn't you?" he demanded.

"If you think so I wouldn't deign to deny," she returned, her chin up.

"Weren't you lookin' up sweet in his face, all one lovely smile, as if you were dyin' to have him see you thought he——"

"I certainly was *not*," she interrupted, when he floundered to an inglorious break.

"I saw you," reiterated Clint.

"Clint Belmet, do you mean you honestly believe I was flirting with that soldier?" she asked, hurriedly, a blush staining her pale face.

"I reckon I do," he rejoined, stubborn even in his fright.

"Very well, I shall tell you the facts," she said, scornfully. "I met Lieutenant Clayborn here in the store. He was kind enough to buy me a box of candy. He put it in my hands. Could I drop it on the floor? I didn't ask it and I didn't want it from him. But I've lived with a fine family since you knew me. I've had training. And I hope I'm a lady. So I had to take the candy and thank him. . . . And if I *was* smiling up sweet at him—that was because he congratulated me on my engagement to you. He'd heard Mr. Maxwell announce it. And he said you had made a name for yourself on the frontier and were a fine chap. . . . There! That's why I smiled so sweetly—you wild buffalo-hunter!"

"Aw, May!" cried Clint, in poignant shame and grief.

But it did not affect her. Turning her back, she started to leave him. Clint caught her, and in low voice begged her forgiveness.

"Why, certainly," she replied, in an icy tone which implied she did not grant anything of the kind.

"Listen," he began, hurriedly, plucking at her sleeve, which she withdrew. "Maxwell got me all excited—crazy for joy over somethin' I—I can't tell you now.

Then I run into Uncle Jim an' he had bad news. Besides, I'm afraid he'd been drinkin'. . . . So when I saw you I was upset an' I—I thought——"

"You told me," she interrupted. "You thought I was flirting. Well, Mr. Buff Belmet, no girl in this world was ever farther from being untrue than I. . . . But the next time you see me with him or—or Lee Murdock, you look out!"

"Oh my Lord! . . . May, don't say that," implored Clint.

"I shall flirt most outrageously with—with anyone."

"It'll kill me," whispered Clint, doubling up as if he had again been pierced by the blade of jealousy.

"Pooh! I'd like to see just what you would do," she retorted, doubtful eyes dark on him.

"Do! I'll do somebody harm," flashed Clint, anger again rising out of the chaos of his feelings.

"You would?" she queried, with the subtlety of woman in her gaze.

"Yes, I would. We're on the frontier now. An' you're my girl."

"I *was*," she said, almost sadly.

"My God! May, you—you won't go back on me?"

She softened at his importunity, though her spirit still ran high.

"No, I wouldn't jilt you," she replied, slowly. "But you need a lesson."

"I've had enough."

"You need a real one. You called me a flirt—absolutely without the slightest reason. . . . And I've l—loved you so dearly. If you knew how the young men in Texas ran after me, you'd be ashamed."

"I don't want to know. I'm ashamed enough right now."

"Ashamed! You just look big and flustered—and want your own way," she replied, with disdain. "I'm disappointed in you. And hurt. It may be a good while until we—we can be married. . . . Every time any young man looks at me—are you going to act like you did, and then rave?"

"I reckon I am," returned Clint, frankly.

"Oh, we'll have a lovely engagement!" she laughed.

"Lovely or not, it'll be only one kind," said Clint. "I suppose I can't keep other fellows from lookin' at you—you're so turrible pretty."

"Am I?" she cried, with the delight of a child. "You never said so before."

"Give me a chance, will you? I've had only a few hours with you. . . . But you're my girl an' I'm sure not goin' to have you makin' eyes at any man."

"Indeed? . . . Just what do you mean by making eyes?"

"Well, the way you was lookin' up at that West Pointer."

"Clint, can't you distinguish between the natural function of a girl's eyes—and deliberate coquetry?"

"Reckon I can't, when they're both natural."

"Meaning I'm a coquette?" she asked, demurely.

"I don't mean just that," replied Clint, hastily. "Truth is, I hardly know what I do mean. You're the first an' only girl I ever had . . . an' my friend Maxwell said, 'You can never tell what a woman will do.'"

"Buff, you take that to heart," replied May, and certain it was she seemed to be trying to suppress merriment.

"But what can I believe?" protested Clint, in despair.

"Believe what you like," she returned, in proud finality, and left him.

Clint simply could not bring himself to answer further impulse, which was to follow her at any cost. If he did, it would only incur her added displeasure. He had already made her the target for gossip of freighters and soldiers, and perhaps even the Indians like Lone Wolf ridiculed him.

While his will was strong he went to his shack and threw himself in a corner on his blankets. He let himself go then, and it was a sorry hour. He might be nearly six feet tall and look like a man, but he knew where a girl and love were concerned he was the merest boy in experience.

When he had beaten himself into some semblance of humility and sense he faced the thing squarely. All in a day he had discovered himself. He loved this bright-eyed girl with all his heart and soul. But she seemed quite a stranger. For that matter, he did not know any girls, and had not exchanged even ordinary conversation with one for years. And May was the only one he had ever really liked since childhood. She had not only changed. She had grown bewilderingly in charm, education, wit, and character. Very far above him she seemed. "You wild buffalo-hunter!" She had called him that, partly in fun and exasperation, perhaps, yet she had struck deeply. Never before had he been ashamed of the nickname Buff; never had he felt the overland freighter to be common, vulgar, on a par with the greasy trapper and the squawman hunter. He had imagined the overland freighter to be a big-hearted, strong, and enduring trail-maker for the pioneer. These Southern people May had lived and associated with came from the best blood of the South. She had been a bright little girl at ten years, and six years of school and association had made her a young lady of quality. He wondered if she would do for this crude raw West. But his loyalty gave him assurance she would. Not, however, for the like of him! It crucified him to confess that bitter fact.

And yet he knew she cared for him, or for the boy she had met by the brook that day long ago and to whom she had affianced herself on a prairie schooner crossing the Great Plains. Perhaps the romance of it had lingered with her, grown with her as she changed and developed, had reached its fruition in the wonder and joy of meeting him again, only to collapse when he failed to measure up to her girlish ideal. She had expected too much of a boy, whose parents were dead, who had no schooling, no home except the camp fire.

Clint thought it all out. He had been a jealous boor. She was a lovely, adorable little lady, whom he had treated shabbily. She had given him her kisses—the

151

memory of which made him rock to and fro, weak and blind, with tumultuous heart—and for that he should have gone down on his knees in gratitude and worship. Instead, he had doubted her, insulted her. Well for her, indeed, that his true colors had come out under stress. Alas for him that he was no fit mate for her!

In his simplicity Clint could see only that she had built a dream around him, which upon reality had burst like a bubble. He took solemn though immature cognizance of her love, and believed it no slight thing. But he was not worthy of it and would only fail to keep it. His pride, a trait he had not known he possessed, had bled to death.

There came a shuffling of heavy boots outside his door, then a knock. He got up to open it. Couch stood there, gloomy and haggard, fire in his eyes, but sober.

"Buff, I been huntin' everywhere for you," he said.

"Uncle Jim, I—I felt bad, an' thought I'd lay down a bit."

"Hope you ain't sick?"

"Yes, I was. . . . Had a row with my girl."

"Wal, it ain't surprisin'. I seen her awhile ago with that lootenant, an' just now with Murdock. She's a dainty lass, an' you can't blame the fellars. Buff, that girl will raise the very hell on the frontier."

"Ahuh! She's raised a little for me already," replied Clint, grimly.

"Wal, don't take it too serious. She's young an' she's excited. I'd bet on her bein' good, Buff."

"Thanks, uncle," said Clint, huskily.

"While I'm thinkin' about it I want to tell you this fellar Murdock sticks in my craw somehow. I've run across him somewheres, or heard about him. An' it ain't to his credit. But I swear I can't place him. I've been worried an' thick. It'll come to me, though."

"It's nothin' to me. Hope that isn't what you hunted me up for."

"Lord! I wish it was. Buff, I just didn't dare lose out on the Aull contract. I've signed. The men are packin' like mad. We leave tomorrow before sunup."

"Without a troop escort?"

"Hell, yes! There ain't a soldier to be had."

"How many wagons?"

"Hundred an' eight, so far. Mebbe there'll be more. But at best only a small caravan. Kit Carson is here. He swore an' said, 'Don't go!' An' I told him I had to. An' then he said, 'Wal, you're not goin' to take that boy Buff.'"

"'Pears Carson an' Maxwell are a lot concerned about me, uncle."

"Wal, they cottoned to you, Buff. You're a likeable lad. Maxwell never had no children. Carson has a half-breed son."

"They're both wonderful men. I look up to them. But I'm afraid it's only a dream—my wantin' to be like them."

"Buff, you'd make a great plainsman. An' that reminds me what I was huntin' you for. Reckon I was cross an' short with you today. I'm sorry. I've come now to say you can stay here with Maxwell an' give up the overland freightin'. Maxwell will give you a job. I'll turn over your money to him. You can marry the little girl. She's a high-steppin' filly an' thoroughbred, but maybe you can manage her. You'd have to get over your softness, though, an' be pretty much of a man. Wal, you can do it. . . . God knows, Clint, I'll miss you, aside from needin' you powerful bad. I never had no son of my own. An' you'd grown like one. . . . An' I'm too fond of you to stand in the way of your happiness. . . . An' that's all, Buff."

"Uncle Jim, I'll go—with you," replied Clint, his voice breaking, and he turned away.

"What!" ejaculated Couch.

"I'll be there, ready to drive out, at daybreak."

"Buff, you're not goin' back on the old man?"

"I should say not."

"But the little girl, Buff. Are you playin' fair with her?"

"Uncle, May is too high-class for me—an' high-steppin', as you said," rejoined Clint.

153

"See here now, you Buff——"

Clint interrupted him hotly and for the first time in their years of intimacy swore roundly at him. Couch expelled a hard breath, as if he had been struck, then beat a hasty retreat.

The die seemed cast for Clint and there could be no backsliding. His heart beat like a muffled drum, as if compressed by pangs within. A lofty exaltation vied with a grim resignation. Black despair haunted the fringe of his mind. But that was only his softness. He would show Uncle Jim. And again mocking words returned, "You wild buffalo-hunter!"

Hurriedly packing his belongings, he carried them round back of the ranch house, and by a cut across the pasture he reached Couch's camp, where he deposited them. The men were packing like beavers, too busy and excited to take note of him. Indians watched the proceedings with interest and speculation. The camp fires were burning. Clint was amazed to see sunset at hand.

No time like the present! He would call at the Clements' camp to say good-by. And as he hurried through the cottonwoods he decided he would send word to Maxwell, thanking his for his hospitality and bidding him farewell. What would that kindly rancher think of him? And the great Kit Carson! He dared not risk seeing them. Perhaps in years to come, if he escaped the fate of most plainsmen, he would tell them how and why he had failed to live up to their hopes.

Dagget's camp was on the other side of the narrow valley, at the upper end, and nearer Maxwell's ranch house. Camps were scattered picturesquely under the cottonwoods. Wagons were standing everywhere. A freighter directed Clint to Clement's camp. He had seen it only by moonlight, but presently he remembered the site, more by its isolation than anything else.

The sun was setting gold in the pass between the ranges, and to the east the gray obscurity hung like a pall over the void where the overland trail wound down into the Great Plains.

Sight of the high freight wagon under the huge cottonwood, where May and he had spent such ecstatic hours—was it only last night?—thrilled and cut Clint alternately.

He saw and smelled wood smoke. The several tents and wagons were grouped among willows and young cottonwoods. Clint strode round a thicket to encounter Clement and his wife at the camp fire. Clint had interrupted a colloquy, to judge by their sudden start, but he was quick to observe that he was more than welcome.

"Where've you been all day?" asked Clement, offering his hand and giving Clint a close scrutiny.

"Lad, it's about time you got here," declared Mrs. Clement, nodding her head significantly.

"I've had a—a bad day," replied Clint, coming to the point at once, hard though it was. "Uncle Jim Couch is packin' to leave at daybreak. . . . An' I'm goin' with him."

"Oh no!" cried Mrs. Clement, and then she too searched his face, which, as always, betrayed him.

"I saw Maxwell today. He had a good deal to say aboot you," said Clement, quietly. "Shore he had no idea you were leavin' us heah. . . . Somethin' has happened."

"Yes, it has. I'm sorry," replied Clint, helplessly responding to their concern and regret, and he smiled as if that might help them to divine his trouble.

"It's May. The little vixen!" declared Mrs. Clement, turning to her husband. "Hall, I told you something was amiss. Gallivanting around all day with Tom, Dick, and Harry—when only last night her engagement was announced!"

"Please don't blame her, Mrs. Clement," begged Clint, hastily. "I—I offended her—insulted her—fell far short of her—her expectations."

"Humph!" ejaculated Mrs. Clement.

"Where is May?" queried Clint, nervously. "I just want to tell her I'm sorry an' say—good-by."

"Son, I'd wait a little while," returned Clement,

easy and cool, after the manner of Texans. "Sit down and let's talk."

"No, I've got to get it over."

"Clint, she has been parading up and down here with Murdock for an hour or more," said Clement. "And I had a hunch she was expecting you. But you came down this way. It's just aboot a bad time for you to run into her, for any reason. She has been on the rampage today. I never knew her to be this way. I don't like Lee Murdock. And I told her, as her engagement to you was known, she should not spend any more time with Murdock. She nearly took my head off. Whew!"

"Reckon that makes it easier," replied Clint. "I'm thankin' you both for your good feelin' toward me. . . . Good-by. I won't be seein' you again."

He left them standing dismayed and aghast, and hurried away toward a gleam of white and gold that shone through a break in the willows. When he cleared the edge of thicket he saw the white was May's dress, and the gold the last glow of the setting sun.

She sat on the wagon tongue of the big freighter, and beside her stood Murdock, leaning attentively over her. Clint instantly divined that May had seen him all the time. The very lines of her graceful form seemed instinct with combat. The spot was well screened from the other camps by a circle of trees and thickets.

Some emotion deep and hot mocked the black, sickening despair with which Clint strode toward May. What a hideous falsehood somewhere! Was it in him? How unreal the picture of her sitting there! She had done precisely what she had threatened. Perhaps she had rather liked being driven to teach him a lesson.

Clint halted before her, bareheaded, without confusion or embarrassment. Before he spoke she read that in his bearing and face which she had not expected. It afforded Clint a melancholy gratification.

He looked straight down into her dark eyes, that

156

mirrored the gold glamour of the glade, that changed, widened, dilated under his.

"Beg pardon, Miss Bell," he began, as cool and drawling as any Texan she had ever met. "I've no wish to interrupt your flirtin', but I'm leavin' on the overland trail at dawn, an' want to say good-by."

She arose, suddenly, her face white as her dress. "OH, CLINT! . . . No! No!"

How the divining love and repentance of her appeal might have softened Clint never transpired, for Murdock gave him a stinging slap in the face.

Clint did not flinch. That second blow from this source was welcome.

"You shore are a wild buffalo-hunter, callin' a lady a flirt," Murdock boomed, with sudden robust voice that indicated his pleasure in this opportunity. He expressed as much satisfaction as disgust. Nevertheless, Texan though he was, he underrated Clint.

"Murdock, do you happen to have a gun on you?" queried Clint, fiercely.

"No," replied Murdock, sharply surprised, and as May screamed he drew himself up.

Swiftly Clint swung a sledge-hammer fist. The sodden blow was accompanied by the rattling of Murdock's teeth. He did not fall. He was propelled down as if by a mace, and he must have been senseless before he thudded to the ground. He never moved. The freighter who had claimed Clint did not know his own strength could hardly vouchsafe so much now.

Clint held the big fist before May's distended eyes.

"Maxwell gave me a hunch that you thought I was a softy. An' I reckon your friend here thought so too."

She made mute denial. She stood shaking, deathly white, shocked at the effect of her willful guilt, too frightened at the astounding suddenness of catastrophe to speak what was clear—her grief, her love, her panic. It was clear even to Clint, with the first rage of manhood upon him.

"Did—you—kill—him?" she faltered, faintly, her quivering hand indicating the fallen man, though her wide eyes seemed transfixed on Clint.

He had no answer for her. To bid good-by to this dainty white creature seemed insupportable. Her white arms and neck were bare. Their loveliness shocked and tortured him. Never had he seen a gown like that. And she had worn it for Murdock! "You can never tell what a woman will do!" How the words seared Clint! He hated Maxwell then, because of what he now believed a bitter mocking truth. Yet to look at May Bell then was to court doubt of his own soul.

Suddenly he snatched her in his arms, unmindful of her little cry, ignorant of his brutal strength, infinitely removed from the intention Maxwell had inspired in him. May Bell was not for him, but he would possess her for one wild, terrible, fleeting moment. Was he mad to imagine he felt a quivering response when he kissed her? Ruthlessly he pressed his lips to her mouth, to cheek, to eyes, and then to mouth again, aware of the torturing sweetness that he tried in vain to take and keep, conscious that this was farewell to beauty, to love, to woman, to the dream of wild hopeful youth.

His madness was as brief as violent. Spent and shaking, he released her, saw her sink to her knees, great wide eyes fixed on his. She swayed back with an inarticulate cry and stretched her white length on the grass.

Clint rushed away through the willows, under the cottonwoods, across the valley, beyond the wagon-train to solitude and night.

In the melancholy dawn, Clint Belmet, armed like all the grim freighters, drove down the winding overland trail toward the Great Plains.

14

It was June on the prairie, high on the Colorado slope, with the purple bulk of mountains dimming behind, and the vast open to the fore. Spring flowers bloomed in the waving grass. The caravan was safely out of the passes and gullies, on the down grade. Even the horses seemed to know. And the lethargic oxen at least made better time.

Couch's caravan encountered many soldiers moving in that part of the country. The war was responsible for this unprecedented condition. The governor of Colorado sent a whole regiment to New Mexico to fight against the Confederacy. At Fort Larned the caravan pulled out quickly, owing to congestion there and lack of feed for the stock. Several days out, two companies of soldiers from Nebraska, bound for Fort Union, camped with the caravan. They were unfamiliar with the country, but had several scouts, one of them a famous character on the plains, known only by the cognomen "Old Bill." He was a story-teller, under favorable circumstances, which meant leisure from scouting duty and the acquisition of a drink or two.

Clint Belmet seldom absented himself from the camp-fire circles these evenings. He was grave and silent, but he listened to the stories and songs, to the talk of soldiers and freighters. The long, lonely ten-hour drive each day always left him in need of the sound of human voices and laughter.

"Wal, once way back in 'fifty-four—or was it 'fifty-two?—I was killin' meat for an outfit an' I had a pardner named Frenshy," began Old Bill, when they had gotten him primed. "It was on the Cimmaron, an' game was plumb scarce. We rode near all day without seein' any buffs. An' long about midafternoon we headed back for camp, an' Frenshy fell into his old habit of wastin' ammunition. He sure liked to shoot.

159

An' he was pretty good, too, but I always beat him. In them days I could hit a runnin' jack rabbit. Wal, we got to jokin' an' then bettin,' an' used up all our ammunition but three loads. We was close to camp then. An' darned if an old buffalo didn't raise up out of a holler. We shot them three loads quicker'n you could say Jack Robinson.

" 'By gosh! you missed him,' said Frenshy, an' I swore I didn't. Anyway, the bull stood there, an' when we rode up close we seen he was bleedin' bad. But the son-of-a-gun wouldn't drop. Frenshy got off his hoss an' pulled his knife.

" 'I'll hamstring the critter,' said Frenshy.

"Wal, the bull laid down accommodatin' like, an' then Frenshy stooped over to cut its throat. But when he just pricked him thar was hell to pay. Thet old bull got up surprisin' quick. Now I'm tellin' you a bull buffalo as big as a hill can move like a streak when he wants to. This one sure wanted to an' he made fer Frenshy. An' in three jumps he was almost on top of Frenshy.

" 'Shoot! Shoot!" bawls Frenshy, an' I yells back I couldn't shoot 'cause my gun was empty. Frenshy dodged, an' to save hisself he grabbed the bull's tail an' held on fer dear life, yellin' like hell.

" 'Kill him!' roars Frenshy, mad an' scared. But I couldn't do nothin' but laff. The bull got goin' round an' round, faster an' faster, till Frenshy was 'most flyin' through the air. Presently he slung Frenshy about forty foot. Lucky then fer my pard, the old bull had shot his bolt. He slowed up an' keeled over. Frenshy went over powerful cautious an' finally cut the bull's throat. Then wavin' the bloody knife at me yelled: 'You —— — — — — —! You laugh over my daid body.'

" 'Frenshy, I couldn't do nothin'. You was so scairt an' funny.'

" ' 'Scairt?' he yells. 'Say, I was scairt only of his tail pullin' out.' "

When the laugh had subsided one of the freighters

gave Old Bill another nip from a bottle, and started the narrator off on another tangent.

"Wal, in 'fifty-eight I was in a queer deal. A band of Comanches went on a raid. You all know Cow Creek. Wal, along the rich bottomland of thet creek some settlers had taken up farms. Sure is strange what chances these fool settlers take. The Comanches murdered every last one of them settlers, wimmen an' kids, too—I don't remember how many, though I did see their scalps. One was from a kid girl's head—long purty gold hair, a pity to see. . . . Wal, somebody reported thet job to Captain Howard at Fort Zarah. An' he ordered Lieutenant Stevens an' sixty troopers to take up the trail of the Comanches. I was ordered along, fer I knowed every foot of thet country. Wal, I figgered I could make a short cut on them redskins. An' I hit their trail about twenty miles on, crossed the big bend of the Arkansas, followed up Cove Creek about twenty miles, an' finally from a ridge top we seen thirty lodges. Stevens sent me alone to find a way to slip up on thet camp. Thar was heavy timber between, an' I had to crawl on my hands an' knees. I went back an' reported I could lead the soldiers right up near the Comanches' lodges. Wal, we tied our hosses, leavin' ten men to guard them, an' slipped easy an' quiet up to thet camp. It was then I seen a string of scalps hangin' on a lodge, an' one of them was thet with the long shiny gold hair. So we knowed for sure these Comanches had murdered the settlers.

"As the Injuns was all in their lodges we crawled closer an' whooped. Then as fast as a Comanche come runnin' out we plugged him. They all had guns an' shot a lot of times, but hurt only two of us, an' thet not bad. We killed twenty-two before they surrendered. An' we got fourteen prisoners, whose hands we tied. Lieutenant let them say good-by to their families, then he ordered us to drag them out of camp, line them up, an' when he gave the word we all fired. Thet was the last of them Comanche braves. It seemed tough to us, but we had to think of them poor settlers. Thet was the only law. We got back all the settlers' stock—eighty-nine hosses, over three hundred head of cattle."

"Wholesale murder on both sides," commented Couch, shaking his head doubtfully.

"Bill, reckon you never did no good in all your years on the frontier," added another of the pessimistic freighters.

Old Bill was highly indignant and more than one nip from the black bottle was necessary to start him off again, and this time he was manifestly inspired to a Homeric recital.

"In 'fifty-four I trapped some on the Medicine Bow, up north. Thar was eight of us, an' I reckon we was 'most as good as a regiment of soldiers. Wal, thet winter we got a big trap of otter, beaver, an' mink hides, an' we knowed they was wuth a lot of money. So we lit out fer the south an' the Arkansas River, packin' our pelts on our hosses an' footin' it ourselves. By July we had hoofed it over seven hundred miles. An', fellars, I ain't lyin' when I say we seen ten million buffalo thet trip. We seen herds fifty miles long, an' I don't know how wide. We calkilated by the time it took them to pass us. Wal, by an' by we come into the land of the Pawnees, who to my mind was in them days the meanest redskins on the plains. One day early we camped at Point of Rocks. We had early supper an' was sittin' round smokin' when we heard a shot. You bet we grabbed our guns an' skedaddled out *pronto*.

"We soon seen a small caravan tryin' to corral their wagons with about sixty howlin' Pawnees circlin' round. They kept shootin' arrows into the oxen to stampede them so they could get at the men easier. We run up fast an' got eight of them Pawnees fust crack. Then we ducked in behind the wagons to load up again. Had only muzzle-loadin' guns them days, but most of us had two revolvers, an' in about ten minnits or so we had twenty-nine savages down. The rest gave up an' rode away.

"Wal, it was a caravan of Mexicans haulin' supplies to Mora, the ranch of Kurnel St. Vrain. We'd

saved them from bein' massacred. We went among
them fallen Pawnees an' scalped them, findin' three
still alive. We knocked two on the head, an' then we
seen the Pawnees racin' back. I yelled to run fer the
wagons. But I picked up thet third live Injun an'
packed him back to the wagon. I never knowed jest
why I did thet. Funny! Wal, the Pawnees fooled
around us some, seen we'd taken all the scalps, an'
they rode away for good.

"The Injun I had picked up was a fine-lookin'
young buck, about eighteen years old. He held out
his hand with palm up, which means friend.

" 'Hey, Reddy,' I says, 'so you're a friend. Wal, you
have a hell of a nice way showin' it.'

"He motioned me to come close. An' I did, as he
had no weapon. He said: 'Me want go home—mother,
father,' an' he spoke tolerable good English. Then he
fainted. He was shot clear through the neck, but the
bullet hadn't hit an artery. My men come up watchin'
me, an Hawkins said: 'You ain't in no hurry to knock
thet reddy on the head. An I said I wasn't an' I'd
like to have him as my private property. They all
laughed, an' agreed. I washed his wound, had a Mexican get me some balsam weed, an' I put a bandage
on. Next mornin' my patient was better, an' I loaded
him on one of the wagons goin' to Fort Bent. We got
there in seven days. My patient was doin' pretty good.
He was thankful fer what I did fer him. He didn't
have thet starin', sneakin' look common to mean redskins. I was curious about him, an' when we got to
the fort I asked him some questions.

" 'What's your name?'

" 'Jim Whitefish,' he said.

" 'Whar you live?'

" 'Big Walnut.'

" 'Are you a Pawnee?'

"He shook his head, but didn't tell me what tribe
he belonged to. Then I asked him if he had been on
the warpath with them Pawnees. He told me he had
been to see his gurl near an' run into them Pawnees.
They made him come along. They kicked him an'

beat him. He had no gun. He wouldn't fight the Mexicans. An' they called him squaw.—Wal, I believed the lad, an' I paid a doctor at the fort to look after him. When I said good-by an' good luck he grabbed my hand.

" 'What's your name?' he asked. •

"I said, 'Old Bill.' He pressed my hand against his breast an' told me he'd know Old Bill. Wal, we sold our pelts an' went back fer more. Along about thet time I did a lot of trappin'. Four years after thet, in the spring of 'fifty-nine, I was with three other trappers workin' down out of the mountains to Raton Pass. We camped at Timpas Creek; had four mules, loaded heavy. Thet night we was attacked by a bunch of redskins. We had to run fer it. I was shot in the leg, but managed to go on till I got another arrow in the back of my neck. Thet tumbled me, an' when I come to I was in a dark place hard to see. I was as weak as a cat. Couldn't lift my hand. Somebody shoved back a blanket an' thet let light in. I seen two Injuns, one a squaw. They held up their hands palms out, an' then I knowed I was with friends. The squaw gave me a drink of somethin' orful. I dropped off again. When I woke up I felt better. An' I recognized the man as the young Injun I'd saved.

" 'You know me? Jim Whitefish.'

"I let him see I did. His mother came with somethin' to eat an' drink. They took care of me fer five weeks. I picked up orful slow. Thet old squaw sure saved my life. Jim told me he was camped on Little Coon Creek, about twenty miles from Fort Larned.

" 'Jim,' I says, 'go to the fort an' tell them to come after me.'

" 'No,' he says, serious like. 'My people no trust me. You wait. When you strong I take you.'

"Wal, I was three weeks longer in thet teepee before I could walk. An' I had Jim's word fer it thet not another Injun beside his mother knew I was there. One night he led me out, an' next day we got to Fort Larned. Jim most carried me, the last few miles. He said: 'Me remember—Old Bill'. . . . I never saw him again."

"Bill, I'm wonderin' if you're not the biggest liar on these hyar plains," said a freighter.

"Boys, thet's the honest God's truth," protested Old Bill. "And believe me or not, I haven't shot straight at an Injun since."

At the Cimmaron Crossing one of Couch's scouts espied mules back in a canyon, and suspected an ambush by savages who had stolen the stock. A reconnoiter proved that the mules were in the charge of twenty-one troopers, who had pitched camp for the night. Naturally, Couch's men took them for Union soldiers. But when investigation proceeded as far as a visit, these troopers turned out to be rebels.

Couch argued with some of his men, who favored merely surrounding the rebels and killing them.

"No, that'd be too much redskin to suit me," concluded the train boss. "Everyone of you pack a gun hid in your pocket, an' we'll drift over there an' hold them up."

His men visited the other camp in groups and at an opportune moment, with most of the rebels round the camp fire, Couch gave the order, and the surprised rebels were soon prisoners.

"You got us where the fur is short," fumed the rebel leader.

Couch's plan was to drive the rebel caravan along with his own, not by any means a task to facilitate his journey toward Westport. As luck would have it a troop of Union soldiers came along, to whom the rebels were turned over.

Some days later, while in camp on Ash Creek, at three o'clock in the morning, Clint awakened and missed Jack. Such a rare occurrence was always prolific of alarm. Clint hurried out in his bare feet to tell Couch, who was on guard with ten men. They awoke all the men and prepared to repel attack. But nothing happened. At dawn, when Jack had not returned, Clint wanted to search for him, but the boss forbade.

At breakfast-time Jack came wagging his tail, leading a strange man into camp, evidently a teamster. He carried a gun.

Couch fastened keen, suspicious eyes on the stranger. A man on foot in that country was either a desperado or an unfortunate traveler.

"Howdy, stranger! Have a bite with us," was Couch's gruff greeting. "An' who may you happen to be?"

"My name's Asher," he said, wiping a clammy forehead. "Teamster on the way to Baruth. I was in a camp about eight miles above you. Fifty-one in the caravan. . . . This mornin' I got up in the moonlight an' went huntin' jack rabbits. When I worked back to camp I heard shootin' an' yellin'. I sneaked close so I could see across the creek. . . . Soon the shootin' stopped, but the yellin' kept up. The wagons began to burn, makin' a bright light. Then I seen a big bunch of Indians. They set fire to all the wagons. I lay low in the brush, knowin' for sure all my outfit was dead an' scalped right then. . . . They rode off, an' I set down the creek. I met this dog. He was sure trailin' them Indians. He fetched me here."

It was the same old story of the plains. But its variations were endless as was its power to blanch the cheek of the stoutest-hearted freighter.

"How many men did you say?" queried Couch, the first to break that stunned silence.

"Fifty-one, all told. . . . If it hadn't been for me bein' wakeful an' goin' huntin' there wouldn't have been anybody to tell the tale."

"Any women an' kids?"

"No, thank God for that."

"Same here. Wal, Asher, reckon you don't feel none like eatin', but since you have to go on—same as all of us—set down an' pitch in."

Next day Couch's caravan drove onto Pawnee Rock, one of Clint's favorite camps along the great trail.

The Arkansas River made a big bend there, which held a million and more acres as level as a floor, where buffalo were always seen grazing. It was a favorite hunting-ground for all the tribes of the plains, and a good deal of the fighting among them took place at this point.

A tribe of Cheyennes came into view of the caravan. They were moving their village, a procedure Clint had observed before and which was very interesting.

When an Indian encampment moved, the squaws did all the work. They dismantled the teepees, packed them on the ponies, and tied the poles on either side. When they were ready to move, they turned the bell mare loose.

This bell mare, an adjunct of every traveling band of Indians, was not only the meanest animal among the mustangs, but also chosen, and in fact trained, to run into a caravan, stampede the stock, and lead them away down the rivers or over the ridges, where the Indians waited for them.

When the horses of an Indian tribe had pretty well cropped off the grass round a village the Indians broke camp and moved to a better location. They were therefore nomadic in habit and followed the buffalo.

This day Couch's men noticed that the bell mare had evidently been steered away from the caravan. The ponies followed with teepee poles tied to their sides, and baskets in which were Indian children, sometimes two or three to a basket. This collection of Cheyennes had numerous dogs, some of which were packing small articles, after the manner of the ponies. Clint thought these dogs had a strain of gray wolf in them.

The Cheyennes came on to a point opposite Couch's camp, where they halted in plain sight. The bell mare, true to her training, splashed across the shallow creek, but when Couch ordered his men in a half circle with rifles ready, some of the Cheyennes rode out and headed her back. Then the braves dismounted and sat down, cross-legged to smoke, while the squaws put up the teepees, laid down robes and blankets, gathered wood and started a fire, cooked the meat, and called their lords to eat it. And this all happened in plain sight, not a stone's throw from where Clint sat and watched them.

But Couch's caravan was not molested, and traveled on to the Little Arkansas, and unfortunately had to halt for the night at a place notorious for ambushes. Pawnees, Cheyennes, Comanches, Arapahoes, and Apaches had attacked many caravans there; and one or the other of these tribes never let a small caravan get by without a fight.

Couch took unusual precautions here, driving a very close corral, placing the six-pound cannon in the most favorable position, and thirty men on guard, stationed all around the circle.

Clint, with his dog Jack, stood the watch with Couch, which was always the worst one—that hour before dawn just at the faintest sign of light in the east. They had a station close to the cannon. Here Clint and Couch, with another guard, walked up and down their beat, with the dog at their heels. The night was cloudy, and warm, threatening rain.

Presently Jack began to whine and lift his nose to sniff the air—a pretty good sign there were Indians somewhere near.

"Wal, we been gettin' off lucky this trip," growled Couch. "Reckon we're in for hell now."

He tied the dog to a wagon wheel, but Jack grew so restless and suspicious that the boss went around, waking all the men. By the time he got back to the cannon, which faced the opening left between the wagons, Jack began to growl fiercely.

"Look sharp everybody," yelled Couch, lighting the fuse.

"HYAR THEY COME!" bawled a scout from a wagon seat.

Suddenly pandemonium broke loose. Couch had at last been surprised. His men were awake, but not all in line, and when a horrid medley of Indian screeches rent the air, only one third of the caravan opened fire.

Clint dove under a wagon, gun thrust forward, his hair stiff, and his skin tight and cold, while the blood gushed back to his heart. The *mêlée* of yells and shots

168

was deafening. Red flashes lit up the dark night, through which swift wild forms sped by. Clint felt wind —a splitting shock—then blankness!

When he opened his eyes he lay on a bed in a strange room. He could see out of a window. Thin snow whitened a roof. Winter! He must be dreaming. His head felt queer, his body like lead. Nothing in sight was familiar. But he reasoned that none of the forts on the plains had a house with a room like this one. He lifted a hand to rap on the wall.

Presently he heard footfalls. A door opened to let in a woman who gave him a look from quick sharp eyes.

"Where am—I?" he asked, and his voice sounded far away.

"Kansas City," she replied, cheerfully, as she bent over him, felt his head, and gazed into his eyes. "Who might you be?"

"I'm Clint Belmet. . . . All that's left of me."

"Good boy! You've come to your senses," she exclaimed, happily. "I never believed it. But the doctor stuck to it—your mind would clear."

"Clear?" echoed Clint, dazedly.

"You've been out of your mind for months," replied the woman, hovering over him. "They fetched you to the hospital in August. And Mr. Couch had you fetched here to my house in late September. It's past Christmas now."

"Christmas? . . . Where am I? Westport?"

"Westport it was. Kansas City now. We're growin'."

"Where's Uncle Jim?"

"You mean Mr. Couch? He left in six days after arrivin'. Led a big caravan out, they said. Over two hundred wagons."

"What—ails me?" went on Clint, fainter.

"Feel that, young man." She took his hand and ran his fingers under his hair, above his temple, where he felt a long deep groove, healed yet still sensitive to touch.

"Bullet hole."

"No. It was an arrow, an' all but scalped you. The

bullet hole was in your shoulder an' pretty bad. But it's healed, too. You're on the road to recovery."

"Where's—my dog—Jack?"

"Mr. Couch told me about him," she replied. "He must have been a wonderful dog. When they found you, as I recall it, an Indian was draggin' you out from under a wagon. An' your dog was fightin' him. Stabbed him with a knife, which no doubt he had intended to use on your scalp. They killed the Indian. Mr. Couch said the dog sure saved your scalp."

"My dog—Jack," murmured Clint, dreamily. He did not feel anything but a dreary recognition of facts.

In February Clint was able to get out of bed and move around the room, and put a stick of wood in the stove now and then. The weather was cold. Mr. Mellon had placed a comfortable armchair in front of the stove, where Clint passed hours. He would read and sleep. He took his meals in that chair, with a board across his lap. His thin hands had long fascinated him, and like a baby he had a habit of holding them up to look at. Day by day they seemed to fill out, to grow less transparent. Uncle Jim had once said Clint's hand was like a ham.

It was in March that Clint began to show marked improvement. The doctor claimed he had at last beaten the blood-poisoning from the bullet wound in his shoulder. Clint's appetite improved slowly, and then by leaps and bounds.

April brought sunny days, green grass, budding leaves, and lilac blossoms on the hedge outside his open window. The birds sang. Spring! But Clint Belmet's blood did not leap with joy. He was no longer a boy and all of life worth living lay in the past.

When he grew able to go outdoors his favorite place was the dock, where he would sit for hours watching the muddy swirling river, the stern-wheelers go sloshing by, belching smoke, or the stevedores at work loading or unloading. Then he would walk along the river bank under the trees, and as he became stronger, out beyond the edge of town, where he would find a lonely place, and rest and watch.

His mind was not active. Something had stultified it. Yet he felt sensitiveness about being the hero of the small boys in Westport. He avoided them when possible. They all knew his story. Buff Belmet! If Clint had killed as many Indians and had as many narrow escapes as these lads credited to his fame he would have been a hundred times Kit Carson.

Summer began to slip by. And Clint took to fishing again, though without the old keen zest. Still it was pleasant to sit on the bank, with his back against a tree, and watch his fishing-line for the bite that never came. Not that it mattered!

Along the end of May the first caravan had started west. In June there were several, all large in number, for the Indians had grown fiercer and more persistent in attack, and the war permitted of no escorts. It was hard for Clint to escape from the influence of the terrific struggle between the North and South. Westport seethed with war talk. Soldiers were always moving. It seemed to Clint there were more people in Westport whose sympathies were with the South than with the North. Sometimes he listened covertly to the guarded talk of negro laborers.

In July more caravans headed out across the plains. Clint never failed to be on hand at the starting hour, and never did he see the oxen wag and heave, the great wagons start to roll, without a yearning to go. Something called him out there to the West. The feeling grew on him. He saw the long winding wagon-train stretching out for miles across the prairie, the vast open on all sides, the waving grass, like a blossoming sea, the birds, the rabbits, the antelope, the deer, the huge horizon-wide herds of buffalo, the long, long gray stretches, monotonous, lonely, and grand. In his mind's eye he was eternally watching the barren leaves, the ridges of high ground, for the sudden rise, as if by magic, of the wild, plumed naked riders of the prairie. He thought of the graves of his loved ones out there, and the grave of his hopes.

For days the first caravan from the west had been expected by Aull & Company. Stage-coaches from

Council Grove and soldiers on the move east from the forts brought rumors of caravans that never arrived. They were going to start, but perhaps they had not done so on time—or perhaps they had been halted.

This spring of 1863 was the most anxious the freighting business had ever experienced. If Aull & Company lost out on their expected caravans of pelts they would crash, and smaller companies were no less in a precarious condition. All business that had no direct connection with the war was bad.

On the morning of July 16th an advance rider galloped into Kansas City and reported to Aull & Company that Nelson's caravan would reach the river some time during the day—one hundred and sixty-nine heavily laden wagons intact, freighters and stock in good shape, and a number of emigrant families that had been rescued at Point of Rocks.

The rejoicing was not confined to Aull & Company. There were a general relief and a renewal of hope for those who had interest in other caravans.

Clint Belmet had been sure Couch would beat any other caravan in. Nelson must have had a fine early spring, of which he had taken exceptional advantage, and then he had undoubtedly been fortunate on the drive.

No doubt the first person in Kansas City to espy Nelson's caravan coming was hawk-eyed Clint Belmet. Sight of it seemed to thrill out the strange deadness that had for months held Clint's emotions. He shook like a leaf. The past seemed to unfold before his eyes—that first drive out from Independence—the brook—little May Bell—the prairie-schooner seat she shared with him—the Indians—the death of mother and father, and all the poignant pictures of the past.

Clint was on hand, foremost in the crowd that welcomed Nelson's caravan. The train of wagons filled all of the open square next to the storehouse of Aull & Company. Clint mingled with the merry, sweating freighters, and exchanged words with one here and there. He spoke a language they understood. Nelson's outfit had been attacked twice. No loss! At Point of

Rocks fifty mounted freighters had driven off a band of Pawnees who were harassing the remnant of an emigrant train. Pawnees, Comanches, Apaches had come out of winter quarters on the warpath, fiercer, stronger than ever. And a new menace had arisen on the Western plains. Desperadoes, deserters from the armies, bandits and Mexican robbers, were now as much to be guarded against as the Indians. A small caravan might slip across, but the chance was only one in a hundred. If both these foes to travel worked east as far as Council Grove the stage-coach lines would be compelled to cease their runs.

That night in Aull & Company's store Clint, who was known there, met the blond giant Nelson, boss of this first caravan.

"Howdy! So you're Buff Belmet. Heerd of you, an' shore glad to shake your hand."

"Do you know my uncle Jim Couch?" asked Clint, eagerly.

"I shore do. Now I place you, Buff. It was Jim who told me about your gettin' shot in thet bad brush Couch had with Comanches. . . . Wal, so you pulled out?"

"Yes, I'm about well again."

"I'm tarnation glad. Let's see. It was near a year ago. Time shore flies. Wal, I reckon you'll be sittin' tight pretty soon, lookin' out over the gray, huh?"

"I don't know, Nelson. Maybe. It depends on Uncle Jim. Can you give me any word of him?"

"Shore. Seen him at Fort Larned last October. He was drivin' to Santa Fé an' Vegas. Expected to winter there."

"Oughtn't he be pullin' into Kansas City soon?"

"He ought an' he shore will be. Don't you worry, Buff, about thet old *hombre*. He takes risks, but he gets there. He's head of the hardest outfit of Injunfighters on the Old Trail. I shore wish I had them. Fact is, if he comes in while I'm loadin' I'll wait an' join caravans with him. . . . Tough freightin' these days, Buff. The strain on men is bad. Watchin' all day, sleepin' with one eye open all night, is as hard as actual fightin.' It breaks a fellar down."

"Did you get—up Maxwell's Ranch—way?" queried Clint, haltingly.

"No. I wintered at Fort Union. Fine open winter an' early spring. Heerd talk, though, about Maxwell. He's not doin' so well. Last fall he lost forty-seven freight wagons. Burned at Cow Creek. Pawnees. An' I understand he was short supplies an' was dependin' on thet train. It never rains but it pours. . . . Wal, the rumor is that Maxwell won't last out the war. He's rich in land an' stock. But if he can't trade—why, he'll have to sell out."

"But wouldn't whoever bought him out be in the same fix?"

"Reckon he would," laughed Nelson.

"Do you know anythin' about Dagget, who drove a caravan into Maxwell's last May a year ago?"

"Yes. He was shot in a gamblin' dive in Vegas last winter. I don't recall who told me. His caravan disbanded, freighters goin' here an' there. Couch got a lot of them."

Clint found speech difficult, his tongue feeling thick and his mouth dry.

"I—I had some friends in Dagget's outfit," went on Clint. "Texans. Name was Clement. Hall Clement was the name. An'——"

"No, Buff, I'm shore sorry," spoke up Nelson, when Clint trailed off. "I didn't hear no word of anybody by thet name."

"There was a fellow in Dagget's outfit, who—who was a Texan, too, but no friend of mine. Name was Lee Murdock. . . . Did you happen to hear his name out there—this winter?"

"Murdock? 'Pears to me I did, Buff," replied Nelson, scratching his head. "I got it. Shore. . . . His name was Murdock, anyhow. I can't vouch for the front handle. Gambler. Pretty handy with guns an' had a bad record. Hailed from Texas. An' if I recollect right he was in Larned last winter."

"Thanks. He might be the fellow I—I mean."

174

"Wal, I wouldn't have told you if you hadn't said this Murdock was no friend of yours. . . . Buff, soon as we unload we're goin' into camp just out of town. Jones' pasture. Come out an' see me. You'll shore be welcome to dinner. I've still got a rump steak of buffalo meat left. Haw! Haw! See him grin. I'll bet ten dollars your mouth's waterin' right now."

"I'm afraid it is," admitted Clint.

"Wal, when a man eats rump steak for a while he never wants no more beef. It's like the hold the Old Trail gets on a fellar."

Clint wandered around awhile, absorbed in thoughts and feelings that seemed like vaguely remembered dreams. He had been waiting for more news than that which concerned Uncle Jim Couch. But he did not voice it to his consciousness. He went back to his room, and paced the floor, and threw himself on his bed. The way it sagged and creaked under him attested to the return of his weight. He spread his right hand before his intent gaze. It was no longer spare— a long thin wide skeleton of a hand. The color was white, but the bulk had returned. He could drive a team tomorrow. The two small scars on his knuckles stood out lividly, permanent brands cut there by Lee Murdock's teeth. Slow stir of blood, slow turgid heat, attended memory of the blow he had given the Texan. The past that had seemed dim, pale, began to gain color and life.

15

Jim Couch, with half a caravan, arrived at Kansas City, late at night on the 2nd of August. Clint did not know of it until morning, when his land-lady informed him that Couch had sent word. Clint left without any breakfast and ran all the way to Aull's freight-yard.

It was a sorry-looking caravan, but Joe Anderson, after a glad hello to Clint, assured him that they had some wounded men, but no dead, and they had brought in all the valuable freight.

Clint found Couch a fit-looking leader for such a caravan. He was grimy and bearded, dirty as a trapper, and he had a bandage caked with blood round his head. He yelled when he saw Clint.

"Buff! By all that's holy!" he exclaimed, seizing him with horny hands. "My God, it makes me glad! . . . You're pale—you're older, but you're well an' fit again."

Clint choked over his warm greeting, then blurted out, "Uncle, have you a—a letter for me?"

"Nope—sorry to say I haven't," replied Couch, suddenly thoughtful.

"Any—news?"

"Lots of news, Buff. Reckon I know what you want to hear first. Last fall when I got back to Maxwell's, your girl May Bell was gone. The Clements went on to Taos. Maxwell told me when he last seen May she was well. But she took your runnin' away turrible hard. Wal, I went on to Santa Fé, an' sent a letter over to Clement, tellin' about you bein' shot an' that I'd left you in a hospital here. I never got no answer. We wintered at Santa Fé, an' didn't get over to Taos. Before we pulled out in the spring, though, I heard the Clements had gone to California."

"Is—that all?" queried Clint, in the grip of crushed hopes, which until that moment he had not realized.

"All about your gurl, an' I reckon it's good news. May Bell took your leavin' hard. She'll be waitin' for you out there some place."

"But—California!"

"It was a damn good idea for Clement to take her out to the Coast. Leastways till this war is over. You ought to be glad, Buff. Why, the Old Trail is a red road through hell!"

"I hadn't thought of that. . . . Did that Murdock go to California?"

"No. He's a gambler, Buff, if nothin' worse. He

176

was at Santa Fé for a while. Thick with Jim Black-stone an' his outfit. Blackstone 'peared to have a heap of money to drink an' gamble with. An' you can bet no rich dad left it to him. I heard a lot of rumors about him. Murdock is in bad company."

"That's a relief," replied Clint, with a forced laugh. "I was horrible jealous of him."

"Wal, you're a darn fool. That little gurl, accordin' to Maxwell, was so crazy in love with you that she couldn't stand one little word of your disapproval."

"Did Maxwell—say that?" asked Clint, inwardly quaking.

"He sure did. I was at the ranch two days, an' whenever I seen him all he could talk about was you an' May. Sort of hipped on it, I reckon. . . . By the way, Buff, Maxwell is in financial straits an' wants to sell out. But everybody on the frontier is at odds an' ends. An' it's bound to grow wuss before it can get better."

"Anderson told me you had some wounded men."

"Yes, there's nine, not countin' me. We was jumped three times comin' across. The last time at Point of Rocks, where I got my head in front of an ounce chunk of lead from a muzzle-loader. An inch lower would have put your uncle Jim in the Happy Huntin'-grounds. Wal, we'd have got licked there if it hadn't been for our six-pounder. Ben Davis took the cannon after I was down. An' two shots sent them Comanches runnin' like skeered jack rabbits. We had to leave some wagons, which was individual loss to the freight-ers who owned them."

"Point of Rocks? Uncle, that's an unlucky camp for us," observed Clint, his memory active.

"Wal, I should smile. Buff, every time Point of Rocks peeps at me over the horizon I get the creeps. . . . As if somethin' bad was goin' to happen to me there! This was the second time."

"Beware of a third, uncle."

"Ahuh. I've had that hunch myself. Wal, we can't help fate, any more than our queer feelin's. . . . Buff,

177

I put your money in the bank here. Did anyone notify you?"

"Yes, an' I've paid all my debts. Got about two thousand left."

"Wal, you leave it there, an' add to it every dollar you get."

"I'm not much of a spender. When are you loadin' again, uncle."

"Right away. Have a big contract. I'll load all the wagons I fetched in an' fifty-odd more. We'll have to put up with some tenderfoot drivers. But my luck holds. There's an army train here, loadin' for Fort Larned. We'll travel together."

"I'm wonderin' if you could use an old overland freighter," drawled Clint, his gaze fixed strangely on the West.

"Haw! Haw! Wal, I might. . . . Buff, get your pack an' guns, an' come out to camp. You want to get some tan before we hit the Injun country. You might get took for a albino."

With a caravan of one hundred and sixty-nine men, not including a troop of soldiers with a supply train, Jim Couch had little to fear from savages on that westward trip.

Seven bands of Indians, some of them large, watched this long caravan pass their lookout points, with never a hostile move. Their silent watchfulness, however, was ominous. Woe betide a small caravan!

Clint Belmet dropped into his old groove, and in a month of driving, hitching up, and chopping wood he was brown and hard again. Not even Couch, however, would have guessed the ever growing state of his suspense and hopefulness. A thousand times while driving, with eyes on the beckoning purple horizon and at night when the coyotes mourned he went over in mind what Couch and Maxwell had said about May Bell.

He could never persuade himself that they were right. But had he been hasty, ruthless, over-jealous,

178

too much, alas! of a wild buffalo-hunter? Had he been unjust to May Bell? Had he done the wrong thing instead of what he had imagined was the best? His doubts increased. Yet in his heart still rankled memory of the scornful flouting she had given him in Maxwell's store, and later, and more bitter, the golden sunset hour when he had discovered her with Lee Murdock. If he could only have had more time! If he had only been wise and self-restrained! Useless as regrets were, they multiplied with the miles. But his hope kindled and burned to a steady fire.

It was November when Couch's caravan arrived at Santa Fé, and snow was falling. The freighters unloaded and went into camp for the winter.

Clint abandoned the idea cherished all during the long trip out—that he would go to Maxwell's Ranch the first opportunity which afforded—for the reason that the colonel was absent in the East. Gold had been discovered on his ranch and rumor had it he was trying to sell out or raise capital.

Next day Clint rode to town to make inquiry about the Clements. He was patient and persistent. At last he was directed to interview a trader from Taos who had recently arrived in Santa Fé. This man's name was Wright.

"I shore did know Hall Clement," he replied, instantly, at Clint's first query. "Fine Texan, and they don't make any better. . . . I'm damn sorry, Belmet, to have to tell you I helped bury him."

"He's dead!" exclaimed Clint.

"Yes. Shot by a gambler named Murdock."

"Murdock! Lee Murdock?" flashed Clint, now with a gasp.

"Never heard his first name. But he was a Texan and knew the Clements. Was sweet on their adopted daughter. . . . I didn't hear much, but what I did was to the point. Hall Clement went to California last year, leavin' his wife an' daughter at Taos. The girl had some reason for not wantin' to go to California. Well, durin' Clement's absence this Murdock nagged the girl

179

till she was ill. When Clement came back he met Murdock an' beat him severely. Later they met in Turner's saloon an' Murdock killed Clement. This Murdock is a dead shot, they say. . . . That was in the summer. In August Mrs. Clement an' the girl left Taos to come here, where they joined a caravan bound for Kansas City."

"*August!* . . . What caravan? Who was the train boss?"

"Bill Kelly, I'm sure. He left Taos in July—had some of my goods. An' I didn't hear of any other caravan leavin' around that time."

"Oh! We missed that train!" cried Clint, in sickening realization. "We took the Dry Trail—the short cut Uncle Jim knows so well. Kelly was on the old road."

Clint rushed out of the hotel and furiously rode his horse back to camp. He had missed May Bell by a few days, for he remembered Couch saying, when they arrived at the fork of the trail, that the tracks of Kelly's caravan were fairly fresh. The freighters took account of such things.

The shock and disappointment seemed unbearable to Clint until it occurred to him that at least May Bell had escaped the importunities of Murdock. There was a nucleus of comfort in this. Kelly had a large caravan and could stand off all save a concerted attack of several tribes. May Bell would most assuredly be safe in Kansas City. It occurred to Clint that she might have received word of his injury and had taken the first caravan east. If that were true! His heart swelled. It would mean she did love him, in spite of everything. The hope would not down.

"If it's so she'll stay there this winter an' wait till I get back next summer," soliloquized Clint, persuading himself that it was not altogether unlikely. "But, oh, the long winter for me—the wait! . . . An' that drive in the spring!"

How could he pass the time—the endless hours of waiting, with nothing to do but remember and yearn, when he could not be certain of anything?

180

Suddenly thought of Murdock flashed across him, and with it the stirring recollection of the two insulting slaps Murdock had given him, and the blow he had returned. Swift on that followed recollection of the several reports about this Murdock, and lastly what the trader Wright had added to them. Clint could imagine just about how Murdock, having failed by permission to win May, had harassed the girl. He would not stop at anything to gain his ends, whether it was marriage or something else. Hall Clement did not beat Murdock for nothing.

"I'll kill Murdock," muttered Clint, suddenly. And then there came a regurgitation of the strange cold ferocity Clint had felt the moment before he struck Murdock.

The deadly resolve furnished Clint food for reflection. He must prepare himself for the inevitable meeting with this Texan; and to that end he began to practice with his revolver. He was already the best pistol-shot among Couch's freighters. With the rifle he was not above the average, but he had the quick eye, the sensitive finger, the knack that made for accuracy. While the weather stayed good Clint went hunting, more with the intent to practice with his revolver than to kill game. Later he would plod out in the snow—into the cottonwood grove—and shoot at targets.

He bought all the ammunition in the store at Santa Fé, and altogether it cost several hundred dollars. The freighters ceased teasing him about this game he was playing. Couch looked serious, shook his shaggy head, but said nothing. When Clint could hit a small tin can every shot at fifty feet he began to think he was getting somewhere. When he could throw one up into the air, and put a bullet through it, three times out of five, he gained confidence in himself.

With this practice there was also included the swiftness of the draw. Kit Carson, who had killed more Indians and men than any other frontiersman of that period, once gave Clint a talk on shooting which he would put to infinite test. So Clint Belmet spent the daylight hours of that winter in keeping a fire burning, cooking, and chopping wood, reading and studying, and lastly perfecting himself in the use of a revolver. Long before spring came he hoped Murdock would return to Santa Fé. But the gambler was working the army camps.

The winter dragged along and spring came late, which fact did not operate cheerfully on the dispositions of the freighters. Some seasons they were able to make two trips each way, but this was exceptional.

Couch did not get started until after the first of June; however, he had command of two hundred and sixty-three wagons, his largest caravan, and that afforded everyone some consolation and lessened the risk.

On the trip across, which was number thirty-eight for Jim Couch, the caravan was circled by four different bands of Indians, the first Kiowas, and the last Pawnees. Couch fired his cannon upon two occasions, causing no casualties, but a decided rout. "Haw! Haw! Run, you red devils!" he would yell, and once he said: "All the same, I'm glad none of them was Comanches. Those varmints have rid up on me more than once— too quick to get the cannon in action."

Clint arrived in Kansas City late in August, happy at last in the certainty of getting track of May Bell. He made so sure of this that he bought a new suit, shoes, hat, shirt, and tie, and arrayed himself as he had never before in his life. In fact, he passed right by Couch and Anderson, who did not give him even a second glance. This pleased Clint exceedingly. He began to have hopes of a decided impression upon May. Yet his old backwardness and doubt assailed him. He resolved, however, if—or when he found her, that if she would only forgive him he would never offend her again, so long as he lived.

At once he got upon the trail of May Bell and Mrs. Clement. They had been at the Hotel Western in the late fall of last year, and upon their return from Texas, where they had traveled by boat, they had spent some

182

weeks in Kansas City. He was informed that Mrs. Clement had relatives there. But Clint's persistent search proved fruitless. It set him, however, upon another track. Mrs. Clement and May had gone by stage to Council Grove.

This upset Clint. His hopes were dashed, and in their place consternation and misgivings began to beset him.

Clint knew something about the stage lines, though he had never actually traveled on one of them. There had been a long route from Fort Union to Santa Fé, and another from Fort Larned to Fort Lyon, three hundred and ten miles, and the same mules had made the whole trip. This line had been discontinued of late, and Clint remembered it only because he had known a man named Clegg at Fort Larned. He had been a stage-coach driver and he told Clint about the trip. "My passengers had to sleep in the coach an' cook their own meals. Shore was tough on them. But when they got to kickin' too blame hard I jest yelled, 'Injuns!' an' thet quieted them down."

The stage line to Council Grove, one hundred and fifty miles, was running intermittently. Clint engaged passage upon the first stage west, a procedure which did not meet with the approval of Jim Couch. Then he had to wait tedious days. It happened, however, that an east-bound stage came in with a driver who had spent several days in Council Grove, owing to a disabled wagon. This man was intelligent and obliging, and he informed Clint that he had met and talked to every person in Council Grove. Mrs. Clement and May Bell were certainly not there. Therefore Clint gave up his plan. It would not be long until Couch's caravan passed Council Grove again, when Clint could inquire for himself.

Meanwhile he resumed his search in Kansas City. At the post office he scraped acquaintance with a clerk who remembered May Bell.

"Reckon I do," he avowed. "She asked for mail here a year ago, about, an' then lately she came sev-

183

eral times. She shore wanted a letter bad. She had great big beautiful eyes like dark velvet. I got so I hated to run over the letters, pretendin' to look for one when I knew it wasn't there. She had a pale face, with sad lips. They were red as cherries, though. I reckon she was about eighteen or nineteen years old."

Clint thanked the loquacious clerk and left the post office. May Bell had recently been in Kansas City, hoping for a letter from him, and she had gone. No doubt about that! But where? It seemed reasonable she would not turn right around and start on the overland trip again. Still Clint feared she had done exactly that. There had been a July caravan and also one in early August, both large and well armed. The only information Aull & Company could give him was that the last caravan, which hauled government supplies for them, had five or six families who had gone along for protection. In fact, all emigrants were persuaded to join either the freight or army caravans.

Clint's next trip overland was the longest he had ever driven. Toward the end of it he would have welcomed a brush with Indians, and for once Point of Rocks failed to cause him apprehension, and he drove through Apache Pass in grim defiance.

Along the main road from Fort Union, just below its juncture with the cut-off called the Dry Trail, Clint saw a short wagon-trail, scarcely half a mile long, working down to the eastward. Such a sight was not unusual, except that in these latter months of the war a short caravan was seldom or never seen.

At camp that night Clint approached Couch with a query: "Uncle, did you see that caravan goin' east on the Dry Trail, about noon today?"

"I shore did, Buff, an' whoever its boss was I shore cussed him proper," replied Couch, with fire in his eye. "Thirty-eight wagons! I counted 'em. Wal, they're plumb ravin' crazy."

Days had to pass, however, before any information about this caravan would reach them.

Upon Couch's arrival at Santa Fé the whole populace, from Aull's agent to the Mexican sheepherder, turned out to welcome a caravan that had been reported mostly all massacred. Such rumor traveled like fire in prairie grass, often by mysterious channels. Seldom, however, as in this case, were there no grounds whatever for a reported attack by Indians. The freighters on the trail and the residents stationed along the line were inclined to take seriously any news at all that was bad. They were skeptical about the good.

"An' where'n hell was we supposed to have been scalped?" demanded Couch, in supreme disgust.

"Point of Rocks," replied Buell. "The greaser didn't talk English very well, but I got that place, positive."

"Point of Rocks? Wal, I'll be damned! They shore got my Jonah. What greaser fetched that report?"

"He rode in here over two weeks ago."

"Alone?"

"No. There were other Mexicans an' several white men in the party. Travelin' light with pack mules."

"Ahuh! Where'd this news about us come from?"

"Fort Union."

"Wal, it was shore tolerable exaggerated," replied Couch, gruffly. "We're here an' we haven't lost a scalp or a sack of beans. . . . Buell, I reckon I don't like that kind of humor. It might be honest, but then again it mightn't."

"Jim, you an' Belmet come in the office," returned Buell, with sober significance. And presently when the three of them were alone he went on: "I had the same sort of hunch. But now you're here all right, I know damn well it smells fishy."

"How do you know?" demanded Couch.

"Wal, when the news got circulated round, Mrs. Clement an' her daughter come rushin' in here——"

"Are they here?" interrupted Clint, with a violent start.

"They've gone."

"Gone!"

"Yes."

"With that little caravan we seen out on the Dry

Trail? Must have left here about ten-eleven days ago."

"Eleven? That's correct. They left on October twenty-third."

"Heavens! Was they tacklin' the trip east that late?"

"No. Fort Larned, where what was left of your caravan was supposed to be."

"Wal! This is somethin' strange."

"It begins to look that way to me, Couch," returned Buell, anxiously, with a worried look. "I tried to persuade Mrs. Clement not to leave. She didn't want to go. But the daughter was terribly upset. Said she would go alone! . . . An' she offered a thousand dollars to anyone who'd take her to Fort Larned. There were some freighters waitin' for a chance to roll out, instead of winterin' here. Then Jim Blackstone was here with his outfit. Ten or a dozen wagons. He took up thet offer of a thousand dollars, an' said he'd be train boss. Mrs. Clement wouldn't let her daughter go alone. They'd practically just got here. Came with Simpson's caravan, thet went on to Taos an' Vegas. So they loaded up thet very day an' left."

"Jim Blackstone! Haven't I heard some talk about him an' his outfit?"

"He's not a freighter, thet's shore."

"Wal, what is he?"

"Been 'most everythin'. Buys some pelts now, tradin' whisky to the Utes. He's reported to be thick with Kiowas, too."

"How many freighters, did you say?"

"Must have been around thirty. Some blamed good men, Couch . . . Davis an' Hennesy, an' Black, an' Tode Williams, all freighters."

"Wal, I know Tode. I reckon he'd be a match for Blackstone any day."

"Buell, has Lee Murdock been here this summer?" blurted out Clint, finding his voice.

"Yes, on an' off. Not since he shot a gambler named Weedon. Murdock hangs out at Fort Larned."

"He'll be there now?"

"Most likely. Larned's a lively place in winter, an' all the gamblers aim to be there, especially for early

186

spring, when the trappers an' hunters come down out of the hills."

Clint turned to Couch. "Uncle, I'm goin' to Fort Larned."

"What! But, Buff, that's out of the question! It's a sure bet no more freighters, or anybody, will start this late."

"I'll go alone."

"Now see here, Buff, you——"

"I'm goin'. I don't care if you've been my guardian. I'm of age. I've got to go. . . . I'll ride at night an' hide durin' the day."

"Wal, if the snow holds off, you might make it," replied Couch, resignedly.

"I'll make it, snow or no snow."

"Buff, you could miss the trail at night, if it snowed. I couldn't keep to it myself."

"I'll go light an' fast. I'll beat the snow," replied Clint, with a steely ring in his voice.

Sunset found him leaving Santa Fé on a big raw-boned horse, with blankets and small pack tied behind. He had dispensed with a pack-horse. He could live on meat and parched corn and dried fruits. He carried two canteens, a Colt's rifle and two revolvers.

Clint had only one thought and that was unwavering—to find May Bell. He had, at last, assurance of her whereabouts, her love, her fidelity, her anguish, and he would find her or die in the attempt.

The night soon encompassed him, cold, starry, and silent. The broad trail was as easy for his keen eyes as if the sun were shining. He ran little risk of encountering Indians after dark. On the soft ground, pulverized by countless wheels and hoofs, his horse made no sound. And with his passion released and augmented by the encouragement of May Bell's faithfulness, with all his senses alert, the hours were nothing. He knew the water holes and towards morning he stopped at one and let the horse drink sparingly. At dawn he halted in a clump of cedars, unpacked and unsaddled the animal and tied him on a long halter where grass was thick. Then, without fire, he ate his meager meal, after which he hid in a thicket and went to sleep.

The sun was westered far when he awoke. He ate and drank again, then crept out of the thicket. The horse had fared well. Clint crawled to a vantagepoint, and swept the country to the fore along the trail. Buffalo, antelope, deer, rabbits, wolves, wild horses crossed his roving sight, but no Indians. He had to fight the temptation to ride out and risk the last hour of daylight, but he resisted it. He had made his plan and would adhere to it. The farther he traveled along this trail the greater must be his caution. The Dry Trail, so seldom traveled late in the summer, on account of the drought, would be less risky. In the still cold twilight he rode out.

16

Some time during the fourth night Clint, coming into the Dry Trail, rode upon wheel and hoof tracks that obliterated most of those that had been made by Blackstone's caravan.

But Clint did not know this until daylight, when he could see them plainly. He studied these tracks and pondered deeply over them, but did not risk himself out on the trail after the day broke. This morning he sat up long to puzzle about this unexpected and decidedly favorable circumstance. Another caravan, and of fairly good size, to judge by the tracks, had turned into the Dry Trail, and not many hours behind Blackstone.

The night of that day a crescent moon shone gold over the black ridge. Clint was making fast time. The tireless animal scarcely needed to be kept to a trot. About midnight in a gloomy spot, overshadowed by low bluff on one side, the horse shied violently and snorted in fright. The instant Clint stopped he smelled putrefying flesh. He knew that odor. Dismounting, and peering keenly ahead, he advanced very cautiously.

Scent of burned hides next assailed his nostrils and sent a shudder down his spine. Indians had attacked either Blackstone's caravan or the one following it and had left death and fire in their wake. Soon Clint came upon the charred skeletons of freight wagons and smoking piles of baled hides. Twenty-two freight wagons in a half circle! That told the story. But which caravan? The cold sweat wet Clint's face and chest.

He searched off the road, guided by his sense of smell, and presently stumbled upon a hideous ghastly row of dead savages, so torn by buzzards and coyotes that it was only with difficulty he identified them as Kiowas. They had not been scalped or stripped. He counted twenty-nine bodies, that had evidently been dragged off the road. The freighters had not buried them, which seemed proof of hurry. Dead horses, too, lay about.

Clint could not find a dead white man, nor any evidence of a grave. This encouraged him, though he knew, of course, that if the freighters had time they would bury their dead. He searched everywhere within a reasonable radius.

Then mounting, he rode on, this time putting the horse to alternate lope and trot. By the first streak of gray dawn in the east he calculated that he had covered thirty miles since the midnight halt.

In the gray gloom he went far off the trail, and found a satisfactory covert, where grass was fair, but water lacking. When he lay down his chest seemed weighted and the clouded condition of mind persisted in sleep. That afternoon, after a survey of the open country, wild and lonely and gray, he built a little fire and roasted strips of buffalo meat, which, with salt and a hard biscuit, satisfied his hunger.

Twilight had fallen when he ventured back to the trail, but he could see distinctly. From long habit his eyes swept the open country ahead, then all around and back. And lastly the trail, the look of which caused him to fall abruptly on his knees. He scrutinized the tracks, he crawled ahead, across, back; and then he arose, shaking in every limb under the realization that the second caravan—the one following on Blackstone's tracks—had turned off. Somewhere and at some hour the night preceding, in the dark, Clint had passed by a fork in the trail, where emigrants bound for Texas turned off. That second caravan could absolutely not have done anything else. The fact increased Clint's perplexities and augmented his fears. He was not an expert tracker, but years of watching the road had taught him much. Ten or a dozen wagons, drawn by horses, and a number of mounted men had proceeded toward Fort Larned.

Clint had undisputable proof now that the loss of wagons had been from Blackstone's caravan. Perhaps the second party had never overtaken the first. And dread gnawed like a wolf at Clint's vitals. He dared not go back, even if that would have been of any avail. He could only speculate on what had happened. As he knew travel along the trail and Indian attacks, the chances favored Blackstone's men having fought and driven off the Kiowas, with more or less loss. No doubt they had abandoned the greater number of their wagons, which the Indians had burned. If any dead white people had been left along the trail, they would have been stripped, scalped, and mutilated.

After that point the nights for Clint were endless and torturing. The snow caught him, squall after squall, but he beat the winter into Fort Larned.

Sunrise of the last day overtook him less than ten miles from the fort, and he rode on in, hungry, weary, haggard, hard, and grim, with infinite respect for the great horse that had carried him through.

Clint rode to Aull's corral, and gave a Mexican lad a dollar to care for his horse. Then he hurried into the store, where he was well known. Beckett, the agent, threw up his hands.

"Buff Belmet! . . . O Lord!—Jim Couch has got it at last!"

"No. I've come alone from Santa Fé," replied Clint. *"Alone!"*

Customers and clerks came at Beckett's call.

"Yes. I rode at night—slept by day," went on Clint, hurriedly.

"You wasn't with Blackstone? He sure never told it, if you was."

"No. I left Santa Fé ten days an' more after Blackstone. I was on his trail. On the Dry Trail I found where another caravan had come in. You see, I rode in on the short cut after night an' never found out about the second caravan until twenty-four hours later. Then I rode on, an' came to burned wagons an' hides an' dead Indians—Kiowas. Twenty-nine of them! . . . Again at night I passed by where the second caravan turned off on the Texas trail."

"Reckon Blackstone never had any idea there was a caravan close behind him. He sure never reported it if he did. . . . An' why in hell was you trailin' after them alone?"

His query strangled the voice in Clint's throat. If all had been well with Mrs. Clement and May Bell— if they had been brought safely on to the fort—this agent would not have been perplexed by Clint's arrival.

"I was—on Blackstone's trail," broke out Clint, hoarsely. "My—sweetheart—May Bell an' her—an' Mrs. Clement—were in that caravan."

"My God! Man, you must be mistaken!" ejaculated Beckett.

"No!" cried Clint, passionately.

"But they didn't come! They're not here. . . . An' Blackstone never said one word about havin' women with him. This is damn strange, Buff. Come with me to the colonel."

"Not yet. Is this Jim Blackstone here at Larned?"

"You bet he is. With his outfit goin' to stay all winter."

"An' Murdock—Lee Murdock?"

"Sure. He was in here half an hour ago."

"Where'll I find them?"

"Ten to one it'll be at Horner's gamblin'. Or loafin' at the hotel, waitin' for dinner. But say, Buff——"

191

Clint stalked out, leaving his rifle where he had leaned it inside the door. The weariness from the long ride, the anxieties, fears, and hopes, the succession of shocks burned into ashes in the tremendous passion which consumed Clint. Yet his mind reverted to the mood inculcated by those winter months in camp at Santa Fé, where he had trained himself for the meeting with Murdock that was now at hand.

Across the square from Aulls' store stood Horner's saloon, a red adobe structure, crumbling and old, with rafters exposed. The letters of a once white sign were half obliterated.

Clint split the double door and strode in. He had been in Horner's many a time. The usual loungers at the bar, the stoical Indians standing like statues, the gamblers at the tables—Clint took these in with one sweeping flash.

His appearance must have been striking, for it seemed the silence began at the head of the bar and communicated itself like a wave to the end of the long room. A freighter's heavy boots crashed down from the stove.

"Buff Belmet!" he shouted.

Ordinarily Clint was a figure to attract attention, but now, white with dust, unwashed and unkempt, black and forbidding of face, he might well have arrested the attention of the wildest of frontier saloons.

"I'm lookin' for Jim Blackstone an' Lee Murdock," he announced in a loud voice.

His challenging speech filled the room, except for a whisper here and shuffle of foot there, and a nervous cough. Only one possible construction could be put upon Clint's presence and his trenchant announcement.

Many faces turned toward a table close to the stove, around which four men sat and three stood. The game of cards had been interrupted. Slowly Clint stepped toward these men, guided by the turning of faces in that direction. Then he espied Murdock, sitting, with restless hands manipulating cards, clean-shaven, handsome face growing set and pale eyes shining. He whispered something, evidently to the man next him, a bearded giant in a buckskin shirt. This individual moved only his eyes. Behind this particular table, in a line with Clint, all the loungers and gangsters stealthily slipped to either side. The reason was manifest, as was the stiffening of Murdock and Blackstone in their chairs.

"I'm Blackstone. What you want?" replied the giant, slow and cool.

"Where are the two women who hired you to drive them to Fort Larned?" demanded Clint, stepping so that he had all the seven men directly in front of him.

"Reckon they were killed or carried off by the Kiowas."

Clint read falsehood in the man's steady, somber eyes. It only confirmed his dreadful suspicious. But few men could lie unbetrayingly in the face of death.

"Blackstone, there's a lie about you somewhere. Why didn't you report the loss of Mrs. Clement an'— Miss May Bell, who paid you a thousand dollars to bring her to Larned?"

"Wal, Belmet, when a man fails bad he hates to give himself away," returned Blackstone, deprecatingly. Under his beard the tan had begun to pale. His eyes quivered with the watchfulness of a man used to crises on the frontier.

"Ahuh! Why didn't you report to headquarters here that another caravan, bound for Texas, caught up with you on the Dry Trail?" queried Clint, piercingly. This was a random shot on Clint's part, but it struck home.

"Who the hell are you to bullyrag me?" shouted Blackstone, suddenly flaring with passion.

"Boss," interposed one of the standing men, low and quick, "he's Jim Couch's driver an' bad medicine."

"That girl was engaged to me," hissed Clint. "An' you haven't got a hell of a long time to tell me where she is."

"So help me Gawd, man, I can't tell you!" rejoined Blackstone, hoarsely, and there might have been truth in that. "The Kiowas jumped us. We had to fight an' run, leavin' most of the outfit an' men behind."

"Blackstone, you're known to be thick with Kiowas—an' you, Lee Murdock—you're known to have hounded May Bell from one place to another."

On the frontier of this day, very much less than that accusation was a gauntlet thrown in the face of men. When Blackstone lurched for his gun Clint's had leaped out of his hand. But the third man of the three standing, who must have unobtrusively drawn his weapon, discharged the first shot, which knocked Clint down.

He raised himself on his left hand, and fired. He downed the man in front of the one who had shot first, and as he staggered to fall over the table Clint's second bullet brought a yell of agony from the coward who had used his comrade for a buffer.

Then Blackstone's gun boomed, and Murdock leaped up, firing rapidly. Clint felt the hot tearing of lead. But his quick aim was true. Murdock threw up his gun and fell backward. Blackstone slid out of his chair, shooting over the table. But he had a large body, and Clint's second shot at him, under the table, found its mark. Blackstone slumped down.

Then, to Clint's deadening ears the rush and yell of excited men grew quiet, and in his dim eyes the fallen men faded, the long room blurred, and grew black.

Before Clint opened his eyes he heard the crackling of a wood fire and he smelled alcohol or some other strong medicine. Then he recalled the fight and at the same instant grew conscious of pain. It took effort to lift his heavy eyelids.

A cheerful blaze leaped in an open stone fireplace. The room was the single one of an adobe cabin, with one window and two doors, the smaller of which led into a kitchen, where some man was bustling about, whistling. The walls of this cabin were covered with

194

pelts, hanging in bundles, and the earth floor bore a number of buffalo robes, the fur side up. Apparently the quarters belonged to a trapper.

It hurt Clint to move his arm even slightly. One arm appeared stiff and useless, but the other was free. His body was like a log.

The whistling man entered, no other than Dick Curtis, the long-haired, buckskinned hunter who had taken Clint on his first buffalo hunt.

"Howdy, Dick!" said Clint, weakly.

"You son-of-a-gun!" ejaculated Curtis, in glad eagerness. "Buff, you've been ravin' like a scalped Chinaman."

"Have I? What about?"

"Ohell! About your girl thet was captured by redskins. Buff, I've had half a dozen girls stolen from me. They were squaws. It's nothin' to go crazy over. Are you comin' to your senses?"

"I hope so, Dick. . . . How am I?"

"Fair to middlin' for a *hombre* who was riddled with lead. Buff, old Doc Culbertson said the Lord must be savin' you for Injun arrows because bullets couldn't kill you."

"I stopped a lot—then?"

"Hellno! Most of them bullets went clear on through, which was lucky. But the one they bounced off your head knocked you silly. Funny how thet bullet hit thet old scar on your head."

"Am I goin' to pull through?"

"Nobody 'cept me an' Doc ever had any idee you would. It was a close shave, Buff. Three weeks ago the fever left you. And then you began to mend, 'cept your ravin'. I'm darn glad. It sort of gave me the willies to listen to you at night. I never in my life seen a man so crazy about a girl. . . . Buff, no one would ever suspect it was in you."

"Maybe I don't know it myself. Where am I, Dick?"

"In my cabin, nice an' cozy for the winter. It's December, somewheres near Christmas or New Year's I forget which. My pards an' me got run out of the hills.

I been gone near two years, Buff. But we saved our ketch. . . . Are you hungry, Buff?"

"I don't feel it if I am."

"Wal, I have been feedin' you best I can. Shore is surprising what little a fellar lives on when he has to. Wal, I reckon you'd like to know what you did to Blackstone's outfit?"

"I'm not over-keen about it," returned Clint.

"Wal, by gosh! you're goin' to hear, anyhow. Buff, we was all wonderin' one night—talkin' thet fight over —how in the hell you ever got to handle a gun like you do. An' there was a freighter here who wintered with Couch over at Santa Fé. An' he told us. You bought all the ammunition in the town. Said you could throw tin cans up an' plug them. Said he'd seen you do it!"

"Reckon I did practice some."

"Haw! Haw! Lucky you did. . . . I shore hated missing thet fight. But my pard, Sandy McClellan, seen it, an' he told me. Buff, there's been a lot bloodier fights than thet. I seen one at Bent's Fort. Two ag'in' nine, an' by gosh! thet was lively. Bullets like bees hummin'."

Clint's memory, probed and stimulated in this way, urged him to sharp yet shrinking curiosity, which he seemed reluctant to voice.

"Sandy seen your fight an' he said it was shore nifty," went on Curtis, in satisfaction, as he straddled a bench and sat down. "When you accused Blackstone of bein' thick with the Kiowas an' Murdock of houndin' your girl, everybody knowed thet you was tellin' them to draw. But McGill had drawed from behind Red Hawkins an' floored you with a bullet. We figgered thet one took you in the shoulder. Wal, from the floor you bored Red, an' when he sunk, you took McGill same place—an' if you want to know thet was right over the top vest pocket on the left side. Meanwhile Murdock leaped up with his gun out, an' Blackstone was shootin' with his hand restin' on the table. Your shot at Murdock was true, Buff, same as the others, but your bullet hit his gun an' glanced up,

196

takin' Murdock on the cheek bone, an' believe me, it left a groove as deep as the Old Trail. Thet put Murdock out, an' Blackstone, the yellow sucker, ducked under the table. Your two shots laid him out, but the bullets went through the board legs of thet table an' didn't do Blackstone much damage. He was around next day."

"How about—Murdock?" asked Clint, with a queer thrill that was quivering pain.

"Close shave there. The bullet took the top of his cheek bone. He was up in a week, but will be disfigured for life. Shore you'll know *him* when you see him again."

"Did they leave Larned?"

"Did they? Haw! Haw! They was told perlite to get out, an' they got. Blackstone, an' fifteen of his outfit, an' Murdock. I never seen a sorer bunch of *hombres*. Blackstone went to the colonel, an' from what I'm told he had to listen to some pert questions which he couldn't answer. They packed an' went south. Thet was three weeks or so ago. Naturally, we all figgered a lot, an' tried to put two an' two together. Blackstone had a bad name, but nobody knew anythin' ag'in' him till you accused him of bein' thick with the Kiowas. Murdock was just a dandy gambler, keen about women, white or red, an' some hasty with his gun. But Blackstone might be one of these caravan bandits thet have developed durin' the war. Wal, anyway, last week Billy Weed, a trapper, came by a Kiowa village over on the Purgatory an' he swears he seen Blackstone there. An' he shore seen other white men. Billy was snoopin' from top of a ridge an' not takin' any chances. Billy has been scout an' plainsman. He's reliable. So whatever Blackstone an' his bunch figgered on the frontier before this caravan job from Santa Fé, they are now outlaws."

"Has any word ever come in about thet Texas caravan?" asked Clint.

"Nary a word. But thet's to be expected. No redskin is goin' to fetch us word, you can bet on thet."

"Aw—an' what's the opinion about Mrs. Clement an' May Bell?" asked Clint, struggling to be coherent. "They left Santa Fé with Blackstone. Buell an' others told me they saw them leave."

"Wal, it ain't hard to take Blackstone's word fer what happened," replied Curtis, thoughtfully. "Shore he's a liar, an' we don't know how low down. But you seen the burned wagons—the dead Kiowas. An' we know Blackstone rode in here with crippled men."

"Dick—you don't get the point. Somebody drove the Kiowas off. They'd never leave their dead. Blackstone sure didn't do the drivin'. He ran for his life. . . . I've a hunch that second caravan came up in time to drive the Kiowas off, perhaps while they were firin' the wagons, or even while the twenty-two freighters from Santa Fé were fightin'. . . . If Blackstone *is* in with the Kiowas, you can gamble he led that caravan into an ambush. An' the second caravan did the fightin'."

"Buff, there's shore a heap in what you say. No one else 'pears to have thought it out like thet. . . . Where are the twenty-two freighters who didn't come in with Blackstone?"

"Dead an' buried or else gone on with the second caravan. Because, Dick, it was a white man who ordered the dead Kiowas dragged back out of sight from the trail. Uncle Jim always did that. He'd stop the train to have a carcass moved out of sight, or buried if he had time."

"Ahuh! You ain't bad at figgerin', Buff. . . . An' it's your hunch there's a chance thet Mrs. Clement an' your sweetheart got away with the Texas caravan?"

"I—I wouldn't call it a hunch—only a hope."

"But such a damn slim one, Buff. You know this here frontier. You better give up right now, else you'll only suffer an' live in hopes, an' die in despair when you *do* find out. Reckon thet'll be next summer. Somebody will give us a line on thet second caravan."

In due time Clint recovered and divided the long hours between the hotel, Aull's store, and Curtis' cabin. Life was slow in winter, except for the gambling fraternity. Clint at times felt the urge to drink and gamble, solely to put his mind off its haunted track. He played checkers, sat beside a stove or before the open fire, read and reread all the reading matter available, and walked out in the open when weather permitted. As winter waned he grew strong again, and heavier than he had ever been. He had no work, not even wood to chop. Curtis had bought firewood already cut. Nevertheless, the days went by tediously in the passing, yet swiftly in retrospect.

In early April the Indians and trappers and hunters began to come down out of the hills with their pelts to trade and sell. Clint obtained credit for the money he had banked at Kansas City, and he bought and traded for a wagonload of very choice furs, which, if he ever got them to a city, would earn quadruple what they had cost.

From that time on the days were not so unbearable, and they gradually grew easier. By May the weather was pleasant, spring was at hand, and soon the first caravan would arrive from the west. Clint knew whose that would be.

Jim Couch was indeed the first, but he did not arrive until June. It so happened that the loquacious Dick Curtis, who had always regarded Clint as his protégé, got to Jim Couch before Clint.

Nevertheless, Clint had to repeat his version of his long lonely ride and the fight in Horner's saloon. The old caravan leader appeared to take it all as a matter of course. Upon meeting Clint, he had hugged him like a grizzly bear, but he wasted no words of praise, as was his wont before Clint had become a man.

"Wal, it's hard to believe any white man would lead his fellow-men into an ambush for the redskins to murder," he said. "Blackstone sure was a hard nut. But let's give him the benefit of a doubt. We'll find out soon enough."

Couch stayed at Fort Larned for two days, adding fifty-odd wagons of pelts to a caravan that was already large. Dr. Culbertson, the army physician at the fort, advised Couch to persuade Clint to rest a few more months. One of Clint's lungs had been nicked by a bullet. The wound had healed, yet it might be wise to give it more time. Clint accepted this advice without any comment. It suited him to remain at Fort Larned until Couch's return trip in October. Clint wanted to interview freighters and soldiers, even Indians, who arrived at Fort Larned from the south and west.

Couch had noted the remains of the burned wagons on the Dry Trail, and the skeletons of horses, but there was nothing to show him that Indians had been killed in this fight. The Kiowas had come back to carry away their dead.

For once Clint saw Couch ride away without suffering any yearnings to go with him. Thereafter every single day dawned welcome to Clint because it might be one that would bring news of some kind. About the end of June, and high time for the first caravan to arrive from the east, a company of soldiers who had been down on the Pecos River arrived at Fort Larned. About a hundred miles south of the Dry Trail they had come upon evidence of the massacre of a medium-sized caravan. Only the iron rims of the wagon wheels remained, with black piles of embers. Thirty ghastly skeletons of what had been white men lay scattered about, some of the bones dismembered by the jackals of the plains. There was nothing to prove the exact time of this massacre, but Captain King's old plainsman said it had been less than a year before, because he had been over that trail with soldiers from Fort Union.

Clint's last tenacious hope died. Bitter as gall—yet a relief! He believed that had been the caravan the movements of which had been of such vital importance to him. The frontier had only taken its toll of two more women. Clint could count hundreds he had known of, and these not rumors. His mother had been the first in his experience. How long ago! He was now a man. The last was May Bell. Mother and sweetheart! May and Mrs. Clement were no better than the many other brave pioneer women who had found lonely graves on the prairie. The difference was to Clint.

Shortly after these soldiers from New Mexico left the fort the first eastern caravan straggled in. It did not take an experienced eye like Clint's more than one glance to see what that caravan had encountered. The feathered shaft of an arrow, imbedded in a wagon, sent a fiery thrill down Clint's spine. And that was the first wagon to roll in. Clint looked no more, but repaired to the store to wait for Eastern newspapers.

Presently Dick Curtis came along with a Kansas City *Daily Times* and a St. Louis *Globe Democrat*.

"Come on home, pard," said Dick, gaily. " 'Cause if we don't go we'll be drunk *pronto*. Papers full of war news. The rebels are licked, an' you bet thet'll go hard with some of the *hombres* here."

Clint did not require a second invitation. Possessing himself of one of the journals, he read as he walked along. Curtis, who deciphered with difficulty, but was proud to show his education, kept reading aloud. Once back in their cabin, they became absorbed in news two months old.

"My Gawd! Buff, the war must be over!" ejaculated Dick for the tenth time.

"You should say, 'Thank God!' " retorted Clint. "An' shut up, will you? I can read."

It took hours, but these two frontiersmen read every word in both papers. Clint, profoundly stirred by the news of the approaching end of the war that had practically ruined the South and broken the North, maintained silence, as was usual with him when deeply roused. Curtis, however, had to talk, and seeing he could make no impression on Clint he went out.

Clint heard some one ask Curtis:

"Say, does Clint Belmet stay here?"

"Sure. But no one knows him by that handle. His name is Buff. He's inside."

This visitor approached and knocked at the open

201

door. Clint rose and guardedly stepped into view. He did not risk chances with strangers. Outside stood a sturdy freighter, ruddy of face and red of beard, with frank blue eyes which took quick stock of Clint.

"Howdy! I'm Clint Belmet. What do you want me for?"

"Glad to meet you, Belmet," replied the freighter. "I've fetched a letter for you. The clerk in the P. O. give it to me. An' he said if I didn't find you on the way out to leave it with Buell at Santa Fé. I'm darned glad I can get rid of it. We had two brushes with Injuns on the drive out, an' I worried like hell wonderin' what'd become of the letter if I got shot."

"Thanks—stranger," said Clint, huskily, stretching out a big hand that shook. A letter for him!

"My name's Paul Davis. I used to drive for Jim Waters. . . . There you are."

He unwrapped soiled ragged paper from a letter and handed it over to Clint with a flourish. He spoke again cheerily, but Clint did not hear what he said nor see when he departed. A thick dirty envelope lay in his hand. A letter—from whom? The handwriting, level and clear, stared at him from the faded soiled paper. The postmark had been obliterated. Whipping out his knife, he slit the envelope. Inside was another, fitting tightly, and this was clean and white. A faint sweet perfume assailed Clint's nostrils. It gave him a shock so that for a moment he was helpless. But his senses were deceiving him. How often had little things hurt terribly! Quickly he opened the second envelope, bent on killing the illusion that mocked him. A sheaf of small thin pages covered with small writing in ink! Wildly he shuffled them to the last, and there, halfway down the page, in a wavering handwriting that denoted spent strength, he read, "Yours faithfully and always—May."

"So help me God!" groaned Clint, staggering into the cabin. He fell into the rude armchair and stared dazedly at the dead gray ashes in the fireplace. He was shot through and through with terror. This letter was old—months old—years old. And he divined that it would all but mean death to him. He stared in fascinated horror at the outside envelope. It gave mute but disputable evidence of having been across the Great Plains time and time again. Sickening to realize—it might have crossed even with his own caravan! Then, in desperation, he drove himself to read.

MAXWELL'S RANCH

DEAREST CLINT:

Oh, why did you run away without giving me a chance to explain! As soon as I could get up I ran after you—in the dark—calling. They found me lost out there.

This morning before the sun rose you were gone. Gone with the caravan! How could I know you would go without seeing me? I thought you a wild jealous boy. I thought you would come back and beg my forgiveness. But you did not— you did not! And my heart is breaking. We go on to Santa Fé, and it will be months before I can see you. But I will send this letter, which I am assured will follow a month behind you. I pray that you may stay long enough in Kansas City to receive it.

Clint, it's nothing now, but I must explain that you hurt my feelings at Maxwell's store. How could you be so rude, so harsh! Even if you were jealous! That thrilled me—the proof you cared so much. But I am not a flirt. I have loved you since I was ten years old, more and more every day of my life. I never went to bed without praying for you, or awoke at dawn without thinking of you first. You did not know that, but *I* did. . . . Then, yesterday, you roused the very devil in me —a devil I didn't even know I possessed. I would teach you a lesson if I had to demean myself to do it.

I planned to have you see me with Lee Murdock. I was mad to do it, for I had no idea of your mood. I meant to make you utterly miserable and then—when you were sufficiently punished, I would make up to you—even more loving than that last night on the wagon seat. Oh, Clint! . . . But the instant you came toward me I realized my mistake. I had not taken you for a man. And when you said you had come to say good-by, my poor heart froze. And—when you asked Lee Murdock if he had his gun I almost fainted. I realized then. But what could I do? I was paralyzed. You looked so stern—so white and terrible. If I had been able to move I would have fallen at your feet. . . . Then you struck him! He lay there on the grass—bloody and still. I didn't care. *That* didn't hurt me. I think I had a strange hot gladness, something new and wild in me—satisfaction.

I don't know what I did or said. Then you seized me like a savage. . . . Oh, my darling! What I am writing now could never have been written *now,* if you had not done that. You frightened me—you took my strength. I *did* return your first kiss. I *did,* Clint. But it had nothing of the love you awakened in me after that. I will cherish those terrible moments through all my life. I love you—I love you! The childish worship—the girlish affection are gone—burned up in a woman's love. It grows as I write. I can stand this agony if only you know.

Sweetheart, I don't blame you now, but you misjudged me. You listened to our kind friend, Mr. Maxwell, who thinks he understands women. You did not wait to find out the truth. Lieutenant Clayborn was nice and amusing. I liked him, even though he was a little sure of conquest. But, Clint, my heart was yours. It *is* yours. As for Murdock, I had grown to fear him, despise him. I never permitted myself to be alone with him, unless some one was near. These natural actions of a young woman are Greek to you. I have already confided in Mr. Clement, this day, and have besought him to have a care of me while Murdock is with us. The moment you read this letter you will know what I would have told you, last night, with my arms round your neck—if you had not been such a wild buffalo-hunter! But Murdock's insult revealed to me that I was proud of my wild buffalo-hunter. I love this glorious West, though it appalls me. I will be true to it and to you. I will not shirk the labor, the loneliness, the peril. Only I must be with you or I cannot endure it.

Mr. Maxwell told me that you were a born plainsman, like Kit Carson. But for such men there would never be any settling of the West. It is a noble, heroic calling. I would not ask you yet to sacrifice that for me. But I am waiting your plainsman's pleasure.

Clint, at the deep of my heart there is assurance of your love and forgiveness. The boy I knew could never have grown into a man too hard and cruel to love and forget. Yet I have been ill since you left—cold with torture and dread—sick with the longing that was dammed up and which you didn't wait for.

Hurry back to me. Remember every mile of the long, long road, of the waving gray prairie we gazed across together, hand in hand—remember I love you with all the heart of a girl who is alone.

Yours faithfully and always,
May.

17

The hopes of the overland freighters that the end of the war would better their condition and lessen their terrible risks proved utterly futile. By 1866 the riffraff from both armies had spread over the frontier, becoming desperadoes of the worst type, as bad as the very worst of the savages.

Charley Bent became the leader of one of the most ruthless and bloodthirsty bands that ever harassed the Old Trail.

Clint Belmet had heard of Charley Bent many times. His name was a camp word on the frontier, and after the government offered a large reward for him alive or dead his story became known.

He was the son of a pioneer named Bent, who lived on the frontier, and who was married Indian fashion to a Cheyenne squaw. He had sent his half-breed son to St. Louis, to be cared for, and later put in school and educated as a white man. Charley Bent, when twenty-one years old, returned to his father. Meanwhile his mother had died. Bent kept a trading store, which he put his son in charge of. The old pioneer was getting on and wanted to retire. One spring day at the end of a good selling season Charley ran off with all the money.

Bent never saw his son again. Charley spoke the Indian languages fluently. He traveled all over. He returned from a long trip to Texas under the name of Lee Murdock, by which he was known until after the fight with Clint Belmet at Horner's saloon in Fort Larned. This turned the keen eyes of the frontier upon him and outlawed him.

He had been playing a double game. He gambled among the whites during the winters; in the summers he developed a gang of from sixty to one hundred Indians and whites. Rumor affiliated Blackstone and his followers with Bent, or Murdock, but up to 1868 no actual proof of this conjecture was available.

This cold-blooded band of mixed villains attacked only stage-coaches and small caravans, murdered all, except young women who were so unfortunate as to be caught in one of these raids, and who were carried off into the mountains, never to be seen or heard of again. The stock and supplies of these caravans were traded to the Indians for pelts.

In the late summer of 1865 information reached

Fort Larned that the caravan which had routed a Kiowa attack on a wagon-train on the Dry Trail had later, on the way south, been set upon by Charley Bent's band and massacred, all except the two women, who were carried away into captivity.

A friendly Ute told this story to a trapper, who brought it to Fort Larned. As the Utes and Kiowas were on good terms, the information gained credence; and in the heart of Clint Belmet ever burned a steady white fire of unquenchable hate.

In 1866 after the reported discovery of gold on Maxwell's Ranch an Eastern syndicate bought all Colonel Maxwell's holdings at a fabulous price. The colonel went East and Clint never saw him again. Rumors reached the freighters that the gold on the ranch had been a flash in the pan; it had failed, leaving the syndicate with a huge ranch which they did not know how to run.

Fatality certainly cast its shadow before it. Point of Rocks, where Jim Couch had suffered two attacks on his caravans, and which the old freighter dreaded more and more, saw a third onset by Comanches. It was a surprise attack, and before the famous cannon could be brought into requisition Couch had been killed. In fact, he fell over the cannon, in the act of firing it. Clint Belmet grasped the fuse from his clutching hand, and fired the charge which turned the tide of battle. Couch, Sanderson, and Hoyle were buried in the shadow of Point of Rocks, along with other freighters of their intrepid breed.

Buff Belmet took charge of Couch's caravan. The best of the old frontiersmen and freighters wanted to drive under him. A fearless leader and a powerful force were imperative now.

In the fall of 1867 Belmet's caravan, working west toward Fort Larned, came upon General Custer's command, and traveled with it to Fort Larned.

This band of Custer's was the most impressive spectacle Belmet had ever seen. There were fully five hundred army wagons and four thousand soldiers. It was a sight Clint never forgot.

207

At the fort the reason for the big force became manifest. General Custer was getting ready for his winter campaign of 1867 and 1868 against the allied tribes from Fort Larned to Fort Riley, and down the Wichita River in the Indian Territory.

No part of the Great Plains had been free from raids, and consternation had spread into the government camps and thence to Washington. The commanders of the different posts had been warned by their scouts; they knew what the Indians were doing, but were powerless. Without soldiers and supplies they could not even leave their forts. And but for the overland freighters, whom the savages could not daunt, they would have fared worse. The sending of General Custer was the first move by the government against these tribes.

At the fort General Custer sent for Clint Belmet. He was in the prime of life then, a yellow-haired, blue-eyed man of great force and most engaging personality.

"Belmet, you have been recommended to me," said Custer. "I will need scouts in this campaign. Would you care to join my command?"

"Thanks, General. But I don't see how I can," replied Clint. "It'll take me a month and more to get my caravan to Santa Fé. Winter will be on us then. I can't get away from Santa Fé till spring."

"You will get back here along in May?"

"I reckon, if it's good weather. By June, anyway."

"Please consider my proposal. It will not be too late in the spring."

"I'll do so. An' I might accept if I can get a boss to handle my men."

"I'd be greatly indebted to you," returned the general, cordially. "I need men who know the country and the Indians, and these renegade rebels who are leading the savages to murder and pillage. I have my reports from post commanders, but very little direct information from scouts like yourself—men who are in constant contact with the conditions out here. Would

208

you be good enough to give me your angle on what I am up against?"

"For the present nothin' of any great moment," rejoined Clint thoughtfully. "There hasn't yet been any considerable bandin' of the tribes together. I would advise breakin' their strength before that consolidation can be effected. Renegade leaders like Murdock—his real name is Charley Bent—are like torches in dry prairie grass."

"Bent? I have a report on him. Do you know where he hangs out?"

"Up in Cimmaron somewhere."

"Belmet, can any of these Indian chieftains be placated—be persuaded to sign treaties?"

"They have been in the past. But they are growin' bitter an' doubtful. They have reason. I've no use for Indians. I lost my mother—my father—my friends —my uncle, all by Indians. But I don't blame them. This is a harsh statement. . . . Let me tell you the kind of thing that makes Indians bitter. Last spring a small caravan of twenty-two wagons went along the trail out here, got to Sand Creek, an' expected to be at the Crossin' of the Cimmaron in three days. Some Kiowas rode into camp—sixteen in all—an' they were hungry. These travelers—they weren't freighters—refused to feed them. The Kiowas started away an' a teamster shot one of them in the back. Killed him. The Kiowas stopped, picked their dead comrade up, an' went on without ever a word. That night a big force of them swooped down on the camp, killed the teamsters, burned the wagons, drove off the stock. . . . Six days later some trappers came down from the hills, found the chain, wagon rims, an' finally twenty-two scalped an' mutilated men. They hurried on here to Larned an' reported the massacre. The colonel sent out a detachment of soldiers, but the Kiowas were never rounded up."

"Well, Belmet, that's the other side of the story, and it is black," replied Custer, sadly.

"General, in my opinion—an' this I got from my uncle Jim Couch, an' Kit Carson—the great danger is that the northern an' southern tribes of the Great Plains will join forces. The Sioux are powerful and we hear rumors. Indian rumors, perhaps, but the more to be reckoned with for that."

Clint went on to Santa Fé with his caravan, spent the winter there, and in the spring started back. Custer was still out on his campaign, which, according to gossip at the fort, had not yet been markedly successful.

When Clint reached Kansas City he learned something that reminded him of his talk with General Custer. The government had made a treaty with the Nez Percé Indians of the Northwest, granting them the Walla Walla Valley forever for their home. The Indians lived up to their agreement. But the whites forced themselves into the valley, and the government ignored their incursions. The Nez Percés went on the warpath, causing a great loss of life and property. And in the end the white men gained possession of the valley under military protection.

Belmet realized that there was no sense in dodging the truth. Government and army, gold-seekers and pioneers, even the freighters in some degree, had been unscrupulous and unkind in their treatment of the red man.

And that very winter, though Clint did not know of it until spring, the government made an appropriation of four hundred thousand dollars to treat with three of the Indian tribes—the Cheyennes, Arapahoes, and Kiowas. Congress failed to live up to the agreement. What became of the money no one on the frontier ever knew. These three tribes, after waiting months and making appeal after appeal to the government through army posts and agents, went on the warpath and spread death and destruction for five hundred miles around.

Clint Belmet saw the worst of 1868 and 1869 on the Old Trail. During these years the government strengthened all the forts in and around New Mexico.

The freighting trade quadrupled, heavy caravans traveling both ways. Belmet became one of the famous train bosses, and the name "Buff" was familiar all along the line.

He had accumulated a considerable amount of money, for with his own and Jim Couch's, which fell to him, he invested in pelts and thus made the freighting business pay him in two ways.

Couch's cannon had belched its slugs many and many a time after its owner's death. Belmet owed his caravan credit for being a magnificent fighting unit, but the cannon backed them up, surely helped them out of many a tight place. None of the Indians but the Comanches could stand a cannon charge. The roar seemed to dispel their courage as much as the slugs. Belmet's band had secured the services of a soldier who had been a gunner in the army. He was a little red-headed Irishman named Benny Ireland. He had no fear of death or devil, and he loved a fight. His one great failing was impatience, which manifested itself in his habit of singing out to the Indians, when the freighters were lying low awaiting a surprise attack, "Cum on, ye red devils, an' I'll blow ye to smithereens!"

The leading factors in Belmet's success in freighting heavy and valuable loads were the hardened and experienced frontiersmen he drew to him, and the fact that he would not handle anything but a large caravan. Then he had grown to be almost as keen on the scent of Indians as the dog Jack, whom he never forgot. It was that he was ready for attacks from the Indians and did not run to avoid them.

Nevertheless, there were other good reasons why Buff Belmet was molested less than other caravan leaders. He invariably remembered the advice of Kit Carson and the methods of Colonel Maxwell with Indians. Belmet never picked a fight; he never turned Indians away hungry; he never dealt in any way but strict honesty with them.

It was indisputable that some of the caravans invited disaster. Kelly's band of two hundred and forty

211

men—a very large caravan—left Taos in the late summer of 1869. At Lower Springs, about five days south of Fort Larned, a small band of Comanches rode into camp and asked for sugar and coffee. There were not more than forty Indians and some of these were in poor condition. The freighters showed the hungry Indians not only sugar and coffee and other appetizing food, but also made faces at them and refused to feed them. Moreover, they drew their rifles and ordered the Comanches to get out.

The Indians moved on. And this large caravan of freighters, secure in numbers, paid little heed to the incident. Before daylight a large band of Comanches stampeded their stock. All the freighters rode out to fight and drive their animals back. They recovered horses and oxen, but they left eight dead comrades and brought in seventeen more wounded. From that time on they had to fight these Comanches day and night for one hundred and fifteen miles. They had one hundred and three oxen killed, and thirty horses. Twenty-seven wagons had to be abandoned. And their casualty list totaled eighty-three dead and seventy-six wounded.

On Buff Belmet's western trip in the fall of that year he fell in with John Hatcher, whose caravan contained forty wagons and about fifty men. Hatcher had been raised in the Shawnee Nation in Kansas. Probably he was the best Indian-fighter on the plains, according to the frontiersmen. Jim Barlow, who had thrown in with Belmet at Kansas City, had sixty-eight wagons and seventy-two men. These caravans added to Belmet's of seventy-four wagons and eighty-one men, and Couch's famous six-pound cannon, constituted a most formidable force.

Beyond Fort Larned they expected an attack every mile of the road. It was due. While making camp early the third day out they saw a band of white men ride by, leading and driving extra horses without packs. Belmet and Hatcher bent hawk eyes on these riders.

"Wal, I see two sick an' crippled men among them," said Hatcher. "What's your idee, Buff?"

"Road agents," declared Belmet. "Jim, I think I'll stop that gang."

"No, siree. Don't do it," returned the old frontiersman. "We can't court trouble. Shore they looked like bad eggs. Them six hosses they're leadin' are stage hosses, if I ever seen any. But we haven't any actual right to stop these men. Suppose they *wasn't* crooked? I'd gamble on thet, but we can't take the risk."

Next morning Hatcher's caravan, which was in the lead, halted to wait for Belmet's to catch up.

An abandoned stage-coach stood on one side of the road. Eight dead men were lying about. The strong box had been broken open and contents taken, as had also the mail sacks. All the bodies had been riddled with bullets; the driver had nine holes in him.

"Wal, Buff, I'm sorry I didn't let you stop them road agents yesterday," said Hatcher. "All we can do now is bury these poor fellows an' report the murder at the fort."

Belmet reported the disaster to the army officials, who at once sent out troops in pursuit of the robbers. They returned the third day, while Belmet was still at the fort. They brought three prisoners. At the rendezvous of the gang the soldiers had killed ten, recovered forty-five stolen horses and eighteen thousand seven hundred and forty dollars in gold, silver, and paper.

Clint Belmet got permission to interview the road agents, and came very near being too late, for when he reached them they had nooses around their necks. Three more hardened wretches would have been difficult to find. The first laughed at Clint's query, the second cursed him, but the third, a young man in his early twenties, replied: "Shore I know Lee Murdock. But thet ain't his right name. Get me out of this necktie an' I'll tell you where he is."

Captain Duncan, the veteran soldier in charge, spoke curtly to Clint:

213

"Sorry, Belmet. It's impossible. . . . Swing 'em up, men!"

The three robbers were jerked off their feet almost before Clint could turn his back. He returned to his caravan, his head bent, his mind darkly on the past. Some day he would run across Lee Murdock. That seemed written in his fate on the plains. Clint had vowed he would never stop freighting until he encountered Murdock and Blackstone, or he knew for sure that they had met their just deserts.

On the way to Santa Fé the caravans were delayed by washouts, due to heavy summer storms. At length Clint and Hatcher decided to take the road to Maxwell's Ranch and avoid all this rough travel. Such a détour meant many more miles, but in the end they would reach Santa Fé as soon as by the main trail.

The road had not been used for years. Weeds and grass had grown up in it, and all the miles along this road Clint knew so well, his mind brooded over the melancholy past.

At length the caravans reached the ranch, to pitch camp in the beautiful grove of cottonwoods. The leaves were turning gold.

Maxwell's Ranch had reverted to the wild. In place of grazing horses and cattle, only buffalo and deer dotted the wide gray pastures. Clint climbed the slope, recalling what he had heard about the operations of the St. Louis Company that had purchased the ranch from Maxwell. They had taken over all the stock, but the object of buying was to work the placer mines. Half a million dollars had been spent there. A forty-mile canal had been dug, to fetch a two-foot stream down to the diggings. But the company found no gold and were ruined.

Clint surveyed the ranch house. What a change! Only a few yeears, yet the fences were all down, the windows were vacant holes, the doors gone, the walls crumbling. Not a living creature to be seen. The rooms were bare, cold, gloomy. Indians had scratched characters on the faded whitewash of the adobe walls. The

dining-hall that had once been the Mecca for all frontiersmen, hunters, trappers, soldiers, and travelers,
and the Indians, was now a den for wolves. Bones
and piles of wolf dung! For Clint Belmet the hall of
Maxwell's banquets was haunted.

After supper he walked along the edge of the cottonwood grove to the spot where Couch's camp had
been located. He could have gone to it blindfolded.
The grove at this point was comparatively lonely, as
his freighters had not driven up so far. Beyond the
clump of willows, precisely the same, stood the spreading cottonwood under which Couch's wagon had stood.
The leaves aloft were sighing. A golden glow from the
reflection of the setting sun mellowed the glade.

Clint's forehead was damp and his hands clammy.
He plunged to the grass and lay back against the trunk
of the cottonwood. The wagon had stood there. He remembered that the high seat, where he had rested with
May Bell, was just under the spreading branch. He
had held her in his arms there, had kissed her sweet
lips and been kissed in return. Just here the tongue of
the wagon had lain upon the ground. May Bell had sat
about there—with a roguish devil in her dark eye. But
he had not understood. He had been only a tortured
youth. . . . Here Murdock had stood, sneering and
cool, and there, close to Clint's hand, he had lain,
bloody-mouthed and senseless.

But that flashing heat of memory did not survive.
Clint sat alone in the place of his dream. And his eyes
grew dim. The hard years since that unforgettable hour
had not killed the sweetness of memory. Never,
though, since he had read May Bell's crucifying letter
had he permitted himself this weakness. He had not
lived solely for revenge, but his search for Murdock
and Blackstone had given the color and vitality to his
trips to and fro on the Old Trail.

But now it was as if only a night had intervened. He
had become a stern, ruthless frontiersman, surviving
by wit and nerve and fierce resistance. Yet in this spot
his heart seemed to burst, and slow salt tears burned
his eyes. Regret, remorse, prayer were unavailing. The

215

iron of the plains had cut deeply into his soul. Yet love lived there still, hidden, unquenchable as the fires of the sun.

The golden glow paled and faded. Lonely, silent twilight settled down. Far up on the ridge a wolf bayed, as if in resentment at the white man's return. The grass was green, the leaves were beautiful, the willows gleamed, the stream babbled behind. But something was gone from the earth. The old cottonwood showed the wear and tear of storms. It had lost something.

Clint knew too much of the horror of frontier life to cavil at his fate, to bemoan it as something more bitter than had been the lot of other frontiersmen. That assumption would have been ignorance and folly. He did believe no man had ever been blessed by such love as May Bell had bestowed upon him, or had known such a sweet and lovely and willful girl. And no fortunate youth had ever been so stupid, so blundering, so jealous, so beset to destroy himself and the girl who worshipped him. But the brutal blows dealt him by the frontier had been no worse than had befallen thousands of men, far more deserving than he. Had not every rod of the Old Trail groaned with the travail of the freighter? How many lonely graves under the waving grass!

Fifteen years now had Buff Belmet held the reins across the prairie land. Few plainsmen had survived so many. The dream that he had treasured once, of giving up the overland toiling and of homesteading a little valley, safe near fort or town, had long been a mocking chimera, to return only in troubled slumbers, gall and wormwood.

Upon arriving at Santa Fé, to Clint's surprise he was greeted as if he were a ghost.

"Buff Belmet?" exclaimed Buell, the agent, who could not believe his eyes.

"Why, of course I'm Buff Belmet!" replied Clint, testily.

"But you were dead!"

"Not quite."

Buell was so astounded that he forgot to shake hands, but there seemed ample proof of gladness that equaled his astonishment.

"Buff, you haven't been in Santa Fé for years. An' you've shore been mourned as dead. I talked with a man who'd seen you dead in Kansas City, an' another who'd seen your grave at some rocky point in the Old Trail."

"Reckon he seen Uncle Jim Couch's. No, my grave hasn't been dug yet that I know of," remarked Clint, dryly, and then an old query forged ahead in his thought.

"Have you seen Murdock an' Blackstone since I left here?"

"Often. They ride in now an' then, when there's no caravan or soldiers around. The Indians keep them posted."

"Ahuh! They must have a hidin'-place in these hills."

"In summer. But they never show up in winter no more."

18

Clint Belmet's fifteen winters on the frontier had been passed in study, reading, hunting, practicing with guns, manual labor, curing hides, and various other less important pursuits.

This winter he spent before the open fireplace, watching the flames, the opal glow, the red embers, thinking, mourning. After the visit to Maxwell's Ranch he felt that he would never be his old self again.

But though sorrow made the days long, it could not hold them back. The winter ended. And spring came with its activities and preparations, its imminence of peril. Scouts and trappers predicted the bloodiest summer ever known on the frontier.

Barlow's caravan departed first, on the way to Fort Lyon. Belmet and Hatcher again joined forces, this trip totaling one hundred and forty-three wagons. Heavily loaded and scarce of ammunition they started out, with their leaders full of apprehension. Tracks of Indian ponies filled the trail, but no other sign of the red men was noted.

"Reckon we'll pay up for this later on," remarked Hatcher, grimly.

"Looks too good to me," replied Clint.

They rolled into Fort Larned without having experienced a single untoward happening, except the tiring of the oxen. Here, before undertaking the long overland journey across the plains, a rest was imperative, and the lightening of loads also. Fort Larned appeared unusually full of spring sellers of pelts and buyers and the hangers-on. Added to these the regular population of soldiers, Mexicans, Indians, and whites made of the town a busy, colorful place.

The first caravan from the east limped in, the freighters of which threw up their hands when questioned about the fun on the Old Trail.

Clint observed a pale youth of about sixteen, who came with the caravan. He carried a box under his arm and did not seem greatly impressed by the excitement at the fort. The freighters were washing up for dinner, but this pale lad sat down on a water-keg, opened his box and, taking out an accordion, he began to play. He played well and seemed to lose himself in the music. Finally Clint spoke to him:

"You get a pretty smart tune out of that. Did you play much comin' across?"

"I played all the time so I wouldn't hear the howling redskins," replied the musician.

Clint wished Hatcher had been present to hear that remark.

"I'm Buff Belmet," said Clint, kindly interested. "What's your name?"

"George," was the mild reply.

What a queer young fellow to journey west, among savage tribes and hardened men!

"Where you from, George?"

"La Crosse, Wisconsin."

"Come west alone?"

"I'm alone now."

"Ahuh! Where's your father an' mother?"

"Buried—back on the trail," replied the youth, in strange calm.

Clint sustained a shock. The new freighters, pioneers, travelers, adventurers kept coming in endless stream across the plains. He sat down beside the young fellow, deeply moved. How long ago it seemed since he was like this! But then he reflected that at twelve he was a teamster, and at the age of this boy a full-fledged Indian-fighter.

"I'm sorry, George. The frontier is a bad place. I know how you feel. Tell me about it," said Clint.

"We had several neighbors who wanted to move to Kansas. My folks didn't care so much to go. We were doing pretty well on the farm. But father gave in, and persuaded mother to. We loaded wagons and started. It was cold and my mother took sick. The Mississippi River was frozen over. We had to cross on the ice. I walked over, sat down on a log, and played 'Yankee Doodle.' The six teams started across. Ours was the last and heaviest. One of the wheels broke through the ice, and then our horses, struggling and frightened, went through too, throwing mother and father into the cold water. The other men pulled them out. Their clothes froze stiff before they got ashore where I was. We built a fire and camped there. We lost everything we owned. I had this accordion. . . . Mother died that night. They buried her up on the high bank. . . . My father took it bad—lay in the wagon—I heard him moan. . . . And died the third day. The neighbors who had coaxed us to come left me to shift for myself at Kansas City. I did not have a cent. I played my accordion to get a bite to eat. And the freighters fetched me along."

"Well! Well! that's a story," ejaculated Clint, nonplused and stirred. "Come with me to dinner, George."

Later Clint got the lad a job in Aull's store and tried to give him some advice, such as he had once received from Kit Carson. But George did not seem to grasp the significance of the frontier.

That night Clint sat toasting his shins before a little red camp fire. Most of the freighters were at the fort, playing, drinking, talking. The early summer night was quite cool at that altitude. Out in the dark the coyotes were yelping. A wind fanned the red embers. Clint spread his big hands to the heat. Tomorrow at sunrise he would start the caravans on the move. Why did he feel a strange portent?

A moccasined footfall broke his reverie. An Indian, wrapped in a blanket, stepped out of the shadow and squatted beside the fire. Clint greeted him with a "howdy," and then gave him a smoke. As he leaned over he recognized the Indian as a Kiowa, called Jim Whitefish, an outcast from his tribe because of his friendship toward the whites. He it was, indeed, who in 1845 had saved the life of the noted scout and trapper, Jim Baker. Clint had heard Baker tell that story. He had saved the Indian from his companions. Jim Whitefish lived in a shack on the edge of the settlement. And Clint had never yet passed through Fort Larned without remembering him. Probably this trip he would not have done so, as his mind was clouded. No doubt Jim Whitefish had called to remind him of this omission. Finally Clint went to his packs and got out sugar, coffee, tobacco, and a piece of buffalo meat—something not to be obtained every day now—and set them beside the Indian.

"There you are, Jim," he said, cheerily.

The Kiowa made an impressive gesture which indicated more than any speech that he had not called on his white friend to beg. Then Jim finished his smoke. Presently he glanced stealthily all around, his inscrutable black orbs piercing as a blade in the moonlight. His lean, sinewy hand gripped Clint's arm.

"White friend take soldiers," he said, in low, guttural, but coherent English, and his other lean hand pointed eastward on the trail. "Blackstone come," and here his hand described a meeting at some place he had in mind. "Charley Bent come," and his flexible fingers drew an imaginary line from another direction. "Heap Kiowas. All meet place of rocks."

Whereupon the Indian rose to stalk away into the gloom.

"Jim!" called Clint, as soon as he could catch his breath. But no answer came. "By thunder!"

It was a most extraordinary proceeding. Clint was so roused over its import that he denied for the moment the wolfish leap of his blood. He had not the slightest doubt but that in those few words Jim Whitefish had saved the Belmet and Hatcher caravans from massacre. The bloody frontier held an Indian here and there who could not let a debt go unpaid. It contained thousands who would give blow for blow. But such Indians as Jim Whitefish made it hard for Clint Belmet to think of killing any Indian, except in the heat of battle, and then that was the instinct of self-preservation.

After a moment of swift thought Clint got up, and in the action his boot kicked over the sacks of sugar and coffee that Jim Whitefish had deigned not to accept. If Clint had required any more significance to impress him it was here. He hurried away toward the fort to find Hatcher. At length some freighter told him the other train boss was playing cards in Horner's saloon. Clint went there and found him.

"Jim, come out of that," he said, and at his tone Hatcher leaped up, and the other three gangsters sat stiff in their seats.

"What the hell?" demanded Hatcher.

"Come out of here."

When they were outside in the dark Clint gripped the brawny arm of his comrade and whispered: "Hatcher, we're to be ambushed at Point of Rocks. Jim Blackstone comin' one way. Charley Bent comin' with Kiowas from another."

"Wal, I'm damned! Shore wondered why the fort was so full of Kiowas. Did you notice thet?"

"Yes. But they were tradin'. I bought out one In-

221

dian myself. . . . Come to think of it, though, there are lots of them."

"Buff, you can see white cunnin' behind this. Who tipped you off?"

"Never mind who. We've got the hunch. What'll we do?"

"Go on! We can't stop. Not for the whole damn caboodle of redskins an' rebels."

"I didn't think of holdin' up. But we might plan somethin'."

"Let's ask the colonel for an escort. By Gad! he'll drop dead, but let's do it."

"All right. But let me do the talking."

Very soon they had audience with the commandant —a Colonel Bailey—fairly new to the extreme Western frontier. He listened coolly to Clint, his cigar, tipped, and then he laughed.

"What's come over you old scouts?" he returned, with derision. "It'd be more fitting for you to escort some of my soldiers."

"Wal, Colonel, come to think aboot it, mebbe it would," drawled Hatcher, as he withdrew.

Outside he cursed roundly. Clint was silent. Some of the army officers were dead wheels in a caravan.

"What'll we do?" demanded Hatcher. "Take no notice of your hunch? I've had one now an' then thet was no good."

"It's no hunch, Jim. It's a tip an' you can gamble on that. . . . Let's figure what they're up to. . . . Point of Rocks again! Jim, you know it's the meanest hole on the whole trail. Indian scouts can sight us from the hills when we're a day's travel away. They can fire-signal or smoke-signal to their outfit below."

"Wal, forewarned is forearmed. We've got a tried an' true outfit. Let's hang over another day—ring in more men—load up with more guns an' ammunition."

"No. That'd give us away. We won't tell the men till we get out to Sand Creek, first camp. Then we'll plan to wag along as usual, till we get to Cottonwood Flat, which is the last water this side of Point of Rocks. But instead of campin' we'll make an all-night drive—

slip up to Point of Rocks in the night instead of day-light."

"Huh! You mean surprise them yellow *hombres* an' their redskins instead of lettin' them surprise us?"

"Yes. It'll be a thirty-mile drive altogether, but we can do it."

"Hard on the stock. But, Buff, I lean your way. Let's sleep on it."

For all Clint could tell, sleeping did not help matters any. In the light of day, however, no venture had the same sinister aspect imparted by the blackness and mystery of night.

At sunrise the caravans rolled out of Fort Larned precisely as upon any ordinary trip. They made eighteen miles, a fair day, during which Clint often stood up on the wagon seat to sweep the plains, especially to the rear, with Jim Couch's field-glass, which Clint always carried. He saw buffalo, but no Indians.

After supper Clint collected his men in a single group, and without betraying the source of his information, acquainted them with the extraordinary menace attached to this particular trip.

"You all know," he concluded, "about the wagon-load of rifles an' ammunition I fetched from Kansas City to trade to the trappers an' hunters at Fort Larned. That was last fall. Well, I picked up what was left—about seventy-five rifles an' five thousand rounds. These are packed in the white wagon just behind mine. I want you all to get an extra rifle an' ammunition, an' keep them at your hand, day an' night."

"Buff, we may have hell, but they can't lick us," spoke up Henry Wells, the oldest frontiersman among them. Several more of the freighters of long experience expressed confidence in their number and equipment. And the gunner, Ireland, swore his cannon was equal to a hundred men.

"I've a plan to work out regardin' the Point of Rocks ambush," added Clint. "Meanwhile we'll travel slow. Save the stock. An' let every one of you be a scout an' guard."

223

Hatcher joined Clint later and expressed satisfaction with the way his men took the menacing news.

"Buff, we're haulin' the most valuable load of furs thet ever left Fort Larned," said Hatcher. "Do you reckon Blackstone an' Charley Bent got wind of thet?"

"You can just bet on it."

"But how?"

"Some slick Indian, or more likely one of the many white men hangin' round the fort. I saw a score I didn't know. Mean-faced adventurers who couldn't look you in the eye. . . . I'm also carryin' important mail, an' sixty thousand dollars for Aull an' Co."

"Whew!" whistled Hatcher. "If this road-agent outfit had ketched us with our pants down, as they're plannin', they'd shore give us a spankin'. I reckon we'll owe a lot to your informant before this trip's over. . . . Buff, the pace is gettin' too hot. I don't mind redskins by themselves so much. But when they're set on by men of our own color an' inflamed by rum, wal, excuse me. If we get through safe I'll let it be my last caravan."

"Jim, you don't say!" ejaculated Clint, in surprise.

"Cleanin' out these robber gangs is a job for the army, not for freighters. General Custer is havin' his hands full with these southern tribes. If he tackles the Sioux he'll get a damn good lickin'. An' who's goin' to do for these desperadoes like Blackstone, an' Bent, an' Broom Field, an' Clanger, an' Lord knows how many others thet are comin' on strong. It's new, this road-agent game. An' it's profitable."

"You're right, Jim," said Clint, ponderingly. "Buell told me Blackstone had stacks of gold. Where'd he get it?"

"Buff, I've a hunch some of these train bosses pick up some extra money by packin' stolen furs to Kansas City. I know one I wouldn't trust. For thet metter, Jim Blackstone was a freighter. He drove for me in 'fifty-eight. In the early 'sixties he was a train boss."

"I know him. Uncle Jim Couch never had any use for Blackstone."

"Wal, neither have I. An' I'll gamble there's not a man in our outfit who wouldn't grin to see a noose go round his neck. Fact is, Buff, the men have taken this news damn serious. They see what we freighters are up against. Injuns is bad enough. If we should happen to have a little fight or two before we get to Point of Rocks, the outfit will be sore as rattlesnakes."

Fifteen miles out of camp next morning a small detachment of soldiers waited for the big caravan to come up. Clint rode at the head of the mile half-circle of wagons—the road took a bend there—and Hatcher brought up the rear.

Clint recognized the sergeant who rode up to his wagon. His name was McMillan.

"Hello, Belmet!" he said. "We've had a bad go with some Pawnees. I split my men up the river, sent them one way while we went another. We've had a scrimmage. I'm worried about Nelson and the ten soldiers who went with him. . . . Get down and come over here to the river with me."

Clint took his glass and strode beside the sergeant. Hatcher came galloping across the level from the road. A few hundred yards on, a line of brush and scrubby trees marked the crest of a considerable declivity. McMillan and Hatcher dismounted. A big basin opened out, with a stream meandering through bottom-lands of willow and cottonwood.

"Belmet, take a squint through your glass at that bunch of horses," directed the sergeant, pointing. "Lost my glass."

Far down along the river, perhaps a mile or more distant, a troop of horses were being driven by mounted Indians. Clint leveled his glass and almost instantly exclaimed:

"Pawnees drivin' a bunch of U. S. Army horses. I see the brand."

Sergeant McMillan cursed vehemently. "— — —! Let me look! . . . Yes, U. S. brand, all right, and they're our horses. . . . Belmet, will you help me round up that bunch of Pawnees?"

"I reckon. What do you say, Jim?" replied Clint, turning to Hatcher.

"Say? Why, I shore say yes. How many men do you need, Sergeant?"

"Each of you get me ten picked men, mounted, and we'll soon corral them."

They returned to the wagon-train, where it was difficult to decide on the men, because they all wanted to go. Finally Jim Hatcher selected his ten men, and said he would stay behind with the caravan. Clint picked ten, and in a very few minutes all the detachments were on the brink of the hill, peeping through the foliage at the Pawnees.

"Belmet, you go down here and follow them," directed McMillan. "I'll ride around with my men and cut in ahead of them. When they see us they'll fight or turn back. In case of a fight you ride up quick. But if they turn back you head them off. Don't let any of them get away. We've been after this bunch for weeks. They've been murdering settlers up the valley."

"How much time do you need to get in front of them?" asked Clint.

"You go right ahead and never mind us."

Clint led his men back along the river to a trail which went down. It was extremely steep, but of soft earth, where the horses slid along without danger, dust, or noise. Once down in the valley, Clint soon struck the heavy trail of the Pawnees and followed it. In less than an hour the pursuers sighted the Indians. And it grew evident that the stolen horses were hard to manage. McMillan and his soldiers appeared on the high bank in front, half a mile ahead of the Pawnees. The Indians halted, undecided what to do, but when the soldiers descended the bank and splashed into the river they turned back.

Almost at once their sharp eyes detected the freighters galloping up. They broke for the river, leaving the stolen horses. But the bank there appeared too steep, and they abandoned any idea of going over. At that juncture the soldiers appeared behind them. Then the Pawnees charged with a wild war whoop.

"Scatter, men, an' shoot low!" yelled Clint.

The Pawnees had rifles and they came thudding on, shooting over the heads of their horses. It was a beautiful sight for the freighters, but not conducive to fine marksmanship. At the first volley only a few Pawnees pitched off their horses.

Clint felt the shock and burn of a bullet in his upper right arm. It dropped weakly and his rifle fell. Halting his horse, he leaped off and pulled his revolver with his left hand. He killed two Pawnees and wounded a third before they wheeled to the left, hoping to make into the heavy brush. But the soldiers were upon them, and the freighters also swerving on their flank. Clint saw a short sharp engagement—a running one, yet at close range; and it ended as suddenly as it had begun.

He examined his wound, and finding it nothing to concern him, except that it bled profusely, he bound it with his scarf, and then led his horse over to his men.

"Buff, I see you're bleedin'," observed Henry Wells. "Any bones broke?"

"No. I'm not hurt. How about you all? . . . Where's the soldiers?"

"Gone after their horses. There's thirty dead red-skins an' nine took prisoner. Sergeant McMillan left orders to line them up an' shoot them."

"Let his own men do that," replied Clint, sharply. "How many of you men hurt?"

"Six, an' none bad, except Heddon, who got a nasty crack in the hip. But I ain't shore the bone is broke."

Clint observed the nine stoical Pawnees standing stripped of weapons, under guard. They were silent, somber. All these plains savages were mystics. They had fought; they had been vanquished; they were ready to receive the fate they would have meted out to their white foes.

Clint put his arm in a sling, then he examined Heddon's wound, which was painful but not dangerous. Some of the freighters, with ropes fastened to their pommels, were hauling the dead Indians to the river bank, where men on foot slid them over to splash sul-

227

lenly and sink out of sight. Clint's sharp eye surely detected life in more than one of them.

When this unpleasant task was ended Sergeant McMillan returned with the recovered horses. Three of his soldiers had been wounded. The comparatively little injury done the white men attested to the advantage of surprise attack.

"Say, didn't I leave orders to shoot them nine prisoners?" demanded McMillan.

"Reckon some one said so, sergeant, but I'm not takin' orders from you," replied Clint, quietly. "We just helped you out."

"You sure did, and I'm much obliged. Thought maybe I could shove the dirty job on some of your men. You all got the reputation of being a bloody lot. Ha! Ha! Ha!"

"It might be deserved, Sergeant. But I reckon we shirk this job."

"Line them Indians up!" yelled McMillan to his soldiers.

The doomed Pawnees did not need to be dragged to the edge of the river bank. And they faced the firing squad. Clint bent lowering gaze on them. He had seen this sort of thing often; he had participated in such justice. But it always seemed so pitiful. What magnificent courage these Pawnees showed!

"Ready! Aim! Fire!"

Some fell backward, dark blank faces terrible to see, and the rest sank down, to be shoved over by the swift soldiers.

The tension of soldiers and freighters relaxed. Some sat down; others looked to their wounds and asked for assistance; still others tended to weapons and saddles. McMillan consulted one of his men about the recovered horses.

Clint's keen eyes caught sight of three Pawnees crawling out of the shallow water across the river. One was crippled, because he had to be helped. The other two had very probably feigned death and had been thrown into the river unhurt. Clint did not betray them.

228

But suddenly one of the soldiers espied them and yelled: "Look!—Three redskins come to life!" And he began to shoot. Plainly his bullets went wide of their mark.

"Sam, you couldn't hit a flock of barns," shouted another soldier, and he opened fire. Several others did likewise. They might have been playing a game. The foremost Pawnee let go his hold upon his injured comrade, and bounding across the sand bar into the willows, he escaped. But the other Indian refused to leave him. Bullets splashed on the water and kicked up the sand. This valiant Pawnee had dragged his brother half out of the water when suddenly he let go. Erect a moment, he swayed back, his dark face gleaming across the river at his foes. He was killed but not conquered. He fell on the sand. The crippled Pawnee too had been hit again. His head sank on his breast; his shoulders stuck to the bank a moment; then gradually he slid into the water out of sight.

The freighters had been held up three hours. "Goodby, Sergeant," said Hatcher. "It's all in the game." And the caravan again headed eastward, making ten more miles that day, mostly down grade to Branch Creek, a spot hardly ever used by caravans. The water was bad.

Outside of that, however, the camp proved comfortable. Next morning at sunrise, Henry Wells reported to Clint.

"Smoke signals to the south, boss," he said.

Clint took a long look with his glass, then sent for Hatcher.

"Wal, shore enough," drawled that worthy. "Let's have breakfast an' skedaddle along."

Before noon one of the scouts, who had been riding a mile or more to the fore, came galloping back.

"Injuns ridin' up, boss," he said.

"Where?"

"Right down the road."

"How many?"

"Big bunch—five hundred, mebbe."

"Comanches?"

"I couldn't tell for sure."

Clint turned and yelled in stentorian voice to the freighters close behind: *"Indians! Runnin' fight! Keep comin'! Pass the word back!"*

Then he addressed the scout: "Ride back to Ben Ireland. Tell him an' Copsy to have the cannon ready an' to fire a couple of times quick, at any chance. An' after that pick out a good bunch to shoot into."

Clint laid his revolver on the seat beside him, lifted his two rifles to the same level, then called to his horses:

"Giddap!"

He drove on, hawk eyes on the horizon line, where the yellow road divided it. Hennesy, the driver behind him, was singing at the top of his voice. Clint peered back a moment. The gaps were closing up, horses accommodating themselves to the slower gait of the oxen. But all were moving briskly.

A long bobbing fringed line rose before the prairie. Clint had never seen the like of that and he experienced a grim thrill. Presently the level line of horsemen topped the grass to come on like the wind. Clint did not remember ever being charged by such numbers, but to his relief they were not Comanches. It appeared to be a mixed band of Arapahoes and Cheyennes. They raced forward, a beautiful shining line, and when within three hundred yards they split on each side of the trail and sheered, to come abreast of the caravan just out of accurate rifle range. Yet they began to fire on the caravan.

Presently Clint had to look back to see them. In a running fight the Indians always kept parallel with a caravan, the more daring riders cutting in here and there, and where they stopped a wagon they were likely to concentrate. Clint saw this very thing happen. Freighters began to shoot, which indicated that Indians somewhere were within range. A group of savages had cut in. Two wagons had been stopped. Clint saw one teamster fall over the seat, and the other huddle up. The next wagon behind came on, going round the two halted ones, and the rest of the caravan kept in order.

There was no confusion. The freighters moved briskly; and all along the line desultory firing began, directed on both sides.

BOOM! The six-pounder! Clint liked to hear that, as did all the freighters. The cannon had been mounted on a wagon, with Ireland in charge, Copsy as assistant, and two teamsters, driving four horses. Clint did not see whether the first charge from the cannon had been effective. Probably it had not been, except to lower the courage of the wild assailants. In exactly two minutes Ireland had reloaded, as Clint well knew by a second BOOM.

The firing swept back along the caravan to Hatcher's end. And this old frontiersman sent up the white puffs of smoke, one for each wagon. This kind of fight was less perilous for the freighters, except when the attackers grew bolder in a massed charge.

Clint had covered a mile by the time the Indians turned to charge back, closer, riding harder and faster, firing oftener, with more audacious braves darting in. The toll of falling Indians began to mount up. These freighters did not waste many shots. Sitting on their reins, they fired while their teams were moving. A yoke of oxen went down. Clint saw the teamster leap off, fire his rifle, and dash back to the next wagon, which came on around and back to the road with but little loss of time.

BOOM! Benny Ireland's cannon roared. A knot of Indians, closing in on the halted wagon, wavered as if struck by heavy wind, and then disintegrated. Riderless mustangs with flying manes ran wild out across the prairie.

The screeching, terrific din of Indian yells, which drowned all save the report of the cannon, gained on the head of the caravan. Clint drove while peering back. Suddenly he thrust the knotted reins under his leg and jerked up one of the rifles. The eighth team behind him was down, a yoke of oxen, and the teamster had disappeared. Then the ninth wagon, trying to clear the eighth, halted, with dead horses and running

231

drivers. The Indians concentrated here, whirled their mounts, rode to and fro.

Clint pulled his team to a stop. Then he began to shoot, now on one side, then on the other. His action halted the head of the caravan. The seven drivers between him and the two teams down followed his example with deadly rifle-fire. The dozen or more teamsters beyond likewise poured a heavy volley into the collecting riders. On each side of the train now the Indians grew bolder and fiercer, insane in their blood lust, daring to the point of destruction. A few more teams down and they would have the caravan order broken.

Clint downed a horse or an Indian for every one of his seven shots, and that with his arm in a sling. He reloaded, although he had the other rifle beside him. He would keep one ready for close quarters. When he looked up again, the Indians had bunched on each side opposite the breach in the caravan. The cannon wagon was off the road, coming at a gallop, the four horses extended, one teamster driving, the other shooting, Copsy also shooting, and Benny Ireland holding on to the cannon. The Indians, frantic at their opportunity, swelled in number at that point. They were about to risk riding through the breach to surround Clint and the other seven wagons.

Fifty yards from the larger group, on the right side of the caravan, Ireland's wagon halted. Clint saw a red belching flame, a leaping tongue of smoke. Boom! the cannon thundered, and like grain before a reaper Indians and horses went down. Clint whooped, as no doubt all the freighters were whooping. All the savages remaining on the right side of the caravan fled as if from a prairie fire. Those on the left side sheered off, but kept riding and shooting. Their golden chance was gone. The freighters behind came up fast, driving two abreast, expecting the order to form a circle. But Clint did not give it, and by the time Hatcher arrived the Indians had circled around to join their fleeing comrades. Far out on the prairie they halted in a dark

232

mass, wild and savage, evidently to consult. But they did not renew the attack.

Swift grimy hands cut out the dead teams and hitched their wagons to the rear of others. The dead freighters were lifted up and covered. Six killed and four wounded. Benny Ireland had a hole through his forearm.

"Hey, boss, shure wasn't thet last shot a hummer?" he shouted.

Fifty-three Indians and almost as many mustangs had gone down to that terrific charge of slugs.

"Irish, you're shure thar with your pepper-pot," shouted a bloody-armed teamster as he took up the reins. Many were the calls vented upon Ireland.

"Drive on!" yelled Belmet.

Once more the caravan leaders moved, and the wagons behind fell in line, and soon the whole cavalcade was in action, stretching along the yellow road. The wheels rolled, the harness creaked, the oxen wagged, the horses settled down, and the freighters drove on toward the vacant, purple, beckoning horizon.

19

Buffalo impeded progress. The straggling ribbons of the immense herd moving north blocked by the caravan, cut it into several sections, surrounded it, and at last brought it to a standstill.

The freighters were not slow to take advantage of their opportunity. Rump steak, their favorite meat, would be the order of the supper that evening, if they were able to move on to camp. By the middle of the afternoon the herd thinned out.

Clint Belmet never tired of watching buffalo. The breath-taking sight of his first buffalo bull, the freezing of his very marrow when Dick Curtis whispered to him to shoot the monster, the tremendous kick that knocked him flat, and then the thrill when he saw the huge black woolly beast down—these youthful impressions had not deadened through the years, and they recurred whenever he saw buffalo. The rumble of thundering hoofs! The prairie-wide pall of dust! Buffalo now as numerous as the grasses of the plains, would some day be only a memory. Clint saw that.

Travel along the Old Trail had lesser problems than Indian attacks, but for all that they were important. Water for man and stock absolutely could not be packed. And after a long pull in the dust, under the sun, the stock needed drink. So that whenever obstacles like the intruding buffalo herd caused delay it was a serious matter.

That night the caravan was eight hours behind and had to camp at another of the unfrequented water holes. In this particular instance, however, the delay was fortunate, because next morning, when they were well under way, they met Pawnees, who after one shot from Ireland's cannon gave them a wide berth. At the regular camp, some miles farther on, the scouts waited in ambush for them.

When Hatcher was told this he threw up his hands with a curse. "Looks like every band of redskins on the plains was layin' for this caravan."

Clint inclined to the same opinion. The mood of the men grew more grimly laconic and defiant as their dangers and troubles increased. For years they had boasted of what might be expected on the Old Trail some day. And in their own particular case the dawn of that day was not remote.

Next morning they were getting well down into the heave and bulge of the last rolling country before the vast level of the prairie land proper. Creeks bisected the region, and from the timbered bottoms thin blue columns of smoke rose against the pale green. They did not sight any Indians, but Hatcher voiced Belmet's conclusion that many a pair of dark savage eyes had watched the caravan from the ridge tops.

This portion of the Great Plains had always been

234

singularly stirring for Clint Belmet. It was the most beautiful and wildest section between the Rockies and the Missouri. Clint was nearing the lonely graves of his father and mother, of Uncle Jim Couch, and of Tom Sidel, the one close friend of his youthful freighting days—the boy who had saved his life.

Afternoon of the day following, so far significant in that no Indians had been sighted when they were known to be in the neighborhood, brought to the far gazing eyes of Clint Belmet the purple and gray mass that was Point of Rocks. Its peculiar shape made it a landmark to those familiar with the country.

Southward fom the position of the rolling caravan the plain ran off into escarpments, some of them rugged, dark with brush, others winding down in gray wavering lines to the blue prairie. Every mile or two a gully opened out of this vast slope, and a green line of willows and cottonwoods wound out to vanish in the level. Northward the last shelf of the mountains sloped endlessly, its grays and purples merging into the distance, which was like a desert or sea.

From the present position of the caravan it was a day and a half of easy travel to Point of Rocks. Sharp Indian eyes must already have sighted the caravan and concluded that the next camp would be at Alder Creek.

Belmet's glass at last located what he had long searched for. From a high ridge dark round puffs of smoke floated from behind the brush. They had a singular regularity. Belmet's teeth set. He knew a crafty Indian was standing over a fire, covering it with a blanket, which he raised at regular intervals to let out a puff of smoke. Somewhere miles away other Indian eyes, sharp as those of a prairie buzzard, saw these signals, and knew that the caravan was passing a certain point.

"Jim Whitefish told the truth," muttered Clint, in gratitude to that outcast friend of the whites. "We're supposed to go in camp at Point of Rocks tomorrow night. An' before mornin'! . . . Well, we'll do a little ambushin' on our own hook."

Belmet sent a scout back along the line to tell every freighter of the signals and that the order was to drive slowly until dark, then briskly on to Point of Rocks. Hatcher sent word forward to Belmet that he had seen an Indian lookout ride across a brow of hill, sit his horse and watch. And the conclusion of Hatcher's message was: "There'll shore be hell to pay an' we want to make Point of Rocks before daylight!"

Toward sunset a marvelous clear light shone over the plains, a beautiful transparent colorless medium, strangely magnifying, and gradually tinging to gold. It still wanted an hour till the setting of the sun. The sturdy horses plodded on, bobbing their heads; the patient oxen wagged their yokes from side to side; the wheels rolled round and round.

Eastward above the gently undulating prairie, where the grass waved in shining ripples, rose the low mound that was Point of Rocks. Clint saw his long shadow moving ahead of him, grotesque and sinister. Away to the south the escarpments ran down dimly into the golden obscurity.

No sign of life! The birds and beasts of the prairie were not in evidence. Over the plains brooded solitude and melancholy, and peace that was an illusion. The sun set behind the caravan, and to the east sky and horizon met, gold and rosy, then paling to gray, and at last dark along the immensity of the level land.

But death lurked out there, like the empty barren distance, so palely gray now, with edges of twilight creeping up from the hollows. The Great Plains! Never had Clint Belmet seen them so vast, so clear, so incredibly old. Long reach after reach, up over the rising bulge toward the ranges, gray and cold as clay, their eternal monotony inescapable and tremendous.

For fifteen years Belmet had watched this phenomenon of changing prairie land—the gold turning gray, the gray to stone, and at last the clear mystery of night over the sea of grass. But this time it seemed more than potent of the purpose of nature and the futilities of man.

At three in the morning Belmet and Hatcher drove their caravans under the dark lea of Point of Rocks, completing the longest drive either of them had ever made. The oxen stood the long haul, but the horses were exhausted. A double circle of wagons, with narrow gateways, at two sides, left only a few acres of grass inside. The horses were fed grain, something always reserved for emergency. The oxen were unyoked and turned loose inside the corral. Scouts were dispatched out on all sides, and Clint Belmet went with Henry Wells to take a look at the bottomlands. All was dark over the wide expanse of timber where the two streams joined, and likewise up the forks. But neither Belmet nor Wells trusted that darkness. They waited, turning strained ears to the low country, listening for Indian dog or horse. A lonesome wolf mourned and a plains owl hooted dismally; the wind rustled the leaves of the cottonwoods, and the soft murmur of water floated by.

Dawn broke. Deer trooped down off the prairie to enter the thickets. Buffalo waded across the shallow streams to climb out on the level.

Wells returned to where Belmet sat. "Buff, if there were any reddys hidin' in the thickets them deer would act different. So would the buffalo. An' we could hear horses a mile. An' by this hour Injuns would be up."

"Henry, we've beat them here," declared Clint.

"Shore have. Let's go back an' get a bite to eat."

Fires had not been lighted. The men had cold buffalo meat, biscuits, and coffee, which had been cooked and brought on for this contingency.

Hatcher came down off the high part of Point of Rocks.

"I left Moore up there with the glass. We can spot them comin' down both creeks, miles away. But nothin' yet."

The last scout rode in late. He had been ten miles to the north.

"Seen suthin' movin' out on the prairie, but couldn't say whether it was Injuns or buffalo," he reported.

"Wal, if the stock wasn't dead on its feet we could pull out of this," remarked Hatcher.

"Boss, we'd never get far," protested Wells.

"Hell! shure we ain't goin' to pass up a foight?" demanded Benny Ireland.

"Buff, I'm goin' round an' ask every man what he thinks about tryin' to travel," said Hatcher.

"But it's poor sense, Jim," declared Belmet, earnestly. "The horses are all in. They've got to have rest. If we started out now they'd drop, one an' two at a time. We couldn't go far before the Indians would catch up. Then we'd be worse off than we possibly can be here."

"Hatcher, he's dead right," declared Wells, and the opinion of this old plainsman carried weight.

"Wal, I'll make a canvass, anyhow," replied Hatcher, gloomily.

Henry Wells showed a surprise he did not speak. Jim Hatcher had never before leaned to a decision like this. Nor did Clint Belmet speak his mind, which he felt at that moment was weighted with catastrophe. In his judgment they absolutely could not go on for at least twenty-four hours.

"Wal, I'll tell you, Buff," spoke up Henry Wells. "It's no shore thing thet we'll be jumped hyar."

"I hope we won't, but I'm afraid we will."

"But we can't be surprised an' thet gives us such an advantage we'll drive 'em off fust charge."

"Henry, if Blackstone an' Murdock *are* leadin' Kiowas to attack us we've *got* to surprise them or be massacred."

"Blackstone an' Murdock?—Charley Bent, you mean? Who'n hell said they was headin' this deal? An' Kiowas, too!—Buff, have you an inside tip on this?"

"Yes. Jim Whitefish told me. You know him. Keep your mouth shut about him. But tell the men whom to expect."

"Gawd Almighty!—Buff, them road agents never tackled a caravan yet they didn't get. Thet's why we never had no proof on them. They haul wagons away

238

an' the white men they kill. An' bury them far off the trails."

"Yes, Henry. Caravans just disappear. It used to be only Indian attacks, wagons burned, an' white men left naked, scalped an' cut. . . . If Blackstone an' Bent lick us here nobody will ever know what became of us. An' the most valuable load we ever hauled!"

"Wal, by Gawd! Blackstone an' Bent will never lick us!"

"So say I. Go among the men an' tell them *who* we suspect is after us."

In a very few moments that camp hummed like a hive of angry bees.

Clint soon climbed to the top of the rocky eminence, where he relieved the man on watch.

"Plenty of deer, buffs, an' coyotes, but no redskins," he reported, relinquishing the field-glass.

"Reckon they have all day to get here *if* they're comin'," said Clint, half to himself. He sat down to study the lay of the land across the junction of the two streams, and the shallow meandering valleys which wound to south and east. With his glass he could command fully five miles of the trail that came from the south and perhaps three up the other to the east. It was logical to conclude that Indians bent on ambushing Point of Rocks would come down by one or both of these trails, because if they traveled on the road they risked detection, and to the north there was no water to camp near. Moreover, the escarpments with their rugged gullies lay to the southward.

"Well, if we *see* them first they are gone goslins," muttered Belmet.

There would be ample time to formulate a plan and carry it out, after the Indians showed up in one or both of the winding valleys. No doubt they had camped at the head of these creeks and were on the march now. The possibility of their not coming stood very remote in Clint's mind. He would have wagered anything on Jim Whitefish's veracity and accuracy. The Kiowa knew. One of his relatives in the tribe or a Pawnee who had drunk firewater with the crafty out-

239

cast had revealed the secret of a long-planned raid, the genius of which had its inception in the subtle heads of renegades. Then the presence of Indians all along the trail, the time and the place, seemed to foreshadow fatality.

Blackstone and Murdock must run their bloody race sooner or later. No desperado of their ilk could long survive the frontier at this period. During the war the stage of the Great Plains had been set for a monstrous drama which was now being exacted. Clint reflected that more caravans had been destroyed in the last two years than in ten before. He tried to recall the number massacred or broken up or vanished or reported lost, but when he got to thirty-three he gave up, appalled. Would this be the last caravan Buff Belmet ever led across the plains? Courage and defiance and reasoning united in a negative, but there was a strange vague presagement set against these, and it intimated that Points of Rocks was to be the end of his overland freighting trail. He endeavored to cast off the shadow, but it continually returned. Like Hatcher, he divined events that cast somber shadows before.

Every moment or so he would lift the glass to his eyes and scan the whole visible length of the south fork of the river, then that of the east. A hundred times or more he scrutinized the valleys, then on the hundred and first his whole frame leaped with a vibrating rush of blood. A thick dark moving band of mounted warriors had turned into the gray valley on the right.

In leaps and bounds he clattered down the rocks to the camp of waiting freighters.

"Men, they're comin'—a big force!" he said, sharply. "Down the right-hand creek, five miles or so up. . . . Hatcher, take twenty-five men an' the cannon. Wade across. Plant the cannon just this side of the cottonwoods an' hide your men all around in the willows. They'll stop there to wait for us an' night. But don't you wait! When they all get bunched in the grove, *shoot!* Keep to your hidin' places an' shoot. . . . Ireland, you an' Copsy stand by the cannon, with another man to back you up. Pick your first shot.

240

Make it count heavy. Then load like hell and keep shootin'."

"Wal, thet suits me, Buff," replied Hatcher, with a gleam of pale fire in his eyes. "What'll you do?"

"I'll take twenty-five men an' go up the left draw. For if Blackstone is to meet Bent an' his Kiowas here he'll come down that draw. If he's late comin' an' we hear you shootin', we'll run back."

"Good! But keep under the bank a little an' come up behind us," said Hatcher. "Wal, thet will leave forty-odd men here to guard the wagons. Suppose another bunch of Injuns would sneak in from this other side?"

"They could come, sure, but sneakin' wouldn't help much. They'd be seen long before they got near. An' I reckon our fight over across the creek will be short an' sweet."

Hatcher got his men moving promptly, and twenty or more of them handled the brass six-pounder as if it were a plaything.

"Wells, you take charge of the men left here," went on Clint. "Have a scout on top, but hidin' mighty low an' careful."

Hatcher, with two revolvers in his heavy belt, which was full of shells, and carrying a Colt's rifle in each hand, approached Clint for a final word.

"Buff, if anythin' happens to me you're to have the money on me," he said.

"Same in my case—if you come out an' I don't," replied Clint.

"It's jest as well we haven't any folks. I often wondered what I was savin' up money for. To quit the plains an' take a rest! But, by Gawd! I've a hunch I waited too long!"

.. What tremendous import of tragedy in Hatcher's simple words! And Clint felt that his own mental state had some similarity to the old freighter's. These early plainsmen were wont to make light of toil, fight, bloodshed, and death. They had undertaken a task wellnigh impossible, and that was to transport across the Great Plains supplies to the forts and trading-posts, and return with the valuable pelts and furs. In the beginning of this business the Indians were more disposed to trade than to fight. But injustice, cheating, broken treaties, murder for nothing, and the slaughter of their buffalo, and at last an army of soldiers sent against them, had made them bitter, ruthless fiends. The white man, of course, owing to numbers and improved weapons, and the spirit characteristic of the pioneer, would conquer in the end. But before that day came there would be many a caravan burned on the prairie, many a brave man dig his toes in the dust.

Clint Belmet's deadly wrath seemed centered more on the renegade desperadoes like Blackstone and Charley Bent. Indeed, the latter was the Simon Girty of the plains. Indians were simple-minded, easily roused, and more easily led. Whatever the crime of the pioneer against them—and it was great—that of the renegade was heinous and unforgivable. Bent had often led his red demons to the destruction of a caravan without risk to himself. Clint believed that this time Bent—or Lee Murdock, as he always thought of him—had overreached himself, and if he were on the way to Point of Rocks he was riding to his doom. Seventy-five freighters, under command of an old frontiersman, each armed with two seven-shot rifles and two six-shot revolvers, and also loaded down with extra ammunition, and lastly the murderous slug-shooting cannon, all ambushed in thick cover, would deal destruction to any force of Indians.

Hatcher's men had disappeared in the willow thicket bordering the right-hand fork of the stream. Clint's men waited for him on the bank. He dared not hold back much longer, but he wanted the last moment possible, in case the scout up on the rock sighted Indians or Blackstone's band, coming from the east fork. And Belmet was tightening his belt when Stevens came sliding down the slope. Rocks rattled ahead of him. With one hand he held aloft Clint's field-glass, and with the other he retarded his descent by clinging to the brush. When he thumped to the ground and looked at Clint with glinting eyes there was hardly need of words.

242

"White men—comin' down the—left draw," he panted. "Eighteen of them, ridin' two abreast!"

"How far?"

"Less'n two miles."

"Good work, Stevens. Go back up an' lay low. Don't forget to keep an eye peeled all around."

Clint, with a rifle in each hand, ran back to join his men.

"White men comin' down this left-hand creek," he said. "Eighteen of them, ridin' two abreast. Must be Blackstone's outfit. Come."

The twenty-five freighters waded behind Clint across the shallow stream and followed him along the sand-bar under the bank for a quarter of a mile. Then Clint mounted the low bank and headed into the willow thicket. It was dense and tangled. At high water this sand-flat, which came to an apex where the two streams joined, was inundated. It sloped up, however, to more open ground where the cottonwoods began. Coming to a well-trodden trail Clint halted, waiting for his men to cluster round him.

"We'll go on to the first open spot an' then hide along the trail," said Clint. "If I'm calculatin' right, this white outfit will get here before the Indians. What we want to do is to capture them without a shot. We'll tie them up an' then hustle across to help Hatcher."

"Boss, Jim Blackstone will be hard to hold up. Capture means only a rope!" said one of the freighters.

"I'm gamblin' on surprise. An' the worst of these bandits will hesitate with a rifle close to his belly. We won't give them time."

Some little distance farther on an oval glade, through the center of which the trail ran, captured Clint's eye as the ideal place to ambush the bandits. All around the glade brush grew high and deep.

"Here!" ordered Clint, halting. Scatter along, twelve men on each side, about the length of a horse apart. Hide an' don't move till I yell. Then jump up with one rifle. . . . Shoot if any man of them makes a move. Otherwise obey orders."

Silently the men melted into the green cover. It afforded perfect protection. Clint, the last to move, backed into the willows at the head of this glade. He could peep through the foliage and see straight up to where the trail entered. And he set his teeth hard. One way or another Jim Blackstone would get his just deserts there. Clint realized that if Lee Murdock accompanied Blackstone it would give a different color to the affair. Murdock would never throw up his hands. He was now about thirty years old and had been a renegade for six or seven years and the wildest and most iron-nerved of the frontier desperadoes. In case that Murdock accompanied Blackstone, which circumstance Clint doubted, the only thing to do was to kill him first and yell afterward. A dead man falling off his horse would not be instantly conducive to his companions drawing weapons. Clint relied upon shock.

He knelt on one knee, careful to note that he was well concealed. He leaned a rifle against the crotch of a willow and held the other well forward with both hands so that he would have but a single move to make. He was breathing with difficulty and was hot with sweat. There was more in this stern hour than just the self-preservation of a freighter. He had often in grim moments held on to life just in the hope of meeting Lee Murdock face to face.

Suddenly Clint heard the thud of hoofs on soft sand. A slight vibration of his body ended in a rigidity that was like ice. Far down the trail, beyond the glade, he saw black hats and indistinct faces of white men, then brawny shoulders, and then the bobbing ears of horses. They came down the trail two abreast. The riders were bunched pretty close, horse to horse, which was a most fortunate circumstance. The leader on the right was a huge man, heavily bearded, and before he rode into the glade Clint recognized him. Uncertainty ceased then for Clint, and even in the dark setting of his mind he remembered the Indian, Jim Whitefish, with passionate gratitude.

They came on, horses walking. They were in no hurry. They talked unreservedly, and one of them let out a hard coarse laugh. They wore buckskin and were armed to the teeth. Not in all Clint's experience had he seen as hard, forbidding, and relentless-looking an outfit. They represented the epitome of wild frontier life of the period. Their indistinct voices grew clearer and finally distinct: "— —hyar ahaid of time," said one of them.

"Wal, Charley aimed to beat the Comanches heah."

Blackstone's deep voice, carrying well, smote Clint's heart with a deadlier import than that indicated by his presence.

"How'n'll did they all git wise to this rich caravan?"

"Aull's been gatherin' ten thousand mink, otter, an' fox hides fer Buff Belmet's caravan."

"Haw! Haw!"

"Wal, you might haw on the other side of your jaw if them Comanches don't get heah, too."

"What's two hundred miles to them ridin' louses?"

When the foremost horses reached to within twenty feet of Clint he rose swiftly, rifle extended.

"HANDS UP!"

The cavalcade froze as one man. The hoofs of the horses beat a nervous tattoo and likewise stilled. Blackstone's face turned a dirty white under his beard.

"Hands up! Hands up!" roared down the glade as the freighters, like grim specters, rose out of the green.

An instant of paralyzed realization—then the hands of every man shot up. It was an instinct. The complete surprise blocked reason. Suggestion was all-powerful.

Clint seized upon the moment with the passion of genius.

"Andy, grab all guns on your side," yelled Clint. *"Sam, you on your side!"*

The two freighters leaped into action, throwing rifles and revolvers to the ground. The stiff upheld hands began to quiver and jerk. Blackstone drew his half-way down.

Clint took two swift strides.

"Up with them! . . . *I'll bore you!"*

For an instant Blackstone's life hung on a quivering

245

balance. His big pale eyes showed sudden fury. His rifle and revolver, jerked from him, lay on the sand. He had decided too late. Black hell then burned in his gaze.

"Keep 'em up! . . . *Don't move!—Damn you, stiff thar!*—If you wink I'll blow your guts out!" So the freighters flashed swift and terrible menace, and many of their rifle barrels were thrust close to the bandits.

"GET DOWN!" bellowed Clint, and he ran up close to Blackstone, prodded him in the abdomen with his cocked rifle. The miracle was that the violence did not discharge the weapon. The bandit leader slid out of the saddle mighty quickly.

Others of his band followed suit. Some, too slow to suit the intense freighters, were summarily jerked out of the saddle. One, clubbed on the head, fell off.

"Punch 'em in line!" yelled Clint, and he gave Blackstone another prod. "Line 'em up! . . . Turn your back, damn you! . . . Now, men, ropes. Two of you cut ropes. Off the saddles! Quick!"

Twenty grim assailants with cocked rifles pushed and beat the band into a line, then stood guard behind them. The other five freighters, inspired and savage, tied the bandits hand and foot, and toppled them to the ground.

"Hey, Belmet, what's your game?" demanded Blackstone, harshly.

"Looks like Fort Larned for you, Blackstone."

Muttered curses rumbled from the prostrate bandits. They were just recovering from a stunning surprise.

"Fort Larned like hell!" burst out a sweaty freighter. BOOM!

The heavy report of the cannon tore through the cottonwoods. It rolled, and banged back in echo.

"Thar she goes!" yelled a lusty-lunged freighter. "Boys, come——"

A thundering crash of rifles drowned his voice. The forest resounded. Then the wild, hoarse yells of fighting men. *Crash!* A shrill strange note pierced it. Yells and cries mingled. Crash!

Clint snatched up his rifle and led his men in mad

246

flight down the trail, into the willows. Crash! The din became tremendous as he neared the scene of conflict. He shouted to his followers to keep to the right, so they would come up behind Hatcher's men. Crash! They understood, though they could hardly have heard. In a few moments Clint reached the trail that Hatcher had made and he headed up it. The rifle-fire now had become continuous, yet above it rose the thudding of many hoofs, the crashing of many horses through the brush, the hoarse bawls of furious men, the piercing shriek of Indians.

Clint felt the zip of a bullet. And he dropped down to crawl. His men were quick to imitate.

BOOM!

Clint yelled with his men. That was music to his ears. The fusillade of slugs tore through the cottonwood grove. Smoke rose in thick clouds ahead. On the far side the heavy firing materially lessened, but to Clint's right it increased. He was working too far to the left. He ran the risk of leading his men in front of Hatcher's fire. A trampling and shrieking of frightened and wounded horses filled the valley with hideous noise. They were close now. Clint sheered to the right, crawling fast, a rifle in each hand. The labor was prodigious. Freighters were not used to running or crawling in such strenuous action as this.

BOOM!

Benny Ireland was keeping to his pace—a cannon shot every two minutes. The roar appeared hollow and thunderous. A blast of iron went tearing through the trees and brush.

Then Clint found himself up to Hatcher's men, on their knees, behind trees, shooting, yelling, crawling forward. Sweat so filled and smarted his eyes that he could not see any Indians. He lay flat, to release his guns and wipe his hot eyes. Presently he got up on one knee. His men came crowding along. The uproar perceptibly diminished. Firing ceased close at hand, grew desultory up the draw and stopped. Hoarse shouts took the place of prolonged yells. The men began to stand up, their hair bristling, their actions daring, nervous, eager, like those of bloodhounds about to be let loose on a trail.

"Hold on!" yelled Hatcher from somewhere. "Wait till that smoke lifts."

Rapidly the smoke wafted aloft and floated away. Horses lay everywhere in the grove, some of them kicking. The ground under the cottonwoods resembled a battlefield. Indians were down everywhere in rows, piles, groups, and singles and many were alive.

"Did Buff Belmet get here?" shouted Hatcher, approaching.

"Reckon we did, but too late to help you," replied Clint.

"Hell! we didn't need help. Reckon you went up the other fork an', hearin' us shoot, you run back?"

"Yes. But before that we held up Blackstone's outfit."

"Holy jumpin' cats!" shouted Hatcher. "We didn't hear no shootin'."

"Jim, we never shot once.—Stevens saw Blackstone's gang from the rock. We hurried up an' ambushed the trail. Got Blackstone an' seventeen men. All hawgtied!"

"Wal, by all thet's wonderful!" ejaculated Hatcher. "Buff, send some men over to guard them bandits. You can never tell what'll happen."

"Andy, take some men an' hurry over there where we left Blackstone," ordered Clint.

Andy yelled, and it appeared that the whole twenty-five men who had executed the coup under Clint's management rushed away through the woods.

"Guard that bunch till I come," shouted Clint after them. But if Andy heard he gave no sign of it.

"Buff, you'll be surprised an' worried. These Injuns are Comanches!"

"Comanches!" echoed Clint.

"Shore are. Look for yourself. . . . Buff, you never seen anythin' like this. Must have been three hundred of them. As you figured, they rode into this open grove. An' they was bunched pretty thick when Benny let go the cannon. My Gawd! . . . I'll bet he put a hundred reddys an' horses down. Then we blazed away, an' it was like mowin' hay. We was all hid an' they didn't know where to turn. Every last man of us got in seven shots before Ben got loaded again. Then, bang! Thet settled it. Hell had busted loose, an' of all mix-ups I ever seen thet one beat them a thousand times. Them thet wasn't hit thought only of escape. An' they run over each other tryin' to get into thet trail. All the time we was pourin' lead into them. An' a big bunch got stuck, tangled, stampeded. Then Ireland let go again! . . . Buff, I'll bet we killed more'n half of them."

"Comanches!—But we were to expect Kiowas?"

"Thet's what I'm aworryin' aboot. Mebbe we ought to expect them yet."

"Listen!" suddenly exclaimed Clint. "As Blackstone came ridin' up I heard one of his men say. 'hyar ahead of time.' . . . An' then Blackstone said, 'Wal, Charley aimed to beat the Comanches here.' "

"My Gawd! mebbe we ain't so lucky yet! We better be aboot our bizness. . . . Hey, men, send all these crippled Injuns to the Happy Huntin'-grounds. An' some of you haul the cannon back across the river."

Dozens of freighters ran forward, swinging their heavy rifles by the barrels and whooping. Ireland with his attendants took up the ropes of the cannon.

"Come on, Buff," said Hatcher. "We might find some Kiowas, an' if we do we'll shore look for Charley Bent."

That stirred a strong urge in Clint, stronger than the repugnance he felt. He became witness to a harrowing scene, dwarfing all others of like nature to which he had been party. All through the glade lay Comanches. Every third or fourth one showed signs of life.

"Smash 'em all," yelled a freighter, clubbing his rifle.

"Haw! Haw!—*Zam!*"

"Playin' possum, huh? Take thet!"

Dull thuds and the cracking of skulls resounded through the grove. And every freighter appeared sinisterly mirthful over the gruesome task. Comanches, of all savages of the Great Plains, they hated and feared most.

"Look for Kiowas," shouted Hatcher. "An' fer a white man painted."

"Put these horses out of misery," ordered Clint.

"Yes, an' make a count while you're doin' it," added Hatcher.

Crippled horses had to be shot. This was a feature of the finishing process that did not appeal to the freighters. Some of them shirked it, but there were others who grinned while cracking an Indian on the skull, and straightway afterward ending the tortures of a mustang. The Comanches, being the finest horsemen of the plains, owned the best horses.

"Ketch all sound ponies," ordered Hatcher.

Few, however, of those still in the grove, were unwounded, and they could not be caught. Clint gazed at so many dark bronze visages without recognizing a Kiowa that at length he gave up. Lee Murdock had not led this band of Indians against the caravan. Therefore he was to be expected. But not from south or east of Point of Rocks! The fleeing Comanches would betray that the caravan had arrived ahead of schedule and had taken the initiative. Chances of Kiowas coming from the north or west along the road were possible, but remote.

In the space of a couple of acres the freighters counted over a hundred dead Comanches. This carnage had been the result of Ireland's first cannon charge, and the rifle-fire following at once. Hardly any force could have rallied after such a frightful first blow. Perhaps many horses received injuries here, yet were able to get away. Several dozen carcasses, however, lay in this zone. Six pounds of iron slugs made almost a bucketful of bullets, and the heavy charge of powder had propelled them terrifically. Trees and brush were riddled. And the savages who had fallen before this murderous instrument presented ghastly spectacles. Mangled bodies and blood reddened almost the whole of that space.

Hatcher met Clint here.

"Shore was a mess. . . . Reckon we'd better clear out an' get back to the wagons."

"Yes. But we've Blackstone's outfit over here."

"Wal, if I know freighters, Blackstone an' his gang won't worry you much by now."

Clint made no reply, but hurried away by a short cut across the flat. He heard Hatcher call his men to follow. When Clint reached the other trail he saw where the freighters had left the cannon on the bank, but had disappeared themselves. Whereupon Clint took to a trot and soon rounded a green corner to reach the long glade. A horrible sight met his gaze. From all the lower branches of the cottonwoods there hung one or two bandits. Some appeared like limp sacks, others were in convulsions, and a few, evidently just hanged, were going through appalling contortions. All this Clint took in at a glance, and at the same instant he heard the loud voice of his men, at his left.

"Andy, cut his feet loose, too, so we can see him kick like the rest of his dirty outfit," called a hoarse voice, in callous mirth.

Then Clint saw Blackstone standing under a spreading cottonwood, with a rope round his neck. It reached up over a branch and down into the outstretched hands of a dozen hard-faced freighters. They had reserved Blackstone for the last.

Clint yelled and rushed over.

"Hold on. Hyar's the boss," shouted Andy.

The stretched rope slackened and all faces turned toward Clint, and toward Hatcher who was approaching rapidly with the crowd of freighters behind.

"Ho, men!" called Clint, before he reached them. "Who ordered these men hanged?"

"Hellsfire! Who needed thet?" declared Andy, suddenly red and fierce. In him spoke the will, the ruthlessness, and all the law that existed on the frontier. Clint realized how superfluous had been his question.

He strode up to confront Blackstone. The bearded giant, ashen under his hair, gloomy-eyed, clammy with sweat, had accepted his fate. Long years of indifferent realization of what awaited him and his kind had steeled his nerve.

"Blackstone, do you know me?" demanded Clint.

"Shore. I've had the pleasure of meetin' you before. I cain't very well offer to shake, Buff."

His voice was husky but steady, and not without humor.

"You were to meet Murdock—Charley Bent here today?"

"So I heerd from your necktie outfit."

"Here, you know damned well you were," replied Clint.

"Belmet, if you know so damn much what do you ask me fer?"

"You gave it away. I heard you. Just before I jumped out of the brush, you said, 'Charley aimed to beat the Comanches here.'"

"Wal, if thet's so he played hell doin' it," returned Blackstone, bitterly.

"Blackstone, I'm not sure I can save your life," went on Clint, hurriedly. "But I'll try—if you tell me the truth about some things."

The bandit leader knew the frontier as well as Clint. Nothing could save his life. The commander of any fort would order him hanged. Evil as he was, he gave out the impression that even if Clint had power to save his life he would not betray a comrade.

"No, I won't answer no questions," he retorted, in dark passion, and his eyes lighted with sinister divination. "But I'll tell you somethin' on my own hook. . . . A few years back me an' Lee Murdock took thet little Bell girl up in the hills where we hid out. We had her one whole winter . . . had her turn aboot!—An' when——"

Clint leaped to brain him, and at the same instant a freighter called, piercingly:

"Up he goes!"

A score of sturdy arms pulled on the lasso. Blackstone's burly form shot up right before Clint's face; in fact he just escaped a violent kick from the bandit's heavy boot. Clint staggered back.

"Swing your pardner, Blackstone," yelled a leather-lunged freighter. "Turn the lady, turn."

Then they held him six feet off the ground, and all faces were turned upward—grim, leering, sweaty, bloody faces, hard as the frontier, yet laconic also in the contemplation of a just retribution.

"Damn your black-stone soul!" called one, breathing hoarsely.

"Now kick."

Blackstone's legs had been untied, as had those of all the other bandits, and there could have been only one interpretation to such action—the freighters wanted to see him kick. And they watched him kick. He was a very large, heavy man, exceedingly powerful, in the prime of life; and no matter what iron will and nerve he had when the spiritual man dominated, his muscular reaction was extraordinarily violent, grotesque, and hideous.

His bearded face, up to the sky, could not be seen, but it must have been too awful for even these avengers to behold. He kicked out with both legs at right angles, just the automatic kick of a jumping-jack. Then all ways, so monstrously that the branch of the tree bent and swung and his body swayed to and fro.

"Ho, men!" yelled Hatcher, from the trail, and his voice had a stirring ring. "Get out of this! Stevens is wavin' from the rock! Shore as Gawd made little apples the Kiowas are comin'!"

Hatcher thudded down the trail, with the watching freighters sudddenly breaking into action. The executioners tied the end of the lasso to a sapling, and leaping to their weapons, grunting and cursing, they stampeded out of the glade.

Clint laid a shaking hand on the lasso. It was tied securely and it would not break. Then he hurried to the trail. But he looked back. Blackstone's writhing had lost energy. It was now a swelling ripple of body. His knees were drawn up. Beyond him hung seventeen dark, limp figures, long-necked and loose, suggestive in their horridness.

Wheeling, Clint ran down the trail after the men.

When he got into the open he espied Stevens frantically waving from the top of the rock. The scout pointed to the north and his gesture inspired terror.

"*Murdock—an' his—Kiowas!*" gasped Clint, and flew over the sandy flat.

Half the hundred men were already across, shouting and calling. About a score were bringing the cannon. They ran with it, splashing, cursing, falling to their knees, plunging on. The men behind carried the rifles for those who were handling the cannon. And four rifles to one man made a burden. Those with the ammunition staggered along, yet made fast time.

Clint plunged into the shallow stream, making long bounds. Suddenly he halted, at the end of a jump. Hatcher, bareheaded, his white locks flying, stood on the bank, cupping his hands round his mouth.

"Come on, boys! Stick to thet cannon!"

20

Hatcher held up all until the men with the cannon and ammunition reached the bank.

"Get your wind," he ordered.

"What's up?" queried Belmet.

"Reckon Bent an' his Kiowas.—Buff, have you any plan?"

"That depends. If we don't know an' haven't time, how can we plan?—Any shootin' yet?"

"Haven't heerd none. I reckon hostilities ain't begun yet."

"Ireland, is the cannon loaded?" asked Clint.

"Shure."

"Lay hold, men—thirty to a rope," ordered Clint. "Rest of you hang close."

He led the way, and the straining freighters followed with the rumbling cannon. When they broke clear of the box-alder brush the going was easier. Clint headed round the left of the bluff, where the way was shorter and less rocky. He thought he heard shouting.

In a few moments Clint rounded the corner. Wagontrain and freighters seemed to burst into view. Three hundred yards out on the plain a strong force of Kiowas paraded to and fro. They were naked and painted, lean, wild young warriors, magnificently mounted and armed. Clint's hawk eye roved to fasten on to a knot of riders gathered round a central figure, strikingly different from the others, even at that distance. The sunlight did not shine off his naked body, which was dark instead of red. His head was not shaven like that of the others.

"Wal, we got hyar first," said Hatcher. "Mean-lookin' outfit, Buff. An' they ain't actin' like Indians. White brains runnin' them Kiowas."

"Charley Bent—or Lee Murdock, as I know him."

"Ahuh, so I reckoned. Wal, shore as this evil day dawned it'll see the end of thet half-breed," returned Hatcher, in terrible passion.

The forty-odd freighters who had been left to guard the wagon-train whooped their welcome.

"Buff, take command," said Hatcher, darkly. How gloomy and strange the old frontiersman! "An' don't forget our agreement."

"Jim, put fifty men up above the wagons among the rocks," replied Clint. "Wait; maybe that's too many. Say thirty. There's cover enough for them."

The freighters did not wait to be selected by Hatcher. With rifles in each hand a score or more rushed for the brushy, rocky slope. Those left free of the cannon dashed to the gate between the wagons. The sixty men at the cannon ropes came trampling after.

The double half-circle of wagons arched from the first rise of the rocky bluff on the west and extended to the sheer cliff wall on the other side, a little north of east. It appeared to be an impregnable defense against the ordinary tactics of plains Indians. Belmet stationed the cannon at the most commanding spot, which was just inside the gate. It could be moved, of course, from

255

place to place. The freighters spread along the inside of the circle of wagons like a flock of quail, and in a few moments not one could be seen.

Ireland and Copsy stood beside their cannon, nonchalant and eager. Stevens mounted to the wheel of the nearest wagon and leveled the field-glass on the Kiowas. Hatcher, Henry Wells, Andy Morgan, and a negro, Jackson, surrounded Clint. Half of the big oval corral had been roped off for the animals, and they were crowded, restless, and hungry.

"Boss, we're outnumbered two to one," said Stevens, in reply to Clint's query.

"Wal, we're good for it," remarked Wells.

"Buff, I don't like the way this Bent outfit looks," complained Hatcher.

"Come down, Stevens, an' let me take a look," said Clint.

"Men, we're shore goin' to learn *how* Charley Bent works a caravan," rejoined Andy Morgan, wagging his sandy head.

"Wal, we'll shore learn, but we may never tell," growled Jim Hatcher, somberly.

They were the last words he was ever heard to utter.

Meanwhile Clint was watching through the glass. He could not make an accurate estimate of the restless Kiowas, but their number far exceeded two hundred. Clint tried to get the glass on the leader, but he was surrounded by his red lieutenants and somewhat hidden. The glass, however, enabled Clint to make a discovery Stevens had missed. These Kiowas were under the influence of rum. Kiowas were wicked enough when normal. But stimulated and maddened by rum— Clint felt his very marrow freeze.

"Men, these Kiowas are half drunk," he announced, tragically.

The absolute silence with which this statement was received attested to its staggering purport. These fiends would have to become sober before they could be beaten.

It struck Clint presently that the Kiowas were riding farther to left and to right. The foremost ones did not wheel and prance their mustangs back. The whole band was spreading out in a long line. This did not mean the familiar circling of plains savages round a caravan. Clint grew anxiously puzzled. The riders spread until the line on the east passed out of Clint's sight. Those going to the left rode in twos and threes, close together, until the line on that side reached clear round to the river, at a point almost even with the bluff.

"Wal, Buff, say somethin'," burst out Henry Wells, who well knew that silence here was ominous.

"By Heaven!" muttered Clint, grinding his teeth. "So that's your game, Lee Murdock!"

Then Clint leaped down.

"Jackson, run along between the wagons," he ordered. "Tell all our men that the Kiowas have been fired by drink. Bent's game is to rush us."

"The lousy half-breed!" ejaculated Andy Morgan.

The negro bounded away to dart between the wagons, from behind which his deep voice sounded.

"Bent has outfigured us," said Clint. "In a close fight we can't use the cannon. But he doesn't know we have two rifles to a man an' a wagon-load of ammunition."

"Reckon we'd better hang by thet wagon," suggested Wells.

"An' the cannon. Because it'll have to be hauled round," added Morgan.

"*Listen!*" suddenly whispered Clint, bending low.

"They're comin'!"

"By Gawd!"

"It's the half-white in Charley Bent thet'll do for us!"

A low, trampling, encircling roar of many hoofs augmented the excited shouts of freighters from the bluff. And suddenly it was drowned by an ear-splitting concatenated war whoop, pointed and sharp, yet prolonged and swelling to hideous proportions.

A band of painted savages riding mustangs as wild as themselves closed in on the caravan. The cannon boomed; the rifles barked. But the sudden gap in the stream of riding demons closed as if by magic, and on they came, pouring in at the gate. Clint and his several companions met that onslaught with deadly fire. Then they dove under the wagons to keep from being run down.

Clint kept firing from behind the heavy wagon wheel, and he saw grimly to it that he did not miss. His keen eye sought among the supple, flitting, painted bodies one that was dark and not red. And at last he got a fleeting glimpse of Charley Bent—the center of a knot of riders, wonderfully swift and wild. Clint's aim was like his superhuman leap of lightning passion. Then through the smoke the demons raced by. They trooped in at the gate, glued to the necks of running mustangs. The roar of conflict spread around the caravan, proving that the Kiowas had not only entered the gate, but were coming over and under the wagons.

An endless smoky hell engulfed Clint Belmet. The battle had been hand to hand for what seemed a bloody age. But it might have been only moments. The milling of terrified horses and oxen, stampeding round and round the corral, unable to get out in any numbers, gave the battle a terrible confusion, and probably saved the freighters from utter annihilation. On foot the nimble daring savages bounded here, there, everywhere; and when a freighter clubbed one down he succumbed to the tomahawk of another. Rifle shots were few and far between, or else unheard in the deafening din. The cannon had never bellowed but once. Wagons were burning. At the far end of the oval the savages pulled out wagons, opening the corral for the bellowing, shrieking stock to pour forth like a dark flood.

Clint plunged through smoke, swinging a broken rifle, trying in the terrific maze to find comrades and keep with them. Smoke blew from the wagons, denser and denser. A circle of fire surrounded the freighters. Here and there in the dim blue haze groups of freighters and savages were contending, shooting, beating, struggling, mad beasts in the grip of blood lust. Clint rushed up to brain a Kiowa that was scalping a white man. He beat down two screeching devils that had set fire to the ammunition wagon.

A score and more of freighters, bloody and unconquerable, with Belmet at their head, gathered for a last stand in the center of the corral. The tide of terrific battle had set in their favor. They stood back to back, shooting the last few of their shells. The smoke was lifting, black and yellow above the roaring flames. A stench of burning hides filled the air. No more shots came from the rocky bluff. The squad of freighters had left it or had been killed.

Near the gate only one wagon was burning and that held the kegs of powder for the cannon and the boxes of ammunition for the rifles. A remnant of Kiowas collected there, fascinated by the chance to fire the last considerable number of wagons. A number lighted torches at the cracking fire which was consuming the ammunition wagon. They danced in a mad circle, torches aloft, in the light of the burning wagon.

A terrific red burst of flame! Crashing thunder! The wagon blew up and a black canopy flew out over the corral.

When the pall of smoke from that blast lifted, the remaining Kiowas were fleeing out over the plain to their horses.

Belmet had twenty-two men left, including himself, all of them wounded, but none admitting their wounds serious.

"Stick together an' we'll make a round of the corral," ordered Clint, huskily.

They found Copsy dead under the cannon, and Ireland lying across the breech, fuse clenched in his stiff hand. Henry Wells and two other freighters lay lifeless inside a circle of dead Kiowas. Jim Hatcher was half under a wagon, stiff and cold. He had been one of the first to go. Clint covered the staring eyes, and then kept his promise to the old caravan leader. The money belt Hatcher had asked Clint to take was thick and heavy. Years of saving—for what!

The dead and wounded were thick on all sides, and significantly, the wounded were always Indians. Once discovered alive, their last moment was brief.

Andy Morgan and Stevens, a little in advance, pulled an Indian from under a wagon. He had called out hoarsely.

"My turn, Steve," said the ironical Andy, with slow deliberation swinging his gory rifle stock aloft.

The Indian had a dark body. Not red! Only red where a bloody stream welled from a bullet hole in his breast! His eyes were terrible in piercing quality, but they were not black. His face bore a ghastly scar!

"Hold on, Andy!" yelled Clint, springing forward just in time to check that battering rifle.

"Belmet!" said the man, weakly, in English.

"Yes, I'm Belmet," replied Clint, and dropped to one knee.

"You know me?"

"I do—Lee Murdock."

"That's not—my real name," came the eager reply, tragic to see in a man mortally wounded. "I'm Charley Bent."

Andy knelt to lift the man's head.

"Have a drink?" he said, offering a black flask.

The renegade with slight gesture waved it aside. He had done with drink.

"Belmet, if you'll do me—a favor—I'll tell you—something."

"I will, if I can," replied Clint, and the awful strife of the last hours seemed to break, leaving him human again.

"My old father is alive—still," whispered the dying man. "Henry Bent. He's in Kansas City. . . . I heard from him a year ago. He believed I had quit—this life. I don't want him ever to know—I hadn't. . . . Will you tell him—or send word——"

"But it'd be a black lie!" exclaimed Clint.

"He's very old—he won't live long," implored the renegade. "He cared—for me!"

"All right, I'll do it," returned Clint.

Intensity flashed out of the man. The tight hold he had on his breast fell limp and the blood welled out.

"May Bell—is in Las Cruces—well—the same. . . . She—believes—you—dead."

Night fell duskily red and lonely. The coyotes began their hue and cry. Slowly the fires died down to smoldering heaps.

The freighters bound up their wounds. Several of them, searching among the rocks, found three wounded comrades, one of whom soon died. A few of the wagons under the bluff had escaped being fired. With food and blankets the last of the freighters repaired to the river bottom, where they ate and rested.

Clint and Andy Morgan, with two other men, went out to find horses. By midnight they rounded up thirty, most of them the saddled animals that had been left by Blackstone's band. Blankets were tied on some, and several were packed with food.

Clint led this silent remnant of a great caravan westward on the trail to Fort Larned. He and Hatcher had failed to deliver the most valuable caravan ever dispatched toward the east. They rode until dawn, hid in a creek bottom by day, and when night came they went on again. Stoical and indomitable they upheld the spirit of the frontier; and with two comrades lost on the way and two dying, they toiled at last into Fort Larned.

21

Next day Clint Belmet joined an army caravan headed for Santa Fé, but as a guest. He lay in an army wagon. He had been shot, stabbed, tomahawked and clubbed. But these injuries were as nothing. His mind could almost have performed a miracle.

The crossing of the Pecos was a circumstance which

gave him supreme joy. Somewhere, way down in New Mexico, west of the Pecos, was the little town of Las Cruces.

In Santa Fé he heard that his old friend and advisor, Kit Carson, was dying at Taos. Hardened as Clint had become to the simplicity and inevitableness of death on the frontier this news struck him deeply.

He rode over to Taos, to learn that Carson had been taken to the nearby army post. Clint made all the haste his condition would permit to go there. It had been many years since he had visited Fort Lyon, but he remembered the country, the post and even the army doctor who had charge of Carson.

"I met Kit Carson when I was a boy many years ago," explained Clint. "He took a shine to me, and advised me how to meet the frontier. I'd not be alive today but for his kindly influence. I'd like to see him—tell him."

"Sure, Belmet," replied the doctor. "Kit will be glad to see you. Everybody who comes along the old trail runs over to see Kit. He's finding out how he is loved by all the West. It's reward enough, he thinks, for his service. But I'm one who thinks otherwise. Come in."

Clint was ushered into a house where Kit Carson lay on a bed of buffalo hides. What a vast change in a man once so virile, so strong! He looked slight, shrunken, and the havoc of the approaching end showed in his haggard face. But not in those eagle eyes!

Carson ceased talking. He sat up. His eyes flashed. The Indian chief beside his bed gazed somberly from him to Clint. The army officers present turned to see who had entered.

"Kit, here's an old friend," said the doctor. "Do you know him?"

"Buff Belmet!" he ejaculated. "Put her thar!"

It needed no more to show Carson's keen remembrance and Clint Belmet's status on the frontier.

Perhaps that warm greeting, as well as the tragedy so surely felt here, had much to do with Clint's deepset emotions. At any rate, seldom, if ever, had he responded to questions as he did to Carson's. Clint told him much of his later experience, and especially of the terrible fight at Pawnee Rock, of Jim Blackstone's doom.

"Wal, you've sure been down the Old Trail, Buff," replied Carson. "The Trail of Lost Wagons! . . . An' now whar you bound?"

Then Clint told of the revelation made by Charley Bent before his death. This communication had a profound effect upon Kit Carson. He seemed to fade away. It was then Clint remembered how dearly Carson had loved his Mexican wife.

"So your sweetheart is alive?" he said, at length, with a beautiful light coming to his eyes. "I remember her. . . . Bell—little May Bell. I was at Maxwell's ranch when you damn near killed Charley Bent. . . . Buff, all's well that ends well. Don't lose any time gettin' to little May."

It was late when Clint got back to Taos, his mind full of the great frontiersman whose days were surely numbered. And he thought that perhaps only the West of his day would ever give Kit Carson the glory due him. For all the old plainsmen, the frontiersmen, knew full well that Kit Carson was the Pathfinder.

At Taos Clint fell in with a wagon-train bound for Las Vegas. When he arrived there he felt almost himself again. He outfitted with pack and saddle horses; and in company with Texans and Mexicans who were on the way south he set out on the last leg of his momentous journey. They were west of the Rockies, far out of the zone of desperadoes who preyed on the caravans, and the savages who rode and fought and burned.

All day long Clint sat his horse and watched the varying aspects of scenery—green and flowery, or rugged and drear, according to the presence or absence of water.

On that ride he seemed to grow both old and young, but toward the end youth resurged and held. He lived over all the long-past precious hours he had spent

263

with May Bell. How few, considering the fifteen years since he had met her beside the brook!

Summer had come to the valley of Las Cruces. It was far south and close to El Paso, at that period a rapidly growing town. White and red adobe houses shone brightly from the green. Level farms, well watered, spread out to the dark hills. Far from Indian trails!

A Mexican kept a store and a tavern. There Clint removed the stains of travel and the beard that had made him so dark and fierce. Would she know him? Could he not relax that stern, intent face?

The first thing he had ascertained was that May Bell really lived in Las Cruces with Mrs. Clement, on a ranch they owned, just out of town. They were rich, the tavern-keeper avowed, and blessed of the saints, for they helped the poor and employed the Mexicans.

Clint walked out, and that was the saddest and happiest walk of all his life.

If May still loved him—had lived and waited for him, despite all—then the future might almost make up for the past.

The white adobe house was set down from the road in a grove of cottonwood trees. There were evidences of Southern influence everywhere. No doubt Mrs. Clement had not forgotten Texas.

With his heart in his throat Clint knocked at the open door. A gray-haired, pleasant-faced, sad-eyed woman appeared. She gasped.

"Mrs. Clement, don't you remember me?" asked Clint.

"Oh, I do—I do!" she cried. "You are Clint Belmet."

"Yes, I'm Clint. . . . Is *she* here?"

"Thank God, she is—well and still faithful to you. But she believes you dead. I always thought you might come to life. I have seen so many strange things on the frontier."

"Where is she?" asked Clint, strangely calm.

"Out in the garden. She loves to dig around and plant."

"You say she is—well?"

"Yes, very well, now. For a long time after our terrible experience in that caravan she was ill. In fact, the whole year we lived with the settler Bennet."

"You left Santa Fé in a caravan under Jim Blackstone."

"Yes, the monster! We were no sooner out on the Dry Trail when Indians appeared and attacked the freighters who had joined us. Blackstone's gang took sides with the Indians. We would have been lost but for a caravan of emigrants on the way to Texas. They drove the Indians off. Blackstone fled, leaving his wagons. The emigrants took us along with them. Baxter, the boss, was an old scout. He knew we were followed. One night he took us down into a valley where a settler named Bennet lived. He was friendly with all Indians. Well, Bennet took us in, and he hid us there for a year. We seldom went out except at night. Then when a big caravan came along we got out. We trailed you to Kansas City and back to Santa Fé. And again we passed you on the way. That nearly killed poor May. Then your death was reported the second time. We saw it in the Kansas City papers. We went back to Texas. I had some property there. I sold it and we went to El Paso, and finally here. May loves the West, but not the plains.

"So she passed me again on the Old Trail!" sighed Clint. "Life seems cruel sometimes. . . . You said she was out in the garden?"

"Come," replied Mrs. Clement, softly.

She led him round the white house to the rear, where cottonwoods were shedding their fluffy cotton-like seeds, and green grass shone, and water gurgled somewhere unseen, and blackbirds sang in the trees.

"There she is. But hadn't I better go first—prepare her?" asked Mrs. Clement, anxiously.

Clint saw something blue out in the garden. It moved. It was a woman of slight form, bending over. Then she stood erect. A sunbonnet hung over her shoulders. Clint recognized that bonny dark head, and all the agony of the years was as if it had never been.

"Mrs. Clement, you say she has—has not forgotten me?" he asked, hesitatingly.

"She believes you dead. But no living man could be more wonderfully loved."

"Aw! . . . It'll not—hurt her—then. I—I want to see her face—when she sees me!"

Mrs. Clement pressed his hand and mutely turned back to the house.

Clint moved out from under the cottonwoods to the edge of the garden. There he halted, not because he wanted to, but because May had turned round toward him. She came walking between the rows, looking down. Her sleeves were rolled up. She held a trowel in her hand.

She grew closer, humming a little tune. When she looked up, twenty short paces did not separate them. A shock caught her in a step, making her a statue. Wide dark staring eyes shook Clint to his depths. He tried to call out.

She dropped the trowel. Her hands flashed to her breast. She swayed a little, her eyes shutting tight and opening wide. Will was stronger than terror. She uttered a wild and rapturous cry and broke toward him, flinging out her arms, running while yet she was stumbling, with glorious light of recognition. "Clint! —Clint! CLINT!"

Sunset! They sat under a cottonwood, strangely like the spreading giant in the valley below Maxwell's Ranch, and watched the western sky. Her head lay on his shoulder and her hand in his.

"God is good. I had almost lost faith in Him and life," she said.

"When will you marry me?" he asked, for the tenth time.

"You will never cross the plains again?" she entreated. "I could not bear that."

"Darlin', I will never go back."

She kissed him gratefully. "Oh, I know how you feel! I shall never forget the prairie land. Endless gray

266

—oh, so far, so lonely, so monotonous—gray and terribly beautiful. Oh, how I loved and hated it!"

"I have had enough, May. I've done my share. . . . Will you marry me?"

"Sí, señor," she replied, shyly.

"When?"

"Sometime. It's very sudden."

"But my longin' for you is as old as the ages."

"Oh, Clint, and mine for you. Promise me you'll never leave me again for a single minute so long as we both shall live."

"I promise, little May."

"You will stay away from trading-posts and forts and trails and Indians and desperadoes?"

"I shall indeed," he laughed.

"Oh, you can laugh! . . . Clint, I'm so happy I shall die. Squeeze me! . . . Kiss me!—You great, calm, cold frontiersman!—And, oh, forgive me again for that one damnable wickedness of my life—when I drove you away at Maxwell's Ranch?"

"I will—when you marry me."

She was silent for a long moment, surrendering.

"There's a padre here at Las Cruces. . . . He will do—yes?"

"Is that last a question—or a consent?"

"Both. . . . Well, Buff, if the padre is good enough for you—you may have me——"

"When?" he gasped.

"Tomorrow—at the very latest," she concluded, merrily.

Clint gathered her into his arms as if he never meant to let her go again. Presently she freed herself with a gasp. "Heavens! Did—I call you—a great, calm, cold frontiersman? . . . But I should have told you sooner. . . . Listen, Clint dear. Let me be serious one moment. I shall marry you tomorrow and all will be well. Ours has been a strange, sad story. But we are both young still. We love the West. We are pioneers and we will be true to that. Let us settle here in this beautiful valley and make our home with Mrs. Clement. She has been a mother to me."

267

"Anythin' you say, little May," he replied, in quiet joy. "I have money to buy a ranch an' stock it. My own, Uncle Jim's, an' poor old Hatcher's. I'm quite rich, May, an' can give you every comfort."

"Why, you wonderful man! I shall coax you to take me to San Antonio—some day," she cried, gaily.

"You won't need to coax. Just one kiss."

"There!" she flashed. "It's paid." And she lay quiet in his arms. Twilight fell. The bees ceased humming. The tinkle of a cow bell lingered musically on the quiet air. A coyote yelped wildly from the hill. And the golden afterglow faded in the west.

THE END